I. G. Mansfield read Natural Sciences at Christ's College, Cambridge. After graduating he joined the civil service in what was then the Department of Trade and Industry and has held a variety of posts in science, energy and trade. Other than writing, his hobbies include reading, chess, hill-walking and ballroom dancing. He lives in London.

IMPERIAL VISIONS

IMPERIAL VISIONS

I. G. MANSFIELD

A CIP catalogue record for this title is

available from the British Library.

First Published in 2010 by Vanguard Press

This Edition Published 2012

To my parents.

For their support in the path to completing this book I would like to thank Jonny Evans and Katy Roberts for early encouragement in writing; Robin Fairey for the creation of the maps; Alex Wright, Susie Roques, Karuna Monteiro, Damian and Bryony Brennan, Steve Burgess and Owen Jones for proof-reading; Jonny Evans and Owen Jones (again) for printing services; and all of the above and Ed Hutchinson, Julia Goedecke, Megan Morys, Neil Roques and Tom Wood for general enthusiasm and support.

Contents

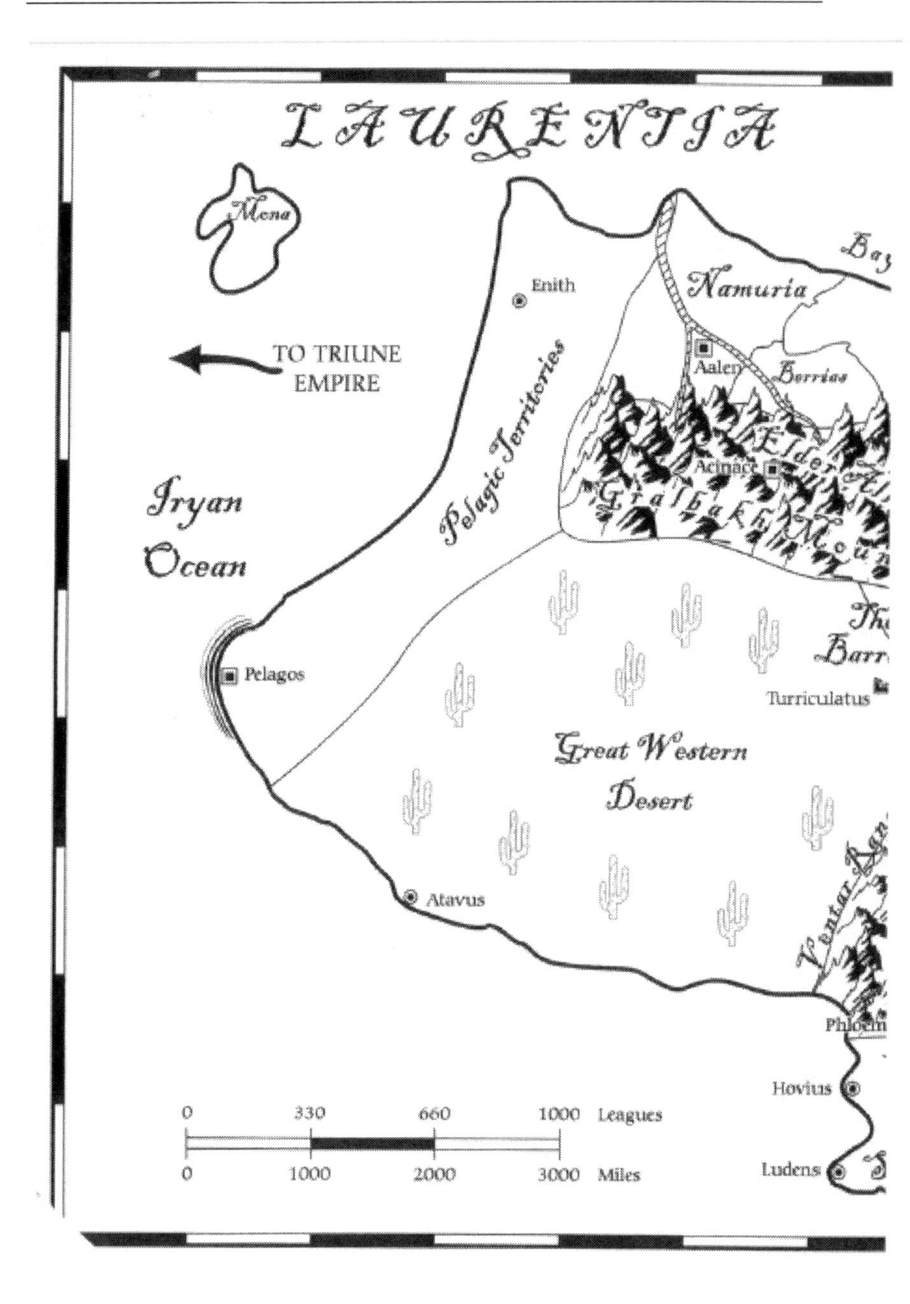
Laurentia
Mena
Enith
Namuria
TO TRIUNE EMPIRE
Aalen
Pelagic Territories
Acinace
Iryan Ocean
Pelagos
Turriculatus
Great Western Desert
Atavus
Hovius
Ludens
0 330 660 1000 Leagues
0 1000 2000 3000 Miles

Bajoc
Rotliegendes
Pridoli
Oszlenka
Loess
Siluria
Zechstein
Zech
Aile
Calyx
(Island of
Dawn)
Debral
Linnarson
Forest of Silence
Karst
Bajada
Greater Torridon
Elaran
Kurdon
Ygerna
Hyrnar
Iskarn
Anille
Erd
Gellin
Givet
Jallenais
Jacon
Druzh
Scandia
Knoydart
Tournais
Aesthen
Sedgwick
Bay of Meneth
Har Meneth
Autigen
N
W
E
S

FLIGHT

"All that walk upon the face of Edrith are known to Our Lady of Silence, and all may be concealed beneath her dark veil."

Konelis Larach – The Annalia, Volume Five

Chapter One

Massacre

The Residency was in flames. Smouldering tongues of fire licked at the side veranda. Smoke billowed from the building as the host of unwashed Gellinese smashed through the door.

The mob had gathered at sundown, crowding into the square before the Residency. There were too many for the square to hold: the overflow spilled into the back-alleys and side streets as far as one could see. Many carried torches or weapons – makeshift cudgels, long knives, butchers' cleavers, even a few antique muskets scattered here and there amongst the crowd – yet despite this they had not seemed so dangerous. There had been murmurs of trouble and unrest before now. Yet the fact that this time the Gellinese guards had mysteriously melted away, whether from design or fear, should have been realised as significant. Only the small Imperial garrison of twenty men had been left to defend the Residency.

Sir Edward had gone out unarmed to meet them in a show of trust. He had spoken with the assemblage, discoursing with them in his cool and cultured voice, trying to persuade them to disperse. For a time they seemed to be listening. Then they were still no longer.

They cut him down. A hulking brute sliced him from shoulder to navel, a cruel sneer on his face as Sir Edward fell. Now the mob was surging forward, a raging horde of anger and hate, crashing over the thin line of green and gold that stood between them and the Residency.

The guards fired once, no more. Then the mob was upon them. It was bayonet and rifle butt against the enemy, a mindless swarm hundreds strong. The soldiers could not prevail. The baying rabble overwhelmed them and beat them down. Those who fell were trampled into the dirt, as were any of the attackers unfortunate enough to lose their footing. Torches were hurled and hungry flames curled up the walls of the Residency even as the Gellinese battered their way into the building, smashing doors and shattering windows.

Inside the destruction continued. The rioters poured through room after room, smashing, looting and murdering as they went. Many of the servants had gathered in the main hall to watch Sir Edward negotiate. They were slaughtered where they stood, their blood spilling out across the once pristine wooden floor.

Even this could not sate the mob's hunger for death and destruction. They tore the Residency apart like a pack of rabid wolves.

Not a man, woman or child was spared. Radburn was beaten to death on the landing, his broken body tossed over the banister to the floor below. Nor did the rioters show mercy to Mrs Derringham, the adjutant's wife, when she confronted them in her bedroom, her eight-month old babe clutched to her breast. So also did they serve Mott, Lowther, Hewisham and all others whom they found. Even the servants, Gellinese almost to a man, did not escape their countrymen's bloody rampage. No mercy was offered to them and so they suffered and died with their masters,

The crimson rivers of blood mingled with the orange of the flames as bitter ruin consumed the Residency. Smoke billowed into the night. With a shudder, the east wing collapsed, weakened timbers ponderously giving way under the inexorable pressure of the heavy roof. Who knows how many of the mob perished beneath its beams? Yet still their fellows rampaged throughout the crumbling Residency, heedless of danger.

Not all of the Residency had yet been destroyed. The uppermost floor had so far suffered comparatively little. Only the most determined of the mob had yet reached it; the fire similarly was more concentrated below, though the fierce flames had engulfed the stairs, trapping both victims and murderers above. In a back bedroom, a knot of frightened servants huddled together, silently praying for deliverance. Sullivan, the deputy commissioner, had shut himself in his office. Head bent over the *variideshar*, he was steadily transmitting an account of events to the Viceroy's staff in Autigen. He might have been sitting in his office back Home: his voice, utterly composed, methodically detailed the events of the last few days, leading up to and including the massacre itself. Even when one of the mob kicked in his door he did not look up. The rioter bellowed at him to move. Sullivan ignored him; a petty distraction, not worthy of his attention. Dedicated to the last to his duty, his calm recital continued unbroken until the rioter, infuriated with his insolence, put a bullet through his brain.

He slumped down over the *variideshar*, killed instantly. As if his death had triggered it, the staircase, already aflame, collapsed, that majestic sweeping edifice breaking within moments into a motley assemblage of smouldering timbers and ash. With an almighty shudder the Residency itself began to follow. Bereft of internal support, the entire building was collapsing under its own weight.

The entire upper storey tilted and went down; a great ship, its rigging aflame after a valiant sea battle, succumbing at last to sink beneath the ocean. The flames roared up to engulf it, consuming man, woman and timbers all, aggressors and victims now partners in fiery death. Hotter and fiercer the fire burned. The surviving rioters crawled from the wreckage to join their wiser fellows outside. The mob licked its wounds, a furious beast no longer but one contented, delighting in the utter destruction that it had wrought.

The fire lit up the night. The screams had ended now; all that remained was the roaring of the fire as it devoured the Residency. Hotter it flamed, burned, scorching with its white hot heat. The pain increased, roasting, scorching, an ardent pain searing through every part of his body. Oh, how it burned!

#

Thomas came to, screaming. A rough hand covered his mouth, holding him down. Dark walls enclosed him, shutting him in. He thrashed wildly.

"Quiet! Be still!" Thomas only struggled more desperately.

"You must be quiet!" Gradually, he recognised Piotr's voice, the thick Rotliegendish accent eventually penetrating his consciousness. He began to relax. The dark walls resolved into nothing more than the banks of the ditch in which they had slept. The sky was grey, filled with the pale, pre-dawn light. They had slept for only a few hours.

His body was cold and wet from the early morning dew. The intense, burning heat of a few moments ago had vanished, leaving no traces – at least none physical. He shuddered uncontrollably as the horrific slaughter, momentarily forced down, flooded up into his mind again.

"It was the vision again?" Piotr's question cut abruptly through his thoughts. He nodded.

"I am sorry," said Piotr. "But we must not be still. They will be following. We must walk. Quickly!"

Thomas turned his head. Piotr was standing, clearly ready to leave immediately. The Rotliegendan appeared entirely unaffected by yesterday's trials. Thomas groaned. Piotr was twice his age, at least. With an effort, Thomas pushed himself to his feet.

Fire of a different kind shot through his body. His thighs and calves burned with pain, crying out against this ill-usage. He staggered but steadied himself against the sides of the ditch.

"Walk," commanded Piotr.

"I can't. Look, I can barely stand."

"Walking will help. Here, take your pack – we must go."

Thomas grabbed the cloth bundle that Piotr thrust towards him. Forcing his protesting muscles into action, he staggered after his companion. He knew he couldn't stand the gruelling pace of the day before.

"How far today?" he called out, his voice tinged with hope. Piotr whirled.

"Silence!" he hissed. "Remember we are not safe here." Thomas shrank back, stung by the harshness of Piotr's anger. That he knew it was justified made the rebuke no less difficult to take.

"To answer your question," continued Piotr quietly, "further than yesterday. We were hunted too closely then to make good time. Today is different. Today we must walk fast, further and faster. We must put good distance between ourselves and the city of Iskarn."

At Piotr's words the day seemed to stretch out before Thomas like an endless tunnel of pain. Further and faster? It would be all he could do to walk a mile. But Piotr was without mercy, already striding out ahead, leaving Thomas to follow as best he could – or to stay and die, as he chose. Wordlessly, Thomas walked.

How their relationship had changed! Only two days before Piotr had been his servant, respectful, helpful and obedient. Now the roles had reversed: Piotr drove him onwards harshly, as if he was a recalcitrant horse – and not a prized one, either. As for respect, not a single honorific had passed Piotr's lips since they had fled the Residency. But then, Piotr had saved his life.

Flinching at this reminder of their danger, Thomas scanned the horizon, glancing from left to right even as he struggled onwards. There were no signs of pursuit: all he could see were the rolling hills, broken by white stone walls, low farm buildings and the occasional more substantial settlement.

Already the dawn sun was burning through the early morning mist. It was a warm land, this nation of Erd Gellin: even now, in late autumn, by noon it would be hot enough to make hard walking unpleasant. Not as sweltering as the jungles of the Imperial province of Scahania to the south – where Thomas had been only once, and then briefly – but still as hot as it would be back in the Empire in midsummer.

It was arid as well. Water here was a precious resource; the hilly slopes had been terraced long ago, the peasants' food crops sustained by the network of thin irrigation ditches that criss-crossed the land, resembling in miniature the great network of canals, masterworks of modern engineering, that in the last century had transformed the face of the Triune Empire.

Here in Erd Gellin, in Laurentia, there were no canals, not yet. Wagon and packhorse remained the primary means of transporting goods, though in these hill villages it was more likely to be by the broad backs of the peasants themselves than either of the former. Piotr had kept them well away from roads or major places of habitation, instead leading them along narrow switchback paths or goat tracks, barely visible amongst the scrubby vegetation and bleached white stone of the hillsides.

Wadis had formed their road more than once. The dried up riverbeds that in spring could be transformed to the raging torrent of a flash flood in heartbeats made for good footpaths in autumn. In some a trickle of water flowed even after the long summer, fed no doubt by underground springs. From a distance one could spot them easily by the thin lines of trees that stood along their banks. Medlar and citron, fig and myrtle, distinct amongst the wiry olive trees scattered across the landscape, their grey-green leaves and gaunt forms so different from the lush, broad-leafed oaks and sycamores of Home.

They were in the same latitudes here as the southern coast of Avalonia, the Imperial Homeland. Erd Gellin however was not on the coast, but in the centre of the giant, heterogeneous and barbarous continent of Laurentia, eleven thousand miles from east to west and over six thousand from north to south. Westward lay the vast expanse of the Great Western Desert, a trackless waste without water or shade for man nor beast. Even the nomads of the Nir Aqinsa only roamed its periphery: none penetrated its heartland habitually and few had ever done so. Erd Gellin was on its fringes; nothing but the Barrens lay between the desert and its western border. At times, it was said, the sirocco could carry the scent of the harsh desert sands clear to the capital of Iskarn, three hundred leagues away. Pure fantasy, yet in his current state of anxiety, senses straining for danger, Thomas almost thought he could smell it now, a pure, hard odour, exotic and merciless.

At least the flanks of the hills remained empty of danger. In truth, if pursuit had been in sight then it would be too late. Two men on foot could never outrun horses, not unless the men happened to be of the Mareischi clans of the Gralbakh Mountains which, Andur knew, he at least decidedly was not. Feared mountain warriors without peer, the men of the eastern Gralbakh eschewed horses. A Mareischi boy was not considered a man until he had run twenty leagues between sun-up and sun-down. A far cry from Thomas's own abilities – it was all he could do now to put one foot in front of the other. Even Piotr, he thought with a snort, would be hard pressed to manage that feat of endurance.

In his heart though, Thomas knew that Piotr, in his current harshness, was performing a more valuable service than any he had had occasion to do in the comfortable months before. Without Piotr's skill they would never have evaded pursuit yesterday, and without his merciless driving Thomas could not have forced himself to go on at such a pace today. He cursed his weakness. Lack of skill was excusable; lack of will was not. He must strengthen his resolve, become as hard and strong as he needed to be. He was all that now remained of the Empire in Erd Gellin now.

Holding fast to this thought Thomas managed to persevere, walking onwards for mile after mile. Though the morning's fiery pain had faded somewhat, the sensation had been replaced by a cold, hard numbness that soaked through his lower body. His thighs ached, his calves ached, the soles of his feet ached. The rolling hills began to seem an almost physical enemy, each summit a fresh battalion of an innumerable host to be mastered and overcome.

How he longed, when they reached one of those crests, to pause and rest, even if only for a few moments. Thomas felt he could lie down, stretch out and sleep for a year, his weary body doing nothing but soak in a bath of delicious idleness.

Only his pride kept him going, his poor stubborn pride. Always ahead, just a score of paces ahead, was Piotr. He knew now that he could not equal Piotr's stamina nor his skills at survival. But he would be buried in a pauper's grave before he begged for mercy from a foreign servant after a mere day and a half's walk, however gruelling. A man of the Empire was a match for any Laurentian native, be he Rotliegendan, Gellinese, Torridonian, Elarani or any of the other half-civilised races that populated the continent. Gaze fixed like a limpet on that retreating back he staggered on, striving to match that remorseless pace.

In all of his later experiences, Thomas would never realise that on this journey Piotr, far from being oblivious to Thomas's difficulties, could in fact not have been more sensitive to his erstwhile master's ability. Throughout the journey Piotr would adjust his pace to Thomas's – always to remain a few steps ahead. The canny Rotliegendan, knowing that even the fastest pace would be lucky to give them an even chance of evading their pursuers, had adroitly judged that this technique would do more to speed their way than any amount of verbal encouragement or goading. He had therefore proceeded to carry it out, as he did almost any other activity he turned his hand to, deftly, skilfully and utterly without mercy.

The day wore on, step after gruelling step. The sun climbed high and the heat grew; not oppressive, fortunately, but still more than enough to make the sweat drip from Thomas's face and forehead. He found himself longing for the next stream, not only for its coolness and the chance to drink freely, but simply for the break in the monotony of pain. Whenever they found one Piotr would make them walk down the centre for a distance, sometimes upstream, sometimes downstream, in order to throw off any pursuit. These welcome breaks came far too infrequently for Thomas – at this time of year, after the long, hot summer, they more frequently found only a dried-up riverbed or a muddy trickle connecting some stagnant standing pools, useless for evading their trackers and folly to drink from. The small waterskins they carried did not contain enough to sate their thirst.

At noon they halted, Piotr pausing briefly in his stride to thrust some food at Thomas.

"Here. Eat," he said in his thick accent, proffering two pieces of flatbread and a handful of dried apricots.

Thomas needed no encouragement. He tore into the food like a man half starved, barely pausing to chew. The simple food was ambrosia. The hard flatbread seemed food fit for a king whilst each apricot burst in his mouth like a juicy morsel of heaven. From the corner of his eye he noticed Piotr. For all his stoic endurance, the Rotliegendan was devouring his own food with similar fervour.

All too soon it was gone, even the crumbs. Thomas looked about hungrily, but he knew from yesterday that no more would be forthcoming. Draining down half of his remaining water, he turned to his companion.

"Where are we going?"

"I am sorry?" Piotr was sipping slowly from his waterskin.

"Where are we going?" repeated Thomas. "Yesterday we were simply trying to escape, to get as far from Iskarn as possible. But today we're heading somewhere specific – at least we should be," a touch of acerbity creeping into his voice.

"Of course." The Rotliegendan was unperturbed. "We are going to Elaran."

"To Elaran?" asked Thomas, dismayed. Elaran was a tiny hill kingdom, even more insignificant, if that were possible, than Erd Gellin. The Triune Empire did not even have a trade representative there, never mind an embassy. "Why not to somewhere more civilised, such as Givet? Or south towards the Imperial territories in the Scahanian peninsula."

"It would not help you – unless you think you could scale the mountains of the Har Meneth. And Givet? Those effete *daszgarta* would as soon shelter you from the Gellinese as a Falani trader would pass by a ripe market. When did they last risk a war? But those are not the reasons."

Thomas waited for Piotr to continue but to no avail. Even at the Residency the taciturn Rotliegendan had seldom volunteered anything. Only when it was clear that no more was forthcoming did Thomas speak again.

"What is the reason then?" he asked, exasperated.

"It is simple. There are sixty-five leagues to the border with Elaran. Maybe sixty now. It will take almost two weeks – on foot, with little food and our enemies following. We will be lucky to get there. To Givet there are over a hundred and fifty leagues; to the other borders even more. You think we could make it? You, who can barely maintain the pace now? We would die."

The anger in his companion's voice was clear. Thomas cast his eyes down, feeling his own anger rise up as well, both at Piotr and at his own stupidity. He had seen maps; he had studied the geography of this thrice-damned region. No wonder Piotr felt contempt for his foolishness. He looked up but Piotr had already turned away, slipping his waterskin inside his bundle in preparation for the afternoon's travails.

If Thomas had thought the morning's walk an agony, the afternoon was agony redoubled. His bile soon vanished; the angry words subsumed by the greater torture of the pace set by his former servant. Yet keep up with that pace Thomas did. The repeated impact of his feet upon the hard rock of the hills struck through to his bones until each downhill step sent jarring shudders through his knees, the pain striking like a hammer blow at the tattered walls of his brain. The stony ground was merciless. Wordlessly, Thomas gathered his hatred, clinging to it and feeding it until it became a malevolent thing, an almost tangible monster that focused in all its fury upon the figure, always twenty paces ahead, of the Rotliegendan.

At that moment Thomas felt he could have killed Piotr. Nevertheless, a core of sanity remained, separating his fantasies of the moment from the reality that he knew was the truth. Even while he was plotting new, excruciating ways of torturing his companion the thought of Piotr carrying his limp body from the burning shell of the Residency was ever present.

"Down!" hissed Piotr suddenly, spinning and dropping low. Bemused, Thomas stumbled on a few steps, bemusedly looking around for the cause of Piotr's anxiety.

"*Bethed Dereszda!* Down I say!" repeated Piotr. Thomas felt the Rotliegendan's broad hand on his back forcing him down to the ground. Unresistingly he cooperated, his sense returning slowly.

"What is it?" he whispered.

"*Tarathin.* To south-west. Lie perfectly still."

Flattening themselves into the side of the wadi they lay there, Piotr's sandy cloak pulled across them. Frozen, they waited. There was nothing else they could do. Barely audible, Thomas could hear Piotr murmuring a barely audible prayer in Rotliegendan and mentally added his own.

A *tarathin*! How long before it reached them? If it was far enough away it might not even pass over, might veer off to left or right and miss them entirely. Then, peering out from beneath the cloak covering him, he saw it. Still far away, at this distance it could have been mistaken for a large bird, its riders too small to resolve.

Tarathin! They, and their larger cousins, the *tarath*, were amongst the more distinctive of the creatures native to Laurentia. Their introduction to the Empire over half a century ago had revolutionised transport. Though the great canals had retained their monopoly upon goods transport, now a man could fly in just two days from Wenlock to Port Medcourt or Ellesae at a price well within the reach of the gentry or the new moneyed industrialists. Not to mention their military uses. The army had been swift to learn from the tactics of the Laurentian nations who had been using the beasts for centuries.

The creature was closer now. Either by design or by chance it appeared to be heading straight for them The two riders could be clearly made out now; small figures, the desert palm upon their tabards, chosen no doubt as much for their slightness of frame as for their skill. *Tarathinakii*, riders of the *tarathin*, had to be light: unlike the great *tarath* who could carry two dozen full grown men with ease, a *tarathin* was more easily overloaded. Scouts, harriers and pursuers, the beasts were bred for speed and agility rather than endurance.

Still it approached, the great wings beating in the *tarathin*'s characteristic syncopated pattern of flap and glide that ate up the miles with deceptive ease. Thomas felt he could almost see the expressions of the lightly armoured riders, the flyer to fore and, seated behind him, the auxiliary, musket in hand, scanning the ground. They were hunting, and it did not take a savant to deduce their prey.

Thomas forced himself even flatter into the rocks of the wadi. Silently he thanked Andur for this continent's primitiveness – had the *tarathinakii* possessed field glasses they would have been undone in an instant, flushed out of hiding from a distance. At least as it was they had a chance, if a slim one.

Then the *tarathin* was above them, its twenty-foot wingspan seeming to fill the sky. Thomas felt naked. Any moment he expected to feel the smashing impact of a bullet through his spine. If they were spotted they would be shot down like dumb beasts, no more able to save themselves than if they were babes. Beside him Piotr was motionless as a rock, a steady stream of Rotliegendan curses pouring sotto voce from his mouth. All they could do was wait, frozen, and pray.

The great leathery wings beat again. Now it was banking, tilting to the left at an impossible angle. No bullet had come. Had they escaped? Hearts in their mouths they watched the great schooner of the air dwindle into the distance. By silent consensus they remained motionless for some minutes after the *tarathin* had vanished from the horizon. When any chance of its return had passed they rose slowly, still shaken from the narrowness of their escape.

That was not the only reason for their disquiet. Neither man was slow in understanding: the Empire did not appoint fools to the Laurentian Service and Piotr was – Piotr.

"You saw the tabards?"

"Yes," spat Piotr. "The desert palm. The symbol of Erd Gellin."

"Then..."

"Yes. The massacre was planned."

Chapter Two

Kindling the Flames

Huddled in a muddy irrigation ditch, Thomas wondered how it had come to this. Who could have anticipated it when he arrived? To think he had cursed his luck for being posted to a flyspeck post in the hinterland where nothing ever happened, rather than to the great Imperial provinces of Scahania or Pelagos! Too much had happened since then by far.

He had left Avalonia in late winter, sailing from Port Medcourt in a Farladan Company merchantman. The voyage had been a swift one. Bypassing Krinth-Turon they had sped across the ocean on the back of the stiff spring gales, arriving in Scahania shortly after the Day of Rebirth. From there time seemed to fly by; a few brief days in the provincial capital of Autigen and then a swift transfer by *tarath* to Erd Gellin.

A small droschky had been waiting for him at the *tarath* field, together with servants for his luggage. With brisk efficiency he had been bundled into the conveyance. He had tried to engage the driver in conversation as they rattled through the streets of Iskarn but his Gellinese had been poor then and the driver had spoken no other language. Instead he'd been left to gaze at the sights on his own, the sun-bleached adobe houses, grand arches and sculpted monuments in the Atavine style all so alien to his eyes, used to the conservative styles of the Empire.

Scurrying, half-clothed natives thronged the streets, begging and hawking their wares. They waited till the last moment before diving out of the way of their carriage or the conveyances of the wealthy Gellinese who, in droshky, sedan chair or tonga went about their own business. In this at least, save for the differences in clothing, the city could have passed for Autigen in Scahania, or for the poorer quarters of Wenlock, Ashgill or Kettingham back Home. Poverty was the same the world over, even in the Empire, despite the introduction of the much-vaunted Poor Laws.

Leaving the poorer quarters with their unwashed swarms of humanity behind, they passed briefly through the inner city. A company of musketeers, gaudy in their livery, stood to attention as they passed. Statues and obelisks crowded the grand squares. Even the cobbled streets were ornamented in designs of grandeur, though the remorseless passage of time had faded them almost beyond recognition, just as it had weathered the statues and crumbled the once smooth lines of the arches. This was an ancient city: one could feel the weight of the long-dead civilizations that had once trod it.

Down a wide street Thomas glimpsed the Iskandin Palace, the desert palm of Erd Gellin flying from every spire. Seat of the Archons, the nine lords who between them governed Erd Gellin, its sinuous lines, cusps and spires gave an eerie impression of the dunes of the desert itself. He had read of it in his studies of the continent. Though it had been razed or burned more than once in the long centuries of existence, it had never failed to be rebuilt. Barring the ruins in the Great Western Desert, the Iskandin palace was the oldest major Atavine building that survived outside of Atavus itself.

The clattering vehicle passed out through the Gate of Humility, leaving the inner city behind. They were almost on the outskirts of the city now, away from its heaving multitudes.

Thomas saw the Residency at last. Set slightly away from the city proper, it stood within a low walled courtyard at the end of a long avenue lined with medlars. Tall, proud and welcoming with the tripartite flag of the Triune Empire flying boldly from its roof, the three storey wooden building with its wings and gables warmed Thomas's heart. In truth, it was a most unprepossessing building compared even to the Imperial constructions in Scahania, let alone to the grand boulevards of Home, yet to Thomas's eyes, saturated by the alien splendours of Iskarn, it seemed the most wonderful building he had ever seen.

Sir Edward, the Commissioner himself, greeted Thomas at the doorway, warmly welcoming him to Erd Gellin before excusing himself and leaving Thomas in the care of Radburn, one of the more junior attachés.

"Well, Maynard, it's always good to have another man here," said Radburn once the usual pleasantries had been exchanged. "Not that we're overworked – you'll find out soon enough yourself how little there is to do here – but it breaks up the monotony, you know. Seeing nothing but the same faces the whole time makes any change welcome."

Thomas's heart sank. What rotten luck to draw a place like this for his first posting! Not a chance for advancement or to show his worth. Still, Radburn seemed pleasant enough, so he made an effort to conceal his disappointment.

"There must be some times when it gets busy," said Thomas. "Emergencies, diplomatic crises?" He strained his memory for any recollection of such an event concerning Erd Gellin.

"Diplomatic crises? You must be joking. These people aren't even interested in trading with us, let alone doing anything that might provoke a crisis. And given that we're almost three thousand miles from the Scahanian provinces – and over a thousand from the next nearest Triune consulate – who can blame them? Oh, the Archons invite us to functions or make a minor request every so often, but I suspect it's just to make us feel wanted. To be honest, the only reason the Colonial Office even has us here is to give the impression that the Empire takes an interest in the whole of Laurentia. Which we do of course, but we take a damn sight more interest in some bits than others.

"Well, these are your quarters. Piotr here will be your manservant; he's Rotliegendan, don't you know – you should be able to find him again easily enough.

"Oh," Radburn added as an afterthought, "the Old Man holds an informal colloquium every Saladar – today, in other words. It will look bad if you're not there. It's your chance to be introduced to the rest of us here – so make sure you're settled and changed by half four."

"The Old Man?"

"Yes – Sir Edward. Four thirty in the drawing room – Piotr will show you the way."

Radburn walked off briskly. Slightly bemused by the torrent of information he had just received, Thomas stood, slightly lost, at the top of the stairs. Fortunately Piotr came to his rescue. Bowing formally, he opened the door to Thomas's quarters and gestured the baggage carriers through.

The Rotliegendan's pallid northern complexion appeared strange, even sickly to Thomas, when compared to the olive-skinned Gellinese or the swarthy colouring more common in the Empire. Still, over the next few weeks he was to find Piotr a steady and reliable servant: taciturn and unobtrusive yet competent and efficient.

Thomas soon settled into the slow, unhurried pace of life at the Residency. Radburn had been right; there was little to do – the Gellinese authorities seldom initiated dialogue and, if they were approached, were invariably polite, courteous and utterly uninterested in any proposal that might be offered. Not that one was offered very often. Even the occasional communication from Home or the Viceroy's office in Scahania only emphasised the paucity of activity.

However, Thomas had no trouble in filling the leisurely days. Learning the language took much of his time – he had learned little Gellinese prior to his appointment, concentrating instead on the more widely spoken Laurentian languages of Silurian and Scahanian. The happy discovery that Piotr spoke Silurian allowed him to practise that tongue also, and the Residency had a relatively well-stocked library with which to further his studies of Laurentia. A year's cramming for the Laurentian Service exams had left him painfully aware that he had only scratched the surface of what there was to know and so many a vacant hour was spent happily absorbing tomes on the history, culture and politics of this vast and backward continent.

The expansionist ambitions of Greater Torridon; the political intrigues of the mage and merchant factions in Linnarson; the glory days of the Zechen-Rotliegendish Commonwealth, long since departed; the ancient Empire of the Atavines, wonders of antiquity with their arcane mysteries; the elusive races of the Elder Alliance; the embracing reach of Mother Church, its tentacles spreading out from the Patriarchy in Aesthen to encompass all Laurentia north of Scahania; all these were grist to the ready mill of his mind. If this post was to bring no glory or quick promotion, neither would he allow these idle days to be wasted when there was so much to be learned.

Nor was all his time spent in study. All told there were only twelve men staffing the Residency, plus the captain of the guard and his adjutant. Five of them had their wives with them; yet that still kept the number below twenty, excluding of course the servants and enlisted men. This was all the society within a thousand miles!

With so few, everyone soon got to know everyone else well, sometimes too well. Yet they whiled away the time well enough. Rides in the countryside, the occasional trip into Iskarn, these and other such pastimes formed the staple of their existence. In the chaplain Thomas discovered a keen sharom player to match his own standard and many a bitter struggle was fought, tooth and nail, within the confines of that hexagonal board. Mrs Sullivan, the deputy commissioner's wife, would organise afternoon tea, the tea arduously transported north from Scahania and the cakes always less than conventional, despite her long-suffering attempts to explain the art of elementary baking to the kitchen staff. And every Saladar were Sir Edward's colloquia, popular with all save the chaplain.

Sir Edward had set up the sessions as a time when all, from himself down to the most junior member on the staff, could openly debate the Residency's position and policy. He believed they served to educate the younger and helped prevent the older –himself included – from becoming complacent. He had brought the practice with him from his previous post and the fact that in Iskarn there was frequently little or nothing to discuss did nothing to dampen their popularity. The discussion would frequently range freely and fiercely over the political events of all Laurentia and of the Empire itself.

It was at one of these colloquia that Thomas first heard of the troubles in the countryside. It was in the new year, a couple of weeks after the midsummer celebrations of High Scriansa. The sherry had been poured – a rather fine moscatel from Siluria – and the assembled company was conversing on inconsequentialities, awaiting Sir Edward's signal to begin.

"Good afternoon, gentleman," said Sir Edward. "Rather too good perhaps for comfort; however, we can thank Andur that here in Erd Gellin it's a dry heat. Just think how our colleagues in Scahania must be suffering.

"And on the subject of suffering, I propose that we open the discussion with the reports of trouble in the countryside. Peasants from around Iskarn have been reporting sights of strange beasts or so they say. Some of you may have heard of this?" There were nods from about half the company, though not from Thomas.

"These 'beasts', as they call them," he continued, "have reputedly destroyed at least two dozen farms, slaying the inhabitants and significant numbers of livestock. The occurrences seem to be increasing across Erd Gellin, though the peasants themselves seldom agree on the nature of their sighting. Sullivan, you've already expressed your views on the matter to me, so perhaps you would like to be the first to comment?"

Indeed, Sullivan's expression could have chewed rocks. His characteristic scowl was even deeper than ever.

"Thank you, Sir Edward. These 'reports' and 'sightings' are nothing but the fevered imagination of superstitious peasantry. We all know the predilection of our own country farmers back Home to such wild imaginings and on this primitive continent it will only be worse. The fact that different peasants seldom agree on what they've seen only confirms it. As soon as they realised that this tale gave them access to the Archons – not to mention the attention it brings – every Tom, Dick or Harry who loses an animal to wolves or carelessness has seen a 'fearsome beast'."

"Thank you for that eloquent summation of your position," said Sir Edward, urbane as ever. "For myself I believe that there may be something in the rumours. Lowther, you wish to comment?"

"Thank you. Sullivan, if you don't believe in these beasts, what do you think is happening? For you can't deny that the city is full of these tales."

"How the devil should I know?" replied Sullivan. "Wolves, lions, perhaps some fell beast from the Great Western Desert or the Gralbakh Mountains has found its way down here. Dangerous, perhaps, but nothing unnatural. The countryside here isn't the tamed garden of Home you know.

"Remember, I firmly believe that no more than one or two of these events are genuine. The idea of dozens or hundreds of attacks as the word on the streets would have it is simply absurd. It's the height of summer; the silly season when such tales abound. It's too hot for people to do anything but gossip and make up stories which spread like wildfire and then die out just as quickly. That's what's happened – the fact that every victim seems to have seen a different beast just confirms it."

Thomas listened, fascinated. He hadn't visited Iskarn since High Scriansâ, over two weeks ago, and it was the first he'd heard of these events. Suddenly, he felt the keen eye of Sir Edward upon him.

"Maynard, you've been moderately quiet in our last few sessions. What do you think?"

Thomas racked his brains, desperately trying to think of something remotely intelligent to say.

"Perhaps," he ventured, "the reason why different sightings report different things is that there isn't just one – or one kind of – beast out there, but a large number."

From the reception of others the comment appeared to be satisfactory. Internally, he breathed a huge sigh of relief. Indeed, Radburn even appeared to be taking his suggestion forward.

"I believe Maynard may have something there," Radburn said. "I've spoken to the servants and they tell me that the rumours speak of all sorts of creatures – and not natural ones either. I've heard mention of demons, even droghkar."

"Mr Radburn, let us please try to keep the discussion to matters of possibility," interjected Sir Edward, the merest hint of steel in his cultured voice. "Demons – yes, this could be caused by demons, though it would surprise me greatly were it to be so, but droghkar? The droghkar are extinct. They were exterminated upon our own continent three hundred years ago and here in Laurentia more than twice that long ago. Perhaps a few lairs survive on Borallia, but nowhere else."

The discussion continued, but little more of substance was said upon the topic. The issue was soon dropped in favour of more relevant topics: the cholera outbreak in Scahania, the Expansionists' chances of holding on to power in the next election and the territorial ambitions of Niavon III of Torridon, to the north. But for an occasional mention by the chaplain over their games of sharom, Thomas would have forgotten about the subject entirely, but the chaplain, who ventured into Iskarn more frequently than most – and had a command of Gellinese fully as good as Sir Edward's – appeared to think that the disquiet amongst the peasantry was gaining strength, rather than the reverse.

The next time the subject formally came to Thomas's attention was at a dinner in late Olmandre, over a month since the colloquium at which he had first heard of the matter. They had been the guests of the Archons the night before, joining them in a grand banquet in celebration of the Feast of Balance. The Iskandin Palace had been a veritable pageant of ostentatiousness, the tables groaning beneath the weight of delicacies and the richly apparelled dignitaries lighting up the night with the glitter of their finery and the sparkle of their conversation.

In consequence, Sir Edward, no doubt at Mrs Sullivan's directions, had ordered only a light repast to be served the following evening. An indifferent consommé had been removed and the fish course, a soupçon of fried smelts in a drawn butter sauce, was being served. Like many around the table, Thomas could only pick at his food, still sated from the previous night's indulgence.

On his left, Hewisham and Radburn were engaged in an animated discussion concerning an arcanist named Galveston. By means of a series of tightly controlled lightning spells, Galveston had apparently succeeded in demonstrating that electricity, previously thought to be a visible form of phlogiston, was in actuality a manifestation of magnetism, the same force that kept a compass needle pointing north. Hewisham, a keen amateur enthusiast, always made a point of keeping abreast of the latest developments in the natural and arcane philosophies and was now busily extolling to the more sceptical Radburn the amazing potential of this new discovery.

"So," asked Thomas, mildly needling Hewisham, "will we be seeing our mills and factories being run by this 'magneto-electric force' in the future?"

"I'd wager not, as far as my money goes," said Radburn decisively, before Hewisham could respond. "Remember when that savant discovered that by burning coal he could get sufficient motive power to run an engine on steam? The dreamers had plans to convert the factories to steam; some spoke of making carriages – or even ships – run on the stuff, until someone reminded them that the price of coal was a significant step above the going price of silver."

"Some still think it might come about," objected Hewisham. "Leighton hopes to find vast, antediluvian deposits of coal in the interior of Borallia or Idriana. Coal's rarity is the only barrier to the scheme."

"I'll not be waiting for them," said Radburn. "Put your trust in water power, that's what I say. That's what the industrialists have done for decades and they're the ones who've made the Triune Empire great. Hard-headed pragmatists; that's what you want, not dreamers."

Hewisham protested, joined by Thomas, as together they held up the role of the natural philosophers and the arcanists in building the Empire. The conversation continued in the same vein of heated, amicable debate, Thomas contributing the odd word here and there. The spark of intellectual discord lent spice to the insipid mushrooms, dry roast beef and surprisingly respectable apple charlotte.

It was not until the ladies had withdrawn and the port was being passed round that Sir Edward called for the company's attention.

"Gentleman," he said, "I have news of some import to convey. Last night I was approached at the feast by High Archon Lykaios. After the usual pleasantries had been exchanged, he mentioned the recent disturbances in the countryside. Though he was most delicate about the matter, the nub of his conversation was a suggestion that we should leave – for our own safety. It appears that, for reasons unknown, the peasantry is blaming outlanders for their recent troubles. Presumably they identify the source of their current troubles as coming from outside and, with a peasant's usual gift for simplicity, have conflated all outlanders into one. Be that as it may, clearly implicit from Lykaios's remarks was that the Archons would bear no responsibility for our protection should an angry mob turn its attention upon us."

Sir Edward paused to observe the response from around the table. At the far end, Derringham was shaking his head vigorously in denial. Others, more polished, were considerably more non-committal though Sir Edward could infer, from their reactions and postures, that at least as many opposed the suggestion as favoured it. The greatest number were simply surprised.

"Many have already left. Perhaps you noticed their absence at the feast?" Nods; they had indeed noticed that. "The Torridonian, Silurian and Givetian ambassadors have all departed. The Patriarchal nuncio left this morning, no doubt following a similar conversation last night."

"Rotliegendes?" asked Sullivan.

"They never had one. Though knowing the Rotliegendans they no doubt have a dozen or more spies in the Iskandin Palace itself."

Thomas was puzzled. Something did not tally. The casual, mild warning that Sir Edward claimed to have received was at odds with the unceremonious departure of the representatives of virtually all the major nations on Laurentia. Either these other ambassadors had learned something more – in which case, what? – or Sir Edward's suggestion to leave had been considerably stronger than he was implying.

Sir Edward was speaking again, his urbane voice suddenly stern and vehement.

"We will not be amongst those who leave. We are Triunes, and men of the Triune Empire do not cut and run at the first sign of danger. Furthermore, we have a duty to our country; a duty to remain and monitor what is happening here, lest it be a danger to the Empire.

"You know as well as I do that, until now, this posting has been largely a sinecure. Will we abandon it as soon a minor difficulty raises its head? We will not. Our role is to remain; to serve the Empire."

There was a pause while the table took in Sir Edward's news and stirring exhortation. Then Hewisham spoke up, respectful yet puzzled.

"Sir Edward, I fully agree with your sentiments – I am in no doubt that we should remain. However, surely you exaggerate the danger to the Empire? What could possibly come out of this backward continent that could seriously endanger it?"

"I do not expect this to be a danger to the Empire," said Sir Edward. "It is far more probable that it is nothing more than local unrest – in which case the Viceroy in Scahania will be glad to know all the information that we can tell him. Knowledge is power, in Laurentia as much as in the corridors of power in Wenlock.

"Nevertheless, the fact remains that there is a chance, however small, that recent events presage something far more serious. You ask what could possibly threaten the Empire. This continent is not Idriana or the Borallian colonies – at most the people are a century or two behind us, and in the arcane philosophies they are our equal. Remember that in the year 179PC, or 1525 Since the Sundering, as they measure it on this continent, the Variscan Imperium was founded in Turriculatus, not so very far from here. I can assure you that they have not forgotten this in Laurentia, nor in the streets and cities back Home, even if you have."

Sir Edward had the whole table behind him now. Thomas, like others of those who had even toyed with the idea that they should leave, felt heartily ashamed.

The Variscan Wars had brought the Empire to its knees. In those days the Empire had only just begun the exploration of Laurentia. In consequence, before they even became aware of Varisca, that militaristic nation had already conquered the majority of the continent.

The next thing the Empire knew, the Variscans had crushed the fledgling Imperial colonies in Scahania and was exploding out of Laurentia into direct conflict with the Empire, the vile sorceries of its necromancers surpassing the Empire's best arcanists and more than countering the Triune's superior weaponry. The Empire had been forced into total war for the first time since its founding. Had the Laurentian nations not seized their chance to rebel against their cruel new masters, shivering the Variscan Imperium into a thousand pieces, the Empire would not have prevailed. As it was, the terrible losses had plunged the Empire into a half-century of isolationism and loosened its grip over a number of former dominions. Some of these had only recently been re-subdued.

"I can assure you, Sir Edward," said Sullivan, breaking through Thomas's thoughts, "that we are all fully in support of your decision to remain. It is clear that our duty to the Empire lies here."

"Thank you for your support," said Sir Edward, including the whole table in his words. "On a different matter: Lowther, what is your opinion of Torridon's latest peace overtures to Siluria?"

The decision settled, the conversation returned to lighter matters. For some time, it seemed that the matter lay buried as life at the Residency continued at its leisurely pace. As summer turned to autumn, the men and women of the Residency continued their trouble-free existence, largely unheeding of the storm that simmered beneath the surface.

However, this golden afternoon was not to last. As the weeks rolled by, the rumours of trouble grew. The feast of Harvest was marred by their presence and, by the Day of Deliverance in mid-autumn, they could no longer be ignored. Whispers no more, the mutters of trouble had turned to roars and the city was alive with the talk of fell beasts stalking the countryside. The Archons did their best to quiet the discontent, but few in the Residency now believed that their turning of public opinion against the Empire was anything other than intentional.

No embassies save the Empire's were left in the city now. Most foreign merchants had likewise left, variously citing either the discontent amongst the populace or the dangers of the countryside as their reason for not returning. It was this that had finally made some in the Residency begin to take the tales of demons and such more seriously, for merchants, particularly Linnarsonian traders, were most decidedly not given to the wild flights of fancy expected from credulous peasants.

On three occasions a mob had gathered before the Residency, on each case dispersed without much trouble by the guards. None now left the Residency without a heavy escort and few save the chaplain left at all. The claustrophobia became intense; the Residency that Thomas had once found so spacious now seemed to close in around him, stifling and smothering his breath. Tempers grew short and more than one previously mild-mannered man or woman found themselves in heated argument over trifles. The fact that none knew the reason or cause for the unrest only added to the unease. No one, not even Sir Edward, could pronounce with certainty upon the nature of the troubles in Erd Gellin, let alone speculate upon their origin or cause. To many, it seemed they had been swept away by the flood of events, without a chance to understand or direct its course.

It was on the morning of 4th Roandre that Thomas overheard the last, fateful conversation between Sullivan and Sir Edward. He was in the library, still a shelter for him from the storms of the outside world and the fear and tension that had by now permeated throughout the Residency. Study was sometimes hard but at least it kept him occupied.

When the Commissioner and Deputy Commissioner first entered he thought nothing of it. It was only when the door had closed behind them and they began to speak that he realised that they had clearly chosen this location for privacy. Tucked away as he was behind a book stack, they were unaware of his presence. For a few moments, Thomas's conscience warred with his curiosity but curiosity, abetted by the knowledge of the awkwardness of announcing his presence now, won out. Careful to make no inadvertent sound, he bent his ears upon the conversation.

"Well, do you think we should accept their offer?" Thomas heard Sir Edward say.

"You can't seriously be considering it!" expostulated Sullivan.

"I'm afraid that I am, David. Despite the bold front we've been putting on, you know as well as I do that our position here is unsustainable. Sooner or later, and probably sooner, the Archons are going to move on us, either directly or via the rabble of the populace. And when they do, that will be it. We have twenty soldiers to defend us, plus however many of the rest of us can fire a gun. At least this way offers a chance."

"A beggar's chance, if that. The offer's a death trap – why else would they make it? All they want is to get us out of the Residency, to save themselves losses and to preserve the building – and its contents – undamaged."

"That is undoubtedly true. But perhaps there is still honour in their offer. Do we not owe it to the women to take any chance we can?"

"I fully agree with you, Edward – that's why I urge you to refuse. Evacuation on foot? How far would we get, crossing Erd Gellin unarmed, with hostile natives, Andur knows what creatures in the countryside, and that's assuming there's no treachery – which there assuredly will be."

"Not quite unarmed," said Sir Edward mildly. "They will allow us to keep a rifle apiece."

"Much good that will do us when we're strung out along a road in the middle of nowhere, facing ten times our number of the Archons' troops. No, if there was any hope of their sincerity they would evacuate us by *tarath*, like gentlemen. Our only hope is to sit tight and call for aid. Maybe the Viceroy in Autigen will stir himself if we catch the attention of the papers back Home."

"Do you really think that's likely?"

"No, Edward, I don't, and you know that I don't. We both know that we're a thousand miles from the nearest Triune outpost and nearly three thousand from the nearest significant garrison. Even if the Triumvirate themselves were here instead of us, there would be nothing more that could be done. If we were on the coast it would be different but we're not, and that's all there is to it. But any hope, even a futile one, is better than none at all. At least here we may make them pay a high price for our lives."

"That's truly spoken." Sir Edward sighed. "You're right, David; I think I always knew you were. I just wanted so much for there to be some way out. The rest of them all think that we have matters in hand, that things will somehow turn out all right in the end. You realise that this will be the worst massacre since Wainwright and his men were cut off at Micraster?"

"We're not dead – yet," said Sullivan grimly. "I just wish I knew why, in Andur's name, the Archons are so hell-bent on clearing us – and everyone else – out of this city. What are they up to?"

"We'll find out. If not us, then whoever they send after us. We've told the Empire enough that they won't be able to ignore this little kingdom from now on. Even the damned Liberals know that we can't afford another Variscan War.

"However, that's by the by. For now I've got to compose our reply to the Archons, telling them that we reject their offer."

The door closed behind them and Thomas allowed himself to relax, pins and needles pricking his legs after so long frozen in position. He was shocked: frightened and stunned at what he had heard. The sheer weariness in Sir Edward's voice had brought home the desperateness of the situation as much as the words themselves.

That had been in the morning. By evening the mob had gathered, a thousand bestial faces baying for blood. It was then that the dizziness started, a spinning queasiness that filled his brain, swirling inside his head until every footstep was a trial and every thought a burden. Detesting himself for his weakness – for what was this but cowardice? – Thomas forced himself to leave his rooms. Staggering, he at last found the doorknob and, with an effort, pushed open the door.

Then he was falling, back and down. Blackness took him and the vision was upon him, searing heat burning his soul.

He saw it all. The brutal mob overpowering the guards; the Residency in flames, burning, falling, the Triune flag that had flown so boldly torn down to die with its inhabitants. Sir Edward cut down on the steps; Sullivan shot dead at the *variideshar,* Radburn beaten to death on the landing. Death, blood and fire, burning, searing and consuming. Soundlessly Thomas screamed.

Somehow he had escaped death – thanks to Piotr. Whilst he had lain there, unconscious, a weakling, the faithful Rotliegendan had carried him bodily out of the Residency. How he had evaded the mob Thomas had no idea: in the two days since the escape they had been constantly on the run, with no time for detailed explanations. Not that Piotr was, in any case, particularly willing to talk. When he had come to, Thomas had found himself wrapped in a cloak somewhere outside the Residency, Piotr watching over. Then – could it really be less than two days ago? – they had begun the gruelling journey.

#

The sound of footsteps recalled Thomas sharply to the here and now. Piotr must be returning. The Rotliegendan had crept off a quarter of an hour ago to investigate the landing of a *tarathin*, the third that had passed them that day. Unlike the previous two, this one had landed, circling down shortly after it had passed overhead.

Crouched in his ditch, Thomas was about to step out when some sudden instinct urged caution. Lifting his head slowly, he turned towards the direction of the noise. What he saw made him thank Andur for his caution. The approaching man was not Piotr but an armsman in the desert palm tabard of Erd Gellin. Had he stood up it would no doubt have been the last thing he would ever have done.

Thomas's sense of relief at his narrow escape died quickly. The soldier was coming straight towards him, walking along the line of the irrigation ditch with musket in hand. Unwillingly, Thomas's hand crept to the pistol tucked inside his cloak.

He had never used a gun before. Duelling had been discouraged in the Empire since before he was born and he had never shot for sport. Now he must shoot – kill – a man. Desperately he clutched at Piotr's words of yesterday.

"Take these," Piotr had said, thrusting the pistol and a dagger at Thomas. "You will need them." Brushing aside Thomas's protestations of ignorance, the Rotliegendan had quickly outlined how to load, cock and fire the pistol.

"Wait until he is close – very close – then point, as if to point your finger. Aim for the body: you will be less likely to miss. Don't shout or give warning, just shoot. And remember your dagger – and his. People have killed and been killed long before guns were invented."

The words flashed through his head as the soldier came closer. The long-barrelled musket glinted wickedly, flashing back echoes of the setting sun. There was no chance now of escaping detection. The soldier was alert, looking down into the ditch as he walked along it. Clearly searching for something – or someone. There could be little doubt as to who that might be.

Now he was only a few paces away. Clutching Piotr's words to him, Thomas pulled out the pistol. It seemed so small, and yet so heavy, a heaviness far beyond its weight. Any moment now he would be discovered. He must act first. Stepping out from the niche in which he had huddled, he raised the pistol, pointed, and squeezed the trigger.

The report was deafening. Thomas saw the Gellinese soldier stagger and fall, his face a mask of almost comical surprise. Then he too was falling as searing heat took him. White hot flames burned through his brain and he knew no more.

Chapter Three

Encounters Unlooked For

He came to just as he had that morning, with Piotr shaking him, the Rotliegendan's pale face a few inches from his own. Still thrashing from the intensity of the vision, Thomas struggled back to consciousness. Despising his own weakness, he forced himself up, ignoring Piotr's efforts to restrain him.

"*Bethed Dereszda!* Kill yourself then!" muttered Piotr as Thomas staggered to his feet.

The first thing that Thomas saw was the body of the dead soldier. It lay stretched out where it had fallen, blood still oozing from the bullet hole in his chest. The corpse was only a few feet away from him.

Queasiness surged inside him. He retched, emptying the contents of his stomach upon the dry bed of the gully. He, Thomas Maynard, had killed this man. The world seemed to spin, the dizziness all but overwhelming him. For one terrifying moment it seemed that the vision would take him again.

Fighting it, he rallied, despite the urge to gag once more. He had killed a man. Shot him down without warning. Shame filled him; he felt like a murderer. As if from a great distance, he heard Piotr speaking to him and clutching at straws, he forced himself to concentrate.

"It was done well," said Piotr. "You kept your nerve. I had tracked down the *tarathin* and dispatched the pilot, but this one had already left. You saved yourself, and me."

Thomas felt warmth at Piotr's praise and hated himself for it. Concentrating upon the words, he asked about the only aspect that seemed to be somewhat removed from death. Anything to keep his mind off that subject.

"What did you do with the *tarathin*?"

"I killed it." Thomas gagged again. Piotr looked at him pityingly.

"Can you fly one?" he asked. Thomas shook his head.

"Neither can I. So what should I do? Let it loose? It might have flown straight home. A skilled neuromancer could have extracted our location straight from its mind. Leave it to starve? I am not cruel without reason. Killing it was a mercy.

"Now move. Your shot may have been heard – we can lose no time. We must walk through the night and may Our Lady of Silence conceal us."

#

The next morning they found the chaplain. So changed was he and so unlikely the meeting that at first Thomas failed to recognise him. Even when he did, it seemed a delusion, a waking dream brought on by his deathly weariness.

For it had been a hard night. They had gone far, wearily forcing themselves onwards when their entire bodies were craving for rest. Oddly, Piotr's final biting words had done more good for Thomas than the previous praise: the criticism, even though for a different reason, helped to assuage his guilt. However, any guilt was soon forgotten in weariness. There is a time for soul-wracking, but when body and mind are being forced to their limits and beyond, even a saint would find it hard to dwell on matters of conscience.

With no moon, their progress was even more arduous. Even Piotr began to show signs of flagging. Tired feet stumbled as they picked their way through the darkness. More than once Thomas fell, sprawling over an obstacle that he had not seen. Befuddled, he lay there, idly wondering why his legs were no longer working. Why wasn't he moving forward any more?

The fourth time this happened – or was it the fifth? – Piotr called a halt. For a few brief hours they rested, sleep enveloping them instantly despite the discomfort of the bare ground.

Immediately it seemed, Thomas was being woken again by Piotr. The sky was only just beginning to lose its pitch-blackness. As was his custom, the Rotliegendan had risen at daybreak. Forced awake, Thomas dragged himself to his feet, knowing in his heart that his companion was right. They must put as much distance as possible between themselves and the events of the day before.

However well his mind might know this, his body told a different story. Limbs protested; the few hours of snatched sleep had not even begun to undo his weariness. So, stumbling onwards like drunkards through the grey light of dawn, the two continued their slow progress across the arid hills of Erd Gellin.

It was then that they came across the chaplain; in the queer half-light when the day had broken but the sun not yet risen above the horizon. The man's clothes were tattered, his body filthy and his face had a look of desolation: a far cry from the spruce appearance he had invariably presented in the Residency. With a shock Thomas realised what he himself must look like.

"Reverend Lawrence!" he called. The chaplain had not yet seen them. At the sound of a human voice he froze, shrinking back like a startled rabbit. Thomas saw him turn round warily, his whole body poised to bolt.

Slowly, recognition dawned in the chaplain's eyes.

"Thomas? Thomas Maynard? Andur be praised!" The chaplain was weeping, tears pouring freely down his face as he half-ran, half-stumbled towards them.

"How did you escape? Wait – don't answer yet. Do you need food?" The expression on the chaplain's face was answer enough. Without hesitation, both Thomas and Piotr drew a piece of flatbread from their scant supply and passed it over.

Ravenously, the chaplain tore into it, huge bites disappearing almost without chewing. It was clear that he was half-starved. Thomas reflected that, save for Piotr, it might have been him in such a situation. He owed the Rotliegendan his life a dozen times over.

"Andur be praised," said the chaplain, finishing the bread. "I can't say how good it is to see another Triune face. I thought no one had got out alive. How did you escape the massacre?"

"Piotr carried me out. We've been on the run since then. But how did you get away? And how did you get here ahead of us?"

"By the grace of Andur I was away at the time or I would have perished with the others. I'd gone to Krithia, a little town around three days' travel north of Iskarn. I wanted to speak to the priest there; he's a godly man, not so wrapped up in saint worship as most of these heretics. I had hoped he might be able to tell me something about those tales of beasts in the countryside we'd been hearing about for so long, whether there was any truth in the matter."

"Did he?"

"Nothing concrete, no, but he swore by his hope of redemption that they weren't just tales. In recent months Krithia has been swamped by refugees from the countryside. Many people are too scared to live outside a town any more. His description of what he'd seen horrified me. He told of terrible wounds; limbs torn away or withered in flame and acid; cruel claw scars stretching the length of a man's torso. The people report demons; winged monstrosities and bestial, goat-like fiends. I fear that the worst we have heard is true."

"Demons and drogkhar," said Piotr. "It is as we feared."

The chaplain looked taken aback that Piotr had spoken. Clearly puzzled as to what to say, he responded by ignoring the interjection. Piotr, naturally, was unperturbed.

"The priest saved me. I told you that he was a godly man. The day I arrived in Krithia, a message arrived from the Archons. The *tarathin* landed only a bare two hours after I arrived – I dread to think what would have happened had I been just that bit slower in my journey.

"The Archons had commanded that all foreigners be immediately imprisoned. The priest and the mayor of each village were responsible for enforcing the order. Fortunately for me, this particular priest considered his duty to Andur more important than his duty to a corrupt temporal authority. The message contained a description of the massacre at the Residency – though they put it somewhat differently of course – so he knew what would happen to me if he turned me in.

"Of course, the whole village knew I was there of course, so there was only one thing to be done. He hid me in the ossuary and told the mayor that I had escaped. You should have seen the consternation that caused! Even from inside the ossuary I could hear the commotion, for it seems that the writ had threatened doubled taxes on any village that allowed a foreigner to escape. The whole village turned out to look for me, scouring the countryside. Of course, they had no luck – and fortunately none suspected the priest of duplicity. When nightfall came and even the most dedicated of the searchers were calling it a day, he smuggled me out of the ossuary – and sent me on my way.

"That was two days ago. I've been wandering ever since – I haven't dared to approach any habitation due to fear of being turned in, so I've been living on what I could find, which isn't much."

"Where were you heading?"

"I don't know. Geography was never my strong point. I was just trying to go somewhere – to get out of Erd Gellin, or meet someone from the Residency."

"We were lucky to meet. Had we been a trifle slower, or your village of Krithia in a different direction, our paths would never have crossed."

"An act of divine providence indeed. Today, if I have not totally lost track of time, is Sodtar, the day of rest. Even if we may not rest, we should at least set aside time to praise and give thanks to Andur, praying that he may continue to guide us through our plight."

Automatically, Thomas glanced at Piotr. What would his companion think of this use of time? To his surprise, he saw that Piotr was nodding approval.

Thomas had forgotten the piety of the people of this continent of Laurentia. Though their practice of Andurism might have some differences to that of the Empire, their devotion outdid all but that of the most ardent of Scriptualists – amongst whose number, he reflected wryly, could undoubtedly be included the chaplain. The great works of the Awakening, the insights of Sinclair, Russell, Laverick and so many others, had yet to percolate to this Dark Continent, burning away the mists of superstition and delusion with their new light of natural, moral and arcane philosophy.

Given Piotr's acquiescence, nay, eagerness, Thomas lent his assent without qualms. After all, Anduranism was as integral to the Triune Empire as honour, duty and loyalty to Triumvirate and Empire. A cornerstone of culture and civilisation.

The chaplain opened the service. This preaching in the open air seemed somehow to suit his temperament more than the heavy, sombre atmosphere of the Residency chapel, steeped, despite its newness, in the shared centuries of tradition. Idly Thomas wondered what Piotr thought of this, accustomed as he must be to the grandeur and formulaic liturgy of Canonical worship.

Yet even before the chaplain had finished the opening prayer, his words were cut off by a distant howl, an eerie, keening ululation that, though so faint as to be on the edge of hearing, nevertheless seemed to tear at the listeners' very souls. Startled, the chaplain stopped, breaking off in mid sentence. Again, the howl rang out, joined this time by another and then by more.

"Run!" cried Piotr, his pale face even whiter than usual. Grabbing his pack, he appeared ready to bolt on the instant. His behaviour chilled Thomas to the marrow. This was Piotr, the man who, alone, had been able to evade the mob at the Residency, who only a few hours ago had calmly shrugged off their killing of two Gellinese soldiers as of no account. What could have brought him to such a pass?

"But the service..." protested the chaplain.

"Forget the *rethesząk* service! There will be time for that later, if we are still alive."

"You forget your place! Thomas, will you allow your servant to speak to me in such a manner? The worship of Andur..."

"Listen to me, Imperial!" Piotr's taut face was bare inches from that of the chaplain. "Continue your service if you wish, but your flesh will be torn from your bones and your soul from your body if you remain here longer. You would do well to take heed when those more knowledgeable are speaking, but the choice is yours!"

On the verge of losing control, the Rotliegendan turned, spitting at the ground. He set off at a fast pace, running westward with a swift jog trot. His companions would follow or not, as they pleased.

"Do what he says," said Thomas, likewise setting off. Behind them, the chaplain was also coming, unwilling to be left alone even if he was not convinced of the danger.

To his astonishment, Thomas found himself not only matching Piotr's pace but gaining on him, terror giving wings to his weary legs. As he drew level, a renewed chorus of unearthly howling broke out behind them, closer this time. Snatching a breath, he turned to Piotr.

"What are they?"

"*Rahvashda* – demon wolves. They have our scent; that last call confirmed it." The strain and fear was evident in his voice. Thomas felt his heart go cold. *Rahvashda* were true demons, not merely some beast that had wrongly gained the appellation.

"How can we outrun them?"

"We can't," said Piotr. "But I think the River Yedisan lies not too far this way – I hope. Pray that I am correct! It's little more than a stream, especially at this time of year, but it may serve."

"What if we don't make it?"

"Then we die."

They continued running, a steady lope that ate up the yards between them and sanctuary. Behind them staggered the chaplain, just managing to keep up, though remaining always a few dozen yards behind. They dared not slacken their pace to accommodate him: only the sight of them ahead allowed him to run so fast. That and the chorus of chilling howls behind; more frequent now, and louder, closer. The very sound drained one's blood of all hope.

Without needing to speak all three quickened their pace. They were cresting a ridge now and beheld the Yedisan before them, a thin trickle, a few feet wide, lined with olive trees and sycamores. This was their hope of salvation?

"Into the water!" cried Piotr. "It is our only chance."

Scrambling down the steep banks they splashed into the river, the swift-flowing water barely covering their knees. The baying of the *rahvashda* spurred them on. Seeking out a low-hanging branch, Piotr hauled himself up into a tree.

"Follow!" he said.

Thomas needed no urging. Grabbing Piotr's outstretched hand he scrambled up. The strength in the Rotliegendan's wiry arms stunned him as he was pulled up with seemingly little effort. The chaplain followed after him. Obeying Piotr's commanding gestures they climber higher and deeper within the branches. The thin foliage seemed a pitiably small concealment.

"This may suffice," said Piotr. "Fortunately we are downwind of them or our scent would have given us away. Be deathly still – their eyesight is poor in daylight, but their hearing is acute.

"We have done what we can. Now all that we can do is pray that the Blessed Ruth, Our Lady of Silence will have mercy and conceal us."

"I will pray to no false goddess," protested the chaplain. "Ruth shares none of the divinity of her Brother..."

"Pray to whomever you will," hissed Piotr, rounding upon him with dagger drawn. "But be silent or I will cut your throat!" Wisely, the chaplain held his tongue. It was probably the first time, Thomas reflected, that anyone had managed to silence him on such an issue.

The baying was louder now, shrill yips interspersing the deeper howls that now came almost constantly. Huddled low on his branch, Thomas's fear was magnified by the dread of the unknown. The exams for the Laurentian Service, though gruelling in their requirements for detailed knowledge of Laurentian history, culture, geography and religion, had been rather less demanding in terms of knowledge of demons. His time at Chelmsthorpe, where he had read classics, had also inexplicably failed to cover the subject. Soon enough he would know far more than he had ever wished to.

Now he saw them cresting the ridge, less than two hundred yards from the river. Great wolf-like beasts speeding along their track faster than a horse could run. Wolf-like yet larger, far larger. To Thomas's eyes they seemed huge, the size of a lion or more, rippling forms of muscle, sinew and tooth. Despite their stature they flowed over the ground like water, all but unhindered by obstacles or gullies. Andur, they could leap the puny rivulet before them in a heartbeat!

Intent on the destruction of their prey the six demonic beasts rushed ever closer. To the water's edge they raced, following the fugitives' scent as unerringly as any bloodhound. There they pulled up short, snarling and coursing up and down the bank, seeking a new trace. They were close enough now that Thomas could see the fiery light of their eyes, the fell demonic glint that spoke of a cunning and intelligence far greater than that of any mere beast. What were they waiting for? They might fear water – that was one of the few facts about demon-kind that Thomas knew – but forget the other bank, one bound could take them into the trees themselves. Thomas had passed through fear now; all that was left was a strange calm, a dull resignation to the end that he knew was near.

A *rahvashda* leaped. Thomas closed his eyes. He was lost. The rending teeth of the beasts would devour him. There was nothing he could do. Then the howls redoubled, the growls of a moment turning to the baying of an animal that has found a scent.

But the teeth never came. To his astonishment, rather than being torn limb from limb Thomas heard their cries diminishing into the distance. He dared to open his eyes. The *rahvashda* were no longer beneath him. Then he saw them, the pack single-mindedly heading westward at speed. Thomas breathed again. They had escaped once more, by the grace of Andur, but how many times could their fortune hold?

For a long while they lay there, pressed close to their tree branches. Only after the last sound of the *rahvashda* had long since died away did the three fugitives dare to stir, levering themselves down from the olive tree that had sheltered them.

"What happened?" asked Thomas. "Why did they leave us so suddenly?"

"They picked up some other scent," said Piotr. "Some luckless peasant no doubt." He spat. "His misfortune has gained us a precious few hours of grace."

"You think then, that they might come back?" said the chaplain.

"No doubt. Unless I stop them. Now silence, both of you."

Reaching into his jerkin, the Rotliegendan pulled out a securely tied, small leather pouch. Opening it, his strong fingers probed inside before drawing out a solid lump of turquoise, as big across as the end of his thumb.

Thomas felt a shiver run through him at the sight of the flawless gem.

"You're an arcanist?" he asked in astonishment.

"A mage, yes," replied Piotr, the slight twitch of his eyes the only sign of his surprise at Thomas's remark. "You recognised the gem – are you talented yourself?"

"No. My studies included a brief grounding in arcane philosophy – or magic, as you call it here – but no, I'm not."

"A pity."

"You studied in Linnarson?" Even as he spoke, Thomas sensed that it was the wrong thing to have said. Piotr's demeanour indefinably hardened.

"I never had that privilege," Piotr said, the edge to his voice unmistakeable. "But I am sure that my skills will suffice. We have some small pool of knowledge in the northeast.

"Now silence. You must not disturb my concentration."

Sliding out of the tree Piotr squatted down on his heels, the turquoise cradled before him in the palms of his hand. Rock-steady, his eyes stared into its green depths, his whole body and mind locked in focus upon the gem.

A few feet away Thomas watched him, hardly daring to breathe. He had never been so close to an arcanist in the casting of a spell before. The petty tricks of the students at Chelmsthorpe did not count. Gemstones, at least gemstones flawless enough to be used for arcane philosophy, were far too rare to be wasted by students: they learned their skills on poor imitations, of no real power. This was true magic, gem magic.

The chaplain stood by his side, similarly transfixed. Together they watched, spellbound, as their companion continued his mysterious work. The turquoise, initially dull, began to pulse with an inner light. At first the glow was so faint that Thomas thought it was bright, throbbing in a steady rhythm.

Piotr was chanting now, a faint, barely audible sound at the edge of hearing. Thomas strained to listen but the words were unintelligible to him; rasping, guttural phrases far removed from the mellifluous strains of Evvenyae or the stately, dignified tones of Dalradian that Thomas had always considered to be the languages of the arcane. Instead the harsh vocalisms continued, punctuated by sharp clicks and fricatives so alien it was hard to believe that they issued from a human mouth.

The chanting came faster now and Piotr's voice became louder, more urgent. Sweat beaded on his forehead. His limbs, formerly steady as a stone, began to tremble as he reached the climax.

A final shouted word and it was done. From east to west the landscape rippled, seemed to shimmer. For a heartbeat Thomas felt as if his soul was being dragged from his body. Then the moment was over: he was himself again. Before him on the ground sprawled Piotr, gasping for breath.

The Rotliegendan looked utterly drained, fatigue writ upon every line of his face in a way, the remnants of turquoise dust trickling through his fingers. Casting the spell, whatever it had been, had clearly exhausted the man in a way that even the two days of gruelling travel had not.

Strangely mellowed by this evidence of humanness in his companion, Thomas offered the Rotliegendan his hand in assistance. Gratefully Piotr took it, wearily pulling himself to his feet.

"My last turquoise," he said ruefully, brushing the last of the dust from his hands.

"What was it that you did?"

"Hidden our trail. If it works. Any signs of our passage will be hidden; no trackers will find us by fair means or foul. Instead, any who try will see the trail heading east."

"How long will it last?"

"At least a day. More if we are lucky."

Thomas marvelled, and said so. He had never heard of any arcane philosophy – or rather magic; he may as well get used to this continent's nomenclature – that could achieve something of that nature.

Piotr shrugged, brushing off the praise.

"You are right – few know how. It's an *isp'te'ran* spell. Their mages are adepts of the arts of defence and protection."

"An *isp'te'ran* spell?" said the chaplain in astonishment. "You've studied in the Elder Alliance?"

"No, thanks be to Andur." He shivered. "By His grace I have been spared that ordeal. The spell was taught to me by another Rotliegendan; I know not whether he himself had studied there or if he had got it, as I did, from another.

"I would not have liked to go there. I met a gryphon once. That was not so bad, barring her sheer size and physical presence, and as for the *mokshtar*, I cannot speak for them. But the *isp'te'ra*? They are..." He broke off, shuddering. "Utterly alien. Callous, totally cold."

"Cruel?"

"No, not cruel. They have that advantage over humanity; they do not fight or kill for pleasure. In both the Variscan and Pelagic wars they fought on the side of the righteous. But they are merciless nonetheless. No man can withstand their tortures, should he have information that they desire. They wage war to win, taking no prisoners, save it benefit them in some other way.

"Nor are they less harsh on their own kind. I have heard it tell that a party of *isp'te'ra* will slay their wounded companions in a retreat, even if there was a chance of survival, if that would maximise the chance of the most surviving. Neither would those slain protest. Individuality truly has no meaning for them; neither does pity, nor cruelty."

Interesting as this interchange might be, a more pressing concern was troubling Thomas. The *isp'te'ra* had been covered in his studies, though it was reassuring nonetheless to hear the books confirmed. Nevertheless, here and now the immediate took precedence.

"Regarding your spell," he interjected, taking advantage of a pause in the conversation. "Won't any following arcani... – mage," he corrected himself, "be able to sense the residue and be able to unravel from that which way we have gone? I'm sure the Gellinese will include mages in those hunting us. Although it buys us some time, as soon as one passes they will be on our tail again."

"You have indeed studied," said Piotr. "But here you are wrong. I have shadowed the residue – no mage will detect its traces, whether man, demon or even *isp'te'ra*. Those of us who follow Our Lady of Silence know many things that others do not."

The chaplain began to open his mouth, but promptly shut it again at a sharp look from Thomas. The man was not entirely a fool.

Though only a few minutes had passed since the spell, already Piotr was getting to his feet, his iron-hard constitution demonstrating itself once more in the speed of his recovery. Only the pace that he set, a hair slower than normal, betrayed his weariness. The hiding of their trail had given them a breathing space, but no more – the three of them were still deep in the heart of enemy territory. They would need skill, endurance and, most of all, luck, if they were to reach Elaran alive.

Chapter Four

Comparative Theology

"I will not take it," said the chaplain stubbornly. Piotr was at the limit of his patience.

"And I say again, why not? You're a fool if you don't!"

"Reverend Lawrence, taking the dagger doesn't mean you have to use it, if you don't see fit," said Thomas, in a conciliatorily tone. "But even if it would have been no use against the *rahvashda*, we may be attacked by others against whom it could be – soldiers of Erd Gellin for example. We know they're still in pursuit."

"So, you would have me slaughter a man whose only crime is to be following the wrong master? I'm surprised at you, young Thomas; you were not so bloodthirsty at the Residency."

"Well," he said abashed, "not exactly, but..."

"Better them than us," broke in Piotr bluntly. Thomas looked at him gratefully for coming to his rescue. "Leave the moral philosophy to armchairs before the fire, Father – out here it's kill or be killed."

"For you perhaps, but Andur teaches us that there is another way. And I have told you before, don't call me 'father'."

"Very well, 'chaplain'. But what of the demons or the droghkar? What of your own Empire's conquest of the heathen in Scahania, for that matter? It's every good Anduran's duty to resist the fiends of hell wherever they may be found."

"Spiritually, mentally or corporeally, you no doubt would say?" said Lawrence, quoting from the Canonical catechism.

"Yes! Look at St. Senren, St. Malbren or St. Harinath of the Lakes. They faced unflinchingly their demons and prevailed, Andur's power triumphant through their righteousness."

"Your saints, not ours," said the chaplain haughtily. "You think that this dagger would be of any use against the *rahvashda*?"

"Through the power of Andur all things are possible – or have you Scriptualists forgotten that, as you have so much else? Men have been killing each other with such as this for millennia before guns were invented."

"Precisely. All things are possible through Andur. 'In His palm we shelter, for His is the hour of our departure.' I put my trust in Andur, not in earthly weapons. Should He wish me to reach Elaran then I will reach it, should all the hosts of hell stand between us. And if he should not so desire it? Then I will obey his will."

A thought suddenly struck Piotr. "Have you sworn a vow of non-violence?" he asked, more respectfully.

"No. We leave such displays of ostentation to you Sanctists."

"Then why, by the broken wheel, won't you take the *retheszic* dagger?" exploded Piotr, his voice flaying Lawrence like a knife. "You're a fool if you think Andur's grace is some sort of physical shield – there are saints and martyrs by the score who will prove otherwise, holier men by far than you. I tell you..."

Thomas could only stand by and listen as the argument raged. It would have been the height of folly to intervene. Piotr was on the edge; it would take only one more straw to push him over into physical violence. As for Lawrence, the chaplain remained quietly stubborn. Not angry, but clearly immovable.

He had always been like that, Thomas reflected, particularly on matters of perceived dogma. Kind and compassionate he might be but when his mind was made up, the chaplain could be stubborn to the point of idiocy. Thomas could remember a time when only a direct order from Sir Edward had made him give way. With no such supreme authority here, he knew that Piotr would not be successful in his remonstrations, no matter what arguments or threats he resorted to.

Lawrence had suffered for it, too, back at the Residency. Not only from his superiors – that could be expected – but from others who, bored with their long exile from Home, found him a ludicrously easy target for mockery. It was not only that his uncompromising views seemed childishly naive to seasoned diplomats such as Sullivan or Lowther, but his fixation upon arcane pieces of theology seemed utterly irrelevant.

To be honest with himself, Thomas agreed with them, though his genuine liking for the chaplain had always made him refrain from joining their mockery. They were all good Andurans, as were the Gellinese and the rest of Laurentia north of the Har Meneth – the populace were hardly pagans like in Scahania or the Borallian colonies. Who cared about a minor difference in the interpretation of scripture? But it was like now: Thomas knew very well that there was nothing in the Book of Andur that forbade Andurans – even ministers – from carrying arms to defend themselves, but if the chaplain thought that there was, well, fish would fly and birds swim before he would be convinced otherwise.

Thomas remembered one particular instance of chaplain-baiting. It had been at dinner a few weeks ago, shortly after the Harvest Festival, celebrated here in Erd Gellin with much more fervour than in the Empire. No doubt in an arid nation on the edge of the desert a safe supply of food seemed both more precious and more fragile than in the Empire's benevolent climes. Few people were dining in the main hall in the following week and that night Thomas had found himself opposite the chaplain.

The meal had started well. Beside him, Derringham and Sullivan had engaged in a lively discussion over the soup on the subject of the Pelagic War. Sullivan had advocated that the tactics and prowess of the Senrenites had been instrumental in forcing the Pelagics to terms whilst Derringham had held to the more conventional view, that the victory had been won by the strategic genius of Caralan Venar. Both men were good speakers who knew their subject well; the conversation remained animated right through the main course, with Thomas himself and others chiming in now and again.

It was only over dessert, a rich fruit cake served with camperdown sauce, that the conversation began to flag. Sullivan, casting about for some new topic of conversation, saw the opportunity for entertainment that lay within the chaplain, who thus far had played little part in the debate.

"So, Reverend Lawrence, what's your opinion of the Senrenites?"

"You know well my opinion, Sullivan. Idolatrous Sanctists, like the rest of their ilk."

"Fine soldiers though," commented Radburn. "They're one of the few chivalric orders who've managed to adapt to modern weaponry. Modern by Laurentian standards that is."

"Does skill in war now justify heresy then? 'Not by force of arms, but by faith in our Redemptor alone may man gain the heavenly kingdom.'"

"Oh, give over, Lawrence – this is the fifth century, not the second. The Senrenites have been a clear force for good for centuries. They're natural allies of the Empire if we expand here: before the interregnum of the Variscan Imperium they'd all but civilised warfare in northern Laurentia."

"A force for good? In a region where there have been more bloody wars in the last century than in all of Imperial history? Where the Niavon dynasty holds sway in Greater Torridon? You've been deceived, Radburn; they may strive for good, but even the best intentions of heretics are doomed to go awry."

"By the Broken Wheel, you can't do expect them to do everything! And even you surely can't blame the Pelagic War on them."

"What do you have against the Canonicals, anyway?" asked Sullivan, needling.

"You step dangerously near to blasphemy, Sullivan."

"Dangerously?" laughed Sullivan, Radburn and the others joining in. Even Thomas could not help smiling.

"As far as I'm concerned," said Radburn, "the Canonicals are good Andurans, same as us. They worship Andur same as us, both as Lord of Order and in his incarnation on Edrith, Andur Astartes, our Redemptor, who died upon the wheel and broke it, thus freeing us from the eternal Wheel of Life. That's all I know about it.

"I'll leave the intricacies to you theologians but I'll tell you, it's refreshing dealing with Andurans, even if they are foreign, as opposed to those thrice-damned heathens in Scahania."

"A heretic is more dangerous than a heathen, who may still be turned to see the justice of Andur. A heretic has already rejected that justice. How can you call these people Andurans? 'I am Andur, Lord of Order, and I alone am your God' says the Book. You know full well that the Sanctists not only pray to their saints but worship Ruth, the sister of our Redemptor. Our Lady of Silence they call her and name her divine, when nowhere in scripture does it even indicate such an outrage. How can they worship a false goddess and still be Andurans?"

"Ah well," said Sullivan, leaning back, "you'd have to read St. Cornelius's *Annalia* for that. Not that I've read it myself, but I understand that he explains the paradox in one of its volumes – if you can call a hundred pages of theology an explanation."

"Konelis Larach was a false saint and a heretic, and the *Annalia* the final nail in the coffin of a church already bed-ridden with lies and superstition!"

"Reverend Lawrence, if you will allow me to interject," said Sir Edward, his attention drawn from the head of the table by the chaplain's raised voice. "I could not help hearing you mention Konelis Larach – St Cornelius as he is known in Dalradian. A fascinating man. Notwithstanding his religious role, it is of course well known that as Abbot of Zarant, he steered the course of the Zechen-Rotliegendish Commonwealth, itself a most intriguing nation."

Like the smooth diplomat that he was, Sir Edward deftly turned the conversation on to less dangerous subjects. Keen to ensure that it did not revert to its former course, Thomas spoke up.

"Sir Edward, I've never understood how he was able to have so much influence, particularly in a country where power was so anarchically distributed as the Commonwealth. Is it possible that historians could have exaggerated his role, in deference to his religious stature?"

"As eminence grise to Dominic the Great, with Silence priests whispering in the ears of half the nobles in the kingdom? No Maynard, it is very clear to see how his power spread.

"Nor do they resent that, in north-east Laurentia. Nowhere is St. Cornelius more revered than in the land that gave him birth. Memories of the Zechen-Rotliegendish Commonwealth die hard in the Tuevic nations; it may have been five hundred years since the last remnants dissolved, but the people still remember the days in which they ruled half a continent in power and glory. Its name could be a powerful rallying cry still – though a dangerous one, as many an ambitious monarch who could not fulfil his promises has found."

The discussion had proceeded on its new course at a level and intensity more suitable for the dinner table. Noticing a similar diminution of noise level in the present, Thomas snapped out of his reverie.

The argument had ceased. Piotr, his face a mask devoid of expression, had resheathed the dagger. Standing with his back to Lawrence, he silently shouldered his pack. Lawrence, on the other hand, stood glowering, looking daggers at the Rotliegendan's back. His hatred was plain to see: if looks could have killed, Piotr would have died that moment.

Thomas knew better than to intervene. He had been there too many times before. As the chaplain turned to follow Piotr, his anger still high, Thomas fell wordlessly in behind them. He thanked Andur that the chaplain was not so far gone in anger as to try to leave. That would have been a certain death sentence, yet Thomas doubted that he could have prevented it.

As the day wore on, the fire of hostility wore off yet a chill remained in the air. Lawrence recovered rapidly. Used to such confrontations, the hot words touched him little. Piotr, on the other hand, was of a different nature. Though in many ways he appeared his former laconic self, exchanging the odd word with both Thomas and Lawrence, it was noticeable to Thomas that not once did he ask Lawrence to do any task. Whether the chaplain had recognised this Thomas did not know; he suspected not, for Lawrence had never been the most perceptive of people in such matters. Yet to Thomas, Piotr's contempt and disdain for the chaplain was painfully obvious.

The subtle hostility continued the next day, distorting the natural air of comradeship that should have grown between the three. However, the rigours of the journey itself and the natural taciturnity of Piotr meant that the tension increasingly slipped to the back of Thomas's mind. There were odd occasions when it rose but for the most part it gave way to more pressing concerns.

The weariness that had beset him remained, exacerbated by the heavy toll that the recent days had taken on his body. His calves and thighs ached, while a long graze on his arm, picked up Andur knew where, throbbed unpleasantly in a counterpart to his tread. The frayed bottom of his shirt was a constant irritant; it had long since rubbed his waist raw. Worst of all, his right knee had been jarred painfully. Each downhill step shot agony through his whole body. More than once he had stumbled, sometimes coming close to falling.

Their pace had slowed; Thomas knew this. He also knew that there had been no other real option. Mortal flesh could only endure so much; perhaps Piotr could have continued their breakneck pace, but he, Thomas Maynard, could not have – and nor could Lawrence. Piotr's spell had at least given them a small amount of breathing space.

Whilst the slower pace might have seemed no less agonising, in actuality the slight let-up meant that all three had the fraction more energy they needed to take note of their surroundings in a way that Thomas at least had not done since the first day.

The landscape was fundamentally unchanged; they had come, in reality, only a very little distance. Harsh, arid scrubland dotted with wiry trees remained their companions, criss-crossed by irrigation ditches and dry, steep-sided wadis. They were still many days' travel from the cooler, wetter foothills of the border country where Erd Gellin ended and Elaran began.

Soon after noon they passed a peddler, a dour-faced man with his long robe pulled tight against the harsh desert wind from the west. Like him, his team of four scrawny mules looked to have seen better times. Neither party spoke. Thomas spared the man a second glance as they passed, the rickety wagon disappearing behind the lee of a great mushroom rock, the sandstone sculpted by centuries of wind into its current distinctive form. Truly, only the desperate were abroad in Erd Gellin in these times.

The afternoon wore slowly on. Just as they had yesterday, a good hour before sundown they began looking for a sheltered place to spend the night. A single night's sleep was not enough to recover from the thirty-six-hour forced march they had made previously. Just the thought of sleep reminded Thomas of how weary he was.

It was as they were making camp that the vision struck again. Once more, burning heat seared through Thomas's brain. The Residency was in flames; again he witnessed the brutal deaths of Sir Edward, Mott, Hewisham and the others. Helplessly, he cried out.

The scenes of horror continued remorselessly, trapping Thomas in a nightmare of torment. The burning pain wracked his body. Screaming, he struggled to escape as white hot pain scorched his skin. Bonds restrained him, holding him fast as he fought to get free.

Then it was over. He began to come to. Gradually, the two blurs above him resolved into Piotr's and Lawrence's faces, bent over him in concern. The restraints against which he had fought so fiercely were Piotr's arms, containing his wild thrashings, lest he injure himself.

It seemed he could still feel the burning pain over his body. When he could move, he felt his skin. It was cool. It felt like it should be burning and blistered, such was the pain he had endured. He shivered, a shuddering spasm that wracked his body, a reaction to the shock of before.

This time it took him longer to recover from the weakness. The world seemed to swim around him, colours and images circling before his eyes. As he lay, recovering, he wondered what was happening. He had never before been troubled by fainting or fits of giddiness. Far off, through the mist of his dizziness, he heard his companions talking.

"This may be the death of him," he heard Piotr say.

"What is it? I never knew him to be prone to fits."

"They're visions, not fits. The same vision – that's the problem. He keeps reliving the burning of the Residency."

"Why? How can we help him?"

"We can't. This is beyond my skill to handle. Perhaps in Elaran there will be one who can help teach him control. I have sent word to others, but they are more distant."

"Sent word? How? Oh, of course – arcanely. Wait a moment – what do you mean, teach him control? I really don't know what you're talking about."

Even through his pain Thomas could not help a wry smile at the chaplain's short temper. Piotr, taciturn at the best of times, would be unlikely to respond to such a demand for information. But to his surprise, Piotr did respond; softly, as if speaking to himself, yet Thomas heard.

"It is so rarely that a True Seer is born," the Rotliegendan mused. "Three centuries since the last, and the previous one five hundred years before that. And the fate of the last shows only too clearly how fragile a vessel one is in which to rest our hopes."

#

Lykaios paced through his rooms. The clutter that adorned them irritated him; state gifts, acquisitions and war loot of previous Archons. Normally their lavishness pleased him – a sign of his wealth and power – but tonight they only served to remind him of all he had yet to achieve, compared to his predecessors.

By the Broken Wheel, what ailed the man! It was most unlike this particular visitor to be late. For the fourth time in ten minutes, Lykaios glanced at the reports on his desk. They were but one of the reasons that he did not relish the upcoming meeting. He told himself that that was the only reason for trepidation, firmly pushing aside the general unease that being in the presence of his ally always caused, an unease not limited to the way in which the man could seemingly evade the wards protecting the palace.

This was nonsense. He was High Archon Lykaios, first among equals of the Archons of Erd Gellin and, in truth, far more than that. No High Archon since before the Variscan Interregnum had possessed his power. He had no need to fear an outlander emissary, no matter what forces he represented.

Tiring of the wait he strode to the window, throwing open the shutters. Unbothered by the cool night air that streamed in he stared out. The splendour of Iskarn lay before him, the sinuous lines of its beauty glinting eerily in the light of the gibbous moon. His quarters lay on the fourth floor of the Iskandin Palace; from here, as befitted the High Archon, he could cast his gaze over fully one half of the city.

Beneath him sentries marched, their vigilance protecting the seat of the Archons from any threat. Within, dozens more guards lay between the entrance and his quarters. Other defences, no less potent for their invisibility, warded the palace against other threats; no magical or ethereal threat could cross those wards without sounding an alarm.

"Lykaios." The crumbling voice sounded like dry dust. The High Archon whirled, trained eyes fixed upon the figure that now occupied one corner of the grand study. Shadows, unnaturally deep, cloaked his new guest, shifting fluidly despite the steady light. As always, Lykaios was unable to determine any aspect of his ally, save for a vague impression of his height and build.

"Yesh'hama," he replied, inclining his head. Slamming closed the shutters, Lykaios strode towards the centre of the room, careful not to come too close to the other. That lesson had been learned early on. Whoever he was, his visitor guarded his privacy closely.

"What news from my allies?" said Lykaios. "Are the preparations proceeding as planned?"

"Your allies' work is proceeding as planned, Lykaios. You need not fear for our side of the bargain. But what of your own part? Has the Imperial cur been tracked down?"

"Not yet, *Yesh'hama*." He had hoped that this would not arise so early. "We are doing our best to pursue him."

"Not yet, Lykaios?" The arid voice was quietly dangerous. "You were granted a pack of *rahvashda* for this task, aside from your own supposedly formidable forces. If your army cannot track down one refugee, why should we believe that it will be able to overwhelm Elaran?"

Lykaios's voice was rock steady in reply, belying his fear. "With respect, *Yesh'hama*, catching a refugee is very different from war, in which I can assure you that our army will have no difficulties. All other foreign powers have been successfully persuaded to abandon the country."

"Then how did this one – a mere stripling, even by your standards – escape?"

"He had aid. A Rotliegendan spy."

"Ah," the harsh voice exhaled. Lykaios could still smell the sterile scent of the desert, despite the window being closed. The sirocco could play odd tricks on a man.

"Ah," his visitor repeated, "a Rotliegendan. They will soon learn that all their intrigue cannot withstand the pure majesty of power. But for now we may have to let this human go." He paused. "I will ensure that the Triune Empire is kept otherwise occupied. Soon they will have far too much to worry about to concern themselves over the fate of one insignificant diplomat."

Lykaios breathed more easily. The sticking point had passed – they would be able to move on to more clement matters.

"*Yesh'hama*, I will be guided by your wisdom." He inclined his head again. "May I ask why you desired to meet today?"

"You may, Lykaios." His guest's voice seemed to convey a hint of amusement. "I came to enquire of the state of your army. Are the commanders ready to receive their...reinforcements?"

"They are." Lykaios's heart beat faster. At last the time had come.

"Then they may begin receiving them – tomorrow. And what of your fellow Archons?"

"All are in agreement, saving only Hathoris whom we have discussed before. Aniketos is ready to step into his place."

"You have done well, Lykaios. Proceed as we have planned."

"When shall I see you again?"

"I will inform you."

"Your will, *Yesh'hama.*" He bowed low. In the corner, the shadows deepened and collapsed, falling in on themselves and dissolving. A rough, abrading wind rushed past him and then Lykaios was alone.

His mind sang with elation. Not an outward sign betrayed his jubilation, trained politician that he was. Even when alone, he had schooled himself to show no outward signs of emotion as a matter of course. Yet inwardly he rejoiced.

Now was the time when the might of Erd Gellin would be unleashed once more – under his command. In triumphant defiance he stared up at the full-length portrait of Akaiakos the Great, High Archon of Erd Gellin in the twelfth century. In his day the nation had been larger by far; from the Iskandin Palace the Archons had ruled half of Varangia, as well as whole swathes of what were now western Givet and Scandia. That was before the desert had encroached, eroding away the rich Gellinese croplands and with them, the source of Erd Gellin's strength.

Now, at last, he could look Akaiakos in the eyes without shame. His leadership, his wisdom and his bargains would make Erd Gellin great once more. With just the aid he had already received, the legions of Erd Gellin would not be stopped – and he had been promised more, oh so much more, for the future.

Dismissing such matters from his mind, Lykaios turned to more pragmatic actions of the plan. A meeting of the Archons must be called for the next evening, with the message to Hathoris to inexplicably not be delivered until too late. There were missives to write to the tagmata commanders and to their subordinates; swift *tarathin* couriers to be dispatched without delay.

And he must summon the First Mage tomorrow morning, to demand an explanation of why the new, strengthened wards had failed to detect or hinder his mysterious visitor. Lykaios, High Archon of Erd Gellin, was never content until all of an adversary's secrets were known. Whether dealing with an enemy or a temporary ally, knowledge was power.

Chapter Five

The Hills in Autumn

Thomas walked freely and easily, savouring the lush vegetation of his surroundings. Though now in late autumn, the landscape here in these parts were still more verdant by far than the arid scrubland of central Erd Gellin. Even the brisk bite of the early morning air only added to his sense of well-being.

It had been twelve days now since the massacre at the Residency. Since the encounter with the *rahvashda* they had encountered no further signs of pursuit. Both luck and Andur's favour had no doubt played a part, but there was little doubt in Thomas's mind that without Piotr's arcane talents their bones would have been bleaching on a hillside a week or more ago. Instead, they had continued their steady progress north-east, bound for their destination as surely as a ship in the Home-coming trades.

At first, progress had been agony. On the fifth day Thomas had wanted to die. Every step was a torture; the gain of each mile a pittance wrested from a brutal enemy. Had he been alone, he could never have continued.

But then a miracle had occurred. The sixth day, instead of being worse than the day before, as had been the case every day until then, had actually been slightly easier. Not by much – his body had still ached, with countless muscles protesting his exertions – but even that slight easing of agony was significant, coming as it did so unexpectedly.

From then on, every day had become better. Soon he was able to think of more than the immediate struggle of walking: to plan for the future and mourn for the past. He even found himself actively appreciating the landscape that they passed through, relishing in the freedom of his newly found fitness as he did so. Though their pace increased as the days progressed, it did so more slowly than his ability, being limited largely by Lawrence. The chaplain, neither as young nor as fit as Thomas, was proving less able to adapt to the rigours of the journey. Even so, he was improving, if more slowly, and his long-suffering endeavour had finally taken the edge off even Piotr's hostility.

Even the visions had caused him less trouble than he had expected. As Piotr had intimated, they were happening less frequently but with greater severity than at first. He had only suffered two more since the day they had met Lawrence.

True, it now took him several hours to recover from each; from the fits of dizziness, the retching and weakness and the feeling of burning pain, but he considered that a fair price to pay for several days of freedom in between.

The state in which one would incapacitate him for a day – or more – was clearly still some time in the future. Thomas had still not told Piotr that he had overheard his and Lawrence's conversation so he had little concrete idea of the implications – if Piotr's outlandish suggestion had been correct.

Thomas had never heard of a true seer! Oh, various arcanists had the ability to dimly perceive the future, weakly, imperfectly and inalterably. They were sometimes referred to as seers, particularly, so he had heard, those belonging to the more mystic monastic orders here in Laurentia. But the concept of a true seer with what, from Piotr's words, appeared to be a rarely born and powerful talent, had never crossed his path, either in conversation or in reading.

That, however, Thomas thought, was a conversation best left for when they had reached Elaran. A pursuit through the wilderness was neither the time nor the place for metaphysical discussions.

His two companions behind him, he crested a rise, pausing briefly to catch his breath. This rolling hill country was a new challenge, stretching and using muscles he had never realised existed. Piotr alone failed to notice the increased arduousness; his legs like pistons eating up the miles like clockwork, untroubled by even the steepest scarps that left Thomas and Lawrence gasping for breath. Had it not been for the rigours of the previous days they two would have found it hard indeed.

And these were but the foothills of the Aripos Hills, and they themselves but molehills beside the great Gralbakh Range that lay beyond. Vast and forbidding, the Gralbakhs stretched lengthwise for over 3000 miles, an impenetrable barrier across northern Laurentia. Its highest peaks dwarfed their Avalonian counterparts. Monarchs amongst mountains, many a climber back Home had yearned to test their mettle against those lofty towers, winning glory for themselves and the Empire by reaching their summit.

None had yet attempted it. Nor was the distance from Home the only reason – men had gone further for less. The Gralbakh Range, however, was the land of the reclusive, powerful *mokshtar,* of the merciless *isp'te'ra* and of the gryphons, deadly and mercurial as quicksilver. These races, as well as innumerable tribes of humans – Zavnarzi, Yale Riders, Serpent Eaters, Kelpurn and countless more – called that mountain fastness home. With the western edge of the Gralbakhs abutting the still fractious Imperial Pelagic provinces, the Triune Empire was understandably keen to respect the Elder Alliance's long-standing history of isolationism. The Imperial authorities would have frowned heavily upon any glory-seeking adventurer who endangered the two nations' treaty of mutual non-interference.

Fortunately the Aripos Hills were less forbidding – though it was true that the hill men of the Har Mareisch could be as hostile to outsiders as the Elder Alliance. But the Har Mareisch was to the far north-east of here; its wild denizens inhabited a forbidding territory that sprawled across the border between Elaran and Torridon, the braided, shawled hill men paying only lip service to their nominal rulers, on either side of the border.

He, Piotr and Lawrence were not, however, going there but rather to Hyrnar, the capital of Elaran. A fortified citadel with a small town nestling around its base, Thomas believed that they would be amongst the first Triune citizens to see it. Not the first of course – Clayton and Booth had passed through in 446, as described in the record of their explorations – but most of the information that the Empire possessed about the city was based on native treatises and descriptions. In his diary Clayton had described it as being located in an isolated valley at the base of a tall mountain, surrounded by hills and reachable only through a snaking canyon, but had said little more about it that Thomas could remember. Truly, there was little to interest the Empire in Elaran, located as it was so far from the Imperial provinces and possessing no great power, wealth nor ambitions. At the moment though, Thomas wished that some geographer back Home had only researched the place out of pure intellectual curiosity – pragmatism was all very well, but it could leave one knowing disturbingly little at times like this.

Still, although there would he was sure a number of strange customs, not to mention an undoubtedly superstitious and backward peasantry in the more remote regions – villagers were always the same in hill regions, even in the Empire – Elaran, was by all accounts, a modern Laurentian nation. Wryly, he reminded himself that this meant it was only a century or two behind the Empire. However, they could at least expect a courteous welcome, basic hospitality and, most crucially, a means of contacting the Empire. Reassuringly, Piotr seemed to have no qualms about their destination and he would certainly know more of the matter than either himself or Lawrence.

Twisting his head round he looked at his companion. The wiry Rotliegendan had become a fraction more communicative during the journey, though still preferring to remain silent unless conversation could not be avoided.

Piotr pulled out his compass and examined it. He gestured; they were to go left. Without comment Thomas obeyed, bearing round the high knoll before them. The narrow deer track skirted the edge of the hillside, wending what felt like a precarious path to the next ridge.

They kept to the heights as much as possible, save where a valley appeared to be going in the right direction. This land was largely uninhabited. The few isolated villages that did exist were easily marked from afar by the patchwork of terraced hillside that surrounded them. It was not difficult to give such settlements a wide berth.

Thomas wondered why there were so few people. Perhaps it was simply a region that had never had reason to be settled, or one that had been bypassed by trade routes and thus withered and faded like a cut flower. Or perhaps its proximity to the border left it undesirable, or it could have been devastated in the Variscan Wars, and never fully resettled.

He shrugged mentally. Who knew why? There were similar regions in the Empire, and right across Laurentia. After all, the land was not that hospitable, even if it was wetter than southern Erd Gellin.

Much wetter in fact. Not only had terraces replaced irrigation ditches around the villages, but they had forded three streams in that morning alone. A smile came to his lips as he remembered the last, a swift flowing brook between deep banks which they had crossed on a natural bridge of rocks and boulders. Piotr had been the first to cross, and thus the one to discover the loose rock. Thomas and Lawrence had struggled to control their laughter as it had tilted beneath him, Rotliegendan curses colouring the crisp autumn air as, arms pin-wheeling, Piotr had, by a hair, maintained his balance. Their highly capable companion had only narrowly escaped a ducking.

After, Thomas had plucked up the courage to tease him about it.

"I see you decided against a bath then."

"I would have, but then remembered that I'd be able to smell you Imperials all the worse if I did."

They had laughed at the swift riposte. Thomas knew he should have known better than to engage Piotr in a battle of wits. Fortunately the next stream was passed without incident and, later that afternoon, they would all receive the much-needed bath. A much larger river, a good thirty yards across, though shallow, blocked their path.

Trousers and packs above their head they waded in, angling their steps up stream against the swift current. The stones of the riverbed, worn smooth from countless years in the flow, rolled beneath their feet, threatening each moment to tip them over. Each step was made with caution; body balanced in midstream, leaning against the current, its rush both enemy and friend.

Now they were past halfway, yet the current had grown, the vagaries of the riverbed channelling its power. The racing water was up to their chests. Thomas hunched forward to raise his pack, keeping his clothes and their food – little enough though it now was – dry. Teetering, he forced his way on, holding fast until a slight shift or lull in the surge let him advance another step.

Then they were through the worst, the current slackening, the water level now up only to their waists, then their thighs. Carefully, still wary of the treacherous stones under foot, they completed the last few steps before hauling themselves out, filled with exuberance, despite their exhaustion.

Stretching out, they basked in the afternoon sun on the great flat boulders that lined the river, waiting to dry rather than pulling their clothes over their wet bodies.

"We were fortunate," said Piotr, once the excitement of the crossing had started to fade. "Had it not been for the dry summer, we would never have made it."

"But we did!" exclaimed Thomas, spirit undampened. The crossing had brought back memories of youthful adventures in the hills of his childhood, but the genuine need and real danger of this crossing had lent it a frisson that elevated it far beyond his boyhood exploits. He saw an answering grin from Lawrence and even a shadow of one from Piotr. The Rotliegendan too was not immune from the exhilaration.

"We must keep going," stated Piotr, his face returning to his habitual lack of expression. Thomas didn't mind. Pulling on their clothes, they set off once more.

The land was definitely changing, the flora reflecting the change in temperature, altitude and water abundance. Grey-green olive trees still dominated the hillsides, but the pomegranates and jujubes of the more arid heartland of Erd Gellin were dwindling, replaced by groves of citron and myrtle that further south had been seen only along the banks of streams. Birds sang; it was only now, once he heard them again that Thomas realised how much he had missed their presence during the long slow months in Iskarn. The keen-eyed desert hawk held sway there. Thomas might not know the names of these hill-land songsters yet their trilling melodies brought joy to his soul.

Autumn flowers dotted the landscape, a last display of nature's beauty before the chill months of winter set in for good. Mullein and emerith sparkled through the coarse grass of the slopes. Even Piotr paused momentarily at the sight of solyana blooming around a jutting outcrop, their delicate petals forming a circlet of gold against the weathered granite.

Crown of Senrens, however, outnumbered all the other flowers by far. Small and hardy, they blossomed profusely across the land. In places, such as the banks of the rivers and streams, they grew so thickly that land itself seemed covered by a carpet of red.

"What are these flowers?" asked Lawrence. They were passing through a meadow filled with the flowers, so dense that their usually delicate scent had become almost sickly in its intensity. Bending, he plucked a bloom, snapping the slim stem neatly and holding the head up to the sun. The seven-petalled flower glistened wetly, blood-red.

"These?" said Piotr. "Crown of Senrens." After a pause he continued, his voice betraying his disbelief. "You didn't know?"

"No, why would I?"

"There's not a great degree of overlap between Laurentian and Avalonian flora," chimed in Thomas, "and I think it would be fair to say that I'm not aware that Lawrence is an expert in identifying even Avalonian flowers." He grinned at the chaplain.

"But every child in northern Laurentia can recognise a Crown of Senren! It's the most holy flower there is; the emblem of the Senrenites, sacred to the memory of St. Senren."

"Why?" asked Thomas, ignoring the chaplain's muttering about 'saints'. "I've heard of him vaguely. Wasn't he a sort of early war leader against the droghkar, up in Aalenium?"

"That was St. Malbren. St. Senren lived near here, less than a week's journey to the west – why do you think there are so many flowers? I thought you'd studied Laurentia."

"I wasn't expected to memorise Ralviin's 'Saintly Lives'," Thomas defended himself. "Funnily enough modern history and politics were considered more relevant."

"*Bethed Dereszda!* The folly of you Imperials…" Piotr trailed off. "Well?" he continued, after a pause. "Do you want to know about him?"

"Yes certainly," said Thomas, surprised. After hesitation, Lawrence also nodded his assent, his sense of curiosity triumphing over dislike of Sanctist mumbo-jumbo. It wasn't often that Piotr volunteered information, particularly when it might mean an extensive explanation. Clearly Lawrence's lack of knowledge had offended the Rotliegendan's sense of piety to the extent that he was willing to take the time to rectify it.

"St. Senren was born in the second century – or more than a millennium before the Triune Empire was founded, as you Imperials like to reckon it. No one knows the exact date, though scholars have debated it for centuries. Record keeping was poor then. But we do know where he was born." Turning slightly, Piotr gestured to the north-west.

"Over there, if you could see beyond that line of hills. Benthos Valley it's called these days and it lies in the south-western tip of Elaran. Erd Gellin claims it; a dozen or more wars have been fought down the long centuries over possession of the valley. Many nations would think a war a small price to pay for St. Senren's birthplace.

"He was a minor lord, but of no nation. As you I hope know, those were the darkest days of the Secession Wars, when the Covenant had been sundered, brigands and droghkar roamed unchecked and each man was master of what he could hold, subject to no law save that of might.

"St. Senren, or Lord Senren as he was in those days, was a just ruler. Many were, or at least tried to be, striving to hold to the values of the Covenant in a world gone mad. However, they were too few and too weak to do more than create oases of calm amidst the turmoil, refuges of calm that all too often were devoured or fell to tyranny the instant the ruler who had established them died or was slain. St. Senren was no different from these others. He fortified the ramparts of Benthos Valley against the storms of turmoil beyond, defending his people with lines of watchtowers and defences. But he could not extend his sway beyond the valley walls, nor hope to subdue the lawless hordes outside." Piotr spat. "*Retheszik dazgharta!*"

"His entire kingdom could be crossed in two days. For all that he ruled it well, he would have been utterly forgotten if not for the demon invasion. Your Scriptualist church admits the existence of demons?" Piotr looked pointedly at Lawrence.

"Of course," said Thomas hurriedly, trying to head off yet another religious confrontation. Piotr waxing lyrical in such a fashion was not an opportunity to be missed.

"Good," continued Piotr, yet he sounded mildly disappointed. "A demon host from the mountains of the north burst through the valley defences and laid waste to one of St. Senren's towns. Survivors told terrible tales of slaughter and destruction. A demon lord, a *Soharadon*, was there in person." Thomas felt shock – a *Soharadon*! The great demon lords had only threatened the world directly a handful of times in the last millennium.

"Yes, a *Soharadon*," said Piotr, seeing Thomas's expression. St. Senren's captains urged flight; no man could stand against such infernal power. But St. Senren, a true follower of Andur, Lord of Order, knew that rulership meant duty; a duty to his people and to the world. Even if Benthos Valley could have been evacuated, where would his people go? They would have been helpless prey to the lawlessness outside. And the *Soharadon* itself would still be present, and would do untold harm before it was finally brought down.

"Taking a handful of retainers, all who would come with him, he rode north to face the *Soharadon*. They found it, so his retainers have recorded, already ten miles south of the border, the earth blackened and burnt where the demon host had past. Whilst his followers desperately engaged the other demons – *sthand*, *goruthang* and *rahvashda* – all fell fiends in their own right, St. Senren, with lance and sword, charged the *Soharadon* itself.

"The *Soharadon*, disdainful of the power of the wretched human before him, took up the challenge. Many and grievous were the blows that they each dealt upon the withered grass, flaming great sword against cold steel. At the last, strength ebbing from a dozen wounds, St. Senren stepped inside the reach of the *Soharadon* and drove his long sword into the demon's chest, killing it instantly."

"He killed it?" exclaimed Thomas, despite himself. "No one could slay a *Soharadon* in single combat! Even the most powerful arcanists would have difficulty."

Piotr's voice grew dangerous. "St. Senren did. Do you dare to doubt? All his surviving retainers concur. He slew it, and perished as he did so, cleaved by the demon's sword and scalded by its blood.

"When he fell, blood gushed from his body, staining the ground red. And then this flower, the Crown of Senren, sprouted from the ground that his blood had stained." Piotr sharply snapped off a flower and thrust it at Thomas.

"Smell it! The scent is sickly this close, isn't it? The sweetness cloying? That is the smell of blood. The blood of the martyr, of St. Senren, his life given for his people that they might know life rather than death, freedom rather than slavery. Just as Andur the Redemptor gave his blood for us, his body broken upon the wheel in order to break the wheel and free us, so did the saint follow his master, his body broken for those over whom he ruled and served."

The heat in his voice ebbed. "Even today, the Crown of Senren blooms widely across Laurentia. Blessed flower; it is the first to reclaim the withered flanks of a volcano or to bloom again on a battlefield.

"Sometimes, rarely, a white flower is found; pure white, unstained by blood..." his voice tailed off.

"Have you ever found one?"

"Me? No. They're rare enough to make a two-legged wolf look common. The Senrenites have a standing bounty of gold upon them. They'll pay fifty crowns – more than a year's wages for a common labourer – to anyone who brings them a white Crown of Senren within forty-eight hours of it being plucked. They believe it has mystic properties."

"Does it?" asked Lawrence.

"How should I know? I assume so or they wouldn't pay so much."

Something had been puzzling Thomas. "You mentioned the Senrenites. If St. Senren died in the battle with the *Soharadon*, how did he found the Senrenites?"

"*Kaszdruthed*! The Senrenites honour St. Senren, they weren't founded by him." Thomas and the chaplain waited expectantly.

"Am I to recount the entire history of Laurentia to you today? Have I not spoken enough already? Study, if you wish to know; read about it in your vaunted Triune libraries!

"On! We've wasted enough time dawdling here already."

Without protest Thomas fell in behind Piotr, Lawrence at his side. Clearly their companion was already regretting his unusual speech. But it had been another side to the Rotliegendan, a passion that Thomas had never seen before. He did not repent having provoked the confidence.

In the valley beneath them a brightly coloured bird darted from an olive grove, its brilliant scarlet wings flashing low over a stream before it disappeared once more in the darkness of the trees. Around their feet the Crown of Senrens clustered as prolifically as ever. In vain Thomas scanned the ground for a white one.

The sun was low to the horizon now. This late in autumn they had only a couple of hours of daylight left. Soon they would make camp for the night; eating their meagre supper. Their supplies were very low now. Despite Piotr's preparations, the addition of Lawrence to their ranks had been an unforeseen circumstance, meaning rations, already lean for two, had to be further stretched to feed three.

They had not dared to scavenge for more. To unnecessarily venture near human habitation was clear folly. One day they had in fact been fortunate; a goat, straying from its customary pastures, had crossed their path as they stopping for the night. A quick shot to the head had felled it instantly and Piotr had expertly butchered it, cooking the meat over a small concealed fire. That had been five days ago though and the last of the meat was long since gone.

A gnarled kumquat tree, its twisted trunk bent curving outwards from beneath an overhanging scarp, provided a welcome treat. A few fruit still clung to its branches despite the lateness of the season, delayed in maturity by the shade of the rock above. The three paused to strip the branches bare, the tart morsels bursting in their mouth with an explosion of flavour. Thomas's mouth puckered from the acid juice. The fruit was refreshing, but ultimately did little to assuage his hunger.

Soon they would be in Elaran. The border could not be more than two days away now. Then there would be food and safety; an end to arduous travail and a refuge from danger. Thomas let his mind drift. He and Lawrence, Piotr too if he wished, would take the first *tarath* flight from Elaran. In under a week he would be back in the Empire; still in Laurentia, it is true, but the Scahanian Peninsula or the Pelagic provinces would seem like Home itself after this barbarism.

Civilisation once more! Decorum, comfort, order; the simple pleasures of associating with other educated men and the knowledge that one was a tiny but integral part of the greatest Empire the world had known since the days of the Covenant.

The Imperial arcanists would solve the mystery of his visions; he would be plagued by them no more. He and Lawrence would be feted as heroes, as the men who had survived the massacre at the Residency. There would be honours, parades, banquets; Piotr would be made a citizen of the Empire. They might even be presented to the Viceroy himself.

Then there would come an expeditionary force; a punitive strike at Erd Gellin. The Empire would never ignore such an affront as this. Inside his head regiments of Triune soldiery besieged Iskarn, blew down the walls and stormed the inner city. The Archons were marched out in humiliation, bending knee in subservience to the might of the Empire. Then he, Thomas Maynard, was there, installed as commissioner: ruler in all but name of their Imperial Majesties' newest colony.

Laughing to himself, he shook his head. Even in his wildest daydreams he knew such fantasies as the extravagant flights of fancy that they were. But that didn't matter. To be safe in civilised territory would be enough. And some of it was true enough – they would be popular heroes for their daring escape, for a few short days until the press tired of them, at least. And the Viceroy would care about the situation in Erd Gellin; the demons, the droghkar and the unrest. He would be noticed, his career would advance, perhaps to First Secretary or Deputy Commissioner initially, but then Commissioner or Ambassador would be only a short step away.

And most importantly, he would be safe. A nice, secure post, deep in the heart of Imperial territory; that is where he would go next.

The Elarani border was just two days away. In just a few days he would be on Triune soil, and it would be many years before he would leave it again.

CITADEL

"A cleft stick, a serpent's tongue, a wolf in shadow. Sometimes blind eyes may see better than the sighted in the darkness."

Konelis Larach – The Annalia, Volume Four

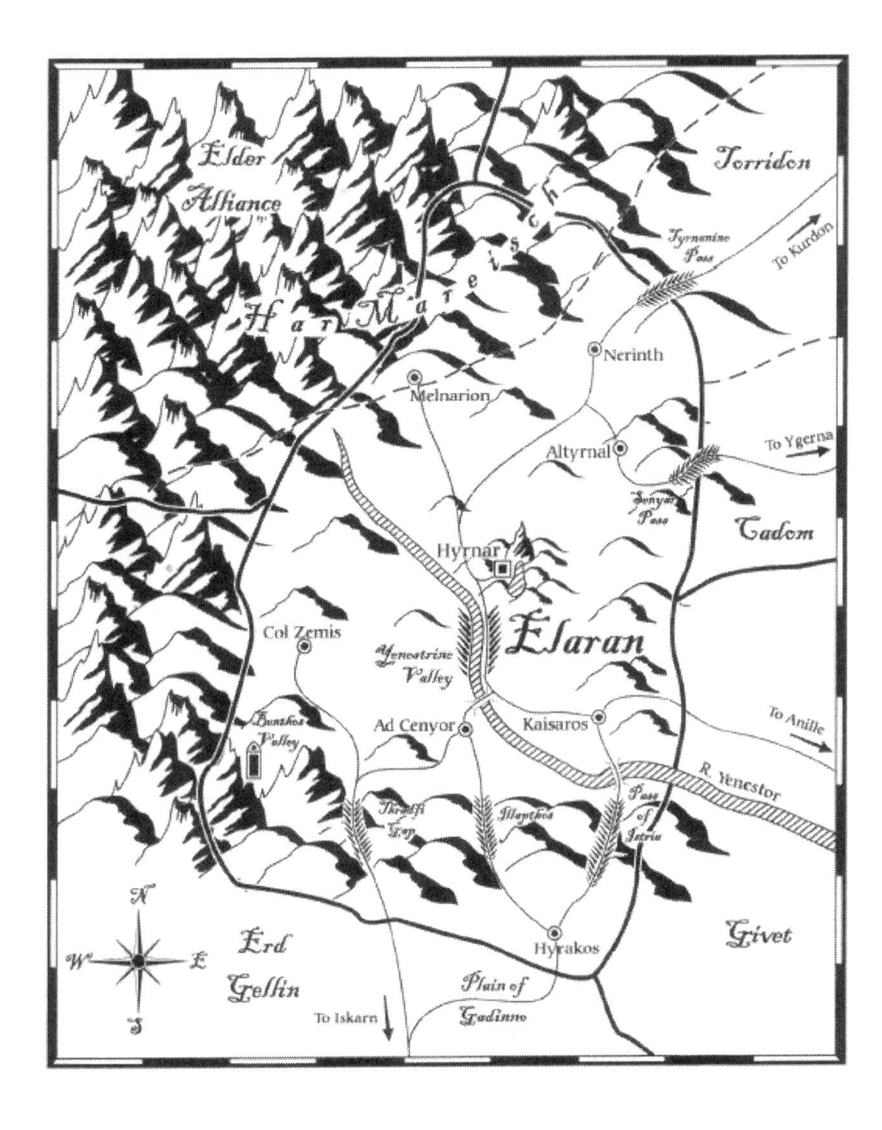
Elder
Alliance
Torriden
To Kurdon
Nerinth
Melnarion
Altyrnal
To Ygerna
Cadom
Hyrnar
Elaran
Col Zemis
Ad Cenyor
Kaisaros
To Anille
R. Yenestor
Hyrakos
Grivet
Erd
Gellin
To Iskarn
N
W
E
S

Chapter Six

Youth and Beauty

"The Torridonian ambassador is here, Your Majesty."

"Bring him through."

"Yes, Your Majesty." The equerry bowed low and backed towards the door.

Seated on her high-backed throne upon the dais, Queen Rianda of Elaran looked every inch the ruler. Clothed in a gown of the finest damascene, the rich cloth masked the slightness of her frame, adding physically to her stature. Beneath the delicate circlet of silver filigree, the crown that she favoured except on state occasions, her face was a mask of serenity, coolly oblivious to the guards and minor functionaries that cluttered the audience room. Beneath her outward poise she was terrified.

"Your Majesty, Ven Atharden of Dorlan, Ambassador Plenipotentiary of Niavon III, Lord Protector of Greater Torridon."

"Your Majesty," he said, bowing, "please allow me to convey the most heartfelt condolences of Lord Niavon, and, indeed, of myself, regarding your father. His tragic death less than three weeks ago at the hands of Gellinese raiders is a great loss to Elaran; we know that he will be sorely missed. Torridon shares your nation's grief."

She gazed forward, the wound of her grief still raw. Abstractedly, she heard herself responding with the necessary platitudes, the training and discipline of years coming to her rescue.

"I thank you and Lord Niavon deeply for your sympathy, Your Excellency. Elaran always welcomes the friendship of its northern neighbour."

"And Torridon likewise welcomes the goodwill of Elaran, Your Majesty. Lord Niavon fervently wishes that your father's untimely demise, tragic as it is, need bring no cessation of Elaran and Torridon growing ever closer in friendship."

Bottling down her grief, Rianda strove to retain her outward mask of calmness. An unctuous man this ambassador; short and stocky like many of his countrymen, yet with a faint aura of menace about him. She had watched him negotiating with her father many times and even the most casual comment held a veiled threat, a trap for the unwary.

"We recognise, of course," he was saying, "that Elaran has suffered grievous losses in recent years in skirmishes on your southern border. You have held your own of course: King Diarad was recognised across the continent as a most talented general. However, Lord Niavon is concerned that, with the new situation, you will be hard-pressed to withstand the superior numbers of the raiders, particularly if Erd Gellin should choose to come north in force.

"This being the case, as gesture of our goodwill, Torridon would like to offer you the assistance of three centuries of soldiers to assist in your defence. All you need do is to give the word and they will be transported by *tarath* to where they are required in under two days."

"We thank Lord Niavon for his kind offer," she replied smoothly. "But Torridonian soldiers, peerless though they are in courage and discipline, may find fighting difficult in our mountains, where a small force can frequently defeat one much larger and better equipped. As the Gellinese are learning, Elaran is no place for conventional armies and siege artillery. First Chiliarch Nomiki, our new commander-in-chief, has matters well in hand."

She paused. "If Torridon is sincere in its protestations of goodwill, then perhaps Your Excellency would be willing to talk of trade."

"Indeed, Your Majesty, commerce is the lifeblood of a nation."

"And yet, Your Excellency, the restrictions between our nations, though they once seemed wise, are stifling that lifeblood in both of us. In this time of amity why should we not remove them, allowing wealth to flow freely between us. Only recently a merchant from your own province of Santon was extolling the potential benefits to us."

"Ah, Your Majesty, that would be...difficult. Regretfully, and I say it in confidence, Siluria is exerting pressure to retain its 'partner of choice' status with us. As I am sure you are aware, it could be costly for us to offend our neighbour to the north." Was she imagining the faintest emphasis upon the "you"? No, she was not. The veiled threats came indeed in every statement.

"But I am sure, Your Majesty" he continued, "that in the meantime your trade with Givet will do much to make up the shortfall with Torridon." Ven Atharden smiled, a crocodile's smile. He knew as well as she did that, under Torridonian pressure, Chenesseau of Givet had imposed tariffs as high or higher than Torridon's.

"Of course, Your Excellency," she smiled in return. "Our trade with Givet is flourishing." The forms had to be observed.

"Needless to say, Your Majesty, if Elaran were to be allied with Torridon then the situation would be very different. Siluria could hardly protest at us granting our ally favourable trading privileges – or, indeed, anything else that they might desire. I have here an alliance accord that I had been discussing with your late father before his much-regretted demise. I believe you are familiar with the document?" At her curt nod he continued. "Lord Niavon, in his wisdom, has given orders that the treaty, with all of its benefits, will take effect immediately upon Your Majesty's signing of the document."

"Your Excellency, whilst I myself might favour the treaty, I will not be so disrespectful to the memory of my noble father as to reverse a decision of his while his ashes are still warm. Please, we can discuss this pact further in a few months, in spring perhaps."

She had seen that so-called alliance pact. A treaty of vassalage in all but name; she would be dead and burned like her father before she signed it. But as long as Torridon still thought there was hope, they might refrain from greater, more costly threats. Squeezed between mightier powers, Rianda was forced into playing games of peril for the highest stakes of all.

"It is of course Your Majesty's decision, but please remember that Torridon has much to offer. I only hope that your southern commitments do not divert you too much from the task of maintaining order. Our border garrisons report rumours of bandit activity along the frontier, particularly in the lawless region of the Har Mareisch, though our well-armed troops have deterred them from making any incursions on to Torridonian soil. Whole villages and even small towns have been burned, or so I have heard."

"I am sure that Elaran can deal with its own internal affairs, Your Excellency," Rianda said steadily.

"See that you do, for Torridon will not tolerate anarchy to the south, nor do we wish to share a border with Erd Gellin. If the situation deteriorates then Torridon will be forced to intervene to preserve our own security. We have recently obtained a sizeable consignment of Triune rifles which could quickly put paid to bandits or the rabble of Erd Gellin."

The threat was hardly veiled now. Either annexation by treaty or by the sword; these were the stark choices that Torridon offered. Her fury and frustration welling up, Rianda rose from her throne, her voice carrying clear and strong across the audience room.

"Your Excellency, you may tell Lord Niavon that should a single Torridonian company cross the border I will place the entire Elarani army in its path. The men of the hills will fight dearly in defence of their homeland and the mountainsides shall be stained with blood before Torridon gains a foothold in Elaran. Even should the south, nay the entire kingdom, be lost to Erd Gellin as a result, still Torridon will not gain one morsel from our demise."

She had shaken him, she could see; for once his ambassadorial suavity had been pierced. The ruler of a minor nation like Elaran did not speak to the ambassador of Greater Torridon in such a way.

"I will report Your Majesty's words to Lord Niavon," he said icily, bowing stiffly. Rianda watched as he retreated from the audience room then sank back, drained, into her tall-backed chair. She barely heard the buzz that rose as the ambassador left; idle courtiers speculating and chattering about the confrontation.

Why had she lost her composure, allowed herself to confront him in such a way? He would make her pay for those words, if he could. But she had unsettled him; perhaps that would be worth something.

She had been born and bred to rule; had been training for it, consciously and unconsciously, for every one of her nineteen short years. But why, she thought despairingly, oh why had the weight of it been thrust upon her so soon?

#

The heavy stones of the Citadel were comforting, in more ways than one. After the debacle with the ambassador, the remainder of the afternoon's court had passed in something of a daze. A succession of tedious minor disputes and petitions, all of which could seemingly only be resolved by her judgement. It had been an effort to devote thought to such trivialities when so many more important matters were at stake. But she did not mean to start her reign with disregard for those she ruled. Her father had taught her that. In the eyes of the petitioners, each case was imbued with an importance surpassing by far that of the Torridonian ambassador, or even the situation with Erd Gellin: and so Rianda had listened, nodded and questioned, as if she too thought that that particular petition was the most crucial thing in the world, before making the judgement. Then again with the next, and the next, on and on in an apparently endless line.

It was a relief when the session finally ended and she was able to escape to these sheltered corridors. Solid pillars supported the heavy arches; the cloisters, part open to the outer air, were cool even in summer. Now, the brisk wind of late autumn brought new vigour to her, deadened as she was after so long indoors.

"Did I do so badly, Euthymios?" she asked, knowing the answer full well.

"It may be better than you fear, my child." Her companion paused, seeing how best to phrase it. "It was unwise, as you well know. But he will set much of your final speech to youthful impetuousness, which may have its advantages also.

"If he believes you to be impetuous, he may yet think that a similar swing of mood could cause you to sign his so-called alliance, or else give other concessions. You will not be able to play on such a belief for long though; Ven Atharden is no fool, much as we might wish it. Sooner or later he will realise how competently you are ruling."

"I will make use of it as long as I can. After all, isn't that all of what we do – one short-term ploy after another, buying our survival one year at a time?"

Euthymios leaned over his crozier, tapping the end on the stones below. The solid thunks echoed through the cloister. "My daughter, you are young to be so bitter."

"Do I not have cause? Rulership thrust upon me so soon; unprepared? Our neighbours, like vultures, not even waiting until my father's ashes are cold before they move in for prey?"

"Yes, truly you have cause enough," he said sadly. "Your father's loss was a blow to us all, but none have felt it as much as you. But he taught you well, Rianda; you do honour to him every day that you sit on his throne."

Suddenly her grief rose up inside her, choking off her voice. Blinking, she tried to keep the tears from her eyes. Even here, in relative privacy, she could not afford such weakness. Euthymios walked wordlessly beside her, aware of her feelings, giving her the time to regain her composure, with tactful understanding.

She had known him for as long as she had been alive; he had become Bishop of Hyrnar years before she was born. An Elarani by birth, he had the genuine humbleness of one who had never expected to rise so high. Nor had he ever sought to rise higher, evidently content to remain bishop of a minor see in order to stay with the people, the country and the king that he loved.

Her father had made him one of his chief councillors, not an unusual move in a time when the princes of the Church frequently wielded as much temporal as spiritual power. The loyalty and devotion with which he had served King Diarad he had transferred wholly to his king's beautiful daughter, a love second only to that which he reserved for Andur, Lord of Order Himself.

Rianda's first memories of him were as the distant, almost daunting figure who presided over the formal rituals in the great cathedral. As she grew older he had become one of her chief tutors in religion, politics and statecraft – the art of ruling. Since the age of twelve she had sat in on her father's privy councils – initially as an observer, until she came of age at fifteen. From the first meeting she had been impressed by Euthymios, at the way his teachings translated into his advice at the council table. Insightful, calm and disinterested; unlike so many of the others his guidance was never swayed by self interest. There was some advantage in having a councillor who did not rule land, even if his loyalty was owed partly to a higher authority.

From the very beginning, too, he had been her confessor, mentor in matters both worldly and spiritual. Now, thrust at such an unripe age into the mantle of queen, she was more grateful than ever for his elderly presence. Though all – she hoped – of her lords were loyal, and not a few served with as much wisdom and zeal, there were no others with whom she could discard, even for a few moments, her crown and talk frankly; as inexperienced princess instead of undaunted queen.

She paused at the thought of her High Council. She had made up her mind as to the decision she must take, though none of her advisors – not even Euthymios – knew, or should know, yet. Tomorrow's council would not be easy, no matter how she presented it.

Turning sharply left they continued their walking, the inner wall of the citadel to their left. Ahead of them on the Har Sarenis rose the cathedral, graceful and strong; behind, on the fractionally higher Har Magisteris, squatted the royal keep, its majestic arches belying its purpose as a fortress of war. The two halves of the Citadel of Hyrnar, heart of the hill kingdom of Elaran. Between the inner and outer walls lay ample room for people, livestock and all manner of goods and provisions. Proud and strong, the Citadel dominated Hyrnar; the houses of the outer city nestled around its walls as mere dwarfs sheltering in its shadow.

Too many times in its history had Elaran become a battleground for competing powers; at times it had been conquered, though never for long. Scars pocked the doughty citadel walls, ugly gashes that contrasted with the well-worn cannon embrasures. Both castle and cathedral had more than once been the site of a last-ditch stand, most recently in the Variscan Wars, two and a half centuries before.

Rianda shivered, the bitter wind that knifed through the Citadel a reminder that that the solid walls were all too slim. She must build defences of words first, that the defences of stone and steel might have a chance to hold.

"Will we hold them this time?" she asked.

"We will try." Euthymios's steely voice belied his age. "I spoke to Nomiki today. He and the other two chiliarchi are in agreement: Erd Gellin is sure to come north in force next year."

"My father's death has made this happen," she said bitterly. "Had he been alive they would never have dared to go so far."

"Do not increase your grief needlessly," he said with compassion. "They have been growing more bold for years. They would be coming regardless; if not next year then the following.

"Nomiki is a bold general, if not quite as capable as your father was. He would not tell me his plans, preferring to tell you directly in Council tomorrow, but I believe he is not without hope. As you have said to the ambassador, our hills wreak havoc with conventional drills and formations."

Rianda's eyes flashed. "As the Torridonians will learn to their cost should they cross the frontier!" More soberly she continued. "But if they do that we are lost, whatever price we make them pay. We can barely fight a war on one front, let alone on two."

"I doubt they will, if you continue the way you have begun. For all we may have said of the audience earlier, it was still a masterly performance. Niavon may squeeze our trade; he may threaten and bluster, but he has no wish to share a border with Erd Gellin. Siluria is enough of a threat; Greater Torridon will not rush to gain a similar foe to the south.

"No, Torridon will hold off until we have done the fighting – and the dying. Only if we are routed will they cross the border to gain the Citadel before Erd Gellin. It is when we are victorious, and weary from our victory, that we must worry in earnest about our friendly neighbour to the north."

"And that, Euthymios, is a problem for another day. What did I say – one year, one month at a time; that is how my father taught me that Elaran survives."

The crozier slammed down in assent. "You are correct, as you so often are." Suddenly more serious, he turned to face her.

"But there is one thing, my queen, that cannot wait until next year."

Rianda halted, arrested by the switch to formality. "Which is, Euthymios?"

"The succession. You have need of an heir, Rianda. As it stands, the crown of Elaran hangs by a thread."

The suggestion appalled her. "Would you have me think of marriage before my father's ashes are cold? It is not two months since he was slain and you would be have me thinking of husbands?"

"All the more reason for haste, Your Majesty. I know you are young, but the circumstances give need for urgency. While your father was alive there seemed time, but his untimely death brought home to us all how fragile is the situation. Illness, an assassin, or simply an accident..."

"Then my cousin would inherit the throne. He is loyal, able and competent – and has two children already."

"Your father's cousin."

"Yes, my father's cousin. He is next in line to the throne, yes?"

"He is, your majesty. And I agree, he would prove a capable ruler. But his mother was Cadomi. With Cadom now a province of Greater Torridon, there are some amongst your lords who might feel that a king who was half Torridonian was...not appropriate, at a time like this."

"Chrysaor is as loyal to Elaran as I am myself – or as you are, My Lord Bishop," she said, outraged. "And none have ever had cause to doubt the Lady Hreith's devotion to my father." Rianda was genuinely shocked – it was the first she had heard of such rumours. "You mean to say that our lords would refuse to follow Chrysaor, a man of true Nemessine blood – as pure as my own – at such a time of strife? To plunge the kingdom into civil war, for the sake of their petty prejudices – or, more likely, their own selfish gain? That would succeed in delivering us into the arms of the Torridonians, as my cousin never would!"

"It is absurd, I know." Euthymios looked somewhat abashed. "I have told them so myself. Chrysaor has proved his worth, and his selflessness, time and again, in counsel and in war. But still some mutter, and voice their disquiet. It is all the more reason for you to find a husband, and produce an heir."

"Do my councillors have nothing better to do than discuss their queen's marital prospects? Am I nothing but a royal brood mare? Who else but Chrysaor would be regent for such a child – or is that also a matter of discussion?"

"Your Majesty, you will need to marry soon in any case, for political if not dynastic reasons. No means of an alliance may be ignored in straits such as ours."

"Do not remind me of my duty, Your Grace." Her voice cut like a knife. "I am aware of my obligations. And I will fulfil them, you need not fear. But what ruler would bind himself to a nation in such a plight as ours – have our good lords considered that? In autumn, when Erd Gellin is defeated and I have shown that I can rule and survive, that will be time to seek an alliance against Torridon. It will not be hard; Torridon's ill-wishers have sons in plenty."

"Your Majesty..."

"Enough!"

He bowed, formally, Bishop of Hyrnar to Queen of Elaran.

"Enough, Euthymios," she said more mildly. "You mean well, I know. But I will not have this subject raised again. My lords and counsellors have better uses for their time."

He bowed again. Turning, Rianda strode back towards the castle, all calm destroyed. Even the wind, whose freshness she had earlier enjoyed, now seemed an enemy. Truly, as her father had said so often, a monarch was always alone.

Chapter Seven

A Choice is Made

Rianda settled herself on her throne. Barring Kadmos, they were all here: the full High Council in session. They waited for her to begin. Silence reigned – all discussions, any clandestine negotiations, cut off mid-flow by the act of her entrance.

Idly, she tapped her right hand upon the table, steadying her composure. She would start in her own time – the act of choosing was power, in a small way. Sunlight lanced through the wide window, sparkling off the inset marble table to illuminate the ancient frescoes behind. The stillness of the privy garden beyond contrasted with the silence of the room; superficially similar, yet one betokened calm, the other conflict.

These were her allies: her loyal lords and generals. Why then, as before, must she play games, much as she played with and deceived the subtle Ven Atharden of Dorlan? Slowly, she scanned the room, ignoring the rich trappings, focusing instead upon the councillors themselves in their high-backed chairs. One by one she found and held their gaze; direct, challenging, before passing on.

Her eyes first sought out Nomiki, First Chiliarch of Elaran, commander of its armies since the death of her father. A tall man, his warrior's eyes met her gaze unflinchingly. Not challenging, but without give – Nomiki knew his power, his competence and his loyalty. Directly opposite her he sat, flanked by his two juniors, the chiliarchi of the north and south. An appropriate place for today; he and they would be first amongst her allies, or her enemies. Which was it to be? Would the others follow Nomiki's lead – whatever that proved to be? Amongst the three chiliarchi he was merely first amongst equals.

The gaze of Lykourgos, to his left *was* a challenge. Unlike Nomiki, the Chiliarch of the South had yet to transfer his allegiance from her dead father to herself. Diarad had been a warrior king, and a nineteen-year-old girl made a poor substitute in the eyes of many. Her mouth twisted. Actaion was another such; his perfunctory nod of the head just short of an insult. Count of Col Zemis, she had not yet dismissed him from the High Council because she could not afford his enmity. The passive opposition of him and his followers could fatally weaken Elaran at such time – better his dissension at Council than that. She knew full well that she could not fill her father's footsteps – but she was queen and he would serve her yet.

She passed quickly over the empty space to be filled by Kadmos – where was the man? – to rest on Euthymios, garbed now in the full purple splendour of his office, mitre on head and crozier in hand. Seated at her right hand, the elderly bishop did not seem to dominate the room; it would only be when he spoke – softly, never raising his voice – that one would realise how the entire assembly hung upon his word. She would have one ally, at least.

Two, she hoped, turning to her left where Chrysaor sat by right of his status as heir. Her cousin owed his allegiance to Elaran itself; above his life, his people or, so some whispered, his monarch. In the skirmishes and border raids of the last decade he had served Diarad fiercely; he had been respected, honoured and served well by his men but, unlike her father, he had not been loved. There was a cold streak of calculation in him that, whilst it made him a feared commander, caused men to keep their distance. It was this that made Rianda optimistic of his support today. Whilst he would not hesitate to oppose her if he disagreed – he had before, and would do so again – it would never, unlike in the case of Actaion or Tarasios be from pettiness, spite or incompetence.

At the thought of Tarasios her lips curled. He was another who should not be on the High Council. The man was an incompetent, a fool who could see no further than a blind scitalis and yet would defend the latest pet theory he had heard as if it were the Book of Andur. But as duke of the largest duchy in Elaran, he must needs be listened to, consulted and placated. The crown could not do without his estate's income or levies, even if it could well do without the man himself. Rianda wished that he was like his father had been, willing to spend his time dissipating himself amongst the pleasures of his home estate; then they would at least have been spared his presence here. Ignorance and folly were poor traits in a lord, but when combined with eagerness the problems were increased thrice over.

Thoughts soured by such reflections, Rianda considered the remaining two members of her High Council. Here at least there was some competence. Not the brilliance and power of Euthymios or Nomiki, but the solid dependability of faithful men who had served long and well. Eliud, March Warden of the Har Mareisch, a stocky, still-powerful man despite his age, the tasselled shawl about his shoulders not his only sign of kinship with the wild men of the hills. And Hesperos, Chiliarch of the North.

Hesperos might not have the strategic insight of Nomiki, nor the inner fire of Lykourgos which caused men to follow him to the jaws of death and beyond. Her father had possessed that gift also. But thirty years of commanding the northern frontier against the unpredictable raids from the outlying tribes of the Elder Alliance, from the probes and so-called bandits of Torridon and in maintaining even a semblance of order in the Har Mareisch, bespoke the quality of his character. He and Eliud and been allies for years, drawn together initially over the matter of the Har Mareisch – for the clans of those rugged hills, on both sides of the border, acknowledged no law but their own and held to no ties but the ties of blood – and then drawn closer through a kinship of temperament. Hesperos's first granddaughter had married Eliud's grandson two years ago – it had been a month to the day after her seventeenth saint-day – and now they as good as thought as one. Stalwarts amongst her nobles, they would hold fast to her so long as she did not disregard the north.

She had come full circle. Holding Nomiki's gaze once more, Rianda decided to begin. The first two items she intended to discuss were of minor importance; Kadmos would be sure to arrive by the time she was in need of allies.

"My Lords of the High Council, I thank you for your attendance today. Before we address the main issue before us, I would…"

Rianda broke off at the sound of scuffling outside the room. The door opened to admit Kadmos, his wolf-like stride rapidly covering the distance to his empty place. Rianda shot daggers at him as he bowed. Sword-Captain of Hyrnar he might be, yet that did not absolve him of such unpunctuality. Whilst his duties – the defence of the Citadel – might be more immediate, all here had their responsibilities. They were not under siege yet.

Resuming, she moved swiftly through the preliminaries. The mild commotion that had been caused by Kadmos's entry quickly ceased as she began once more.

The first two items were dispatched rapidly. Rianda had neither the time nor the patience to waste upon trivialities today. A trade pact with Linnarson and a border dispute between minor nobles were hardly topics that would be spoken of down the centuries. The first was important, true, but uncontroversial and of no need to discuss if not for the sums of money involved. The second was even less worthy of attention. The lords concerned were vassals of Tarasios and their quarrel an absurdity relating to a petty patch of land that he had nevertheless insisted must be brought before the High Council. Well, she would humour him. Throughout, Actaion sat with his head in his hands. Save for a single scathing comment the Count of Col Zemis did nothing to even pretend an interest in the matter at hand.

It was almost a relief, despite her forebodings, when the issue was finally concluded and she was able to move on to the principal business of the day.

"My Lords, let us move on to more urgent matters. Erd Gellin marshals its forces on our southern border; there can be no doubt that they mean to come north in force in spring. Fortunately, by the grace of Andur, we have some small breathing space – even the Gellinese are not foolhardy enough to invade the hills of Elaran in winter."

"Would that they were," said Eliud.

"Would that they were indeed. But the Archons are wiser than that, or at least their generals are. And so we have a bare few months in which to ready our defences.

"Nomiki, we have the three chiliadi, of one thousand men apiece. How many more men can we raise?"

"My fellow chiliarchi and I are in agreement. If we strip our other frontiers, leaving only a token garrison," – he paused questioningly, continuing at Rianda's impatient nod – "and call a full muster of the peasantry, we can raise almost an additional two thousand. Over half of these would be untrained; likely men who had never held a musket before."

"They will learn," Rianda said harshly. "They know the land; that is weapon enough."

"But, Your Majesty," interjected Actaion, "that will leave our borders unguarded. What of bandits? Torridon may seize the opportunity to invade, or even Givet."

"My Lord, we will not broadcast our weakness to the world. You think Givet will invade? When did that effete nation last go to war in earnest? At most a token probe. As for bandits and raiders; our people will simply have to hold fast. Even the worst storms can be endured for a season. Far better than for them to languish under the heels of the Archons." Her voice was hard – she could not afford to show weakness here, no more than before the Torridonian. Every word felt a betrayal of her people – yet all she said was true. She had naught to offer Elaran but the lesser of two evils. And she would do worse too, before this council was over.

"And Torridon?"

"Torridon will not invade whilst we are fighting its battles for it. It has no greater love of Erd Gellin than we do. Even were we to leave the north fully garrisoned, do you think that our good Chiliarch of the North, loyal and valiant though he is, could hold against three or more legions of Torridon? For that is the minimum that Niavon would send against us, make no mistake. And not a man can be spared from the south." Hesperos nodded awkwardly; he knew well enough that he could not do the impossible; he had fretted over that very eventuality for years.

"How many men will the Archons send against us, Nomiki?"

"Three tagmata are marshalling on the Plains of Gadinno: over ten thousand men."

"You see, Actaion? Ten thousand men or more, all hardened warriors, and we have a bare five thousand – brave, it is true, but poorly equipped and many untried. Outnumbered two to one we will be hard pressed to secure victory; to lengthen the odds still further would be the height of folly."

Actaion bowed his head. "I am convinced by your wisdom, Your Majesty." The Count of Col Zemis knew when he was defeated; the mood of the High Council had turned against him. The galling fact, Rianda, reflected, was that in her place he would have made the same decision as she had. The man was no fool as a strategist.

She had no time to brood on such matters now. Turning to Kadmos, she stifled her irritation at the Sword-Captain's late entry.

"And how many from Hyrnar itself?"

"Two hundred, Your Majesty, all well disciplined." That last went without saying. None but the elite joined the Household Guard of Hyrnar, and they got little chance to become soft under Kadmos's demanding training. Even in peacetime, the lean Sword-Captain set as gruelling a regime for his soldiers as he did for himself.

Kadmos was uneasy, though none but those who knew him well could have guessed from his impassive face. "I planned to leave one hundred to guard the Citadel. We are not so far from the border that a bold *tarath* raid could not penetrate, and any fewer would be insufficient to man the walls."

Rianda nodded sharply. "It would avail us little to defeat Erd Gellin and return to a smoking ruin. Agreed.

"And what of the Har Mareisch?"

"Little good news," said Eliud. Lines criss-crossed his weathered face. He seemed old today: his years showing. "They will send no men."

"That was to be expected," said Chrysaor. Rianda looked sharply at her cousin but allowed him to continue. "What of raids?"

"The principal clans have agreed not to raid outside their territory, Your Grace. Though what they consider their territory does not entirely co-align with our own views."

"You claim kinship with these people, do you not? What good are such ties if not in times as these?"

Eliud readjusted his shawl, fingering the intricate pattern of knotted braids that indicated clan markings. "We of Melnarion have never been considered truly of the Har Mareisch, Your Grace. My presence here and our loyalty to the Crown confirms that in the eyes of the true Mareischi hill men. And in any case, each clan is a nation unto itself. No man of the Har Mareisch will hark to one outside his clan."

"Family before clan, clan before Mareischi...and Mareischi before outsiders," murmured Hesperos. "Well do we of the north know that creed."

"What surety do we have of their oaths?" Chrysaor was visibly doubtful.

"It is enough, cousin," said Rianda, firmly. "The clansmen have their own honour. The March Warden has done well, and more than well. It is over a century and a half since so firm a truce was concluded. Their help in arms was never more than the faintest hope. It is enough that the north may enjoy relative calm and that one section of our border at least is secure from Torridon."

Eliud smiled grimly. "Aye, I pity the Torridonian who attempts to force those passes. The clansmen are demons incarnate when roused, and their long-barrelled jezails shoot as straight as a Triune rifle. Niavon's men will fare ill indeed should they venture there."

There were nods of agreement from around the table. Many in that room had served on the northern borders at some point in their past and knew first hand the terror of a Mareischi raid, screaming clansmen riding their yales pouring out of nowhere from a bare hillside. Then they would be gone, the goods seized and the attackers melting back into the hills, leaving organised pursuits to find nothing but empty passes and the steady attrition of sniping musket fire from the hillsides.

Even for those, such as Rianda and Euthymios, who had not so served, the reputation of the Mareischi hill men was well known. Euthymios watched as Eliud rearranged his shawl once more. Distinct though the men of Melnarion might claim to be from they of the Har Mareisch, the kinship between them was written in every line of his face. Unconsciously Euthymios fingered the rich, dyed wool of his own robes, armour of a different sort.

"We have spoken much of troops in this Council, your Majesty, but what of mages?" said Actaion, tiring of the discussion of the Har Mareisch. Col Zemis lay in the west of Elaran. "They are as vital to our success as cannon, or more."

Rianda gestured to Nomiki to respond.

"We have seven, My Lord," he said. "All stand ready to defend our homeland."

"Seven?" said Actaion. His face showed his contempt. "Erd Gellin have more than twice that number in a single tagma; Torridon even more, at one per century. How can you hope to withstand odds of over six to one?"

"If I might interject, Your Majesty?" Euthymios looked questioningly at her. "We have a further sixteen mages unaffiliated to the army in the country and over twice that many students and apprentices. I have spoken to the nine here in Hyrnar and all have shown a willingness to assist in whatever way they are able."

Nomiki brightened. "They would be invaluable, Your Grace. They might be untrained – from a military perspective that is – but their raw power could be used in gestalt by our mages to strengthen defences or bolster our shields against scrying. Some may have their own talents as well." He looked questioningly at Rianda.

"Take them all," she said. "All who will come willingly and conscript those who will not. I will sign the decree today – this is no time for half measures. Our terrain is our life, and secrecy of the essence: if the Gellinese can scry out our movements we are all lost.

"Euthymios, see that a list of the mages and their dwelling places are given to the First Chiliarch."

"Yes, Your Majesty."

"Well, My Lord of Col Zemis?" she said, turning to Actaion. "Does this assuage your fears?"

He nodded, judiciously. "It may be enough. Two to one are the standard odds in magecraft, at which a weaker force can withhold a stronger. We will have that many – barely.

"But I have another question for our chiliarchi: what of Hyrakos?"

There was a hush as they considered Hyrakos. Euthymios looked troubled, Chrysaor impassive, Lykourgos defiant. The Aripos Hills covered the whole of Elaran, stretching from the southern border to the northerly ranges of the Har Mareisch and the great Gralbakh Mountains, of which they were but foothills. No enemy could hope to penetrate far until spring, and even then with difficulty. This is what the chiliarchi – what they all – were counting upon; what gave them the valuable breathing space they needed to raise the muster and then the possibility, slim though it might be, of holding off superior numbers of the better-armed Gellinese forces.

Not so Hyrakos. Nestled on the southern flanks of the Aripos Hills, the city lay right on the border, where the country was rolling but not yet precipitous. Sprawling and wealthy, Hyrakos was a valuable asset: Elaran's gateway to the nations of the south.

Rianda felt a tightening inside: this was the moment she had feared. And yet someone else had raised the subject, and an adversary rather than an ally at that. A gift from Andur indeed; a small one perhaps, but in her situation even the smallest was a boon. A monarch of Elaran might in theory be all-powerful, but one who tried to rule without the broad support of her High Council was a neutered power without doubt. Her father had told her so, many times.

She waited, wondering how the chiliarchi would answer.

"I will be flying to Hyrakos as soon as this council is complete to take charge of the defence," said Lykourgos, Chiliarch of the South. "The southern chiliad, one thousand strong, is already fortifying the city and First Chiliarch Nomiki has agreed that two *hekatontadi* of the first chiliad be flown down to support them."

Chrysaor leaned forward. "Those are brave words, and I commend your courage. But will they be enough against the might of Erd Gellin? Is there a way for us to obtain more reinforcements?"

"Not quickly. We have only eight *tarath* available and they will need rest after such a long flight. It is possible that we could purchase more from civilian use..."

"Out of the question," said Euthymios tersely. "The treasury is not a bottomless pit. What funds we have will be sorely needed for more vital needs – arms for the muster, shot for our cannon, gems for our mages."

"Accepted. That is what we had thought. In that case we could potentially transport another two hundred within two to three weeks – if Hyrakos still holds. With the onset of winter, marching by foot through the passes would be risky – we have too few men to risk losing any – though we may hope that some of the southern muster may be raised before Hyrakos comes under attack."

"The matter still disturbs me," said Chrysaor. "Twelve hundred men, against over ten thousand Gellinese? Granted that our men are brave, but we have not the materiel of the enemy, nor will you have the advantage of terrain."

"It will not be an easy task, you are right. It may even be impossible. But we will make them pay dearly for its capture, and perhaps we may buy some time for the rest of Elaran to rearm."

Rianda knew the time had come.

"I forbid it!" Her words cut sharply across the crowded room. Every head turned to her in shock at her words.

"I forbid it!" she repeated. "You propose to throw away more than a third of our army – and for what gain? A thousand dead Gellinese? It will mean nothing to them. Any time you buy is likewise meaningless; Erd Gellin will not attack beyond Hyrakos until spring, by which point the defence would long have succumbed."

"What then, Your Majesty, do you suggest?" challenged Lykourgos. "I have explained that it is impossible for us to reinforce it further."

"Evacuation. The southern chiliad must be evacuated immediately – by *tarath* and by foot."

The room burst out in a hubbub of noise; everyone speaking at once, all decorum forgotten.

"Quiet!" The noise level fell at Rianda's command, though some muttering continued. "We will discuss this like civilised folk, not a rabble of Gralbakha.

"Chiliarch Lykourgos, you have objections to my proposal?"

The Chiliarch of the South struggled to contain himself. "You write us off too easily, Your Majesty," he said angrily. "The men of the south served your father loyally: allow us to serve you the same way. Erd Gellin will lose men by the score to gain every square foot of Hyrakos."

"Your men's loyalty is not in question, Lykourgos. It is for that reason that I would not have them die to no avail."

She turned to the First Chiliarch. "What of you, Nomiki? Do you share the Chiliarch of the South's opinion – can we put up a meaningful defence of Hyrakos?"

The answer Nomiki wished to give warred with the truth. Eventually he answered.

"No, Your Majesty," he said, resignedly, "we cannot. Outnumbered ten to one, with no allies, no means of escape and no support? Hyrakos's walls were not built to withstand the bombardment of cannon." Tarasios, as always, was struggling to comprehend, but Eliud and Hesperos nodded agreement as he spoke.

"Militarily there are no two ways about it," agreed Chrysaor.

"But what of the people of Hyrakos?" broke in Lykourgos. "We cannot just abandon them to their fate!"

Chrysaor clasped his hands, leaning back. "I am afraid that they will have to take their chances. We must do what is best for Elaran."

"Those are my people!" Slamming his fist upon the table he rose to his feet. "You suggest we leave them to die – not even shed a drop of blood in their defence? They deserve better than that. I tell you, My Lords, Your Majesty, the southern chiliad will not stand for these orders: and nor will I."

"Sit down!" Rianda's voice cut like a whip, the voice of one trained to command and used to being obeyed. Belatedly she had remembered that Lykourgos himself came from Hyrakos; had a wife and children there.

"You swore an oath to the throne of Elaran, My Lord; an oath to the Nemessine line. Will you dishonour those vows you made to my father and to myself?"

Shamed, Lykourgos sank back into his chair. Now was the time for her to press forward; now, whilst the Council was still on her side. Softening her voice she continued.

"Better for the people of Hyrakos to lie under Gellinese rule for one winter, than for all Elaran to suffer their tyranny in perpetuity. A season of taxation and curfews can be endured. If no resistance is offered the Gellinese will not be too harsh; the Hyrakosi will be spared the travails of siege and the butchery and looting that would come if the city was sacked.

"Well, my Lords, do I have your agreement? The southern chiliad must be out of Hyrakos within the week."

A series of reluctant nods came from around the table. Most of the High Council agreed the necessity – even Lykourgos knew it in his heart – but none could like such a move. Euthymios and Eliud in particular showed distress, whilst most of the others looked uncomfortable. Of all who were sat at the oval table, only Tarasios and Chrysaor appeared unconcerned; the former too foolish, the latter cushioned by hid overriding devotion to Elaran, at whatever cost.

In truth, though she was careful to conceal it, her own heart was similarly in turmoil. Why had her father been taken at such a time? She might speak glibly of enduring a season of hardship, but who could tell how the Gellinese would act? Her heart wept for the people of Hyrakos, yet her resolution could not falter. Without the southern chiliad– one third of her trained forces – Elaran would fall in spring, without a doubt. Elaran must not fall; therefore, Hyrakos must be abandoned. The logic was chilling, but inevitable.

As the Council dispersed, she heard Actaion murmur to Tarasios, sotto voce yet she knew he intended her to overhear.

"So, our little queen has her victory, for now, but what will come of it?"

How she wished she knew.

#

Ven Atharden of Dorlan folded the letter into four, carefully pressing down each crease as he did so. Pausing briefly, he labelled the envelope appropriately before tucking it inside the large package of papers that would be winging its way to Kurdon on the next *tarath*.

Queen Rianda thought that she could threaten him, did she; thought that Elaran could stand alone against the might of Erd Gellin? Well, perhaps it could. But not without leaving itself open to the might of Greater Torridon to the north.

He poured himself another glass of wine. An adequate bottle; Silurian, of course. A shame that Torridon's greatest enemy produced the best vintages on the continent. Not even the new imported Triune vintages could compete, for all their favour with the nobility. The Triunes themselves knew the truth of course: it was Imperial consumption that was responsible for driving up the price of Silurian wines so much in the last few years.

This little kingdom would soon learn its lesson. No matter what the self-important High Council, currently sitting, decided, Elaran would soon learn that its days of independence were numbered. The time of the little nations was fading. Greater Torridon, Siluria, Scandia; all had grown in the last century. The revolts against the Varisca had splintered the continent into a hundred tiny pieces, but those days were over – the coming of first the Falani and now the Triune Empire had hastened the process, perhaps, but it had always been inevitable. All that was left to decide for the fly-speck kingdoms was whether to go gracefully, or to be crushed.

Not for the first time, he felt pride that he was a Torridonian, a citizen of the mightiest nation in Laurentia, no matter what those fools in Siluria might say. Hastily, he put the thought of the Triune Empire out of his mind. That was a different matter, he told himself, reshuffling the order of the diplomatic documents in the package. They were not truly of Laurentia, whatever their temporary presence here.

The pack was complete. Details of the Elarani military strength, the defences of Hyrnar and many other matters, significant and trivial, pertaining to the nation of Elaran. And in the long envelope, marked for the eyes of Niavon III himself, Lord Protector of Greater Torridon, a transcript of his latest meeting with Queen Rianda, of her futile defiance and her rejection of Torridon's latest offer. A summary of his recommendations filled the rest of the letter; contingencies and possibilities outlined and assessed.

He stood up. Before two Longest Nights had passed the black boar of Torridon would wave over the Citadel of Hyrnar, with Elaran the latest Torridonian vassal. And then – what reward for Ven Atharden of Dorlan, the ambassador who had made it happen? Grand Duke of Elaran? No, that would be too much of an elevation. Duke of Hyrnar perhaps; he would settle for that. Or perhaps even a position at the court in Kurdon?

Whatever the reward, it hardly mattered. That was not why he did it, but for the glory of Torridon. Ringing the bell for his secretary he directed the man to take care of the package. There was no time to rest on his laurels – the work of an ambassador was never done.

Chapter Eight

When Worlds Collide

Rianda closed her eyes and leaned back, letting the peace of the garden envelop her. The calm was bliss. Not a sound could be heard, save for the call of a late-year hoopoe. The tumult and pressures of the Citadel, of ruling, seemed for these few moments at least to be a world away.

The evening breeze stirred, a cool breath passing over her, carrying the poignant scent of telvain with it. Eyes closed, she could picture their ephemeral blooms, opening only at dusk for these few weeks at the tail-end of autumn. Emerith vines twined delicately among them, powder blue flowers set like jewels amongst the dark green foliage of the telvain. Even now, at the very gateway of winter, the privy garden was a beautiful place.

Soft footsteps sounded behind her. Which dullard official had decided now that she could not be spared, even for a few moments? Annoyed at how easily her calm had been shattered, Rianda took a deep breath. Now, of all times, she needed her composure and, vitally, a few moments away from the demands of the court and council. She should have left orders she was not to be disturbed.

Behind her, the footsteps halted. Forcing down her disappointment, she turned, to look into a fair face almost as familiar as her own. Rianda broke into a genuine smile, all irritation vanished.

"Come, sit by me, cousin," she said warmly, patting the space beside her.

The older woman slid gracefully on to the stone bench and smiled.

"I see I was not the only one who sought out the peace of these gardens tonight."

"And grateful for your company I am, to be sure," Rianda said. "Though I confess, I would have received far less graciously any other who disturbed me." She watched as Elena settled herself, delicately rearranging her skirts as she sat. As Chrysaor's wife, the royal duchess might be separated from Rianda by a generation, but in age fewer than a dozen years separated them.

Elena had first appeared when Rianda was six, her cousin's young bride, dazzling the court with her beauty and young life. Like most who met her, the young princess had instantly succumbed to the new bride's charm, an impossible blessing of an older sister, kind, gentle and fun, who always made time for her young cousin by marriage. As Rianda had grown their relationship had matured, growing stronger, with Elena playing by turns the role of elder sister, aunt, counsellor and friend. Since Rianda's ascension to the throne, Elena and Euthymios had been, in their different ways, two rocks without which she would surely have fallen.

Elena twined an errant stem of emerith about her fingers, the delicate blue flowers shadowed against her hands. Her beauty had not faded over the years; raven hair, unbleached by time, still framed her gentle face, delicate and lovely.

"These gardens are still restful, even now," she said. "I am not surprised that you sought them out tonight."

Rianda looked at her questioningly.

"Chrysaor told me of the High Council. I am glad that such decisions are not mine."

"You would make a better queen than I, Elena." In her heart she knew it was not true; her statement was born of the desire, a desire that could never be fulfilled, to have her burden lifted – no more. Elena would never have acted as she, Rianda, had today; therefore Elena could not be a better queen, for today's actions had been the right ones. So she had to believe; the alternative led to madness and despair.

Even as these thoughts flowed through her mind, Elena was speaking, echoing her thoughts out loud.

"No, Rianda. Your father taught you well, but that alone would not be enough. The strength of the Nemessine line runs in you, and the wisdom too. They do not in mine – nor in Chrysaor's, though he is of your line."

Rianda was shocked. "He is a great man," she protested. "He rules his duchy well – perfectly, some would say – and Elaran never had a more staunch defender in battle."

"Yes, he is all of that. But he could not be the king that your father was – nor does he seek to be. I do not say this to lessen him, for he would tell you the same. He is devoted to Elaran – utterly – and served your father loyally, as he will serve you.

"He is like me, in fact – we are both of us happiest supporting others, not in the place of honour ourselves." She smiled. "We are like each other in so many ways, though outsiders often do not believe it."

Rianda's smile echoed hers. It was impossible to do otherwise – Elena's inner joy was infectious. She and Chrysaor enjoyed that rarest of circumstances: a marriage of state that had resulted in love. Though some wondered at it, the hard Duke of Altyrnal and his gentle wife were devoted to one another.

"What of the twins?" asked Rianda. After two miscarriages and a baby that had not survived birth by a week, three years ago Elena had finally managed to provide her husband with an heir. Her happiness was deeper now, and richer; tinged with the wisdom of one who has known sorrow, as well as joy.

"Sleeping now, by the grace of Andur," Elena replied with a wry smile. "It's the only time Our Lady of Silence manages to make her presence felt in their lives. They're walking now, and talking, and utterly irrepressible."

"Don't pretend that you would have it any other way, cousin."

"Then I won't," she said, blissfully serene. Rianda sighed. Young Fotis and his sister Amaltheia were the delight of her eyes too, though she had far less time than she would wish to see them.

"How I envy you, Elena."

"They've been pressing you to marry again?" her cousin said, perceptive as ever.

"Yes," admitted Rianda. "Euthymios is the only one who has mentioned it openly, though he says he's only voicing what the others say behind my back. But the hints are always there from them, nonetheless.

"Why do they do it?" she burst out angrily. "I know my duty to Elaran; I will marry in due course, and for reasons of state. But may I not have at least a year to mourn my father? It's not as if the succession were not clear."

"You have no child."

"Not you too, Elena! Your own husband is my heir – a legitimate male of the Nemessine line, you said so yourself. And he has heirs himself; Fotis to follow, and Amaltheia after, should mischance befall."

"Andur forgive that it should ever come to that. And Chrysaor has no desire for the throne; he does not wish to rule."

"I dare say not, but my nobles would care little for that. He is neither tyrant nor fool – Elaran has seen many a worse king, has it not?"

"Ye-es," said Elena slowly. "But you have no heir. And that," her voice turned compassionate, "is what counts in the eyes of your lords."

Rianda sagged, her anger collapsing to despair like a puppet with its strings cut.

"By the Broken Wheel," she cried softly, "is that really how they all see me still? Am I really naught but a royal brood mare?"

"Not all, cousin, not all." Elena took her hands her gently. "And even in the worst, not entirely. But they desire stability; if you were a man it would be no different. The monarch must have an heir."

"Must I give way then?"

"No, of course not." Rianda looked up, startled by the firm, no-nonsense tone from Elena. "But you must not expect them to stop pressing for it either. But then, lords are always pushing their ruler to do something, aren't they? It may as well be this as anything else. And while they're wasting their energy, they won't be opposing you as strongly on your other plans, will they?"

Rianda laughed, despite herself. "What would I do without you, cousin? I think I'd go mad."

"Perhaps you would – after all, there's a long history of it in the Nemessine line," retorted Elena, knowing full well there was nothing of the kind. The conversation successfully lightened, the two women's talk turned to other matters, letting out the tensions of the day in restful discourse.

The telvain were fading now, petals falling from their fragile blossoms as the evening darkened. Soon only empty stems would remain, bare against the dark foliage. The other flowers were closing too; mullein and emerith, the pale blue of the latter now grey in the dim light. Rianda shivered, drawing her cloak more tightly about herself.

Again, footsteps sounded on the path; a rapid patter of feet. A young page hurried towards them, slowing as he approached.

"Your Majesty, Your Grace," he said, bowing low. "Your Majesty, the Sword-Captain requests your presence in the Queens' Room. He says it is of the utmost importance."

"He does, does he? And does the Sword-Captain say what the matter is?"

"No, Your Majesty," said the page, stammering slightly. "Only that it concerns Erd Gellin."

Of course, Kadmos would hardly be likely to tell of the news to a young whelp like this; the news would be all over the Citadel before dawn. However, he was not one to waste her time unnecessarily. Reluctantly, Rianda got to her feet.

"Very well, tell the Sword-Captain that I will be following imminently."

"Shall I come also?" asked Elena as the page dashed off.

"No, cousin; only one of us need lose our evening. I thank you for the offer though, and more for your company this evening. A quite unlooked-for blessing."

Striding through the royal keep, her guards behind, Rianda pondered over what this could mean. She would know soon enough. Sweeping into the Queens' Room she saw Kadmos lounging against a pillar, an aura of excitement visible beneath his habitual demeanour of self-assured command. Euthymios stood beside him, similarly tense. Four full dekani of the household guard lined the room, muskets in hand.

"What is the meaning of this, Kadmos? Are you planning a palace coup?"

"No, Your Majesty." He sketched a hasty bow. "We have captured prisoners – two of them, from Erd Gellin."

"We have prisoners by the dozen from Erd Gellin. Who are these two – the High Archon and his wife?"

"They say they are Triune citizens, Your Majesty. They claim that the Gellinese razed their embassy, massacring everyone but them. Six days ago they – and one other – were intercepted by one of our border patrols. Fortunately the commander of that sector recognised their importance and reported them: they were flown to Hyrnar post-haste."

"Massacring a Triune embassy? Even the Archons aren't so stupid. Do these so-called Triunes think we are fools?"

"They appear to be genuine, Your Majesty. I haven't questioned them extensively – I thought you would wish to speak to them yourself, first – but from what little they've said they appear to be telling the truth. They certainly don't *look* Gellinese. Perhaps the Archons think they are far enough from Triune territory to treat the Empire with impunity."

"Or perhaps their hubris has simply crossed the line into folly. If the prisoners are who they claim, then why the guards? I presume that they have been disarmed."

"Of course, Your Majesty." He paused, uneasily. "I believe that the prisoners are who they say they are. But there is always the possibility that I am wrong – it would not be unlike the Archons to attempt an assassination at this juncture. There is also the question of the third man."

"The third man?" she queried.

"The third man who was captured with them. A Rotliegendan, he claimed; he escaped the very first night."

"Surely that would support the truth of their story," interjected Euthymios.

"Perhaps," said Kadmos dubiously. "But it could equally indicate danger of a different sort. The Rotliegendans play a deep game, and who knows what their current schemes are?"

"We will hardly find out more without questioning them," said Rianda crisply. "Bring them in." Kadmos's suspicious nature and attention to detail were invaluable traits for one in his position. Together with the superb discipline and fervour he instilled in his men it meant that she could not have hoped for a better Sword-Captain. The Citadel was safe in his hands. But sometimes his nature got the better of him – there was a time for caution, but a time for action also.

"This could be an unlooked-for boon," whispered Euthymios as Kadmos gave the order. Rianda nodded peremptorily. She did not need his help to spot a *tarathín* in a cloudless sky.

She watched the two prisoners as they were brought in, stumbling slightly, hands loosely bound in front of them. Both bore the signs of hard travel: dirt and grazes still visible on their haggard bodies. A brief rest could not erase the hardships of two weeks or more. Their tattered clothes were not of Gellinese cut, though that told nothing, in itself. Such details could be counterfeited.

They bowed low before her, the younger with more grace than the older. She studied him. Somewhat taller than his companion, his ragged locks and spare frame did nothing to disguise his youth. He could be at most a few years older than she herself. The other was older: in his mid-thirties or thereabouts. It was hard to tell. Kadmos was right – the two did not look Gellinese. They were swarthier and there was more – their features were subtly different; less angular than those of Elaran or Erd Gellin. Rianda had never seen a Triune but she could well believe that these men were from a different continent.

Their first words confirmed her impression. It was the younger who spoke, surprisingly. He spoke in Dalradian of course: language of the long-dead Covenant, lingua franca of the educated of two continents. But while the words were understandable enough, the accent was alien. Not bad, as one sometimes heard – his articulation was consistent and his fluency and diction made it clear the man was no novice – but as if he had been taught in a totally divergent school of pronunciation.

"Your Majesty, why are we being treated as prisoners? We mean no harm to you or your kingdom."

"We are at war with Erd Gellin, or will be soon. Anyone crossing the border must be treated as suspect."

"Rest assured, young Triune, that if we truly thought you Gellinese spies your condition would be significantly worse than it is now," said Kadmos.

"In the meantime," continued Rianda, "you would do well to remember that you are our prisoners, and whether you remain so is entirely dependent on our goodwill."

The younger stepped forward angrily. "But..." he began before freezing. Two score muskets had snapped up, levelled directly at him. Slowly, he stepped back, careful to make no sudden moves.

"Yes, Your Majesty," he said, subsiding.

"So, let us start at the beginning. Who are you, and what are your names?"

"Thomas Maynard, Your Majesty. Junior attaché to Their Imperial Majesties' embassy in Erd Gellin."

"John Lawrence, chaplain to Their Imperial Majesties' embassy in Erd Gellin. Your Majesty," he added. His Dalradian was more halting than the first's.

"Very well," said Rianda. "So tell us: why are you here and what do you wish from us? It is beyond living memory since a man of the Triune Empire has entered Elaran."

Rianda listened as the men began their tale of destruction, slaughter and flight. Only once did she interject, to query them over Piotr.

"This Piotr, your Rotliegendish servant – you say he was a mage, as well as his other talents? And you never had an inkling of this, when he was your servant?"

"No, Your Majesty." He answered calmly. "I realised he was more educated than most, but that was all."

"And where is he now?"

Thomas looked genuinely anxious, clearly fearing he would not be believed. "I don't know. He said nothing to us of his plans to escape. We were as surprised as your men to find him gone."

Kadmos turned to her. "You believe this tripe?" he growled in Elarani. "Don't worry – neither of them can speak our language; I've tested them extensively." He grinned wickedly.

"It may be true, Kadmos. His words have a ring of truth. You said yourself that Rotliegendes plays a deep game. These Triunes could be nothing but pawns. Does the rest of their story tally with what they have said before?"

"Yes," he admitted. "And not word for word either, which would have argued for a memorised tale. My gut instinct still argues for caution though."

"We cannot be too cautious though, if we hope to gain their trust," said Euthymios. "If these men are Triunes, with such reason to be hostile to Erd Gellin, they could be a great asset both in what they know themselves, and perhaps even in aid from the Empire."

"The former is more likely to be forthcoming than the latter, but even so they will be greatly valuable. It will be a fine line to tread." She turned once more to the captives.

"I do apologise," she said to them graciously, switching back to Dalradian. "Please continue."

"This is preposterous," burst in Kadmos, as soon as they had finished. Rianda had noticed that her Sword-Captain had been restraining himself with some effort. "You had spoken of your pursuit by *rahvashda* before and that I accept – I can well believe that the Archons are dabbling with infernal matters. But you speak of demons in such numbers as to decimate the countryside. And drogkhar! The drogkhar have been extinct since shortly after the time of St. Cornelius."

"You may be right about the numbers involved," admitted Lawrence. "But the villagers of Krithia were quite positive in their identification of drogkhar."

"The word of villagers!"

"We do not doubt their sincerity," said Euthymios, more mildly. "But can uneducated villagers be considered to be reliably able to identify drogkhar, when the species has been extinct for over half a millennium? More likely, surely, that they had seen some form of vile demon that bore a scant resemblance to the drogkhar of the ancient tales."

"Perhaps so," said Thomas. "But I warn you that we in the Residency made the same mistake of underestimating our enemies."

"Enough of this." Rianda cut them off – such discussions could wait until a later date. "I can assure you that we will not make such mistakes. Kadmos," – she switched to Elarani – "inform First Chiliarch Nomiki of these rumours as soon as we adjourn."

The two men stood passively before her, more confident than when they had been brought in. Not that the vigilance of the guards was any lower – Kadmos maintained a superlative degree of discipline in the Household Guard. The hour grew late and the room cold; the Triunes' story had not been short in the telling and the Queens' Room not designed for night-time use. Too many windows allowed the heat to seep out. In their rags the captives must feel it more than she in her gown and cloak, particularly coming as they had from the warmer climes of Erd Gellin.

She turned to Kadmos. "Untie their bonds. It is time to show that we trust their word."

"Very well, Your Majesty." The Sword-Captain's studiously blank face betrayed his feelings about the order.

"Men of the Triune Empire," she said, addressing them for the first time with this appellation. "We believe your tale. In the name of Andur and of His sister Ruth we welcome you to Elaran and state our friendship with the distant Triune Empire."

They stood stolidly whilst their bonds were cut. The elder betrayed signs of irritation at her speech, whilst the younger just stood there, relieved. Well, she told herself, what had she expected – cheering?

"You are free to go if you wish, whereas as long as you remain in Hyrnar you will be our honoured guests."

"Thank you, Your Majesty," the younger – Thomas, she thought it was – said courteously. "As representatives of the Empire, might we request right of passage upon the next *tarath* flight heading towards Imperial territory?"

Rianda made her expression downcast. The trap was sprung. They had accepted her terms – they were playing her game now. Euthymios, she knew, was appreciating the delicate balancing of forces, the trap wrought of steel filigree that could provide the Empire with no reasonable grounds for complaint over how its citizens had been treated.

"I regret that that will be difficult, much as I would wish it otherwise. You know, of course, that we are preparing for a war with Erd Gellin. Your tidings only confirm their hostile intent. Every *tarath* we own is being used to transport men and supplies for the war."

"It may be possible for you to gain passage on a privately owned *tarath*," said Euthymios, playing his part as smoothly as if rehearsed. "I believe the House of Gelrin from Linnarson has a *tarath* in the city, and perhaps there are others." Of course, as Rianda and he both knew, the Imperials would find no *tarath* able to convey them. "Oh, so sorry," would be the refrain as one excuse after another met their ear. A queen, even one of Elaran, could still arrange some things. Merchants of Linnarson would do anything for money.

"What of other means? By road, perhaps?"

"I would strongly advise against attempting to cross Elaran by foot at this time of year," answered Euthymios. "The first snow has already fallen in the higher hills; soon the passes will be closed until spring. Is that not so, Sword-Captain?"

"It is, Your Grace. Only yesterday I received word that the Tyrnanine Pass had been rendered impassable. The First Chiliarch is cursing the saints themselves.

"I believe, my friends," Kadmos grinned wolfishly, "that you may be forced to endure our hospitality this winter."

Lawrence opened his mouth angrily to protest, but desisted at a refraining touch on the arm from Thomas. Rianda approved. One at least of these Imperials knew what could be bargained for and what could not.

"It seems that the season leaves us no alternative, Your Majesty," Thomas said to her, bowing slightly. "But I am sure that you will take care of our needs most graciously.

"As we are unable to leave until spring, may I ask a boon? The Empire will wish news of the massacre in Erd Gellin – as yet, they may have heard nothing. Will you allow us to send a message by *variideshar*?"

"Of course," said Rianda. "We have no direct link to the Triune Empire – as you know, you two are only the second direct contact we have had with your nation."

"The Bay of Meneth would in any case block a direct line from Hyrnar to Autigen," said Euthymios.

"That is true. However, we do have links to other nations who will be able to relay the message to the Triune embassy there. I think perhaps Linnarson might be best – one can always be sure of their neutrality. I assume the Triune Empire has a presence there?"

"It does, Your Majesty. We thank you."

"Euthymios, please accompany them to the *variidesharium*."

They left at the dismissal, following behind the bishop, accompanied only by two guards rather than the former four dozen. The elder appeared somewhat bemused by the rapidity of their change in circumstances but the younger was maintaining his composure well.

"Kadmos," said Rianda, as soon as they had left. "Please set someone to arrange quarters for them. They should be secure, but not obviously so – they are free to move around the Citadel, but we should maintain a discreet watch on them nonetheless."

"Of course, Your Majesty." As he left, Rianda wondered how the arrival of these two Imperials would change matters. They offered no direct military advantage and yet, as she well knew, information could be as powerful as any cannon. There would, of course, be great advantages in close ties with the Triunes, but such far-off fruits would come to naught, unless Elaran first withstood the onslaught that would arrive with the spring.

Chapter Nine

Counsels

Thomas lay down on the bed, stretching luxuriously. He smiled as he let his muscles relax into the softness, letting his body go limp. It seemed an age since he had enjoyed such comfort, rather than a bare two months.

The Elarani certainly had not been lying about them being treated as honoured guests. These quarters were fit for a king – or at least for an ambassador. Sitting up, his eyes swept over the frescoed walls and marble frontage, lingering on the lush divan that occupied the centre of the main room, just visible through the half-open door. Cabinets and wardrobes of burnished cedar completed the room, adorned with the delicate statues of fired ceramic favoured by the Elarani.

In truth, it was a considerable step up from his quarters as a junior attaché in Iskarn, and seemed a ten-fold improvement by dint of his recent hardships. Truly, he thought, he wouldn't mind spending a week or two here, even a month, before heading for the Imperial provinces, particularly if they were to be treated throughout in the manner these rooms suggested. Though he and Lawrence had sent the *variideshar* message before retiring, suddenly the question of when they would receive an answer seemed to become a good deal less urgent.

A hammering at the door interrupted Thomas's reverie. Groaning, he forced himself off the bed, peeved slightly at this interruption. What could the Elarani want now? Suddenly his sense of humour reasserted itself. How little it took to change one's mindset from being a captive to feeling at home! Fewer than six hours ago he had been a captive of these people, and now he had the temerity to feel aggrieved at an interruption – and a relatively polite one at that, for all the noise. After all, they could have just walked in.

Shaking his head at his own folly, Thomas pulled open the door. It was Lawrence. His aggrievedness returned with a vengeance at the sight of the former chaplain. They'd only parted half an hour ago. Andur Astartes, hadn't they spent enough time together over the last two weeks? Thomas was not pleased to have his first chance to truly relax disturbed. He had been on the run ever since the Residency had been destroyed; at no time totally free of fear. Events had moved so fast that there had never really been the time to take everything in; too many things had been pushed aside in the struggle to survive. Thomas needed the time to lie back alone in safety and think, to truly digest and come to terms with what had happened.

"Come in," he said, ungraciously. Lawrence needed no urging. By the time Thomas had finished speaking Lawrence was already halfway across the room. Thomas reluctantly pulled up a chair as his unwanted guest plumped himself down upon the divan. There was no need to encourage this visit to last any longer than necessary, but he supposed that to remain standing would have been rather too discourteous.

"Look here, Thomas," said Lawrence, "what are we going to do about all this?"

"Do? We seem fairly well set here for a couple of weeks. Enjoy the comfort, get our strength back and tell the queen and her lords anything they want to know about Erd Gellin."

"You're seriously content to wait out the winter here?" said Lawrence in disbelief.

"I hardly think it will come to that – we've sent off our message, and no doubt soon enough we'll find a passage back to civilisation."

"You think the Elarani will let us go so easily? We're prisoners here in all but name. I tell you..."

"Don't be absurd, John." Thomas's voice cut off Lawrence's rising voice mid-flow. "Queen Rianda is concerned that we don't leave until her councillors have pumped us for all we know about Erd Gellin – you're right enough there – but how much do we know? Precious little. I'm happy to help all I can and I'd advise you to do the same – anything to strike a blow against the Archons. But once that's done, what do they gain from restraining us? They don't want the Empire's enmity and this is a chance for them to gain its friendship."

"You're naive. But there's no sense arguing – there's nothing we can do either way but wait for the *variideshar* reply." He sank further into the divan. Thomas sighed. The last two weeks had done nothing to soften the chaplain's stubborn mind. At least he wasn't – yet – ranting over the religious beliefs of the Elarani.

For his part, Thomas couldn't see the problem. As he had said, he was more than happy to give any information of use to the Elarani before they left, and in the meantime they certainly didn't seem to be being mistreated. Unfortunately, if Lawrence wasn't going to change his mind, nor did he show any signs of imminent departure.

"Well, as you can say, we can discuss it again then. What are your own quarters like?" asked Thomas, hoping Lawrence would take the hint.

"Much as these. Slightly smaller, I think. I didn't really stay to examine them." Lawrence levered himself around until he was looking Thomas straight in the eye. Speaking deliberately, he said, "Look, there's one thing here that no one's mentioning."

"Piotr?"

"Exactly. What's his game? Why did he disappear when we met the Elarani?"

"Does it matter? We both owe him our lives. I don't blame him at all for escaping when he did – we were captives, after all." Thomas voice was firm as he defended his one-time servant.

"Why didn't he take us with him then?"

"He might not have been able to. I'm sure that it would have been much easier for him to get away alone than dragging us two along with him. Would we have even wanted to? Where would we have gone? I think you're forgetting that he didn't owe us a thing; quite the reverse in fact. And if he didn't wish to be detained, or had just tired of yoking his path to ours, that's his business, not ours."

"I think you're the one who's forgetting something, and that's how little we know of him. I say again, what game is he playing? A servant with his skills – languages, arcane philosophy, weapon craft?"

"Servant or spy, he got us away."

"Yes," said Lawrence, "But where is he now?"

#

"That," said Euthymios, "is the question. Where is he now?"

"And what is he doing?" added Rianda. They were back in the Queens' Room, the portraits of the eight previous ruling queens of Elaran gazing down upon them in majesty. Rianda would be the ninth. Looking up at the portraits she prayed she would do better than Euthalia, whose misrule had all but destroyed Elaran in civil war when her discontented nobles had attempted to depose her in favour of her cousin. The fact that she had ultimately won was no comfort – Rianda would not have victory at such a cost.

She forced her thoughts back to the new arrivals. "Do you think they are telling the truth?"

"About the Rotliegendan?" queried Euthymios.

"I meant overall, but yes, we can start with the Rotliegendan."

"I do, Your Majesty. Neither of them seem to know much about him – they even thought he was just a servant until the massacre. We've both said many times how deep a game Rotliegendes plays – I'm afraid those two young Triunes were likely just babes in his hands."

Rianda thought that the two Triunes weren't so young as all that. But of course they would be unfamiliar with Laurentia.

"The bigger question," continued Euthymios pensively, "is whether this Piotr – if that's his real name, of course – was spying for Rotliegendes or if he's a member of the Pillar of Zech."

"Does it matter? The Pillar as good as controls Rotliegendes. The king's a puppet and those of the nobility that aren't members themselves are firmly under the thumb."

"The Pillar does have great control in Rotliegendes, you're right – and it has almost as much in the other Tuevic nations, particularly Zechstein and the former Duchy of Toarcia. But there is a difference. If Piotr's a Pillarian, he won't be acting for national interest – the Pillar plays an even deeper game than the Rotliegendish and, Andur knows, they have more influence, if not as much as direct power. They've friends in unexpected places, all over the north-east and even as far south as here, and they've been working indirectly for the same agenda for centuries now."

"When will the Tuevic nations let this folly go? The Zechen-Rotliegendish Commonwealth has been dead for five centuries, and it was on its knees long before the Pajderza War finished it off. How can they hope to revive it?"

"Yes, my daughter, the Zechen-Rotliegendish Commonwealth is long dead, but memories run deep. Would you forget Elaran and fail to seek her revival, even were your forces crushed, Hyrnar captured and you yourself a refugee in the wilderness, without resource or power? Would you not strive for her restoration and freedom, until your dying day? And would not your son do the same, and his son, and his daughter and all of the Nemessine line, until Elaran was free once more? The Pillar is no different."

"Be that as it may," said Rianda uncomfortably, "we're unlikely to find out whether or not this particular Rotliegendan is a member. Or what he was up to." She nodded sharply. "So I suggest we turn our attention to the two Triunes who we actually have. What were your impressions as you took them to the *variidesharium*?"

Euthymios smiled inwardly at his queen's rapid change of subject. His young protégée sometimes applied the techniques of the Council chamber rather too readily to avoid topics in more normal conversation. Ah well, he reflected, such was the privilege of majesty.

He pondered how best to answer her question. "They are taking it...differently, Your Majesty. And not the way you might expect. I am somewhat surprised."

"Differently how? Don't make me drag it from you, Euthymios" she said in exasperation.

"My apologies, Majesty. It is somewhat hard to describe. The younger is very content; he is calm and appears satisfied by your decision. He answered my questions about himself and Erd Gellin without hesitation."

"What did he say?" interjected Rianda sharply.

"Oh, nothing substantive. I was only testing the waters. But he appears receptive. And it was he who composed most of the *variideshar* message – that was standard enough, just describing what had happened to them and where they were. I gave them two minutes of time, which I thought was justified."

"Generous, but yes, you were right. What of the elder?"

"Quite different. Much more resentful. He practically reeked with hostility. He obviously considers himself nothing better than a prisoner, whereas the younger is at least willing to go along with the fiction that they are honoured guests."

"They are honoured guests," said Rianda. "As long as they don't try to leave too soon. They will be treated as representatives of the Triune Empire. In any case, where would they go and how?"

She tapped her fingers pensively against one of the marble pillars. The rhythm against the cool stone was restful. The queens of antiquity gazed down upon her as she pondered.

"You will have to gain their confidence, Euthymios. Starting with the elder – we cannot have him infecting the younger with his hostility."

"Ah, Majesty, that may be awkward." The bishop gathered his vestments about him. "The elder is a chaplain..."

"Yes, he said so. All the better; he will trust a bishop."

"Quite the opposite, I'm afraid. The Triunes are from Avalonia; they are Scriptualists who accept neither Canonical doctrine nor the authority of the Patriarch in Aesthen. The fact that I am a man of cloth will do more to earn his enmity than anything else I could do."

"Are the differences really so severe? We have had so little contact with the Triunes."

"Severe? You could say that," Euthymios said dryly. "They did cause the Sundering of the Covenant and start the Secession Wars."

"I know that, Euthymios. But that was almost two thousand years ago. I thought that both sides might have mellowed a bit by then."

"You're right, of course." He had been wrong to chide her. "The Synod has debated it a number of times, but the obstructions to reconciliation are mainly on their side.

"In truth, we've no trouble with many Triunes. For most people, belief in Andur is enough, and they're not too disturbed by points of doctrine; in fact, a lot of the Triunes are quite disturbingly secular. I'm quite sure I'll be able to win the confidence of the younger one – Thomas Maynard, his name was – and the religious differences won't concern him in the slightest.

"But unfortunately, the chaplain seems to be rather fervent. Just from a few things he said when we were together it's quite clear that he thinks us as good as heretics and myself, as a Canonical bishop, the next thing to an arch-demon."

Rianda looked pensive. This made things rather more complicated. She had counted upon Euthymios being able to befriend these strangers. The elderly bishop, with a genuinely warm manner and generous heart, would have made a far better confidant than any of her other close advisers. Kadmos was simply too fervent, whilst First Chiliarch Nomiki or Chrysaor, her cousin, were too reserved to hope to gain the outlanders' confidence. In any case, their other duties were far too pressing with war approaching. The same held true for Hesperos and Eliud, who might have been possibilities, and for Lykourgos, who would not have been. Tarasios of course was too foolish and Actaion could simply not be trusted. He would have been as likely to conceal anything he learned as report it too her. Troubled, she began to hum tunelessly to herself; an old lay of Elaran that her father had been wont to quote from.

"What do you suggest then?" she asked.

"I've been thinking about it. I'll still take care of Maynard of course, but as for Lawrence – the chaplain – I wondered if you'd considered Ven Tychon."

"Who is he?" The name seemed faintly familiar.

"Air Captain Tychon? He commands the *tarathinakii*?"

"Of course. I remember seeing him." She paused suddenly. "Are you sure?" she asked dubiously. "What would a man like him have in common with a Triune chaplain?"

Euthymios spread his hands. "I'm not entirely sure. But the man is extremely personable and is said to have a quite phenomenal charisma. His men worship him, and the *tarathinakii* are a fairly intelligent group. Notoriously independent too. And they're about the same age..." He stopped, aware that he was rambling.

"Your Majesty," he admitted, "I don't know if it will work. But my instinct tells me it's worth a try. Tychon will be in Hyrnar over the winter anyway; the *tarathin* forces won't need to move until the last movement, and they'll be of more use here. And, to be honest, I can't think of anyone else who might pull it off."

"We can but attempt it, I suppose." She sighed. It almost seemed that they were investing far too much effort in these two Triunes – but then high prizes demanded high stakes. And truly, they were not risking or spending much, save Euthymios's time. Though that in itself was precious.

"Is there anything else I should be imminently concerned about, Euthymios?" Rianda asked. "The withdrawal from Hyrakos – how goes that? Is Lykourgos cooperating?"

"He carps, but he obeys, Your Majesty. He is still your servant, even if he dislikes the order, and there is no vein of subtlety in him as there is in Actaion. First Chiliarch Nomiki and Chiliarch Hesperos also see the necessity for their action, and he respects them. I believe the three of them are planning the withdrawal as we speak."

"Lykourgos respects them. But he does not respect me."

"I did not say that, Your Majesty."

"You implied it."

"Your Majesty, Lykourgos honours and respects you as a ruler and queen. But we must face the truth: whilst he would always obey you, on military matters the views of his fellow chiliarchi are bound to sway his own mind more than your own words – or more than mine, for like you, I have no first-hand experience of warfare and make no secret of it."

That was the truth, and Rianda knew it, but it was a bitter cup to swallow, especially when in a bare few months the decisions she would need to be making would be largely military. Still, it was for this, amongst so many other things, that she valued Euthymios. Kind, caring, compassionate; he nonetheless would not mince words nor perform the false kindness of sheltering her from the truth. A queen could not afford illusions.

The bright candlelight of the chandeliers remained as steady as ever, their multifaceted, crystalline radiance illuminating the former queens of Elaran with a steady, warm glow. Evening had already been drawing in when Kadmos had first called Rianda in to examine their new guests and much time had passed since then. Outside, through the western window, the moon was already high, casting its silvery sheen upon the grounds of the Citadel, gently illumining the flowers that had given Rianda such pleasure, their petals now closed in slumber.

Weariness called her, the tiredness that overcame her now at the end of each day since she had become queen. She had plunged herself into self-enforced busyness upon the shock of her father's death, hoping that exhaustion could dull the sharp pain of grief. But the deliberate effort had hardly been necessary. Weeks later, her days were still filled from dawn till dusk. Every moment of her day had a dozen demands on it; the Citadel was filled with people whose work could seemingly not progress without a few minutes of Rianda's time. Even from those matters that she herself considered important she could have filled her days thrice over. And then there was the unexpected; whether disasters, or merely new complications such as tonight's, they still inexorably ate away at her days.

She sighed. "Was it always this way, Euthymios? I seem to remember a time when I was younger and things were simpler; the Citadel happy, my father at peace and Elaran not needing to fight for its life."

Euthymios looked down at her with compassion. He marvelled at how her slight frame with intricately coiled hair twined above that delicate face could withstand all this and, so far at least, master it. She was so young still, so seemingly frail. But old enough, he prayed, and strong enough too.

"No, my daughter," he said gently. "It has always been this way in Elaran. It was just that before you were too young to realise it."

#

"Quickly now!" snapped Lykourgos. The aide dashed off along the corridors of the citadel. Lykourgos turned back to his companion.

"Only six of the *tarath*, you say?"

"Yes," said Nomiki. The two chiliarchi were in the Map Room, the military heart of the Citadel, where for five and a half centuries the chiliarchi of Elaran had planned their defence of the kingdom. "There is less urgency now that we are evacuating, not reinforcing, so I believe it would be useful to keep two here at Hyrnar, in case of emergency."

"You're right," Lykourgos said grudgingly. "Even six will still be considerable aid." He cursed savagely. "But those *tarath* should be going south laden, not empty. Retreat? What does our child-queen know of war?"

"Girl she may be, but she is queen nonetheless and no man's puppet," said the First Chiliarch sharply. "Cross her and you will find she brooks no disobedience. In any case," he continued more mildly, "I like the plan as little as you, but surely you can see its necessity?"

"Perhaps. But what price Elarani honour?" Lykourgos strode to the great map that covered fully half one wall of the room, giving the room its name.

"Look at this," he said, gesturing vehemently. Nomiki looked. As First Chiliarch he had studied that map for years. The vividly textured detail of the kingdom of Elaran and borders was engraved into his mind; by now he could have sketched it from memory. The beautifully rendered ruggedness of the Aripos Hills that covered almost the entire nation, sloping down to the flatlands of the south-east border where Hyrakos lay and, in the other direction, climbing steeply to the highland fastness of the Har Mareisch and the precipitous scarps of the Gralbakh Mountains, of which the Aripos Hills were only foothills, though mighty foothills indeed.

Even after so many years, the talent of the crafters still took Nomiki's breath away. The land was so detailed it seemed to stand out from the wall itself: a three-dimensional image of reality. Roads were picked out in shards of black onyx, glistening liquidly, whilst sultry garnets and carnelians marked the principal towns, smouldering redly with their inner light. Hyrnar itself was a magnificent ruby, fully a thumb's width thick, set in its crowning glory below Mount Karnitha in the centre of the kingdom. The gems were not quite spell-quality of course, but their perfection came close; they were flawless to the naked eye. Their lustre multiplied the map's beauty, as did the scattering of jewel dust, fragments of crystalline zircon and tawny topaz, verdant turquoise, azure lapiz lazuli and ruddy agate, that glistened upon the peaks and valleys of this portrayal of Elaran, bringing to life its forests, stones and streams.

Countless hours of craftsmen had been devoted to this map. And not only craftsmen, Nomiki reminded himself, but soldiers, explorers and cartographers. The brainchild of Hypatios II, third Nemessine King, the map was uncannily accurate. Every path and track known was marked upon it, and each new one was added when discovered. The map had survived the Givetian conquest and the more recent Variscan Interregnum: in both cases the invaders had recognised its value.

Lykourgos's voice broke into his reverie. "From the Har Mareisch to the Plain of Gadinno this map shows Elarani soil. Not one stone; not one stone I say, should be given up unfought."

Nomiki's eyes strayed south to the passes; the Thradfi Gap, Illapthos, the Pass of Istria, the last already closed by weather. There were others of course, but it was through one of these that a Gellinese army must come. Hyrakos lay on the other side of them, naked.

"You are right in principle, Lykourgos. To surrender Hyrakos unfought grieves me deeply, but look." He waved his hand towards the map. "How can we hope to defend it? In spring, when our forces are marshalled, we have a chance of stopping the Gellinese at the passes. But to fight them in the open, outnumbered ten to one. Neither the queen nor I will let you throw the southern chiliad away for no cause.

"What of the city? The people of Hyrakos are Elarani too; the blood of our country runs through their veins. What will they, or others, think if we give up an entire city for 'tactical reasons'?"

"It must be done."

"Must it?" Lykourgos whirled, striding away to the far edge of the room. Nomiki winced as he saw him collide with the order table, a harassed scribe scrabbling to recover and sort the documents scattered by the collision. More composed, Nomiki followed his fellow chiliarch.

Lykourgos turned to face him as he drew near. "Our little queen speaks glibly of the Hyrakosi living under the rule of the Archons for a winter," he said bitterly, "but what does she know of enemy occupation?"

Nomiki struggled for an answer, but Lykourgos was already continuing. "And how will we have the force to reconquer it next year? You and I both know that we will be hard-pressed to beat back the invasion at all, let alone take the offensive.

"No, if we abandon Hyrakos now, we abandon it for years, perhaps for ever. And we abandon those living there to the tender mercies of the Archons."

"Your family need not be amongst them," said Nomiki, with some sympathy. "Get them out. None of your men will begrudge them the space on a *tarath*."

"How can I? You say that none would begrudge them the space, but what of the people of Hyrakos? Chiliarch Lykourgos evacuating his family – they would take to the hills at once. Perhaps it would be better if they did," he said bitterly.

"No, I cannot do that. They must stay, with the rest, and we must pray that our queen's words are true." His breath came out harshly, chokingly. "But..." he tailed off.

"Lykourgos, you will not stay!" Nomiki was alarmed. His subordinate was on the brink, torn between conflicting senses of duty, and his stiff-necked honour would not allow him to take even the small step – the removal of his family to safety – that might somewhat assuage it. Nomiki grappled for the words he must say.

"You told me to look at this map before," he said. "Well, you look now!" Grabbing Lykourgos by the shoulders, Nomiki physically forced the man towards the map. His height had advantages at times. By the saints, he needed this man! Since the death of King Diarad, no other commander in Elaran came close in the fervour and devotion Lykourgos inspired in his men, and in tactics only Chrysaor and Nomiki himself could surpass him.

"See there? You said it yourself, not two minutes ago. We will be hard pressed to defeat the Archons, let alone counter-attack." Nomiki gestured at the wall, towards the southern passes.

"How can I defend these hills without the southern chiliad – without *you*? Forget Elaran; forget the child-queen on her throne: *I* need you." Nomiki felt Lykourgos's shoulders sag beneath his hands. The fight had gone out of him.

"I will not stay and fight," said Lykourgos steadily. "I swore an oath. I will withdraw, and return to Hyrnar, and leave Hyrakos to its fate."

Nomiki said nothing. Wordlessly, Lykourgos turned from him and picked up the next sheaf of papers from the order table. In an unnaturally calm voice he said,

"*Hekatontarch* Phaidros reports that the chiliad has insufficient mules to carry enough food to get further than Kaisaris, if they retain all of their cannon and equipment."

"That can be arranged," said Nomiki. "On no account can we abandon armaments to the Gellinese. Resupply trains can be routed to meet them. It is Tarasios's lands – we will need to speak to him."

"I'm sure that even he should be capable of such an order, if we explain it slowly enough."

As if nothing had happened, the two chiliarchi bent over the order table, methodically processing the vast array of detail involved in moving an army at short notice. As they worked, Nomiki heard Lykourgos murmur again, as if unconscious that he was doing so.

"I swore an oath."

Chapter Ten

Sentence

Sunlight lanced through the high window, transforming the dull *variideshari* into shimmering spheres of light. The room seemed to come alive, changing in an instant from a dreary attic to a place of laughter and life. Colours flashed from the *variideshari*'s precious centres, the flawless diamonds suspended arcanely in the perfect centre of each sphere, imbued with the force that gave them powers. Scintillating, they scattered the sun's rays across the room, flashing arrays of colour that danced across the shadows.

Then it was over, the sun disappearing behind the grey-white clouds that blanketed most of the sky. Once more, the *variideshar* were apparently no more than glass spheres sitting upon their plinths, the central gem only visible to one who looked. Only those nearest the window still sparkled faintly, a mere shadow of what they had been only a moment before.

Eleven of them. A small number, Thomas thought, if one compared it with how many there would be in Linnarson, Kurdon or Autigen, let alone Wenlock. The great Parliamentary *variidesharium* contained almost two hundred of the devices, connecting the Triune capital to its districts and provinces, knitting together the Empire with ephemeral cables of light, strong as steel. Only the ocean proved a barrier to their range, an obstacle that so far had thwarted the best efforts of countless arcanists.

Yet notwithstanding the comparison, those eleven spheres probably represented more wealth than existed anywhere else in Elaran, other than perhaps in the crown jewels themselves. Thomas estimated that a single *variideshar* would cost upwards of a year's revenue for a small hill nation such as Elaran – twice that, of course, for the internal links, where Elaran would have to bear the full cost of their creation. No wonder they were kept so carefully, each cushioned and secure upon its plinth of polished walnut, here in this room deep in the heart of the Citadel. Only the one high, narrow window was present for light and air, and that only because the room looked inwards, towards the Har Sarenis and the cathedral, rather than outwards to the world outside. Four guards were present. They had been here each time he came; dour faced men with muskets and swords, surrounding the clerk and clerk's runner who operated the devices.

A *variideshar* began pulsing, the first on the far wall. The gem at the centre seeming to expand and contract in steady rhythm, scattering shimmers of light –

green, pastel blue, the deepest rose and more – across the surface of the sphere. It was a reverse of the light show of a few minutes before, but with the light now coming, impossibly, from within. The first time Thomas had seen one he had been stunned, but he had been much younger then, only in his second year at Chelmsthorpe.

Swiftly the clerk stepped up to it, deftly tapping the surface in the ritual sequence that would activate it for reception. That had been the great genius of their creator, whosoever that great arcanist might be, lost now in the depths of history. *Variideshari* had been known in the time of the Covenant itself, and the secret never lost. But the fact that any person, with training, could use them was their great virtue, for what use such a device if it could only be used by arcanists?

The clerk had almost finished now, each movement smooth and sure. Despite the best efforts of the arcanists, *variideshari* remained heartbreakingly fragile. What might look like imperishable crystal was naught but the most fragile glass. The *anaedeshi*, as the clerks who operated them were known, were an elite corps to which none gained entrance without years of training. This one here was no exception.

Thomas watched him as he completed the sequence, sweeping his curved hand around the sphere in a deceptively casual motion. Activated, the pulsing stabilised, the *variideshar* glowing now with a steady internal light as its message poured out. The crystalline notes chimed through Thomas's bones, painfully beautiful; a mountain stream of quicksilver set to music. As always, no trace or characteristics of the initial voice were transmitted, yet the words remained clearly distinct, each syllable falling resonantly into place.

Despite this messages could be surprisingly difficult to understand. Though the *anaedeshi* were trained in how to speak clearly, the alien timbre imparted by the devices could make even the simplest of messages obscure to the untrained ear. This was one of the clearest that Thomas had heard: there was little of the distortion, resonance and beating that all too often set in, culminating in the single high tone, heartachingly pure, that occurred if too large a body of water lay between. It was from Anille, capital of Givet, only a short way to the south-east, so the clarity was only to be expected.

Thomas had asked the link-locations of all the *variideshar* here. Though he could not yet recognise, as the more experienced *anaedeshi* could, a sphere by the characteristics of its chromatic display, he had, more prosaically, memorised them.

Torridon, Siluria, the Elder Alliance. Thomas mentally ran through the list once more as the message continued, a tedious description, for all its beauty, of trade negotiations and distant politics. He recognised its importance but such matters were hardly the most engaging for one not intimately involved.

Linnarson came next. Another predictable link; the merchants of the city state dominated the trade of northern Laurentia, whilst its university was the centre for arcane learning on the continent. Those four globes completed the window wall; now he turned to the three spheres on their padded plinths that occupied the crossbar of the horseshoe, the shorter wall perpendicular to the first.

Givet and Erd Gellin, Elaran's southern neighbours. His stomach still turned at the thought of the latter and its proximity, of their harrowing flight that, less than a week ago, had seen him a fugitive in a hostile country. Firmly, he put the thought aside, continuing. Aesthen came next, seat of the Patriarchy. No Canonical nation would be without this link. From the Holy See, the frail Patriarch had absolute sway over the spiritual welfare of the continent – barring a few enclaves of pagans – not to mention his dominance over the kingdom of Scandia, a theocracy in all but name.

Thomas edged forward to get a better sight of the last wall. He took care to remain well behind the painted line, beyond which none save the *anaedesh* was permitted to go. There had almost been an unpleasant incident on his first day here, for Elaran took no chances with its *variideshar*: the four guards had clear orders in case of transgression. Still, from a couple of feet behind the line he could see the remaining three clearly enough.

First Ygerna, the capital of Cadom province. That had been a surprise, initially: why would Elaran, with so few *variideshar*, have two links to a single country, even one as important as Torridon? And why to Ygerna, when Cadom was such a minor province? The clerk had not known but Thomas had asked Euthymios, and learned that the queen's great aunt, the mother of the current Duke of Altyrnal, Chrysaor, had been a princess of Cadom. She had always missed her homeland, and the *variideshar* had been part of her royal dower.

Finally came Rotliegendes, the last, save for the two internal links that connected Hyrnar to the north and south of the kingdom. Rotliegendes was also not such an obvious link, though in hindsight was less surprising, for while Rotliegendes's power was small, its webs of intrigue reputedly covered Laurentia. As always, the thought of Rotliegendes turned Thomas's thoughts to Piotr, his erstwhile servant, rescuer, companion and guide. Where was he now? No doubt reporting to a superior on the events in Erd Gellin. It had been almost a week since he had disappeared, the night after their interception by Elarani border guards.

Still, Thomas wished him well, wherever he was now. It was impossible to bear the acerbic Rotliengendan any ill will at all, despite the fact that he had undoubtedly been spying on the Triune Empire from his servant's position in the Residency. But Piotr had had no reason at all to risk his life to save Thomas from the massacre, nor to have shepherded him halfway across Erd Gellin. It had assuredly made his own escape more difficult, yet the Rotliegendan had not hesitated to put himself in greater danger for the sake of common humanity.

Unless. Thomas paused mentally. Unless the half-heard, half-imagined conversation that Thomas remembered had some truth to it. Piotr had spoken of a true seer, of Thomas being the first born with this talent for centuries. It would explain Piotr's efforts to keep him alive – and the reason why it was he, hardly the most senior member of the Triune embassy, whom Piotr had been serving. Of course, Thomas's more sceptical side reminded him, that could simply have been because he was the only person whom Piotr had been able to contrive to serve.

Thomas shook his head. The whole thing was absurd. He, Thomas Maynard, a true seer? Whatever that might be. Piotr had never mentioned it again and, after all, he had been falling into the depths of one of his visions when he had heard it. More likely he was delusional, spinning a fantasy out of the ether to explain away his problem.

On the other hand there had to be something in it. He had never truly seen the blaze of destruction that played itself out repeatedly in his mind's eye. But then wasn't it just what he would imagine if asked to describe a bloody massacre? Or perhaps he had seen it, before blanking out, and now his mind was suppressing the memory, pushing it down until it forced its way out uncontrollably, rendering him unconscious. Some of the moral philosophers were working on such theories. That would mean that really he was just going mad, with these delusions of grandeur nothing but one more symptom.

Sometimes he despaired, playing the arguments round and round in his head. The arduous journey had taken his mind off such things; by day the struggle and pain of maintaining the pace had prevented him from thinking too deeply and at night he was so weary that he fell asleep the instant his head hit the ground, despite the discomfort. But here in Hyrnar he had all too much time to think.

Since arriving, there had been little for him or Lawrence to do. Kadmos had questioned him more than once on conditions in Erd Gellin, as had Nomiki. Trapped between these two soldiers, the wolf-like Sword-Captain and the tall and imposing First Chiliarch, Thomas had never felt more insignificant. Things hadn't been helped by the fact that, although he had done his best to answer their questions, he simply couldn't tell them the things they wanted to know. He was an administrator, not a soldier. Facts such as the state of equipment or morale of the Gellinese soldiery – things that those two could have determined in a glance – were as much beyond his possession as the dark side of the moon. Oh, there were some things he could tell – the presence and type of the demons, the situation in Iskarn, but for every question he answered, there were five more at which he could only shake his head helplessly.

In some ways though, even those sessions were a relief. At least it was something to do; a time when people wanted him. There was little else to fill his days. He had tried to explore but the Citadel was a veritable maze of corridors and passages. Asking directions was hopeless – though he might be able to converse with the queen and her counsellors in Dalradian, the guards and servants spoke only Elarani, a language he had never seen the need to learn, spoken as it was only in this one small nation far from Triune influence. His quarters might be luxurious, but there was a limit to how much time could be spent in them before boredom set in. He had thought he would relish such freedom after the harrowing escape, but the mind, Thomas admitted to himself, is a contrary thing.

He had no idea how Lawrence was spending his days – after two weeks in close proximity Thomas needed a break from the chaplain's company. The journey had not made them closer. As for himself he spent much of his time here, haunting the *variidesharium*, waiting for a reply from the Empire. Why this need for an answer had become such an obsession he was not sure. Perhaps because it was that it would let him know how he was to return to the Imperial territories, or perhaps the reason was subtler: a subconscious desire to reassure himself that the entire Empire hadn't perished in the madness at Iskarn. Or perhaps it was just that he needed solitude, a place where, unlike his quarters, he would not be disturbed. Whatever the reason, the days here had provided ample time to mull over recent events.

Some time later, his reverie was disturbed by the sound of the door opening behind him. Thomas turned to look. It was Euthymios, dressed as always in his full episcopal robes, mitre on head and crozier in hand. Thomas wondered, as he had before, why he never put them aside, for the bishop did not seem to be a man who stood on ceremony.

It was not the first time Euthymios had been in. As one might expect of the queen's chief counsellor, he would check in more than once a day, ensuring that no new transmissions had been received that could result in Rianda – or himself – being caught flat-footed. He always found the time to speak to Thomas, enquiring if he was well and whether all his needs were being taken care of. Of course, Thomas always replied in the affirmative; in truth, he was being well looked after and to complain of boredom or restlessness would seem absurd. What he really wanted – return to the Empire, or failing that, knowing when he could go – the Bishop could not provide.

This time was no different. Euthymios nodded to him on entry and, after glancing the transcripts of the most recent transmissions to ensure that none were urgent, he enquired after Thomas's well-being. They were exchanging pleasantries – it had snowed that morning in Hyrnar, ragged flurries descending over the Citadel, though it did not settle – when one of the *variideshari* pulsed into action, shimmers of light scattering through the room.

Thomas's stomach tightened. It was the fourth from the end; the link with Linnarson. Relax, he told himself, relax. There had been a dozen or more transmissions from Linnarson in the last few days, and none had been a relayed reply from the Empire. Still the tension remained, as he watched the *anaedesh* play his hands over the sphere in the sequence of activation, subtly different for each *variideshar*. Thomas and Euthymios had broken off their conversation, both eager to hear the news from Linnarson.

The crystalline message was short and concise.

"First Secretary Selsb for Triune Ambassador, Linnarson. Maynard to remain in Hyrnar as Imperial Ambassador to Elaran. Acting rank deputy secretary. To report weekly. Lawrence to likewise remain; junior ambassador; acting rank assistant secretary. Triune Empire looks with favour at Elaran. Conclude."

Thomas was in shock. His legs trembled uncontrollably. Try as he might, he could not stop them quivering violently.

No return Home! Not even to Scahania or Pelagos. Stuck here, as good as alone, thousands of miles from civilisation in a country about to be plunged into a bloody war it could not win. This refuge was no more than a gilded trap. Too numb to speak, he staggered. He thought he might throw up.

Slowly the shock receded. His legs were trembling less now; Thomas felt that perhaps he could try to walk, if he wanted to. Gradually, as his mind settled, he became aware of a hand on his shoulder. He had totally forgotten Euthymios's presence. For those few minutes nothing had existed in the world save himself and the image of the prison that walled him in, stretching out from now to the future until it dwindled out of sight, he still trapped within it.

How long had Euthymios stood by him, hand resting compassionately upon his shoulder? Thomas wasn't sure. The bishop stood by him, offering wordless support but not imposing, allowing Thomas to regain his composure without disturbing him with unhelpful inanities. Only after some minutes, when Thomas had begun to feel himself again, did Euthymios speak.

"So, now you are our first Triune ambassador." He paused. "It would, in any case, have been spring before you could leave, and who knows what may have changed come spring?" There was a deep understanding in his voice that made Thomas want to weep. Inconsequentially, he thought again that he would never get used to the way the Elarani spoke Laurentian, as if they were speaking around a wad of cloth.

"Come," Euthymios continued when Thomas made no reply. "If you are to be here for a while, it is best that we get to know each other." Thomas made no protest as Euthymios shepherded him out of the *variidesharium* and down the stairs, mutely following the bishop through the twists and turns of the Citadel's corridors. Despair filled his mind. What was the point? Another time he might have welcomed the news; the promotion, the glory, the adventure. Had this not been what he had dreamed of when he joined the Laurentian service? But too much had happened too quickly; terror, hardship, the brutal death of all whom he had known; now he wanted nothing more than the assurance of safety and the companionship of his own kind.

They crossed a high, arched bridge, walled and roofed, the chill wind whistling through the narrow slits that passed for windows. Dimly Thomas registered that this meant they were leaving the palace, crossing from the Har Magisteris to the Har Serenis. Well, it made sense that the bishop would have his quarters in the cathedral. Then they were there, Euthymios gently leading him into the room, settling him down into a low easy chair.

A servant entered, carrying a lacquered tray. Euthymios pressed a demitasse of coffee into Thomas's hand. Thomas looked at it with distaste. It was strong and black, thickened almost to syrup with sugar. His mouth curled up at the cloying sweetness as he sipped. What wouldn't he have given for a decent cup of tea, but they seemed not to drink it here, nor in Erd Gellin, though at least there the Residency had had its private supply.

Still, the coffee warmed him, that and the blazing fire churning out heat like a mill churned out cloth. As the chill faded from his bones, the melancholy started to fade from his spirit and he sat up and began to look around him.

It was the first time he had been in someone's private quarters in Hyrnar, save for his own and Lawrence's. This was of the same mould as his; the Elarani style shone through, like the Gellinese but with no trace of Atavine influence. There were no sinuous lines here: the Elarani favoured sharper, straight-edged designs or else stylised scenes from history or legend. Frescos and mosaics filled the white walls with the fabled exploits of saints and heroes whilst luxurious rugs recapitulated the theme on the stone floor. So far, it could have been a twin of his own: a surprise – they must have meant what they said about housing him as an honoured guest, for his quarters to be comparable to that of the queen's first counsellor.

Euthymios had personalised this room though, increasing the warmth ten-fold by giving it the unmistakeable stamp of someone's home. An impressive collection of books filled a stout cedar bookcase and overflowed onto a couple of nearby shelves. There must have been over fifty – almost a hundred – bound in leather and vellum, some plain, others elaborately decorated. Thomas scanned the spines. They were mainly in Dalradian, as one would expect, but some in Elarani and in the flowing abugida of Evvenyae, and even a few in Silurian and what he thought was Rotliegendish. Of those in Dalradian and Evvenyae he recognised several; one or two he had even read.

The rest of the shelves and surfaces held an assortment of objects, arranged haphazardly, yet giving no impression of clutter or untidiness. Decorated pottery and urns; a sculpted figure of a Mareischi yale rider, spear upraised, carved out of jet; a number of fossils, carefully polished and mounted. Thomas recognised an ammonite, its coiled shell unmistakeable, and smiled at the memories it brought back. He and his sister had spent many a childhood day in the limestone quarry near their village hunting out the stone remains. The largest they had found had been almost a foot across: at the time it had seemed half their own size, for they couldn't have been more than eight or ten.

An elegant sharom board reminded Thomas of more adult pastimes. Did Euthymios play, he wondered, or was it simply an ornament? It certainly served the latter purpose admirably; each piece intricately carved from ebony or mahogany. The whole rested upon a marble coffee table of a type that Thomas had never seen before. From what he could see, the table appeared to be divided into dozens of segments, each made of a different coloured marble – green, purple, orange, cream – marbles that he had never even known existed, to produce a geometric design of stunning beauty.

Euthymios had settled himself upon the divan opposite Thomas, sinking comfortably into the cushions. With his trappings of office, it was easy to forget just how old the bishop was. To Thomas's surprise, Euthymios did not begin by questioning him on the new role that had been thrust upon him.

"I left Elaran once, you know," said Euthymios, reflecting. "It must have been a half-century or more ago now. I was only fourteen, and had just been sent to the great seminary at Bajada. I had been told to remember it was an honour, for Bajada houses the best seminary in the north, the best outside Aesthen itself. But mostly I remember wanting to be back in Elaran. They say that the hills are in our blood; our food, our water, our air, our very life. So it was for me, at least."

"And you've never left since?" said Thomas, unsure what else to say.

"Not once. King Diarad – Rianda's father – made few state visits and when he did I always managed to stay behind. There had to be someone to mind the Citadel, keep the kingdom running smoothly in his absence. That's what I used to say, anyway. In reality, of course, Kadmos or his predecessor could have probably done a perfectly good job, but Diarad always used to accept the excuse.

"The synod asked me to move once too," he continued pensively. "That was much later on, of course; I had been bishop for a decade or more. They asked me if I'd be willing to accept the office of Suffragan Bishop of Pridoli. It would have most likely meant succession to the archdiocese within a few years, one of the most prestigious sees in Laurentia.

"I told them no, of course. Rianda had been born by then; I was already beginning to instruct her in statecraft, and Diarad still needed me. In any case, Siluria is a long way from here, and flat, too flat. Hill men weren't meant to be by the sea.

"So I turned them down, and young Marnlen took my place. He's one of the Lord Servants now and sits on the Grand Synod. Rather him than me. But enough of an old man's maundering; what of you? What is it like where you're from?"

"Not at all like Elaran, I'm afraid. Trandale's largely flat; cropland, with the odd lake scattered here and there. The wolds are twenty miles or so to the west, but even they're nothing like the Aripos Hills. A few hundred feet high at most."

"You're not from Wenlock then? Even here we hear tales of it. They say it's even larger than Kurdon."

"The stories are true. Over a million people live there, more than twice as many as Kurdon. I've never lived there, though I've been there of course. Chelmsthorpe, where I studied, is much smaller. The size of Hyrnar perhaps, though totally different: it's a university town, not a capital. I guess it might be like Linnarson without the merchants – not that I've ever been there either of course." In truth, Thomas didn't know at all what Linnarson was like, though from his studies he could have recited the details of its political governance and economy. However, Euthymios seemed to take what he said at face value.

"Well, we each love the land where we were raised. To you, know doubt, these hills are as alien as your wolds would be to me. But what about you, your family? Do you have brothers, sisters?"

"A sister, yes, Edith."

"A lovely name, that," interjected Euthymios. "Your Triune names are so melodic."

"She's always been grateful for it, yes." Thomas laughed. "Mother won out in choosing it. She said my father had got his way with me – Thomas was his own father's name."

"We must always be grateful for Andur's mercies," said the bishop, with a smile. "Both the great and the small. Here in Elaran she would not have been so lucky: by custom the father names any daughters and the mother the sons. We sometimes get strange looks from foreigners when the mother speaks in the anointing ceremony, but that's the way it has always been here.

"It sounds as if the two of you are close. Are you near in age?"

"She's two years younger than me. And yes, we were close, particularly when we were younger. We grew apart, of course, once I went away to school, but not through anger or quarrels.

"She married last year, just before I left for Laurentia. The latest letter told me they're expecting their first child in the spring."

The conversation continued, Euthymios doing his best to put the young Triune at ease; interspersing his gently probing questions with anecdotes and reminiscences of his own life. Almost without realising it, Thomas found himself describing his life in great detail: Home, his family, his time at Chelmsthorpe and his first few months in Laurentia. For the first time since arriving in Hyrnar he felt at ease, relaxed. The bishop, for all that Thomas was aware of his power at court, seemed such a gentle, unthreatening figure that one could not help trusting him.

Months later, when Thomas had got to know Euthymios far better, he would realise just how naive this initial assessment had been. Whilst it was true that the bishop was gentle and kind, it was also true that he was an astute and experienced diplomat and counsellor. Whilst he would not have lied to or manipulated others for his own ambitions – these had long since been subsumed into his devotion to Elaran – he would not hesitate in using what he knew for Elaran's benefit. His country, his queen and his God – these were Euthymios's three pillars, bridged by an arch of moral probity, honesty and compassion.

At the moment though Thomas knew nothing of this, and guessed little. The hours passed by rapidly and he was somewhat surprised to notice his hunger when Euthymios rang for his servant and asked him to bring in some refreshments.

"I think that we could both do with something to eat," said Euthymios and Thomas heartily agreed. Now it had been brought to his mind, his stomach was definitely rumbling.

The food, when it arrived, proved to be pieces of hard white cheese and olives, crusty white bread and a large dish of some cold, brownish paste which proved upon enquiry to be a mix of aubergine, tomato and garlic. The enquiry was a somewhat more convoluted process than he had anticipated, aubergine not being the most frequent word in the classic Dalradian texts, and thus missing from Thomas's vocabulary.

Thomas ate hungrily. He had developed a taste for the hard cheese since arriving here, and though still somewhat suspicious of made dishes, he found the aubergine to be relatively tolerable, even pleasant.

"I couldn't help noticing," said Euthymios, as they ate, "that you eyed the sharom board as you came in. Do you play?"

Surprised, Thomas nodded enthusiastically, making up for the full mouth that prevented him from answering.

"Would you like a game?"

"Yes, definitely," said Thomas with genuine enthusiasm. "Lawrence and I played at the Residency, but we haven't seen much of each other since arriving here. And didn't have a board, in any case."

"That I can supply, as you can see." Picking up the tray of food he drew a chair up to the sharom table.

"We should probably make sure our rules are the same before starting. It would be embarrassing to discover part-way through that we'd been reading off different hymnals."

Thomas frowned as he sat down. "There shouldn't be a problem, should there? The game's pre-Covenantal, after all."

"Yes, but these things can diverge sometimes. Look at the Church."

Unlike in the Church, a quick comparison found that in sharom at least there were no differences between the two continents. Setting up the pieces, Thomas again admired their intricacy. He had drawn red, and the smooth warmth of the mahogany felt welcoming to his hands. A master carver had devoted many weeks to this job.

Euthymios noticed his admiration. "They are magnificent, aren't they? King Diarad gave it to me on my consecration as bishop. He said that everyone else would be giving me spiritual gifts and that if he couldn't give me something temporal, who could? In his defence, I've always said that sharom nurtures the mind, and the spirit through it."

Thomas nodded abstractedly. After the almost obligatory removal of his *tarathin*, he had moved swiftly to the attack, swinging his chariots and *isp'te'ra* out to the flanks. It was the fast, aggressive style of play that he favoured, particularly when playing red.

The bishop had responded methodically, declining the gambits offered in favour of a steady advance in the centre, pushing his pikemen and spearmen forward slowly but methodically, supported by mages.

Thomas studied the hexagonal board. The ebony pieces formed a solid bulge reaching almost to the halfway point, with his own pieces in a red arc around them. Well, he could deal with that. Advancing his knight, he traced the forthcoming sequence of moves in his mind.

Euthymios took a bite of bread, slipping an elephant to one side. Thomas studied it. The move appeared innocuous enough. Decisively he once more advanced his knight, capturing a spearman in a sacrifice that would split Euthymios's formation and leave the bishop down by a chariot – or more.

Without hesitation the bishop responded, capturing the knight with his isp'te'ra. Ignoring it – for now – Thomas smoothly continued the orchestrated sequence of moves, slicing his left chariot in to pick off a now unguarded knight.

Capture followed capture in quick succession until the third move of the sequence. Euthymios, instead of advancing a pikeman as Thomas had expected, slipped his elephant forward two spaces, threatening the chariot, releasing the power of his general and enabling a mage attack on Thomas's own general.

Thomas froze in the process of reaching for his next piece. Slowly, he withdrew his hand. How had he missed this? Searching for a way out, he found none. He would have to retreat his general. Grimacing, he made the best of bad job and swept it back along the long diagonal to the corner. From here it could still influence the bloodbath in the centre, but he had ceded the initiative to Euthymios.

The bishop lost no time in cementing his advantage. Caught exposed by the attack on his general, Thomas was forced to defend desperately just to preserve his own. When the dust had settled, far from being ahead Thomas found himself two spearmen and a knight down, with his opponent controlling not only the centre but the west flank of the board.

The tempo eased then, the game shifting from a sword fight to a wrestling match, subtle changes of positions marking the struggle as Euthymios strived to bring his now heavier weight to bear. He edged a mage forward, patiently.

"I wonder," the bishop mused, "if your Piotr could play. Rotliegendans are traditionally good at sharom – and so are spies, for that matter."

"Probably," said Thomas. "Though I must confess I never found out – I didn't think to ask. But he had so many other talents that he never told me of, I wouldn't be surprised."

"Yes, you told me of his magecraft. Where is he now, do you know?"

Thomas considered his next move. Retreating a chariot, he said, "I often wonder that. I knew so little about him."

"Rotliegendes? Torridon? Here in Elaran?" Euthymios probed.

"I really have no idea. He could be anywhere. I don't even know how long he'd been in Elaran before I arrived. I never thought to ask – he was just a servant, you know, at first and then after the massacre it didn't seem important."

"That at least is something I can tell you. He arrived in the month of Ellawen – less than two months before you arrived. A...friend...alerted us to the fact."

Thomas sat back, surprised. That was something he hadn't known. Euthymios had just taken his priest, sacrificing an *isp'te'ra* for the piece. The ring of steel was closing in around Thomas's king.

"Why did he save you? That's what I've wondered." The bishop was pressing harder now, sealing off the last routes of escape. "It must have been challenging, even for one of his capabilities."

"Perhaps he liked me," suggested Thomas inanely. His head was starting to pulse in an all too familiar way.

"Isn't that stretching it a little too far? Personal loyalty is all very well, but it's rather out of character for a Rotliegendish spy to risk his life for someone he'd known only six months, don't you think? You said yourself you had never treated him as anything other than a servant."

Thomas floundered, trying to think of an answer. Seeking a way out he turned his attention to the board. A sudden flurry of moves and his king fell, caught in a three-way pincer attack from Euthymios's chariots and general. The pulsing in Thomas's head intensified as he crowned his prince, the new king now stranded, exposed in the centre of the board. Desperately, he landed his *tarathin*.

"Come now, you must have some idea of why you're so important to the Rotliegendans."

He could barely think now, the pain in his head throbbing stronger as a wave of dizziness engulfed him. He felt sick. Through blurring vision he fought it, ordering his pieces in a futile defence. His general fell; an elephant; his last *isp'te'ra*. His *tarathin* had long since gone. He wanted to be sick. Fighting nausea, he watched Euthymios obliterate his final defences, setting down the final piece with a solid thud.

"Sharom," said the bishop, with finality.

As Thomas toppled his king, the vision took him, white heat obliterating his existence.

Pain engulfed him.

Chapter Eleven

The Fires Build

Thomas came to slowly. A wet coolness crossed his forehead, blessed relief against the pain. He still burned, but it was fading into memory as his consciousness returned. Groaning, he opened his eyes, blinking. Something obstructed his vision; all he could see were dim shadows. His questing hand explored, seeking the problem. A damp cloth covered his eyes, the source of the cool moisture that soothed his head.

He pushed it aside. The cloth gone, he saw Euthymios bending over him, genuine concern on his lined face. Ignoring the bishop's steadying hand Thomas struggled to sit up: fighting, as he did every time, against the weakness that overcame him after a vision. This one had been particularly bad. They did indeed seem to be getting worse with each bout.

Defeated, Thomas sank back, exhausted, on to the divan.

"Don't force yourself," said Euthymios gently. "I don't know what happened, but whatever it is, you need to recover." Angrily, Thomas shook his head, but his futile attempts to raise more than his head off the divan proved Euthymios's words only too accurate.

Resignedly, he gave up the attempt. "How long was I gone for?"

"Well over six hours." Euthymios pointed to the closed shutters. "It's close to midnight." Thomas groaned, in despair as much as in pain. His whole body ached; the days of rest might as well not have occurred. He had hoped that reaching safety might have seen an end to the visions, but the several untroubled days had proved nothing but an illusion of deliverance.

"Has this happened before?" When Thomas did not reply, Euthymios repeated the question.

"You may as well tell me if it has. We're not entirely ignorant of such things in the clergy, and it may be I can help. The telling may be bad, but reliving it again will be worse."

Thomas winced. His screams must have made it all too clear what was happening. He considered. Euthymios had pulled up a chair and sat down. Hands crossed lightly on his lap, the bishop gazed peacefully into the distance, attention seemingly happily absorbed by the frescoes on the far wall. It was quite clear he was content to wait all day.

Well, it could hardly do any harm. After all, Euthymios probably already thought that he was weak minded. What matter if he confirmed it?

With an effort, Thomas rolled himself on to his side. "It's been happening since the massacre." Quickly, he rushed on before his resolve could fade. "Once when I was almost unconscious I heard Piotr say something about a 'true seer'. But it might be nothing; I could have been delirious."

Euthymios sat up sharply, but to Thomas's surprise the expression on his face was shock, not pity or contempt.

"A True Seer? Are you sure?"

Thomas was taken aback by the reaction. "You've heard the term before?"

"You haven't? I would have thought that that lore would be known on both continents."

"The years of barbarism lasted over a millennium on Avalonia," said Thomas, somewhat defensively. "Since the Founding the Empire has done its best, but much was lost beyond recovery."

"I suppose that there are no records of any True Seers from before the Sundering. And Our Lady of Silence would be unlikely to bless a continent which owns her not.

"Why didn't you mention this as soon as you arrived?"

"I didn't even know if I'd really heard it, let alone what it meant. I still don't! What is a True Seer, anyway? You all speak as if it was something terribly important. Piotr said something about the last being three centuries ago."

"Ah yes; Arafin of Tournais. Murdered by the Variscans before he reached the age of eight." Euthymios paused thoughtfully. "How often have these visions been occurring?"

"Almost every day at first, but they've been getting less frequent, but worse. But..."

"Always the same one?"

Thomas shuddered. "Yes."

"It fits; it fits the pattern, as far as it is known. And it would explain so much else."

Thomas managed to lever himself upright. He was beginning to become irritated.

"What pattern? What else does it explain? Will you please tell me what a True Seer is?" he demanded. "I've heard of arcanists and mystics who call themselves seers, diviners, augurers, what have you, trying to probe the future. Their predictions are always so vague to be near useless – that's what you say I am?"

"No! Those you describe may call themselves seers, but their visions come from arduous rituals and arcane ability. It is no innate talent – not that what they discover does not sometimes have value; no, not at all," he said pensively.

"But a True Seer is different. They are born, not made, and born rarely at that. A True Seer, in full possession of his talent, can course the full spectrum of the fixed past and the flux of the future."

"And the present?"

"Of course. What is the present but the past of a moment's time, or the future of a second ago?"

Thomas was stunned. And this was what they thought he was? It was an ability he had never heard of; one beyond the most powerful arcanists' wildest dreams.

"But couldn't the visions just be, well, delusions?" he protested weakly. "I've heard of others having such flashbacks. And they're not True Seers." They're just half-mad, he added, silently.

"Normally, I'd say yes, notwithstanding the fact that yours are decreasing in frequency and increasing in severity, just as a True Seer's do. But there is more here than meets the eye. Piotr believed you were a True Seer, and the Rotliegendans have a way of knowing things that others do not. We will not know for sure until – unless – you become able to control the visions."

The thought gave Thomas new strength. To be able to control the visions; to see what he wished, to not be trapped in an eternal vision of fire and pain.

"Will it be difficult?" he asked.

"I imagine so. So little is known, and I know only a fraction of that." Thomas could hear Euthymios's frustration. "St. Cornelius writes that to control the visions takes deep mental focus and discipline – but the same could be said of magecraft. But learn it you must, or it will kill you."

Kill him. Thomas could well imagine it. The pain of the visions was already unbearable. How much more could he take?

"How many..." He restarted. "How does it happen?"

"We know so little," the bishop said again. "Unless brought on by a horrific experience such as your own, a True Seer's talent develops less violently, with gentler visions of the past, present and future. They may be disorientating, but they're not dangerous. Of those True Seers who reached maturity – and remember that since the Sundering there have been only eight, not including yourself – only two have gone through what you appear to be suffering. Of these, the first experienced steadily more intense visions until he died; with the second, knowing of the example of the first, the problem was recognised quickly and his talent brought under control. But I have no idea how difficult it was, or of the timescale."

Thomas tried to ignore the 'of those who reached maturity'. Given his own recent history, he thought he could guess why that might be. He shuddered. But the resolve that had carried him through the flight across Erd Gellin was not far away.

"And you can help me to learn this control?" he asked in a calm voice.

"Not I," said the bishop. "I have no arcane abilities, and know only what little I've read. But there are others who might be able to. The Velnerines have a hospice here in Hyrnar..."

"Velnerines?"

"One of the newer religious orders, though amongst the fastest growing. They're renowned for their understanding of the mind: they follow the example of St. Velnery the Pure, who cured Niavon I of his madness in the Pelagic Wars."

"That was less than a century ago."

"Yes. St. Velnery was martyred in 1772 of course, and the order sprang up soon after."

Something about the Velnerines tickled the back of Thomas's mind. "Are they the ones who accompany armies to war?" He thought Linnarson came into it too, but he wasn't sure where. They had seemed a minor order at the time he had read of them and he had committed little of the detail to memory.

"That's right," answered Euthymios. "St. Velnery revolutionised battlefield healing in the armies of the so-called Grand Coalition. The practice had been in an appalling state before then.

"We'll be very glad of their presence come spring," he added soberly. With a visible effort, Euthymios pushed the thought aside. "But that is not your problem. It is your visions we must be concerned with now.

"You'll be able to walk in the morning?" Thomas nodded. "We'll go then. You must sleep here tonight.

"No," he continued at Thomas's protests, "you can barely move. Aiolos will make you up a bed in here with no trouble at all."

Ringing the bell for his servant, Euthymios watched as Aiolos quickly and efficiently laid out a pallet, blankets and cushions on the floor and transferred

Thomas to it. The young man was bearing up well for now, but the morrow would bring what it would bring.

#

Despite the circumstances, Rianda could not help but take pleasure in being in the Map Room. Perhaps it was its association with childhood memories, which no amount of grave discussions could entirely erode.

Her father had possessed a similar love of the room, and would often spend time there, talking to his chiliarchi. He had brought her with him often when there was nothing of import to discuss, even before she had formally begun attending Council. Too young to have an interest in the adults' conversation, she remembered well the fascination that the great map had had for her. She had been able to spend hours enthralled before it, tracing the paths of roads, rivers and streams, and could still remember vividly the time when her over-enthusiastic hands, wanting to touch, had knocked off one of the jewels. What a fuss that had caused! It had been the town of Nerinth, she remembered, and it had become the subject of much teasing from her father as she grew older, whenever the town was mentioned.

The map still possessed a certain spellbinding quality; its shimmering beauty and marvellous craftsmanship uplifting even when it was being used to discuss the invasion of her country.

A flying visit by *tarath* had brought back Lykourgos to update her and Nomiki on the evacuation of Hyrakos. Chrysaor, her cousin, was also present. The royal duke was as experienced and hardened a warrior as any of her chiliarchi; like them, he had commanded men under her father for more than two decades. Both she and Nomiki trusted and valued his abilities.

Lykourgos had finished his briefing. He looked exhausted. Rianda realised that she had never seen him look that way before, but three days of frantic evacuation, coupled with the emotional drain of abandoning his hometown and family to the enemy, had taken their toll. It was thanks to his efforts – his commitment, despite his desires to the contrary – that the southern chiliad was through the Pass of Istria and on its way to safety. As he pointed out the positions of the chiliad, its rearguard and baggage train, describing the arrangements for resupply and transportation, his sagging frame bore testament that the smoothness of this retreat had not just come about by happenstance.

Nomiki and Chrysaor questioned him on points of detail, but Rianda was satisfied. The retreat was going well. But there was another, more important, consideration troubling her, one that had not yet been mentioned.

"Has there been any word from Hyrakos?"

"None, Your Majesty," said Lykourgos. "And I considered it – unwise, given the circumstances, to spare a *tarathin* to scout."

"Unwise?"

"Do you think the people of that city would relish the sight of an Elarani *tarathin* above them? That we had not only abandoned them, but were sending someone to watch and gloat? Win or lose this war, Your Majesty, your name will be cursed upon the streets of Hyrakos for decades!"

"You go too far, Lykourgos," replied Rianda icily. "I trust you had better reasons than that for your decision to leave us in the dark."

Lykourgos got his temper back under control. "I did. Your Majesty." He bit off the words savagely. "Erd Gellin will move in days. Hyrakos is lost, and our *tarathin* are too few to risk one to know whether the day is tomorrow or next week. My scouts will warn if the Gellinese come further. Do my reasons satisfy you?"

"What do you say to that, Nomiki? Or you, Chrysaor?" Those two had stayed silent thus far in the exchange, slightly ashamed on behalf of their fellow commander. All three men in the room knew that, whatever was said, they would do Rianda's will, for she was queen. The fact that, in the case of Hyrakos, two of them thought she was right, and one wrong, made no difference at all; it had been otherwise in the past and would be again. Lykourgos had done the honourable – the only possible – thing and fulfilled his oath, carrying out his duty to the best of his abilities. To be expressing his dissatisfaction with it now to Rianda demonstrated an almost embarrassing lack of control.

"The Chiliarch of the South's decision was valid, Your Majesty," said Chrysaor. "Though it is not the one I would have made myself."

Nomiki nodded, adding, "I would probably have done as Lykourgos did, Your Majesty." Neither commented on the impeccable way in which he had carried out the retreat itself. Rianda did not need the obvious pointed out to her.

"You have done well, Lykourgos," she said, punctilious but no less appreciative for that. Ordering the retreat had cut her to the bone – how much worse must it have been to actually carry it out? In private, she could well forgive Lykourgos's resentment, even if to him and others she must be cold.

The discussion turned to the defence of the Citadel. This was folly: none of them could add anything meaningful to the topic, important though it was.

"Kadmos will be returning from the outer town shortly," Rianda said firmly. "It is he who will need to be informed of this. Lykourgos, you must see him before you return to the south.

"Now, when will the other chiliadi move south?"

"Not yet," said Chrysaor. "Whatever Niavon's protestations of friendship, we do not wish to leave our northern border unguarded for a day longer than necessary."

"Agreed," said Rianda. "They would pour over the border like ants with a scent of honey. So, when? Nomiki?"

"In living memory the snow has never melted on the southern passes before the month of Pilter. The Gellinese cannot move before then. On the first day of Doren Mur, the northern chiliad will begin moving south. When it reaches Hyrnar, the first chiliad will join it. At the same time, the southern chiliad will move out from Ad Cenyor to the Pass of Istria. By the Day of Rebirth, all three will be in position.

"And may Andur have mercy upon us all." There was nothing more to be said.

#

Time and again Fotis ran determinedly towards his goal. Each time, just before he reached it, he would be intercepted. Amaltheia, that fraction taller and steadier on her feet, would unfailingly catch him just in time. Chrysaor thought wryly that he wished some of his border guards were half as reliable as his daughter.

It didn't matter which of the five tall poplars that Fotis chose for his target. Whichever one he aimed for his sister would plunge in front of him and they would both go down in a heap, laughing and struggling to get up again whilst keeping the other down. In contrast to their abilities when running, Fotis was slightly better at this, but whilst he could have then easily reached the tree he was now close to, the rules of the game appeared to demand that he was then obliged to run for one of the other four, which he dutifully did, giving the time for Amaltheia to also rise, run after and catch him. As far as Fotis knew, the game and its unspoken protocols had never been discussed; it had simply arisen, as is the manner of such things amongst three-year-olds, particularly twins.

Elena smiled at him, her happiness shining from her eyes. Since the birth of the twins she had been happy in a way that she had not been since the first few years of their marriage. Oh, none other than those closest to her had noticed it; had realised that the lively, cheerful young princess that they looked on was increasingly a thin facade over a river of sorrow. But then, apart from Elena few had noticed his own grief; would have believed how deeply the hard, cold Duke of Altyrnal – he knew well enough how others thought of him – grieved over his wife's sorry and his own. Diarad had known of course. He and his brother had always been close, an intimacy that neither their different temperaments nor Diarad's kingship had ever changed.

He still felt Diarad's absence, a mourning that time only made more poignant. With every passing month, it became only too clear what Diarad's loss had meant. Elaran was sliding into the abyss, and despite her accomplishments, compared to the boisterous warrior king that his brother had been Rianda seemed but a thin reed with which to fend off the gathering wolves. Since spring he had spent all too little time with his children or his wife, and he would spend even less in the coming months. War was coming, a bloody struggle in which victory would be won at huge cost, if it were won at all, and yet these precious months were denied him.

Gently, Elena stroked his arm. His spirit lifted, a fraction. His wife had always been able to sense when the black moods were upon him and just her presence could ease them. Today, though, the darkness would not be shifted so easily. Even the sight of his children's play was bittersweet.

"In less than five months I will be leaving for the south," Chrysaor said flatly. "The chiliadi must be in place by the Day of Rebirth."

"What chance do we have?"

"Little." He did not spare the truth from his wife. Throughout their marriage, he had not done so, and nor would she have wished it now. Had he tried, he could not have maintained such a deception for long. He might as well have tried to deceive himself.

"The Archons will have at least twice our number, probably closer to thrice. To set against their numbers and armaments we have only our knowledge of the hills. Almost half our men will be militia conscripts; peasants with poor equipment and worse discipline."

"Peasants may surprise us yet," said Elena gently. "Their fervour may count for much when their homeland is in danger."

"If not, then we are all lost. We will all suffer Hyrakos's fate."

"It is truly abandoned then?"

"It is." Chrysaor's face was bleak. "And may Andur have mercy upon us. But it is only thanks to that that we have any chance at all come spring."

"I still cannot quite believe that Rianda ordered it. Until her ascension, I had always believed that her father was the harder of the two; that Rianda was the more thoughtful, but also the more compassionate."

Chrysaor shook his head. "Diarad was compassionate. Rianda can be harder than Diarad ever was. I believe she grieves for Hyrakos, but she never flinched from forcing the decision through Council."

"She can't harden herself by act of will alone," said Elena, horrified. "She'll destroy herself."

"She might do," admitted Chrysaor. "But she must make the decisions nonetheless. She is the queen."

Elena tried to reconcile this with the earnest, gentle Rianda who she had known since girlhood. They had spoken only four days ago. She understood the necessity, but this must be tearing Rianda apart.

She was shocked, also, by her husband's calm acceptance of it. But then, perhaps because he was of Nemessine blood himself, Chrysaor's loyalty had always been subtly different from others. Their focus was the royal line; the Nemessine king or queen that stood at the heart of the nation. Nomiki, Eliud, Euthymios and the rest; all these had transferred their allegiance without difficulty from Diarad to Rianda.

Not so Chrysaor. He had loved Diarad, his cousin, but he had none of the same intimacy with his niece. Whilst Elena and Rianda had been growing closer, Chrysaor had more frequently been fighting on the frontiers with Diarad – or holding the lines, whilst Diarad was in the Citadel, dealing with matters of state. Nor did Chrysaor share the other counsellors' almost mystical loyalty to the monarch; he knew that only an accident of birth had spared him the king's seat himself.

Chrysaor's devotion was to the land itself, to the country and people of Elaran. He would die for them; he had already risked his life a dozen times over. With some bitterness, for she loved her niece dearly, Elena faced the fact that her husband would willingly see Rianda sacrifice herself for Elaran. The fact that Rianda would gladly do so herself never crossed her mind.

The night was drawing in now, the chill growing more intense. It was past time for the twins to be put to bed. They would have been happy playing here longer, if left to their own wishes: already, this patch of garden was becoming known across the Citadel as "The Twins' Garden". Neither as large nor as beautiful as the Privy Garden, the small patch of greenery provided the perfect play spot for a pair of rambunctious three-year-olds.

Sighing, she began to stand to call them in. Before she could do so though, Chrysaor leaned towards her suddenly.

"If the southern passes are lost," he said in Dalradian, "take the twins and flee to Torridon. Go to my cousins in Cadom; they will look after you."

Shocked, Elena stammered incoherently about leaving Elaran.

"I mean it. A siege is no place for four-year-olds. You will be well treated in Torridon: Niavon may seek concessions, but he is too civilised to harm either you or our children."

"The twins will go. But I will not leave here. If the Citadel falls, we will flee north together."

"If the Citadel falls, I will be dead," said Chrysaor harshly. "And if the passes are lost, the Citadel cannot stand." Fotis and Amaltheia, standing near, had drawn back at their father's words. Though they could not yet understand Dalradian, the tone of his voice, even though not directed at them, was all too clear.

"I want your promise, Elena. For their sake, for yours, for mine; and for Elaran's. Would you have the last of the Nemessine line grow up with neither mother nor father? Kadmos has told me, Elena: this fortress cannot stand. I would have something that I have loved survive."

Biting her lip, Elena nodded. "You have my word, father of my children. Husband of my heart." Taking refuge in formality, she bowed her head low. Then, wordlessly, she stood up, gathering her children to her. Equally silent, Chrysaor joined her. Fotis and Amaltheia knew that all was not well. Their tongues, too, were unusually muted, as the four headed back to their royal quarters.

#

Lord Trevelyan crumpled the paper in his hand. Andur Astartes! Another disaster. It was a bare fortnight since he'd received news of the Iskarn massacre. And now this. He slammed back his chair. Where was Parrington?

A cold fury wrapped him as he strode through the corridors, brushing off the lackeys and native servants who buzzed around him with their unwanted offers of assistance. No Laurentian Viceroy had suffered even one debacle such as this since the turn of the century, and that had been shortly after the Assimilation, when a few minor fracases were to be expected.

By the Broken Wheel, they'd hang him out to dry once they heard of this back Home! To those sitting in their comfort and safety in Wenlock there were no excuses; any setback abroad could only be explained by rank incompetence in the presiding Imperial representative. Half of the imbeciles in the House had never even left Avalonia. Amongst those who had, there were precious few with a level head on their shoulders, or who weren't in the pay of the Farladan Company or another of the great lobbies. The Expansionists would cry timidity, the Conservatives incompetence, whilst the Liberals wrung their hands over the civilian deaths. The portrait of the current First Lord of the Treasury seemed to mock him as he passed. The House was no more than a pack of hounds: united by the slightest sniff of blood.

His only hope would have been intervention by the Triumvirate, but he had never been one for sycophancy at court. Even if he had, the Triumvirate had little influence in these times of so-called peace; the House kept the powers of the Imperial Throne strongly in check except in times of national emergency.

Throwing open Parrington's door he shouted out for the man. No reply. Damn! The chief arcanist was not in his quarters. Reluctantly, Trevelyan admitted to himself that it was reasonable for the man to be at his work in the middle of the day. The thought did little to stem his impatience. Turning back to the door he called down a guard.

"Get me Parrington," he commanded. "I want him here immediately."

"Yes, My Lord."

"Immediately, you understand? I don't care what he's doing or if he's talking to the Archangel Halrii or the King of Hell himself – immediately!"

As the soldier hurried off as though a pack of *rahvashda* were on his tail, Trevelyan paced restlessly across Parrington's quarters. His mood would not allow him to sit. There wasn't even anything he could do in response. It might be different if there was. A quick campaign in reprisal, offending cities captured, fines levied, hostages taken and trade concessions granted and the crowds back Home would soon be cheering him in the streets instead of calling for his head.

But all his forces, land or sea, were as good as useless. Iskarn was in the centre of the continent, thousands of miles from the nearest garrison, let alone the nearest substantial military force. And he didn't even know what was happening in Atavus! The city might be a flyspeck along the desert coast, but it was the only friendly port between the Scahanian Peninsula and the Pelagic provinces. What news had come through before the *variideshar* had been smashed was confused and nonsensical. He didn't even know if the city was still standing.

What was keeping Parrington? Trevelyan glanced at the junk strewn about the arcanist's quarters. Various instruments: lenses, measuring devices and the like – it looked more suitable to belong to a ship's navigator than an arcanist. But no naval officer would allow a room to be so untidy. Various carved trinkets and curiosities dotted shelves, scattered amongst piles of minor gems. They had to be flawed – he hoped not even Sir Walter Parrington would be fool enough to leave spell-quality gems lying about unguarded. A heap of strange geometric shapes: polyhedra, regular and irregular, carved from a variety of materials, many of which Trevelyan could not recognise; one-sided hoops; aperiodic tessellations; sinuously shaped glass retorts which the eye traced, watering, until it realised that they did indeed have only one side – what did arcanists do with all this stuff?

They had their uses of course, and not only in war, or he wouldn't be waiting here, cooling his heels for Parrington to arrive. The Empire was supported by its mastery of the natural and arcane sciences. It had better be of some use now.

He heard the sound of hurrying footsteps. At last! As Parrington entered, breathless, Trevelyan turned to face him. The chief arcanist was an unprepossessing man, on the short side of average. His suit was of a fair cut – good but not exceptional – though he had clearly not stopped to make himself less dishevelled on the way here. That pleased Trevelyan – this was no time for fripperies.

"Atavus has been attacked by sand elementals," barked Trevelyan as soon as Parrington had come to a halt.

"By sand elementals? But that's..." Lord Trevelyan's mood suddenly registered on Parrington and he altered his sentence mid-flow. "...unheard of," he continued, recovering well. "How severe is the damage?"

"I don't know! The *variideshar* was smashed in the first assault. It could be a minor raid or the entire city could have been razed to the ground for all I know."

"Were they able to send details of the sand elementals? How big were they? Did they give a description of their appearance?"

"Never mind the thrice-damned elementals! I need to know what's going on there. Get me a scry portal focused on the city and you can stare at the elementals to your heart's content."

"Yes, My Lord. It should be doable. The Atavine Bay lies between us of course..."

"I don't care how you do it – you're the chief arcanist, not me. But get me that portal within two days."

"Yes, My Lord." As Trevelyan strode out Parrington reflected that he had never seen the Viceroy in such a temper, or so impatient. Usually he was only too ready to chat about the arcane sciences, particularly their philosophy.

Such thoughts faded into the distance as the import of Trevelyan's news sunk home. Sand elementals! How marvellous. Wainwright's Theory of Elements had been gaining credence ever since Blenkinsop and Janovsky had proved the existence of the Ether by measuring the movement of Edrith with respect to it. Phlogiston had long since been isolated, leaving only two out of four of the predicted tertiary elements – Caloric and Vital Essence – to be discovered.

All six of the secondary elements had long since been isolated, of course, though some naysayers still insisted that they were compounds, particularly since the discovery of Primordial Slime elements in the caverns of the Mappel Ralpura had been exposed as a fake. The existence of sand elementals would provide the final confirmation of Wainwright – get his name in the Proceedings of the Imperial Society for sure.

This could be the landmark discovery he needed to get him true recognition, to elevate him from his humdrum status as a competent arcanist to a position of greatness. If he played his cards right with the press the discovery of a new element could have him feted by the common man. Combined with the genuinely ground-breaking nature of this discovery he could have it all. Fortune, fame, and a steady climb to the upper echelons of the Imperial Society. His name would go down in history as the man who had finally proved the Theory of Elements beyond all doubt.

If, that is, these were sand elementals, not air elementals misdescribed by an over-excited layman.

He would soon know. He spread out his work map of Laurentia and rooted in drawers for the necessary tools and drawing instruments to carry out Trevelyan's task. Parrington grimaced. Carefully, he ruled a number of lines, measuring off distances with a pair of dividers and comparing them with his altitude charts.

It was not going to be easy. The Atavine Bay lay square in his direct line to Atavus, not to mention the usual problems involved in operating from this cursed peninsula-on-a-peninsula. Sometimes the need of the Viceroy's predecessor to have his capital city in a militarily defensible position had a lot to answer for. Scrying – any arcane radiation for that matter – could not operate across water.

Frowning, he sketched a few more possible ray paths, adjusting for refraction by eye. That might work; it had potential, certainly. The routing station at Rom, of course, then using a secondary focus at Aesthen with the Har Meneth used as a refractive plane. The beam splitting point would be the apex of the Ventar Range of course. Scribbling down the equations he began to calculate it more precisely.

Yes, it would work. The sympathetic resonance from the Aesthen/Ventar dummy leg would stabilise the whole structure – they'd need that for a long-term portal such as this. Now, how about the power? It was going to be fiendishly draining with the need to sustain the two foci. A zircon and two amber – no, three would be safer – for gestalt. A couple of acolytes should be enough to keep it going once it was established, but he'd want at least four, plus another arcanist to set it up. Hammond would do; he was talented and powerful enough without suffering too greatly from ambition.

Parrington didn't mean to share the sight of these sand elementals with others until after he'd sent the dispatch Home. No one would steal this discovery from him.

In his pursuit of discovery, he had almost forgotten that an entire city had perhaps been razed to the ground by the creatures.

Chapter Twelve

Heresies

Thomas hunched down, pulling his head within the hood of his coat. He had slept poorly – he always did, following a vision – and the rattling motion of the droshky didn't help. His head felt woozy, half dead, and his mouth dry.

Euthymios seemed utterly unaffected sitting upright beside him, seemingly heedless of the weather. But then, he had probably not spent a sleepless night with a head spinning with residual nausea. The bishop, his arms crossed lightly in his lap, smoothly rode out every bump of the droshky's passage whilst Thomas jolted up and down, arrhythmically, each jarring motion a mallet striking through his body.

The crisp, late-autumn weather of the day before had vanished overnight, leaving grey skies and a sleeting rain that chilled to the bone. It was Thomas's first trip outside the Citadel since arriving but the huddled town held no appeal for him. Through the grey lines of sleet the stuccoed houses were dingy and drab, of little attraction and less interest. Why couldn't these people pave their roads properly? In any case, he had more pressing matters on his mind.

After a night's sleeplessness Euthymios's words, which had seemed so reasonable the night before, had taken on a character of absurdity. The bishop's casual acceptance that Thomas might be a True Seer seemed somewhat implausible. Was it not more likely, thought Thomas, that Euthymios had simply been humouring him? They were going to these Velnerine monks now not to seek his training as a True Seer, but to treat the mental malady from which Euthymios, probably correctly, believed him to be suffering.

There was something disturbing, in any case, about monks. Like all Triune citizens, Thomas's Scriptualist upbringing had bequeathed him a deep-seated suspicion of cloistered orders: they reeked of mysticism, of hypocrisy, of secret rituals and hidden agenda. Not being particularly religious, it is doubtful that he could have advanced a coherent argument for his feelings; in fact he barely thought of them consciously. That didn't alter the fact that monks were untrustworthy.

"How can anyone even know I'm a True Seer?" Thomas asked suddenly.

Startled, Euthymios turned to him. They had both sat in silence until then.

"I'm sorry?"

Thomas elaborated. "You said last night that if I was a True Seer it would make sense that Piotr watched me and rescued me. How could he know? I didn't know so how could he? The same for the Archons – if that's why they attacked?"

"How did they know? Well, that's quite simple. Through those same seers, diviners and augurers that we were disparaging yesterday."

The bishop's calmness was maddening. Determinedly, Thomas made himself sit upright, trying to emulate Euthymios's posture. A particularly jarring bump rather ruined the effect, causing Thomas's jaws to clack together painfully whilst Euthymios smoothly rode it out. Gritting his teeth, Thomas persevered as the bishop continued his explanation.

"Although they may lack the scope and power of a True Seer, that doesn't mean that these lesser seers can't do work of value. It may take much effort, true: many years of training and many days of ritual and preparation. But they can obtain glimpses of the future, though shadowed and imperfect. With sufficiently many such diviners concentrating upon a single event – the next True Seer – it's not inconceivable that one or more faction may have determined the person.

"That makes some sense," said Thomas dubiously. "But how would they even know to start looking? Why should a new True Seer be born now, rather than in a decade or a century's time?"

"Now that is the question. Scholars and philosophers have speculated on that matter for centuries. St. Cornelius believed they were a blessing of Ruth to the world, in times of its need – in which case, we may all have cause to fear. But his suggestion is strongly disputed by others, who see it as merely random: though I must say I lean towards St. Cornelius's point of view.

"But I digress. How people would know is much simpler. In the *Annalia*, St. Cornelius left directions, obscure – he was often obscure – as to when the next True Seers would appear."

Thomas was surprised. "St. Cornelius was a True Seer?" Somehow he had never made the connection.

"Of course. The last but one. Being one himself, he saw the value of others being able to identify and train the next True Seer early. He could have pinpointed who it would be exactly but he also saw the dangers of doing so: remember, it was he who believed they were intended to lend aid to Laurentia in times of dire need. So, as he did with much of the *Annalia*, he made the references so obscure that only those learned in the Mysteries of Silence would be able to interpret them, and then only shortly before the event itself.

"Unfortunately, even saints are not infallible. The last reference was not as obscure as he had hoped. As I mentioned yesterday, the Variscan Imperium hunted down and murdered Arafin of Tournais when he was only eight years old. Had they not, perhaps the Confederacy of the Lakes would have prevailed. Who can say? This time, at least, if the Rotliegendan involvement means anything, events seem to be progressing more according to plan."

Thomas shivered, and not only because of the cold. He was still not used to this thought of real, personal danger.

"What was St. Cornelius's plan?"

"I don't know. The Rotliegendans may know, if anyone does. Or no one may. But remember, his plan may not be entirely what yours or mine might be."

The droshky halted suddenly. Surprisingly daintily, Euthymios stepped, crozier first, from the low conveyance.

"We have to walk from here. It's not far."

Slipping down from the droshky, Thomas followed. Euthymios walked at a steady, measured pace, as heedless of the sleet as he had been of the motion of the droshky.

"I don't see how," said Thomas, as he caught up, "how St. Cornelius and the others can predict things five centuries or more into the future. You've been speaking as though the future was set in stone. But surely we can change things. What of free will, after all?"

"Of course we can change things. What good would it be to predict the future, if we couldn't change it?

"You can think of it this way. Consider a skein of yarn…no…look, have you read the *Annalia?"*

"No."

"It would make it easier if you had. In Linnarson it's on every curriculum, lay or clerical."

"In the Empire it's considered a work of heresy," said Thomas, somewhat defensively. "It was banned until last century. In any case, I studied classics: Atavine and Covenantal works mainly. Then things of relevance to modern Laurentia for my Laurentian Service examinations."

"If the *Annalia* isn't of relevance to modern Laurentia, what is? You can't hope to understand Silence worship without it: it was the book that led Patriarch Johan IV to formally incorporate the veneration of the Blessed Ruth as an integral part of the Anduran doctrine. Not to mention its contribution to history and moral and natural philosophy."

Thomas felt both embarrassed and annoyed. He wasn't a historian or theologian; he couldn't be expected to have read everything.

"This way." Euthymios gestured sharply towards a covered ginnel. "It'll be more sheltered." More sheltered it might be, but the passage was barely wide enough for them to walk abreast.

"You were describing the nature of foretelling," ventured Thomas hesitantly.

"Yes, well." He thought. "St. Cornelius uses a number of metaphors, but the simplest is possibly in Volume Six, where he compares it to a river. The road and the skein analogies are confusing, and Volume Two is far too abstruse. That's where he discusses the true nature of time.

"You can think of time as a river, branching out towards the sea. Behind us, in the past, is the river, solid and unbroken. In the future, it branches into a myriad of channels, each of which also branch themselves.

"The most likely futures, those that are probably going to occur, are represented by the widest channels. Those that are unlikely are small channels. Then there are the things that are impossible: I won't, for example, wake up tomorrow to find I've turned into a wyvern. Those are the pieces of ground between the channels – where water cannot flow. Is this making sense?"

"More or less."

"Good. When I say branching, of course, the channels can also converge. For example, in a one-sided battle between two nations, the river may split into a thousand different channels depending on who precisely is killed. But all the channels flow close to each other – in the vast majority of cases the same side wins the battle – and in ten years time, any of these branches will give much the same future. That is how St. Cornelius and others were able to survey the centuries ahead: details may change, but only a relatively few people or events are significant enough to dramatically shift the course of history.

"Now, the amount of water flowing at any point along the river stays constant, no matter how many branches it splits into. It has to, really: you can't create more water from nothing. What a lesser seer does is essentially the equivalent of casting his consciousness into the river at the point where he's standing, and then allow it to flow downstream before looking at the vision. He has no control over which of the channels he enters, but of course he is most likely to end up in one of the larger – the most probable – ones, simply because it *is* more probable. In our analogy, more water flows into it so, simply by chance, he is more likely to see it.

"If a seer – or a number of seers – do the same thing, over and again, and also examine the points leading up to it and beyond it, they can get some sense of the likely paths of the future. But it's time consuming and difficult. The rituals are notoriously inaccurate: not only is it hard to pinpoint how far in the future you want to be, but some seers have reported visions of the present or of the distant past. Frequently, the vision itself is the best guide to when it took place."

"And True Seers?"

"A True Seer can navigate at will this system of channels. They can pause where so ever they wish and view that branch of the future, surveying time and space at their whim. Somehow they can sense both the width of the channels and their nature. All that limits them is time, for it takes the same amount of time to view a vision of the future or the past as it would to live it."

A thought struck Thomas. "What about channels that we've passed?"

"What do you mean?"

"If we move forward into the future, the branching channels that we didn't go down will be passed – but do they still exist? Could a True Seer go back to the branching point and then forward again, to see how the present might have been?"

"I'm not sure," admitted Euthymios honestly. "You'd have to read the *Annalia* – though I can't remember seeing it there. Remember, of course, that this river analogy is only a metaphor; the true nature of time is quite different. But what you suggest might still hold true.

"Of course," he added, with a rare touch of levity. "If you are a True Seer, you won't need to read the *Annalia* to find out – you can just try."

They continued their way through the town, Thomas following Euthymios's lead through a maze of a back alleys and side streets. A couple of times they crossed wider streets and once a small square; quite tiny, just a few dozen feet on either side. There was nothing to compare with the great plazas of Iskarn, or of Autigen in the far south. All the grandeur of Hyrnar lay on the two hills within its Citadel.

In another of the larger streets Euthymios stopped unexpectedly, before a large white building. Even in this weather, it gleamed.

"You mean, this is it?" asked Thomas. Despite the breathtaking whiteness of its walls, it looked nothing like his mental picture of a monastery. What it resembled, in fact, was a merchant's townhouse. Save for its cleanliness, it could not have been told from its neighbours.

"Yes. The order obtained the house when they moved down here about twenty years ago – a benefaction of the Delaclare family, I believe. They've been here ever since.

"Now," Euthymios cautioned, as they entered, "let me explain things, or we may waste a lot of time. I know the Abbot well, and they'll let us in to see him quickly, without having to explain too much. The last thing we want is to spread this news all over town. The Abbot's a good man, even if he is Torridonian, but most of his monks are from Torridon or Linnarson, and even a vocation can't breed the propensity for intrigue out of a Linnarsonian."

True to Euthymios's word, a quick sentence from him had the monks at the door bowing low, ushering the two of them in. They were halted just inside the entrance. Puzzled, Thomas turned to Euthymios.

"Your shoes," the bishop murmured. "Take them off." He had already removed his own.

Thomas realised that the doorkeepers were, indeed, proffering them shoes of a sort; half-open, thin-soled affairs, coated on top in white wool. Shrugging, he slipped them on.

Once their new footwear was in place they were allowed out of the anteroom, past the white-robed brethren and the groups of petitioners. Inside as well as outside the hospice shone. The floors and walls were polished to perfection, the woollen clothes of the monks washed until they shone like white samite. The necessity for the shoe exchange was obvious: without it visitors would rapidly have made the floor filthy.

Thomas marvelled at the work it must take to keep it in such a state. It seemed a needless extravagance. Whilst few in the Empire still believed that washing caused disease, the association with weakness lingered on. If Thomas had known that the Velnerines' pioneering approach had reduced deaths from gangrene by two thirds during the Pelagic War, their obsession with cleanliness might have seemed more understandable, but he did not.

Without another word their escorts led them straight to the back of the building and up a small flight of stairs that must, Thomas thought, have originally been the servants' staircase. Clearly, the monks themselves must live on the top two floors. Glancing through a door on their way through he saw that much of the ground floor was given over to rooms where the sick were being treated. He looked away quickly, feeling the irrational fear and distaste of the sick that is so often found in the always healthy. With a twinge of shame but a larger one of relief he headed up the stairs, glad that they would not be staying down here.

The Abbot rose to meet them as they entered his study. He was an elderly man; perhaps a few years younger than Euthymios, Thomas judged. The two embraced warmly.

"Andur's blessings on you, Euthymios," said the Abbot. "What brings you here today? At times like these I can hardly believe that it is simply the pleasure of seeing an old friend."

"Would I need any other reason? Though I fear that the times mean we will soon be seeing all too much of you and your order. Grateful though we will be for your presence, better still that your skills were not required at all.

"However, sadly you are right. It is more than a wish to see you that finds me here, pleasant though it would be to sit and while away the hours as we did in better days. By Andur's grace mayhap we will see such times again soon."

The Abbot shook his head. "Perhaps." He gestured to a long bench.

"But come, sit down. Standing may be good for the soul, but the body need only take so much mortification. Come, why are you here? Could it have anything to do with your young companion, a Triune by his countenance?" He bowed elaborately to Thomas.

Abruptly his expression turned serious. "Whatever it is, Euthymios, if it lies in my power to help you, I will."

"You have guessed right, my friend." Euthymios sighed. "This 'young Triune', as you term him, is indeed the source of my troubles, and perhaps of our salvation, also." Leaning forward, the bishop gripped his crozier firmly.

"Jarlod, he may be a True Seer."

Thomas saw Jarlod's eyes widen slightly. Beyond that small gesture, the Abbot betrayed no indication of his shock or surprise.

"I can tell by your voice that you believe this, Euthymios. I know you too well to take you other than seriously, though Andur knows, there are few who would do, with this message. What's led you to your conclusion?"

Swiftly and succinctly, Euthymios explained the situation. Jarlod listened, all trace of his former levity gone.

A long silence followed. Thomas felt the urge to say something but managed to restrain himself. After what seemed an age the Abbot spoke.

"It may be that there is something I can do. I believe that at least I will be able to determine whether or not he is a True Seer." Thomas twitched. He wished the two of them would stop discussing him as if he wasn't even here.

"And if he is?" asked Euthymios.

"Then we will do our best. But you know as well I, old friend, that we will then be in almost entirely unknown territory. We must pray that Ruth will guide our steps; it would be capricious of her indeed to simply abandon one of her Seers."

"Our Lady of Silence is not known for giving what she considers unnecessary aid," warned Euthymios. "Cryptic warnings; an unlooked-for blessing or aid, yes, but she only intervenes when *she* believes it is needed. If mortal ingenuity cannot supply the rest, then success is undeserved. So the *Annalia* teaches us, at least."

"In that case," said Jarlod, with a flash of his former humour, "we will just have to rely on her Brother, won't we?

"Now," he continued, returning to business, "it will take me a little time to assemble those I need. A task such as this calls for a careful balance of minds in the ritual: powerful, perfectly balanced and complementary. In particular, I would have the aid of Prior Gildrue, one of the most accomplished amongst us. He is in town and will need to be recalled before we can start. And of course I cannot say how long the ritual itself will last.

"Will you stay?"

"No. There is too much to do back at the Citadel. I have sadly neglected my duties at the cathedral in the last week. In any case, I would only be in your way, here.

"You work too hard, Euthymios."

"No harder than I must, Jarlod. Andur calls upon us to not spare ourselves in our service to Him."

"And your service to Rianda?"

"Rianda needs me," said Euthymios flatly. "I am Elarani born and bred, Jarlod. I will not spare myself in service to my queen or country, any more than I would in service to our God."

An awkward pause followed. Breaking the silence, Euthymios addressed Thomas.

"Thomas, I will be leaving you in the Abbot's more than capable hands. You will be in my prayers. I have no doubt that if anyone this side of Aesthen can help you, he will be able to."

Thomas just nodded. As Euthymios left he suddenly realised how much comfort he had begun to take from the presence of the elderly bishop. Bereft of his strong, supportive presence, Thomas felt utterly alone. He might have known Euthymios for only a few days, but the conversation they had shared yesterday had built up a closeness that, however ephemeral, was nevertheless a staff to lean upon here in this strange, unknown land.

Around him, the Abbot was busily making his preparations; calling people in, conferring and giving orders with smooth efficiency. Thomas might as well have been invisible; a stream of monks flowed around him without a word. Against his will his body began trembling: a physical outpouring of the combination of loneliness, trepidation and unfamiliar surroundings. He was not sure what he had dreaded most: that these Velnerines would be unable to help him, meaning that the visions would continue unchecked, or that they would help, proving him a True Seer. The very concept made him tremble.

The Abbot re-emerged from the vestry into which he had momentarily disappeared. He had changed his vestments; the new robes, though still of the purest white, were considerably more formal. The sleeves were covered in a geometric design of the finest silver filigree; the body embroidered with symbols of the Anduran faith: the five-spoked wheel, the double-barred A, the sword and scales of justice. In his hands he carried a strange object, a tortuous band of metal, twisted and folded back upon itself, in a convoluted pattern that seemed to have only one end. In the centre of the object was a small rod of a pale, smooth material. Thomas grimaced as he realised that it must be bone; the object itself some sort of grisly relic.

At the Abbot's gesture Thomas followed him to a small side chapel, a small train of monks in tow. It had once been a bedroom, or perhaps a store room, but, like the rest of the building, had been converted from its original purpose when the Velnerines moved in.

The original furnishings had been stripped, the dark cedar walls polished until they glowed with a dark, vital light, reflecting the shimmer from the candles placed in brass brackets around the room. A marble statue of St. Velnery the Pure looked down from above the altar, one hand reaching up, the other down, to symbolise the saint's succour of both the high and the low. A depiction of the Wheel had been inlaid in bronze in the floor, the symbol representing each of the apostles set at the end of each of the five spokes; the boar of St. Gregory, the lion of St. Brantos, the winged bull of St. Daniel, the wyvern of St. Luderand and, closest to the altar, the loyal hound of St. Johan, first and most favoured disciple of Andur Astartes.

"Thomas," said the Abbot, addressing him for the first time, "if you would move to the centre of the wheel, please. Sit on the floor, and make your mind as calm and composed as you can." Thomas did as he was told, though his mind could not have felt less composed. He had never been particularly religious; nor had he had much contact with the arcane sciences, save for what was ordinarily encountered in day to day life in a modern nation like the Empire. Here, in this ornate chapel, isolated, alone and the centre of who knew what Sanctist ritual, he was finding goose pimples rising on his flesh.

Four of the older, more senior looking monks took up positions at the ends of the spokes, with the Abbot himself standing in the place of St. Johan in what Thomas guessed to be the primary position. They wore vestments of the finest white, less ornate but of the same mode as the Abbot's, and each leaned upon a short staff made of a tawny wood, carved with a spiral design. The Abbot was the exception. Instead of a staff, he held out, in hands cupped as if in offering, the misshapen relic that Thomas had seen earlier.

Outside the circle, a novice began swinging a thurible of incense, the sweet, heavy aroma spreading across the room. An eerie chanting began, as the outer monks took up a haunting, atonal plainsong that did nothing to settle Thomas's nerves.

"We will begin when I give the word," said the Abbot, in Silurian. The ordinary voice seemed to bring with it a sudden restoration of normality, bringing Thomas to his senses. "Those of you outside the circle, stand ready to restrain him, should he grow violent."

"That will not be necessary," said Thomas, jumping up, his voice coming out in an awkward half-yell.

"I'm sorry," said the Abbot, looking genuinely embarrassed. "I hadn't realised you understood Silurian." But a dam had broken within Thomas, and he was not to be so easily silenced.

"Well, I do. And it would be nice if you could explain what was going on. What is this ritual? What are you going to do? And what is that?" Pointing at the relic of twisted metal and bone, Thomas was unable to keep the distaste out of his voice.

"I'm sorry," the Abbot said again. He gestured for the monks to cease chanting. "I had thought Euthymios would have explained things to you, but I see that he left it to us.

"We are, as I think you know, skilled at mental healing?" At Thomas's nod he continued. "Assuming that Euthymios was right and that you are indeed a True Seer, your vision, your mental eye as it were, has become fixed upon one incident. We must dislodge it, but this will take power: a large degree of mental inertia will have accumulated by now.

"That's the reason for the ritual and for the numbers involved: to contribute their strength. Essentially we are praying for Andur's intervention, through the medium of his holy saint, Velnery the Pure, to intercede and free your mind. If you are not a True Seer, we will be attempting to cure the fixation anyway."

"And what happens then?"

"If you are a True Seer, you mean? If you're not, you're simply having flashbacks. But if you are, then your mental eye will be free. You'll still get visions, but they will be of many things, from the past, present or future, usually – from what I have read – of scenes relevant in some way to your own life – or your future life. In time you will, we hope, learn the skill of focusing those visions and navigating the river of time, to view what and where you wish. But that will come later."

Thomas was not sure he relished the prospect of continued visions of his past and future, but decided to let it pass for now. It had to be better than reliving the massacre again. However, the Abbot still hadn't answered his question about the relic.

"And what is the purpose of that?" he asked again, gesturing.

"This?" said the Abbot in surprise. "Ah, of course. I had forgotten that you Scriptualists do not make use of relics, nor do you venerate the saints." Thomas thought he could detect a hint of disapproval in his voice.

"This," continued the Abbot "is a representation of the *lathâele*. After St. Velnery's martyrdom, when the faithful returned to examine the spot where he was slain, all that remained were his bones, scoured clean but perfectly preserved despite the fire, and this, the remains of his sword, twisted and tortured by the forces involved into the form that you see here. Upon testing, his followers found that the metal had been transformed; no longer steel, no force could bend or break it, nor could the metal lose its sheen: dirt and stains simply ran off. It was christened the *lathâele,* an Evvenyae word meaning 'the soul indomitable', and is one of the most holy relics of our Order."

How in the nine circles of hell was he killed, Thomas wondered, mind taking refuge in trivialities to escape from the thought of what he was getting himself into. He had thought that St. Velnery had been a healer. Then he remembered that Euthymios had mentioned that the saint had brought his healing talents to the Pelagic Wars: no doubt that explained much, for gruesome things could happen in war, even to non-combatants.

"And this is the sword?" Despite himself, he had been quite impressed by the tale.

"No," answered the Abbot. "This is merely a representation. The true *lathâele* is in our motherhouse in Kurdon, and may only be touched by the Minister General or by his special dispensation. But ours does contain one of the saint's finger bones, as you can see. It is still imbued with the power of the blessed Velnery.

"Now, are you ready to begin?"

"I think so."

"Good. You will need to clear your mind; make it calm, peaceful, empty. Recite the creed."

"What?" Thomas was startled.

"The creed. You do know it, don't you?

"Well, yes, of course, but..."

"Just recite it, then." His voice softened. "I would it were otherwise, but unless you wish to spend several years studying Velnerine lore, there are some things which you will have to simply take on trust.

"Recite it, over and over again. Clear your mind of all else, focus only the words you are speaking, not their meaning, not what is happening elsewhere. Let the words be all there is in the world to you."

Somewhat nervously, Thomas nodded. The eerie plainsong started once more as he began.

> "I believe in Andur, Lord of Order
>
> God of power and might.
>
> Through his great strength he created Edrith.
>
> By his pure wisdom he formed mankind.
>
> In his perfect justice he bound us to the Wheel,
>
> bound us to live and die and live again,
>
> world and time without end.
>
> Bound us, as the pagans are bound still.
>
> I believe in the Wheel of Life, eternal, unchanging,
>
> that binds all life upon its turning,
>
> binds it through birth and death
>
> to infinite lives of suffering.
>
> Andur's perfect servant,
>
> the epitome of Order.
>
> Without Order there is no righteousness.
>
> Without righteousness there is no honour.
>
> Without honour there is no justice.
>
> Without justice there is no Order:
>
> Order above all; the source, the summit, the centre.
>
> I believe in Andur Astartes, Redemptor of mankind,
>
> Andur's incarnation on Edrith.

Sinless, perfect, divine;
Andur as Andur above.
For our souls he suffered torment,
was bound and tortured upon the wheel.
At midnight, he broke the wheel,
broke it, as his body had been broken,
broke the Wheel of Life as he broke that wheel of mortal hands.
Night became day.
Light shone through the darkness.
Chains were cast away, fetters unshackled.
I believe in the grace of Andur,
that those who have faith in Him shall have eternal bliss,
freed forever from the torment of the Wheel.
I believe in the judgement of Andur,
the ultimate judge, with perfect justice, with perfect mercy.
He shall save those that have faith;
they will be placed by his side in heaven.
He shall cast the unbelievers back upon the Wheel,
there to suffer once more
some greater, some lesser, in accordance with their deeds.
I believe in the Book of Andur,
divinely inspired, infallible,
that guides the church of Andur,
founded by the apostles, in accordance with His will.
I believe in one anointing in the faith,
in the confession of my unworthiness,
in the forgiveness of sins,
and the life of the world to come.
Exantior.

"Again," the Abbot murmured as he finished.

"I believe in Andur, Lord of Order..."

"It is not the right creed," he heard one of the monks whisper, concerned. "There is no mention of the saints, nor of the divinity of Our Lady of Silence!

"By his perfect justice..."

"Peace, Prior Gildrue. It is the Falanine creed; the Scriptualists have used it since the Sundering."

"Order above all..."

"It matters not the form of the words; it is the process of recitation that is needed here."

The words came distantly now, far off, through a deep haze. When he finished the recitation for a second time he began again without prompting. The words echoed like solid blocks in the empty cavern of his mind.

"I believe in Andur, Lord of Order..."

The Abbot was chanting now, call and response with the other four around the wheel, the plainsong a haunting counterpoint. There were no lights, no flashes of power, no displays of arcane power searing across the room from staff to *lathâele*. Just a steadily building force; a waxing pressure upon the borders of his mind, gentle yet inexorable. The last thought that crossed Thomas's mind before unconsciousness took him was to wonder, incongruously, what Lawrence would say to this.

#

With dazzling speed he shot along the Harnelin Way. Past the gleaming mansions and townhouses of the wealthy he flew, bursting out into Murchison's Square above the great equestrian statue of the Duke of Tavinshire. Trumpets sounded along Prian Street. A procession was beginning: coaches and cavalry processing along the grand plane-tree-lined avenue.

He headed higher, seeking a better view. Behind him lay the Greensward, the white domes of the Government offices that crowded it sparkling in the sun, and beyond it rose Bethwark Cathedral, proud towers standing tall.

The procession drew in to sight, wending its way through the city to the cathedral. An escort of cavalry, resplendent in green and gold, led the way followed by the coaches of state carrying the three persons of the Triumvirate. More cavalry followed and foot soldiers; drummers, a band. The nobility and the civic dignitaries of Wenlock. All the pomp and circumstance of the Triune Empire assembled in parade.

With a start, Thomas recognised the banners. This was the birthday of Corithin Andar, founder of the Empire. He had been to watch this procession once before, during his time at Chelmsthorpe. But that meant it was Trenwen: late spring, a fact amply confirmed as he glanced around.

Wenlock was in bloom, springing with new life. Across the river, in the park, banks of tulips stood in full flower, blooming amidst lissuin and tall hanyitië. The avoligna were in full flower, delicate golden blossom silhouetted against their iridescent silver bark.

Like a hammer blow it hit Thomas that he was in a vision – and that the vision was not of the massacre. No searing heat, no scenes of destruction and pain. Here in the vision, his physical senses and awareness were dulled, as if he were feeling them from a long way away, but even so the knowledge sent a tingle of excitement and trepidation down his spine.

Then he was zooming out, whether involuntarily or by some subconscious prompting he knew not. The city shrank away; the domes, the houses, the great river Medon dwindling to tinyness; Wenlock itself a splodge in the surrounding countryside. From far higher than the highest eagle he surveyed the Empire: its towns and cities mere dots, the mighty rivers wending their way across the vasty plains. From the great northern forest of Ellesae to the Bay of Caradoc; from the mountains of Nurn to the cities of the western plains it lay before him.

Straining, he tried to make out Chelmsthorpe, but he was too far out. A thought stuck him suddenly: when was this? Last spring, or next spring? Perhaps some other spring entirely, decades, even centuries in the past or future. He chided himself; he was not thinking clearly. The three Triumviri were those that had been enthroned when he left. That set the date as no more than twelve years ago – or up to a few decades, at most, in the future.

Now he was moving again, slipping inwards and sideways. The motion – if such it could be called – was strangely nauseous, though no sound, no rush of air betrayed any sign that he was moving. Downwards he soared, the land coming into focus beneath him. Patchwork fields emerged; roads, streams and villages. This was Trandale, his own county! With some poignancy he recognised the land that he had known since childhood. What wouldn't he give to be there now. There was Erbenby, and Dalham; there was the old quarry that he had only yesterday been telling Euthymios about.

Hernchester moved into view, the county town. A crowd was gathered before the church. There were his parents! They looked well – and the same age as when he had left, save for an extra line or two of grey in his father's hair. Looking closer at the crowd he spotted his sister and her husband, people crowding around.

Edith cradled a babe in her arms. He started. His sister with a child? This must be next spring, the baby the child that his mother had written of in her last letter. His sister looked radiant; the babe healthy, the oil from the anointing still visible on its forehead, though with the shape of the wheel now somewhat smudged.

Thomas wanted to grin with happiness and to smile at the bizarreness of it all. It had just sunk in that, from halfway across the world, he was looking at his own unborn nephew.

Chapter Thirteen

Within a High Tower

Time passed quickly from then on. Though Thomas still saw little of Lawrence, the Citadel of Hyrnar began to seem less lonely. He saw Euthymios frequently and, prompted he suspected by the bishop, Kadmos had mellowed towards him. Their initial sessions of questions had long since ended, with the frustrated Sword-Captain finally admitting that Thomas had told all he could. Little enough though it was, Kadmos nonetheless realised – even if Thomas did not – just how valuable to him and the chiliarchi even those few scraps were.

It was on Kadmos's instructions, Thomas knew, that the hard-faced guards of the Citadel turned a blind eye to his wanderings and exploring, allowing him to investigate all the nooks and crannies of the place, from the servants' quarters to the battlements. Only the royal quarters and the armouries were barred against him, as they were to every inhabitant of the Citadel save those authorised by the Queen or Sword-Captain.

There was no doubt that this exploring contributed greatly to the easing of Thomas's initial loneliness. As the passages of the Citadel unravelled before him, the dusty passages began to feel almost like home. He grew accustomed to the decorations: the geometric designs, the frescoes of the beasts and the saints. The stocky grandeur of the Har Magisteris, the graceful power of the Har Serenis, the bustling activity of the servants that underlaid it all; to each, in their different ways, he began to feel not only familiarity, but even an affection.

As he roamed the Citadel he was beginning to pick up some of the language of the inhabitants. He was still far from fluent: despite his talent for languages, Elarani was a strange tongue, preserved relatively unchanged by its hilly isolation whilst, outside, the protean languages of the flatlands had merged, blended and changed. It seemed to be more related to Evvenyae than to anything else and that long-dead language had never been one of his strengths. Still, he had picked up enough Elarani by now to make himself understood, if with difficulty, and to catch the gist of what was said around him. Just the ability to make out some sense in what was said; to change the flowing, meaningless babble to conversation between fellow people, had ended Thomas's isolation in their midst. The more he understood, the more he came to understand not only the very real anxieties of these people, high and low, but their equally real determination to resist the advance of Erd Gellin to their last breath.

Punctuating the exploration of the Citadel there were, of course, his visits to the Velnerines. These had taken place regularly, slightly more than once a week, since that first visit in the month of Roandre. Though initially filled with trepidation, Thomas had come to find them enjoyable. The Abbot, though very different from Euthymios, was both skilled and devout and Thomas had come to appreciate his sometimes scathing humour. Not that the Abbot was ever less than professional upon matters of seriousness, but even the briefest moment of laughter was a balm given the increasing sombreness of mood within the Citadel itself.

Only occasionally did that atmosphere penetrate the walls of the hospice. Their business was to treat the sick and to worship Andur, and for this they had no need for external complications. A cloistered order of healers would naturally be immune from the attention of all but the most uncivilised of aggressors and, with most of the monks from Torridon or Linnarson, few had any personal stake in the troubles of Elaran. Only those from outside, like Thomas himself, brought that funereal wind into the hospice.

One visitor in particular seemed to chill the room with his presence. Indeed, from what little he had seen, the man seemed to be directing a hostility at Thomas himself, though for what reason he could not guess. Thomas had seen him more than once on his trips to the hospice: the man had to be a devotee of St. Velnery for he was clearly not unwell. Short and stockily built, the man moved like a dancer and yet exuded an almost tangible aura of power. A warrior, almost certainly, and a hardened one at that. What the man's exact role within the Citadel was, Thomas didn't know, but his glower was the only blot upon Thomas's visits to the Velnerines.

Even the treatment itself was not unpleasant. There was a solace to be had in the calm and tranquillity of the procedure. Thomas had to do little but allow his mind to go vacant. He would have put up with far worse to have been rid of the visions. Jarlod sometimes spoke of a more active phase of treatment, when he would actually be learning to control the visions, but for now Thomas was content to let events take their course. The monks would tell him when they required more.

Whatever they had done was working, that was what counted. Thomas didn't entirely know why, nor did he entirely care. After two weeks of almost constant trepidation it was an ecstasy to be free. Since the vision of Home on his first visit, he had only had two more in almost as many months. Just two, and neither was of the massacre: there was no pain, no burning, nor did they cause him to lie debilitated for hours afterwards.

True, neither had been entirely comforting, but he could live with that. In the first he had begun as he had in the vision of Home, floating high above Edrith, seeing the world spread out in its glory before him. This time the continent below him had not been Avalonia but Laurentia, its mountains, deserts and forests all displayed for him to see. It was the first time he had really appreciated its size.

The Imperial provinces of Scahania and Pelagos, for all their seemingly great extent, made up but the tiniest fraction of this vast landmass. Here in Elaran, in the centre of Laurentia, he and Lawrence were a very long way away from friendly lands.

As he watched he realised that something was changing. At first he could not work out what it was, so subtle was the change. But then he realised. The Great Western Desert was growing. Almost imperceptibly it nibbled at its boundaries, edging into the Barrens and crowding the semi-arid lands around Atavus.

There was splendour in the stark beauty of those glistening sands. A white death; waterless and pure. Looking back to the borders the growth had accelerated. The Barrens were all but gone; the waves of sand lapping now at the borders of Erd Gellin. Gathering pace, the desert swelled. Inexorable, unstoppable, a tidal wave of sand sweeping over the world. Elaran vanished beneath the torrent, and Torridon, Givet and Rotliegendes followed in quick succession. Sweeping onwards, north, east and south the sands roared. The desert lands of Scandia fell next, their rich golden sands, filled with hidden life, smothered beneath the barren onslaught. Beneath the heights of the Har Meneth the sands halted, piling up against those giant redoubts, but then they were over, the lush lands of Scahania exposed helplessly before them. In a heartbeat, they too were buried and all was sand. Between the Iryan Ocean and the Island of Dawn only the highest peaks of the Gralbakh Range could be seen protruding amidst the lifeless sands.

The second vision, although not so disturbing, was no less strange. Thomas had seen the Viceroy walking alone, bereft of all the dignity and trappings of office. The landscape through which he walked was not the lush jungles and exotic cities of southern Scahania, but instead a starker, emptier land. Somehow Thomas had known that it was Pelagos, the Empire's northern province upon Laurentia, rather than the bleak Starkenfells or a scene from Avalonia or elsewhere.

Nothing else happened. In contrast to the tumult and fury of the expanding desert, this vision was calm, dominated by the lonely silhouette of the solitary Viceroy. Overlaying the scene Thomas could feel a deep grieving: that of a man wronged and cast out. But though he watched and waited, no explanation came.

But though the visions were perplexing, they did not seriously disturb him. After all, from what Euthymios had said, they could be from any time in the past, present or future. He had told the bishop of them, of course, but he had been unable to make any sense of them either.

"I wouldn't worry," he had said. "The chance of interpreting an arbitrary vision, without context or guidance, must surely be slim, even for an experienced True Seer."

"Which I certainly am not."

"Quite. But that will come in time. It will not be until you learn to navigate the channels of time that your talent will truly come into its own."

Thomas had felt comforted by this, despite the subtext of needing to push forward and learn more. He had squashed that thought to the back of his mind: the Velnerines would tell him when the time was right to progress. No doubt Lawrence would also have told him to push harder – but he had barely seen Lawrence for weeks. Euthymios's urging was easy to resist: the bishop was too courteous to offer more than the gentlest of hints to a guest, and Thomas still found it relatively easy to ignore the slight pangs of guilt that stung him when he thought of it.

He knew why Euthymios was pushing. It was not simply intellectual curiosity, though no doubt the bishop would have found the subject fascinating. Although he tried to conceal it, Euthymios was deathly worried about the coming spring campaign. Thomas had been long enough in Hyrnar to realise that all but the most bombastic inhabitants of the citadel recognised that the Elarani forces would be sorely overmatched by those of the Gellinese, and Euthymios was nothing if not a realist. Thomas's talent, if he could but master it, could give Elaran the vital edge it needed to survive.

Hadn't he been through enough recently, though? A few weeks of relative relaxation would do no harm. Euthymios himself admitted that he had no idea how long it would take to learn the Seer's arts; it could be weeks, could be years. Years seemed more likely considering the length of time arcanists studied.

He would start in earnest after Longest Night, Thomas told himself. Another couple of weeks would make little difference. So the sessions with Euthymios continued; talking, listening, playing sharom. Save for that one grain of awkwardness over mastering the visions, both enjoyed each other's company. As well as a shared love of sharom, in which Euthymios enjoyed a slight advantage, both had a deep interest in learning of the other's country and history. Each took for granted so much that the other didn't know that their conversations were frequently a fascinating meander through history, politics, religion and geography.

More than once Elena joined them. She and Euthymios had been friendly since she had arrived in Hyrnar. To some, their friendship had seemed unlikely – the elderly clergyman, not young even then, and the bright and charming new bride – but in both ran deep currents of kindliness, compassion and a lively intelligence.

Like everyone else, Thomas took to the royal duchess immediately. Her lively tongue added exuberance to their discussions and, though less learned than the bishop, her quick mind penetrated as deeply as his into the myriad facets of life in the Triune Empire. Why, she had once asked about the historical basis for how each of the three constituent kingdoms chose their triumvir and Thomas had been unable to answer.

For some reason he had always felt entirely at ease in her presence. She treated him as what he was – a young man, somewhat out of his depth, but neither stupid nor irrelevant. She never patronised him, but nor did she treat him with the false formality that would have been his due had he truly deserved his nominal rank of ambassador. Intellectually, she treated both him and Euthymios as equals and they responded in kind. The bishop said that she had always been that way from when she had first arrived: lively, with a way of making all who spoke to her feel at home; gentle and considerate, but with a personal confidence that was neither hidden nor in doubt.

If Thomas found himself at home with Elena, that was more than he could say for her cousin. Perhaps that was to be expected: Rianda was a queen, after all. Even if it was only of a tiny Laurentian country – he no longer thought of it as barbaric – burden of sovereignty must weigh no less heavily on her for all that.

Euthymios had arranged a weekly meeting between Thomas and Rianda; a recognition of Thomas's formal status as Triune ambassador. No doubt he hoped to tie Thomas more deeply to Elaran, for any information that Thomas had to give could more easily have been passed by way of Kadmos or through Euthymios himself.

The audiences reflected this. Thomas sat awkwardly, facing Rianda in her circlet and robes of state. Both sides were well aware of the truth. Ambassador he might be, but the title was honorary only: he had no power to commit the Empire to anything. His only role was to relay messages back, keeping the Empire informed of the strange goings on in the centre of the continent.

Just her presence daunted him. Though she was even younger than he, Rianda had been trained for the throne since earliest girlhood and had ruled this land in her own name for months now. Thomas was powerless, a helpless refugee dependent on Rianda's charity – and the long shadow of the Empire's power. Rianda commanded armies; she was bracing her land against a forthcoming invasion. It might have been different had he actually had something to say – a clear role to fulfil – but he didn't. Therefore the meetings passed in a stilted conversation, in which Rianda asked if he was being well looked after and Thomas asserted that he was, describing his meetings with Euthymios and his trips to the Velnerines. Rianda would give him a formal update on Elaran's preparedness for him to relay to the Empire, and would ask him if there was any word or message from them in return. There never was. Then it was over; his formal bow, her nod in response, and he would be escorted out of the audience room in relief, leaving Rianda to deal with business that was actually important.

For if the days passed easily for Thomas, that was not the case for Rianda. From dawn until dusk, and often long after, her days were spent in preparing Elaran for the coming struggle. To the myriad of tasks that ordinarily filled the time of a ruler were added new problems: organising the muster, dealing with recalcitrant nobles, each of whom believed he and he alone knew best how to defend Elaran, and, always, balancing the need to marshal her forces southwards whilst still fending off the ever-present threat of Torridon to the north. By the end of each day she was utterly drained.

Once, Thomas had spied her from a high tower, walking in the privy garden with Elena. Though he didn't know it, she had just concluded a successful deal with the Givetian ambassador, securing the supply of much-needed materiel for the coming campaign. It had taken days and all of Rianda's and Euthymios's skill at bargaining to reach acceptable terms; settling at last on a cost that, although steep, was not quite ruinous for Elaran. Just one more stitch in the tapestry of the land's defence.

Wearied as ever, Rianda had sought solace from her labours, just a few moments' peace in the tranquillity of her gardens. Even from so far up Thomas could see the exhaustion that bowed her shoulders as she entered and the visible way in which she straightened, came alive, as she cast off the cares of state. He couldn't hear their conversation, nor did he wish to. Even just watching made him feel guilty of eavesdropping, of infringing her privacy, but somehow he could not draw away.

Rianda had put aside her state robes and crown. Beneath, she was dressed simply, in a cleanly cut gown of myrtle green that seemed to glow with life against the dull winter foliage of the garden. Beside it, Elena's appearance seemed almost subdued, though the older woman was usually accounted the greater beauty. To Thomas it appeared that only here had Rianda truly come alive, away from the caging demands of the throne that trapped and crushed her with its burden.

Still talking, the two women passed behind the almond trees and out of Thomas's vision. When they emerged they would no longer be visible from this window. Resisting the urge to seek a new vantage point, he headed down the winding stairs, his thoughts filled with the young, brave, beautiful queen. He prayed that the wisdom and courage of her actions would be enough to save this country.

Rianda, also, prayed for this, but with a less flattering interpretation of her own actions than that which Thomas so blithely granted her. All too often, she believed, she was walking on the edge of a precipice, with only one false step needed to send her plunging into the abyss.

Always the subject of Hyrakos leered at her from the shadows. It dogged her constantly, even on matters where there seemed to be no connection. As the weeks went by and no news came from the south, a growing coterie of nobles began to mutter their dissatisfaction at her actions.

Lykourgos had gone south, Andur be thanked, to see to the preparation of the southern chiliad, now settled in Ad Cenyor for the winter. Without him the dissidents had no focus for their discontent. Yet their discontent showed itself nonetheless in many ways: more men now were reluctant to adhere to her decisions without debate; few propositions she put forward in Council went unchallenged. Small things, perhaps; insignificant in themselves. But together, they signified something much more worrying. Had it not been for the unquestioning support of Euthymios, Kadmos and Nomiki, the muster might have stalled in its tracks.

If only some word – any word – would come north. The city had fallen, there could be no question of that, but the silence let men's minds breed demons worse than any likely reality. One solid report, no matter how bad, would have done much to quiet the mutterings. It would also have eased the ache of her own heart.

Though she must defend her actions in public, not a day went by that she did not question her decision to abandon Hyrakos. It was the right decision; she had believed that at the time and still did, but what would be the cost? Could any cost be too high to pay for the preservation of Elaran? Her head told her no, as did her heart; but inside her soul wept.

The die was cast now. There was no choice but to persevere, trusting that the men preserved by the retreat from Hyrakos – the southern chiliad, fully one third of her trained forces – would be enough to tip the balance in the coming struggle. That was the gamble she had taken and that must run true if the sacrifice of Hyrakos were to mean anything at all.

"Blessed Ruth, Our Lady of Silence, intercede for me now," Rianda prayed, gazing up the statue of Ruth that dominated the west transept. "May Andur show his mercy to the people of Hyrakos. Shelter them in their innocence. If punishment is needed, may the hand of Andur, Lord of Order, infinite in his justice, fall upon me, not them."

Unwilling tears rolled down her face. The flicker of the candles blurred, a shimmering veil.

"If only I could know how my people fared," she cried out in despair. "You are the mistress of knowledge, Ruth. The mysteries of the past and the future are laid bare before your eyes! Why will you not let me know?"

The blind gaze of the Lady of Silence gazed down upon her enigmatically. Even the statue mocked her. Shining forth with a cold lustre, the statue's pale marble face glistened in its framing of polished jet, the mineral sculpted so finely that it seemed formed of living hair. Robes of the deepest indigo, cloaking the sister of Andur Astartes in her shroud of midnight.

Rianda continued to pray, ignoring the mocking reply of her soul. Some day soon she would know the truth, would know whether Hyrakos lived or died. Perhaps the town was well; no news was good news, so they said. She could not make herself believe that platitude. Until the day that news came; until the spring; until the forces of Elaran had held or perished against the hordes of Erd Gellin; until then, she must be strong. Though her heart lay buried in Hyrakos, Elaran would prevail.

Chapter Fourteen

Through a Dark Veil

The great bell tolled.

Sound rolled out over the silent city, echoing through the ruins, smothering the darkened streets in a deep, rich blanket of noise. Over the shattered remains of houses, the bleak, gaping shells of what had once been proud churches and monuments, the peal echoed. The timbre of mourning filled the air.

Beneath him, in the ruined city, shadowy figures began to converge. Half-seen, they scuttled through the mist-filled alleys. Twisted, misshapen bodies mixed on equal terms with clawed beasts and powerful, hulking frames born in the fires of hell. A *rahvashda* slunk through a narrow passage. Wolf-like jaws open ravenously, it padded softly through the streets, hunting for food.

Not a human soul could be seen amongst the desolation. Even in the cathedral they had found no refuge. Its three domed towers lay smashed, gaping hollow spheres open to the night air. Shattered, they seemed to stand in mockery of the illusion of Andur's power.

A face at a window. Hope surged within him. So life did exist here. Hidden indoors; crouched in a basement, who knew how many still survived?

The window quivered; shattered, glass exploding in a thousand splinters. Out of it the creature lurched; the face stretched mindlessly in a hideous rictus of unnatural hunger. This was no fragile survivor but one of the predators. His hope died stillborn, leaving nothing but ashes in its wake.

The bitter truth was that none had survived here. The desolation was complete; it was only a delusion to think otherwise. Those who had not been carted off had long since perished, hunted down, tortured and slain like vermin. Hunger had eventually driven out even those who had initially evaded the sharp noses of the *rahvashda* and the fell powers of the *goruthang*. Once in the open they were easy prey. *Mernal*, *sthand* and *nasku* stalked the streets, or crawled, or flew: there was no escape. The infernal creatures fed on pain and death; mortal suffering was their ambrosia. Even drogkhar would not survive long here. Perhaps some human life survived in the sewers, reduced to the level of rats in order to survive, but even there the end could not be long postponed.

The clatter of hoofs sounded on the stone streets. A natural noise that sounded as out of place here as a profanity in a sermon; a breath of cool air on a hot summer's day. One almost expected a group of gentlemen out for an afternoon's ride to appear and the desolation of the city to vanish like a dream before their warm normality.

It was not to be. From the dark mists of the alley appeared a figure, mounted upon a black horse a full seventeen hands high. Behind him followed two dozen soldiers riding in two disciplined columns. Garbed in black, grim visages looked out from under steel, high-crested helms. Muskets lay across their saddles; swords at their side. They carried no banner, wore no markings.

Their leader halted abruptly, his troop stopping immediately with eerily precise exactness. Slowly, the commander surveyed his surroundings. Before that gaze, the demons slunk away, fading back into the shadows and crevices of the ruined city that was now their lair. What mortal could cow horrors such as these?

A shifting veil of shadows concealed his features. His cloak was not woven of ordinary cloth like those of his followers but of living darkness, a rippling pool of protean night that shrouded his body, but could not conceal the bulk and power of the man shrouded within.

From his breath came a reek of sand. Not the richness of the Scandian desert, hinting of spices, luxury and hidden life, but the sterile scent of the Western Barrens, where no life could live.

"It has begun well," the figure said in a voice of crumbling dust. The now empty streets appeared to meet his satisfaction. The head turned, seeming to look directly at the far-off vantage point from which Thomas, bodiless, viewed the scene. The power in that gaze! Even from so far off, in a mere vision, he felt its intensity, beating down upon him like the remorseless heat of the midday desert sun.

Though his eyes could see no change, somehow the figure seemed to smile cruelly. It knew well its own strength. What is more, it knew its opponents' weakness. This desolation was only the beginning.

#

It was impossible to get to sleep after that. Determinedly Thomas lay on his bed, eyes closed, but try as he might drowsiness would not come. The longer he lay there, the more awake be became.

He could feel the bone of his hip sticking into the bed. Rolling he tried to get comfortable. Faint noises – noises that normally would barely even register on his consciousness – seemed to never cease. No matter what he tried to concentrate on the memory of the most recent vision came crowding back.

Deliberately he avoided thinking of what it could mean or signify. Some things were best considered in the clear light of day. If it had only been a matter of clearing his mind of this then sleep might well have come, though it would have been a troubled one, restless and disturbed by dreams of what he had just seen.

It was more than that though: he simply wasn't sleepy. Thomas had had this problem before: although a sound sleeper, if something did wake him he found it very tricky to fall asleep again. By the time he had listened to the cathedral clock chime first the half and then the three-quarter hour – of what hour he didn't know – he had had enough.

If he was going to be awake he might as well do something more than just lie here. At the very least moving around might make him tired enough that when he came back to bed his body could overcome his perverse mind which was insisting, despite all the evidence of the time of night, that he was wide awake.

Rolling out of bed he pulled on some clothes, not forgetting a thick coat. The corridors were empty as he padded through them; even the servants were still abed at this ungodly hour. The occasional guard was the only other person he saw, but if they wondered what he was doing, their impassive faces said nothing. If the Triune ambassador chose to wander around in the middle of the night well, as long as he kept to the allowed areas, that was his business. Everyone knew that outlanders were eccentric.

The very emptiness gave the Citadel an eerie feel. Thomas was used to it bustling, well lit, thronging with life. Now the darkened corridors seemed almost ghostly, the cool wind blowing hauntingly through the stone passages. One could feel the weight of ages. The long centuries that this place had been lived in, had sheltered its inhabitants, had been fought over, damaged and restored seemed only a moment away. It felt as if one could turn a corner and suddenly appear in a thirteenth- or fourteenth-century Citadel.

It was that aura that made Thomas feel comfortable, if in a slightly peculiar way. This was a place full of life; asleep, not dead. The clock struck two as he descended the stairs, confirming this. The flow of air through the Citadel could have been the breath of a great creature, waiting only for the new day to come alive again. In every way, the Citadel's emptiness was utterly different from the desolation of the city in his dream.

Drawing his cloak around him he stepped out into the gardens and shivered. He had forgotten how cold it would be. It was only two days before Longest Night, the heart of winter, and winters closed in fast here in these hill lands. A silver filigree of frost had begun to form over the ancient stonework, an icy lace that clasped the Citadel and gardens in a fragile embrace. It was a cold, clear night. The moon, just a few days past full, shone its pale light down into the gardens, glinting off the new-formed frost and turning the trees and bushes to shades of grey.

Emboldened, Thomas stepped out from under the lintel and made his way into the garden. The icy grass was crisp beneath his feet. He walked slowly, listening to the faint crackle of every step he took. Above him the stars glinted, the familiar constellations of Home, though moved by distance to an unusual position for this time of year. He had always been fascinated by astronomy.

There was the Hammer, the star of its cross point signifying north, but the Wyvern was in the east, not the north, and Jayaran and the Leopard were similarly displaced. He sought out the Piinaenii, that perfect pentagon of five stars that the superstitious still believed to be the house of Andur. They should have been high in the sky by now, but instead they were glimmering just above the eastern horizon. He had star-gazed frequently from the Residency in Iskarn, but had never gotten used to the strange distortion of the constellations' positions. Oh, he knew the reason *why*, of course. Everyone knew how Edrith spun on its axis and moved through the heavens, and it was logical that one should view a different portion of the celestial sphere when one travelled a quarter of the way around Edrith. But though his head might accept logic, deep down it still just felt wrong.

The heavens seemed so peaceful compared to all that happened below. Who knew what sights these distant stars looked down upon? As he stood there in contemplation Thomas felt a light touch upon his shoulders.

With a start he let out a yelp, involuntarily jumping half a foot into the air. He had not heard anyone approach behind him. Twisting around he stepped back in surprise. It was Rianda.

"I had not thought anyone else was awake at this hour," she said, smiling faintly.

"I'm sorry," Thomas stammered. "I didn't mean to...I wasn't..."

"I meant no accusation," the queen said, lifting her hand slightly as if in dismissal of the thought. "I am only surprised that you, also, are too troubled to sleep. Or is it simply restlessness and a love of the night sky that drives you from your bed?"

"Well, the stars are..." He tailed off. His training began to reassert itself. Remembering his manners, he stepped back and bowed.

"You also are troubled, Your Majesty?"

"Rianda, please." She looked irritated. "It's the middle of the night. If we cannot dispense with formality at this time then we're at a pretty pass indeed.

"Come, let us walk. It is too cold a night for standing."

He fell in beside her. She wore a white gown of finest organdie that fell smoothly to her ankles. Set with scatterings of opals and seed pearls it sparkled in the pale moonlight. A woollen shawl of textured cream and brown was wrapped about her shoulders for warmth, though despite her words she did not appear cold.

They walked together through the garden. To Thomas, there seemed to be an almost unearthly quality about it: the clear sky above, the peace of the garden, the beauty and poise of the young woman – a queen, no less – beside him. He did not dare to speak lest just a single word shatter the magical spell of the moment.

It was Rianda who first broke the silence.

"So tell me, Thomas." she asked gently, "what brings you here at this time?" With her words the world outside came flooding back. The garden was no less tranquil, the night no less crisp, but something of the enchantment of the moment was dispelled none the less.

"A vision," said Thomas reluctantly. His eyes took on a haunted, far away look, as the memory of what he had seen played again across his memory.

"What of? I had thought that you had been freed from the vision which had been troubling you when you first arrived."

"I have. But this was no better, save that it wasn't of people I knew. And I hope that it won't recur, like the last did.

"I was watching a city – I don't know where, but I think from this part of the world, judging by the buildings. It had been destroyed. Utterly desolated. And not by any ordinary battle. There were demons stalking the streets. Horrible things, terrifying. I recognised the *rahvashda* that chased us in Erd Gellin and there were others, all sorts. I don't know what they all were.

"But there weren't any people, that was what was worst of all." He had needed to talk of this. Somehow, this meeting here, outside of the normal activity of the day, removed the formality that formed a barrier between himself and Rianda. He felt he could talk to her now quite naturally, almost as if she were an old friend.

"There weren't any people," he repeated. "I looked, but couldn't see any. Nothing but the demons and this thick mist that covered everything, at least until the riders came up."

"Riders?"

"They were all dressed in black, but seemed to be ordinary humans, except for the leader. They wouldn't have looked out of place in the Empire's cavalry – or yours – except that their uniform and standard bore no devices. But the leader, I don't know what he was, but no human, that I'm sure of. The demons shrank back away from him as he passed. He reeked of the sand. And at the end, he turned and looked at me – straight at me it seemed, though I don't know if he really saw me." Thomas shuddered.

"But that was just at the end. And in some ways it was better than the rest: at least you'd know where you were if you were facing him. The rest: it had just all been destroyed. Total desolation. Even the cathedral was ruined. It had domed spires like all the churches do here, three of them, and they were all shattered. It seemed a mockery. Hell must be like that: Andur's power put to mockery by a host of demons."

Thomas stopped, realising that Rianda was no longer at his side. He turned round. She had halted mid-stride, a few paces back. Her expression was ghastly. He had never before seen her show emotion so vividly.

"Your Majesty? Rianda? Are you alright?"

She looked up at him with a face like death. It had been drained of all colour: pallid in the moonlight.

"You've described Hyrakos," she said hollowly. "The triple dome of the cathedral was renowned throughout the land. There was none like it in Laurentia. The meaning of your vision is unmistakeable."

Hyrakos. Thomas knew the name. Euthymios had told him of it. It was the city that had been abandoned to Erd Gellin at the start of winter.

"You believe that the Gellinese have done this?" The thought sent chills down Thomas's spine. What he had seen might be happening now, not in some far off future or land. He thought of the preparations for the coming invasion currently being made all over Elaran and prayed with renewed fervour that they would be successful.

"No," answered Rianda. "It is I who have done this." Though her voice remained level, a slight quiver betrayed how close she was to losing control of it. If she did so, she would break down completely.

"I made the decision to abandon Hyrakos," she continued bitterly. "I forced it through, against the advice of my counsellors. I abandoned them to their fate.

"I can still remember my words. 'Better for the people of Hyrakos to lie under Gellinese rule for one winter, than for all Elaran to suffer their tyranny in perpetuity.' That's what I said, secure in my palace here in Hyrnar. But it is they who have paid the price."

"Perhaps it may not have happened," offered Thomas, clutching at straws. "Euthymios has said the visions sometimes show what might be, instead of what is. And I haven't yet learned how to tell the difference."

"No. It has happened – it is happening now. Did Euthymios not also say that the more likely a thing is, the more likely it is to appear? And though you may have visions of false futures, you will not see false pasts. I have no doubt you viewed it at this very moment. I will not cling to false hope. I have betrayed Hyrakos; at the least, I can face my guilt with honour."

"But you could not have known..."

"I should have known – I am the queen!" The silence that followed that self-accusatory cry seemed almost solid in its thick weight. "The clues were all there. You had told me of the demons that pursued you; we had all heard the rumours.

"Do you think excuses matter to those who have died, or worse? Mine is the responsibility, just as mine was the authority that condemned them. All that is left now is to pray that their sacrifice will be enough to save the rest of Elaran from a like fate."

Thomas realised he was standing close to her. Involuntarily he had moved towards her, wanting to comfort her somehow in her despair but unsure how. Rianda, too, suddenly seemed to realise their proximity. Taking a step backwards she took refuge from her grief in formality.

"I would appreciate it if you did not speak of this vision to others. My people are troubled and I would not have them disturbed unnecessarily by matters that they can do nothing about. Similarly, I would ask your permission to speak of what you have told me to Euthymios and others of my High Council."

"Of course, Your Majesty," Thomas replied, stiffly. The sudden change of tone had taken him aback. "I would also wish to tell Abbot Jarlod, of the Velnerine Order, of the vision. He has impressed upon me the importance of telling him the full details of any vision if he is to make progress with my teaching."

"You may do so. Euthymios assures me that the Abbot's discretion can be relied upon.

"I will now return to my quarters. I thank you for what you have told me."

Still somewhat bemused by the turn the conversation had taken, Thomas watched her walk back to the palace. She carried herself with poise, a smooth glide with her body and head erect. Only as she passed around the corner – no doubt she thought she had passed out of his sight – did she relax her control, her body sagging suddenly as if all the life had gone out of it.

#

The spectacle below did nothing to shift Lord Trevelyan's black mood. To outward appearances he was the quintessence of authority and dignity, but had any of those watching looked closely at his eyes, the listless indifference within would have been quickly revealed. The very finery of his office seemed a mockery and the pomp and circumstance of this naval review was only an added knife in the wound. Those around him – those who counted, at least – knew full his well his circumstances. Yet still they all, himself included, maintained the polite pretence, going through the motions of ceremony and governance as if the debacles had never occurred.

Sometimes it suited him. He stared out over the parapet. The same westerly wind that stiffened the sails of the Imperial fleet below sped another ship, less welcome, ever closer.

A mail packet had been sighted yesterday off Millisa Head. The first ship from Home since winter; the first that could bring word of how the disasters that had beset him – the Iskarn massacre, the sack of Atavus – had been received. In under two weeks it would be docking at Autigen and Trevelyan had no illusions as to the message it carried.

Dismissal and disgrace. Without a doubt he would be stripped of his rank and office. What, he wondered bleakly, would be the reason given? Rank incompetence? Unlikely – even from their armchairs in Wenlock they might find that hard to stomach. No, it would be something like 'insufficiently rigorous analysis of the strategic position, leading to the occurrence of undesirable events that could otherwise have been prevented'. The usual civil service verbal circumlocutions, saying nothing at all, yet saying everything.

There would be no evading the bullet. One such catastrophe could – possibly – have been tolerated, but not two. No viceroy since the reconquest had suffered such a setback and been so unable to take punitive measures against those responsible.

Such a failing was particularly inexcusable in peacetime. For it was peacetime: a naval review such as the one taking place now was only possible in times of peace. Five ships of the line led the way, spearheaded by the flagship Dauntless, a fine seventy-two gun three-decker with a complement of over five hundred men. A round dozen frigates followed, with a smattering of sloops and smaller craft making up the tail. Over eighty percent of the Southern Laurentian Fleet was displayed before him now; in the north, he knew, a similar display of the Northern Laurentian Fleet would be simultaneously taking place off Pelagin. In war such an assemblage would be impossible; the ships would be dispersed along the coast of the enemy, blockading their ports and scouring the trade routes for merchant shipping.

The Haldane, the Triumph, the Redoubtable: the names of the ships brought little comfort either. Well, what did he expect, he told himself. Wallowing in self-pity would do little good. Even in the depths of his despair he hardly expected them to change the names of the ships for him!

The Iilanthaed brought a wry smile to his face. Now that was a name more suited to his mood. Named after the admiral, of course, the hero of the Battle of Relladan, but those like him who still knew Alanyae could make out the name's original provenance: "bringer of ill-fate". An unfortunate name for a man, he reflected, particularly in those days when knowledge of Alanyae was more common. Now, of course, there was probably not one man in a thousand who could speak it.

Why did his own knowledge of it make him proud? It was a bastard tongue; a hybrid of the noble Evvenyae that every schoolboy learned and Avallan, the language of the Triune Empire today.

It had already been in decline five hundred years ago when the Empire had been founded. Its slow slide into disuse had only accelerated after the Charter of Unification had been signed and the three major nations of Avalonia were knotted into the Triune Empire. With Avallan the language of both Kett and Regensheim, both more populous than Venyaemos, it became almost by default the lingua franca of the Empire, though Dalradian of course survived as a scholarly tongue. The greater movement of people, particularly the move from the countryside to the cities as first agriculture, then industry, began to modernise only hastened its demise.

However, it was the Variscan War that plunged the last nail into Alanyae's coffin. In the wake of that ruinous struggle, in which the Empire had only just survived, much weakened, few wished to cling to things that marked them out as different. Alanyae was only one of many relics discarded as people cleaved to a sense of belonging in the Empire as a whole. Now, a hundred and fifty years on, it was only spoken by a few peasants in the more backward areas, a handful of scholars and the members of a couple of dozen old Venyaemic families that had kept the tradition alive.

Why, then, did he feel proud of the knowledge? He didn't know. But it gave a man something to cling to; particularly now, when he had failed the Empire and all that he had devoted his life to. Not that it gave him any more to fall back on.

What would happen to him if he returned to the Empire? There would be the inevitable hearing before a Select Committee of the House which would, no doubt, largely exonerate him, attributing the matter to circumstances beyond his control, with the caveat that he had – so they would say – done his best when given a responsibility beyond his capabilities. Some sinecure would be found for him; one of the innumerable offices with no real power or responsibility, just an impressive sounding title for the impressing of the ignorant. On the surface, life would go on as before – his acquaintances were far too civilised to cut him openly – but somehow, things would be different: he would be subtly excluded, apologetically but firmly left out of the things that mattered. The Scahanian princes had had a method of torture by which the victim was driven to madness by the endless repetition of a thousand feather blows; they could have taken lessons from the Triune establishment. Oh, that life might be well enough for the idle or the vain but for Trevelyan it did not bear thinking about. With an angry shake of his head he dismissed it from his mind.

The thought of retiring to Northcote House, his family estate, was no more appealing. Both an empty life of country sports and the local society and the more contemplative existence of scholarship and gardening were each equally unappealing. He had none of the compensations that would make an existence of growing roses palatable. His wife had died of cholera in his third year in Scahania and their marriage had borne no fruit.

No, there was nothing for him back Home. Better by far to humble himself to the new Viceroy and accept a lesser position here. It would take some getting used to: the Scahanian Viceroy exercised a degree of control over the Empire's Laurentian holdings that dwarfed the power of any other administrator – in terms of day-to-day checks on his authority, he had far fewer than many of those above him, even the Triumvirate and Prime Minister.

Although accepting a lesser position might be unconventional, it was not unheard of. It would have to be somewhere outside of Autigen: it would be too galling to see another mismanaging things in the palace where he had so recently ruled. Pelagos province would do nicely: though technically under the aegis of the viceroy, the north-western province was far enough away from the core Scahanian provinces of the Empire in Laurentia to enjoy a fair degree of autonomy. He had, in any case, always gotten on well with the current governor.

There was even, he thought, allowing himself just the barest hint of a smile, the possibility that whoever displaced him might find himself equally overtaken by circumstances. He had been reading the reports of young Maynard, now comfortably ensconced in Elaran, and, unless he was much mistaken, with the spring winds would come a firestorm.

That would be small comfort if he was seeking a reinstatement: the Colonial office might forgive, but it did not forget. Extenuating circumstances do not excuse a blunder: that way lies decadence. How often in the past had he repeated that same maxim?

No, reinstatement was an impossible dream – but there were other compensations. The Great Western Desert, it was clear to him, lay at the centre of these unexpected events. To the east of it lay the Barrens of old Varisca, Erd Gellin and Elaran, where demons had been sighted, an Imperial outpost massacred and where Erd Gellin was launching a war of aggression backed by dark forces. To the west of the desert lay Atavus, decimated two months ago by mythical sand elementals in an attack that had come from nowhere. Trevelyan had not yet put all the pieces together, but he was in no doubt that the same sinister power lay behind both disturbances. The only question was: what would it do next?

He could do nothing to help the Elarani against Erd Gellin. Most of the other borders of the Great Western Desert were closed: in the south it was bounded by the Atavine Bay and to much of the north lay the Gralbakh Mountains. But in the north-west the mountains fell away to hills and then to flat, fertile plain: the southern border of the Imperial province of Pelagos. An obvious target for the next invasion. It should be easy enough to obtain an appropriate position there. It was enough of a step down that the world would interpret it as a gesture of humility and a continued desire to serve, despite his disgrace.

With him there Pelagos would not be unprepared. It would feel very good to strike a blow against whatever powers had cast him down. It would be interesting, he thought with anticipation, to see how this mysterious foe fared against the readied might of an Imperial province.

Chapter Fifteen

Blessings From Above

"The mysterious figure in Thomas's vision continues to disturb me."

"Must we dwell forever on the subject, Euthymios?" said Rianda wearily. "We've discussed the vision endlessly from every possible angle and made no progress. Whilst terrible, it has no material effect on our plans, save to reinforce the imperative of resisting successfully. And that was something we didn't need. No one has questioned our will, only our ability."

"Do not be too bitter, my daughter. There is hope yet."

"Slim hope."

"But even a slim hope is far better than none at all. That's why I dwell on this figure: it is the one aspect of young Thomas's vision that provides more information as to Erd Gellin's mysterious new power. The Archons have always been rapacious, but never before have they had demons and drogkhar to carry out their schemes.

"I had been puzzled. It is simply not feasible for a nation to gain skill in the dark arts with such rapidity. I had wondered if they'd reawakened some dormant power that had lain buried in dead Varisca and that may still be so. But the vision suggests something else."

"What?" Rianda was curious, in spite of herself.

"Thomas said the figure reeked of sand; of the sterile wastes of the Great Western Desert. Does this not suggest something to you, my daughter?" Euthymios's voice grew animated. Without giving her space to reply he continued.

"The Forces of the Sand! Our own myths speak of them in whispers, as do those of our neighbours to the south and west. And it is known that the Atavine Empire was overcome by their actions, though that was so long ago that we know little of the details of the event.

"In the days of the Atavines the desert was less than half the size it is now; it is less than five hundred years since it overran the western plains of Erd Gellin. Could it be hungry again?"

"I can see that you have given the matter much thought, Euthymios. And perhaps it may help us in the long term. But in the short term we must first survive the spring offensive.

"Ever since word was confirmed of demons our wizards have been considering ways to counter them whilst still maintaining a robust screen against more conventional battle magics. Unless there is something more they can do against these Forces of the Sand, this vision of Thomas Maynard is nothing but a distraction."

Euthymios sighed. "You are right, my queen. But still, I cannot help taking the longer view – there may be a time in the not so distant future that we will be glad of such knowledge."

"We may indeed," said Rianda. "Then we shall be glad indeed of your knowledge. But first we must survive the spring." Standing suddenly she strode across the room.

"What a gift that man has! If only he could control it. To see at will what the enemy forces were doing: that would be worth an entire chiliad, if not more."

"I know." Euthymios joined her at the window. "The vision of a True Seer passes all magical boundaries. Even the best defences of the Gellinese mages would not prevent their secrets from lying bare before us. Thank the Blessed Ruth that she has bestowed her servant upon us, but for all her munificence it is a boon that brings small comfort as yet."

"How does the Abbot say he's progressing?"

"Slowly, but some progress. In truth he does not know. Not that I blame him: he is like a blind man leading the sighted through a dark tunnel: neither can see an inch, but at least the blind has more experience of how to approach the conditions.

"It could be worse. At least we seem to be winning his loyalty, or at least his sympathy. Imagine if the Gellinese had tried to do the same instead of trying to kill him?"

Rianda felt her stomach clench. The possibility did not bear thinking about.

"Their own arrogance put that beyond their reach. The Archons are confident enough in their own strength to feel no need of such aids – all that they desired was to deny him to us.

"But the Imperials have, all unknowingly, granted us a great gift. By ordering him to remain here we have gained the space to win him over. Had they brought him straight back..."

"He would have died," said Euthymios bluntly. "The Imperials have no lore of the True Seers, and even the most talented of their arcanists could scarcely have unravelled the mysteries in time to save him. There are..."

He broke off as the door burst open. Who would intrude upon the queen without knocking? Kadmos perhaps – but the breathless figure who entered was not the Sword Marshal, but a young servant who Euthymios recognised as one of the *anaedesh's* runners, an initiate into the brotherhood who tended the communication orbs.

"Your Majesty. Your Grace." The young man bowed low, remembering his manners despite his hurry. He had clearly been running.

"A message from the Linnarson *variideshar,* Your Majesty. The *anaedesh* said I was to bring the transcript as fast as I could." Still panting, he handed over the carefully folded paper, marked with the *anaedesh's* seal, to Rianda. Had the seal been broken the runner could have faced charges of treason. It was a harsh discipline but a necessary one: charged with receiving and transmitting the secrets of kingdoms, *anaedeshi* had to be beyond trustworthy and their apprenticeship was accordingly hard.

Surprised, Rianda cracked the seal with her thumb and unfolded the message. It was rare for a transmission to demand such urgency. Had it been from Kurdon or the northern border she would have feared the worst – but what bad news could possibly come from tiny, wealthy, scrupulously neutral Linnarson?

She scanned down the document. Euthymios waited for some indication of its contents. As he watched, Rianda began to tremble. She reached the end of the message and began to read it once more; then again for a third time. Eventually, even Euthymios's patience could bear it no longer.

"What is it, my daughter?"

Wordlessly she handed over the message. Soon he was in as much shock as Rianda.

"To Her Nemessine Majesty, Rianda of Elaran, by the Grace of Andur Queen of Elaran, Lord of the Har Mareisch," it began formally, "I approach you as a most humble servant of holy St. Senren, honoured vassal of the most high Andur, Lord of Order." Startled, Euthymios began to quickly scan down the rest of the message.

"Whereas it is the duty of every Senrenite knight to serve order and justice above all...Andur, the seat and summit of all moral law...to honour Andur and St. Senren through valour in just war, on the side of righteousness...the confirmed reports of demons, droghkar and other foul beasts of hell amongst the legions of Erd Gellin...and the fact that Benthos Valley, birth place of the blessed St. Senren and the ground where his holy flower first bloomed, lies within the confines of Elaran...would be a source of eternal shame to our order were its hallowed ground sullied by the feet of the wicked...do therefore pledge myself, together with my entire Hand of Senren, fully one hundred and fourteen knights, to your service and the defence of Elaran."

"Signed Sir Hanyarmé Morentes, Servant Captain of the Knights of the Most Holy Order of St. Senren," breathed Euthymios. "An entire Senrenite Hand to our aid! Even as soldiers alone they will be worth five times their number; their mystic prowess will double that. For the first time I no longer dread the onslaught of the Gellinese's unnatural allies."

"I can hardly believe it," said Rianda, still trembling. "Even a dozen would have been a boon beyond price, but an entire hand, unasked for?"

Suddenly unsure, she asked, "They are definitely coming, aren't they?"

Euthymios looked again at the transcript. "Yes," he answered. "Sir Hanyarmé states that the Vicar General has already granted his assent. He and his hand will be arriving in early spring, shortly before the fast of Doren Mur. Just in time, in fact. Though the snows that are delaying the Gellinese will also, of course, prevent the Senrenites from arriving any earlier."

"I still cannot believe it," Rianda breathed. "And all because St. Senren's birthplace lies within our boundaries. What a matter on which to turn the fate of a nation!"

"Well, it was not the only factor, my daughter," said Euthymios didactically. "The presence of demons and drogkhar undoubtedly played a great part in initially attracting the Senrenites' interest."

Rianda ignored this. "Announce it to the Citadel, Euthymios. We will hold a grand ball in their honour to celebrate the Day of Rebirth, the coming of new life and a new hope. The jackals of Torridon will see we are unbowed by the coming threat. We must not lose face before them: any appearance of weakness will cause them to leap upon us and tear us apart. Let all the world know of our new allies and undaunted spirit; that lets us celebrate even on the very eve of war.

"And let my people celebrate the good news. They have need of hope in these dark times."

#

Where was Lawrence? Thomas hurried through the Citadel corridors. He wasn't in his quarters – not that that was surprising, he'd barely seen him for weeks. Thomas was now realising that he had little idea where he might find him. What had the chaplain been doing with his days whilst Thomas had been spending time with Euthymios and the Velnerines?

Even on Longest Night they had not seen each other. Despite it being a relatively major holy day here in Elaran Thomas had not attended. Nor, if he had, did he imagine that he would have seen the chaplain: Lawrence would have been even less likely to attend than he had himself.

In Avalonia the day was the nadir of the year, the midpoint, when the powers of darkness and evil were strongest. Men huddled into houses and churches, praying to the power of Andur to keep them safe from harm. Though few these days believed that demons and spirits really haunted the land, the symbolism remained.

Here in Laurentia though, Longest Night seemed to have been adopted by the devotees of Ruth – Our Lady of Silence, as they called her. Rather than symbolising the power of evil, the darkness represented Ruth's shroud of silence, the enigmatic mystery and concealment of the blind and deaf sister of Andur Astartes.

The whole concept of Ruth worship mystified Thomas. In the Scriptualist tradition, Ruth was no more than a minor player in the Book of Andur. Andur Astartes's twin, it was mentioned that she was born blind and deaf: other than that she made few appearances, usually in conjunction with other members of His family. The Book certainly didn't say she was a goddess.

Euthymios had tried to explain it to him once, referring to books of the Book of Andur that Thomas had never heard of and, inevitably, to Larach's *Annalia*. According to him, Ruth was divine, but of a lesser divinity than her brother's, who was Andur's incarnation – and thus Andur Himself. That was why, so the bishop said, that, though immortal, she had not been assumed into Heaven but still walked the earth today. Supposedly Rianda's grandfather had seen her in his youth, though he had not recognised it until after the fact.

Thomas had to admit that his mind boggled a bit at the last statement – an immortal demi-goddess who wandered mysteriously across Laurentia? – but, to be honest, he had never been much of a one for religion or theology. He paid his dues to Andur each Sodtar and then left the rest up to Him. As for the Laurentians, Lawrence and others might launch polemics against the heresies of Canonical doctrine but for Thomas – like most other Triunes in this day and age – they worshipped Andur, so that was enough for him. Not like the pagans down in Scahania or in the Yang-Tsu Empire and the Kingdom of Imako on Borallia.

Despite that, Longest Night seemed a step too far. It was not that he violently objected to Ruthine worship in the way Lawrence did – if the ceremony had been at some other point he would no doubt have gone along. He just would have been profoundly uncomfortable to be sitting there in that sort of silent contemplation on Longest Night, given its usual connotations back Home. Particularly when the forces of darkness seemed all too close; just a couple of hundred miles away over the southern border.

However, as well as avoiding the company of others on that day, he and Lawrence had also avoided the company of each other. It was strange, Thomas reflected. Back in Iskarn they had been relatively friendly acquaintances but the close proximity into which they had been forced by their recent hardships had served to drive them apart rather than bind them together. The journey had caused both to see the other more clearly, in particular the differences between them. Once in Hyrnar they had both, almost deliberately, gone their separate ways.

But now, for the first time in weeks, Thomas felt a need to talk to a fellow countryman. The news of the Senrenites – and of the grand ball – had spread like wildfire through the Citadel. For the first time since he had arrived, Thomas could sense people's optimism. The air was heady with it.

Thomas had also felt swept up in the pervasive mood. Even if it was all more peripheral to him, it was hard not to care about a place in which you had spent two months – and which had been so welcoming. In addition, Thomas did not like to think of the slim chance that he and Lawrence would have of ever reaching Imperial territory again if Elaran was defeated and overwhelmed. It would be the flight from the Residency all over again.

It was hard to be excited if there was no one to share it with. Understandably, the news had meant that Euthymios was now busier than ever, the few small hours of spare time he had had vanishing in the necessity of preparing for the Senrenites. The same was true of Kadmos and the others who spoke Dalradian. Thomas's Elarani was still too poor for him to have ever spoken much to the servants and other common folk of the Citadel. With Lawrence he could revel in the good news; together they could discuss its implications and savour with anticipation the time, only a few months away now, that they would be Home once more – or, at least, back in Imperial territory.

However, a fruitless wandering through corridors and rooms had brought Thomas full circle, back to Lawrence's quarters. If he was honest with himself the search had been an exercise in hope – if Lawrence had frequented this area of the Citadel, other than to sleep, they would have bumped into each other more frequently in the weeks they had been here. Remembering the chaplain's habits in Iskarn, Thomas wondered if perhaps Lawrence had been venturing into the town below the Citadel. If so he could search all day with no success.

"*Iinala*!" he called, catching the attention of a passing servant. "*Âealiri-na Lawrence*?"

"*Qii*?"

"*Lawrence. Âealiri-na*?" He was sure that was right. Third person singular interrogative, with the suffix to indicate it was place that was questioned. This language had the same counter-intuitive sentence structure as Evvenyae.

"*Lawrence*?" The man still seemed not to understand.

"*Lawrence.*" He pointed at the former chaplain's room.

"*Ii, Lawrence.*" The servant pronounced it differently; the vowel sounds drawn out and diphthongised. A torrent of Elarani poured out from him. Thomas could comprehend perhaps one word in six, if that.

"*Laealaasii,*" Thomas managed to interject at last. Slowly. Bit by bit, he managed to make sense of some of what the servant had been trying to tell him. A couple of months was no time to learn a language properly, but he wished now he had spent more time practising in Elarani with Euthymios, instead of conversing entirely in Dalradian, a second language to both, but one in which they were both fluent.

It appeared that Lawrence was likely to found in an area called the Paddock. Thomas had heard it mentioned before – it was to the south-east of the palace, beyond the formal gardens and only just within the confines of the Citadel proper. The Citadel's livestock was kept there, if he remembered correctly. Thomas hadn't been there yet: the weather since their arrival had made explorations outside less than appealing.

For that matter, he wondered what Lawrence was doing there. Whilst the chaplain had never paid much heed to wind or weather, he had also never, so far as Thomas was aware, been interested in horses. However, asking the servant merely provoked another flood of incomprehensible Elarani.

The language barrier was too great for Thomas to try to surpass it again. He would no doubt find out soon enough what Lawrence was doing there when he arrived. So, after ascertaining from the servant that a person named Ven Tychon was likely to be in authority, Thomas thanked him – he could say that much, at least, without difficulty – and bade him farewell.

The Paddock, when he reached it, was both large and bare. The closest part of it was also relatively flat, something unusual in this Citadel upon two hills. Thomas wondered to what extent it was artificial. Beyond this section the Paddock sloped away to the south-west, longer by far than it was wide.

Someone had laboriously cleared snow off the flattish part, an area at least one hundred yards on each side. Beneath, the grass lay dead, the blackened blades mirroring the leafless trees that formed a line between the Paddock and the palace, shielding it from view.

Nearby, beside the line of trees, stood eight great barns, each more than two hundred feet wide. These, thought Thomas, must be the living quarters of the great *tarath*. Beyond them, he could make out more numerous, smaller constructions, no doubt the stables of the *tarath's* smaller cousins, the *tarathin*. He hadn't realised that these beasts were housed here, although in retrospect his assumption that the Paddock was only for horses seemed naive. The Elarani would hardly house such valuable beasts of war as *tarath* and *tarathin* outside the defences of the Citadel.

From where he stood the field seemed deserted. Unsure what else to do Thomas began to make his way over to the *tarath* barns. Surely there would be someone there who could direct him to either Lawrence or Ven Tychon.

His cheeks burned from the cold. He had thought that he had wrapped up warmly, but clearly not warmly enough. It was still only a few days past Longest Night, the mid-point of the year, and the weather was bitter indeed for one raised in the Triune Empire. This, thought Thomas wryly, remembering his examinations for the Laurentian Civil Service, was what a continental weather system at high altitude meant in practice. The bitter temperatures of double digits below freezing had seemed more distant when writing about the climatic influences on trade winds in a warm examination hall in Wenlock.

As he approached the barns two *tarathin* appeared from the south-west. No doubt they had spied him from above and now hastened to see who this stranger was in the Paddock. Thomas squinted to try to make out their riders but the afternoon sun lay directly behind them. It was impossible to make out any details through the glare.

Almost directly above, the beasts began to spiral down, the leathery wings banked in a slow glide. They were close enough now for Thomas to see the riders clearly. The first was a short, stocky man who wore the uniform of the army of

Elaran. To Thomas he seemed somewhat familiar; he tried to remember where he had seen the man before. But then such thoughts were forgotten at the sight of the second rider. It was Lawrence.

Thomas was stunned. The *tarathin* landed, Lawrence slipping down from his mount's back with the same practised ease and grace as his companion. In the air he had similarly displayed the easy competence of a professional. Was this the same Lawrence who had been nervous and uneasy around horses: the worst rider in the Residency?

Laughing, Lawrence, staved off the host of questions that poured overflowing from Thomas.

"Enough, enough," Lawrence said, hands up in mock surrender. "I'll tell you everything in a moment; just give me time to catch breath. First though let me introduce you to Ven Tychon, Elaran's Air Captain, to whom I am profoundly indebted for his teaching and patience. Tychon, as I'm sure you've guessed, this is Thomas Maynard, my companion on the way here, who I've often mentioned."

Somewhat coldly, Ven Tychon shook Thomas's hand. With a start Thomas recognised him as the Elarani officer whom he had seen a number of times on his visits to the Velnerine hospice. On those occasions too, the man had looked at him somewhat unwelcomingly. Thomas wondered what Lawrence had said of him.

However, such thoughts were soon swept away by the flood of questions inside him. Lawrence's whole demeanour had altered; he was now visibly more confident, physically self-assured in a way that he had not been before. The diffidence mixed with defensiveness that had always characterised him in the past was nowhere to be seen.

"It's amazing," said Thomas tritely. "I would never have imagined you as a *tarathinaki*. How did you begin learning?"

"Serendipitously." Lawrence smiled. "Or perhaps it wasn't entirely a coincidence. Ven Tychon took me in hand shortly after we arrived, just I hear that Euthymios did for you. After I'd begun to settle in, one day he suggested I accompany him on a *tarathin*.

"I'll admit, I was dubious when he suggested I take the reins. But as soon as I'd done so I forgot my trepidation. Tychon was right behind me if anything had gone wrong, but nothing did: it was one of the most exhilarating experiences of my life."

"He took to it like a yale to a mountain ridge," interjected Tychon. "I've almost never seen someone so good."

"Since then we've spent most of our time down here in the Paddock. I've been able to join the other *tarathinakii* in their training. Without it I think I would have gone mad: there are none here who share our faith and your heretic bishop won't allow me to preach in his cathedral. But here I feel there is really something I can be doing. Flying – I just can't describe it. The feeling I get is the closest one could get physically to being with Andur.

"But I'm sure this wasn't what first brought you in search of me. Is there news from the Empire?"

Thomas smiled to himself. There was still a little of the old Lawrence left, but it seemed new vistas had opened up inside the chaplain.

"Well, your news of what you've been doing is at least as unexpected as what I'd come to tell you. You'll have to give me a demonstration soon.

"But yes, I do bring news. Not from the Empire, unfortunately, but important nonetheless. Ven Tychon, you will be interested in this as well." Swiftly, Thomas explained the details – at least what he knew of them – of the Senrenites' offer of aid.

"That's astonishing," said Tychon. "Unlooked-for aid of the highest quality. One hundred Senrenites! My grandfather fought in the Pelagic wars and often told me of the glory of a Senrenite charge. This might be enough to turn the tide."

He turned to Lawrence. "Lawrence, I'm afraid that I must leave you. First Chiliarch Nomiki may wish to speak to me of the plans for the coming campaign. I don't think that the presence of the Senrenites will greatly affect Nomiki's plans for the *tarathinakii*, but there may still be matters he wishes to discuss. I assume you will be continuing your practice – and do feel free to show your countryman anything that he wishes."

Shaking hands, more warmly this time, with Thomas, Ven Tychon spun smoothly and strode off in the direction of the Har Magisteris. His walk was fluid, graceful and swift; he was soon lost to sight beyond the line of trees.

"Well," said Thomas, feeling slightly awkward. The sudden departure of Tychon had left Thomas and Lawrence alone, and Thomas was feeling slightly unsure of what to say. It had, after all, been over a month since they had seen each other properly.

"Shall I show you what I've learned?" asked Lawrence. His keenness to demonstrate his newfound skill at flying overcame any similar awkwardness that he might have been feeling.

"Yes, definitely," answered Thomas, seizing the offered line gratefully. Doing something concrete was always an aid to conversation.

Lawrence moved towards his *tarathin*, then stopped as he realised Thomas was not following.

"Well, come on," he said.

"You mean, actually fly on it?" Thomas said nervously. He hadn't counted on this when Lawrence had first suggested it – he had assumed he'd be watching from the ground.

"Of course. How can I show you anything properly from down here? You've flown on *tarath*, haven't you? This really is no different – you'll just be a passenger, and the harness is quite secure."

With some trepidation Thomas edged towards the beast. It was true, he had indeed flown on a *tarath*, a number of times in fact, but those great beasts were considerably larger than their smaller cousins. With its broad back and wingspan of nigh on two hundred feet, being on a *tarath* felt relatively secure. For one thing, you couldn't see the ground.

This, on the other hand, would be quite different. Sitting astride its body like a horse, your legs would be dangling in mid air. Thomas didn't feel the stirrups and harness would be much comfort. Though a twenty-foot wingspan might sound a lot, looking at it now it seemed awfully little to hold up two people, as well as the beast itself.

The *tarathin*, oblivious to the less than flattering scrutiny to which it was being subjected, continued placidly to feed, cropping the grass with firm sideways tugs of its long, ridged beak. At Lawrence's coaxing it lowered its wings, previously swept back into a high arch over its back, to allow its two riders on board.

"Well, it seems secure enough," said Thomas dubiously, testing the strength of the harness. Lawrence had deftly and expertly bound him into place, fastening the buckles and tying the knots with the swiftness of one fully accustomed to the procedure before following suit for himself. Although the arrangement seemed satisfactory enough, Thomas still wasn't entirely convinced it would restrain his full weight should he lurch sideways out of the saddle whilst in midair.

"What of Tychon's *tarathin*?" he asked, trying to find an excuse for delaying their takeoff. "Are we just going to leave it here?"

"Don't worry about it. It's well trained enough not to stray. Handlers will be along soon to take it into its barn." Indeed, two figures were already approaching them from the line of trees, no doubt instructed to do so by Ven Tychon on his way back to the Har Magisteris.

There was nothing more that could be done to delay it. Thomas told himself firmly to make the best of it. After all, hadn't he faced worse things – far worse, in fact? Still, he couldn't put to rest the knot of fear that was clenched inside his stomach. But he couldn't back out now. He suspected that Lawrence – who clearly had no such anxieties about heights – already knew exactly what he was feeling, and he'd be judged before Andur before giving him any more satisfaction. Going through with it couldn't be that bad.

Despite his intense concentration, the moment of takeoff still took him by surprise. As the leathery beast launched itself skyward Thomas's stomach dropped away. He bit down hard to prevent a scream and then the air was rushing by and his body was straining against the ropes of the harness, almost horizontal, or so it felt, as Lawrence banked the *tarathin* in a wide sweeping spiral upwards.

At first Thomas could do nothing but grip, white-knuckled, to the straps of his harness. The ride was as terrifying and exposed as he had feared. The *tarathin*'s relative smallness changed the entire motion of the flight. Rather than the steady glide, the measured wing beats of *tarath* flight, the *tarathin* surged forward with each wing beat, jolting and jarring its passengers.

Or jarring Thomas at least. He noticed that Lawrence, in front of him, rode out each wing beat smoothly, body moving in synchrony with the beast. Then he gasped again as Lawrence took the *tarathin* into a long, low glide, skimming almost to the ground before rising high once more.

Consciously, Thomas made himself relax his grip. This was safe; people did it every day. He forced himself to breathe slowly and steadily, calming his mind. Though the physical discomfort did not decrease his thought became clearer, no longer bound by clasps of fear. For the first time he dared to properly look down at the view below.

And what a view! The entire Citadel lay resplendent below them, dazzling in lines of crystalline white. Snowbound, the frost had transformed it from a squat fortress to a thing of beauty. Palace and cathedral both stood outlined in lace, a masterwork of winter's finest art. Not even the winter's snow could hide the strength and resilience that lay within. The underlying strength could not be concealed, an iron heart just beneath the surface that enhanced rather than diminished the majesty of the scene beneath. Resolute and enduring, the Citadel was Elaran's high tower of resistance.

One final time they swept over the Citadel's twin hills. Then they were off, Lawrence urging their steed to greater efforts. The wings beat faster; in a flash they had covered the full length of the Paddock. A copse reared up before them, one moment distant, the next beneath them. Lawrence expertly guided the *tarathin* down, landing gently on the edge of the trees.

"What did you think?" asked Lawrence, face shining with glee.

"Superb!" answered Thomas. Nor was he merely being polite. In the second half of the flight the exhilaration of the rushing air had seized him, catching him up in the wild abandon of the flight's speed. It had been terrifying, but glorious – though it would not be for him, he could understand why Lawrence had fallen in love with it.

As he fumbled with his harness, Lawrence had already slipped off the *tarathin*'s back and was tethering it to the tree. Before Thomas was even halfway through, Lawrence was at his side, swiftly unfastening the remaining straps. Together they wandered into the copse, seeking a place to sit sheltered from the wind.

The flight seemed to have broken down all the artificial restraints between them. Sitting on a long log a few feet within the tree line they talked freely, easily; it was as if they were back at the Residency, discussing the ways of the world over a game of sharom. In fact, Thomas reflected, he and Lawrence had always got on well, save for when the strain of two weeks of constant proximity had become slightly too much for both of them. Their lack of communication of the past couple of months undoubtedly had as much to do with their business and the different circles they had found themselves in, here in Hyrnar, rather than any conscious decision – at least after the first few days – to avoid each other. And that, he acknowledged, owed no small part to the efforts of their hosts. Being separated from each other yet welcomed by Euthymios and Ven Tychon had no doubt helped the Elarani to forge the chains of sympathy that now bound both of them to Elaran.

For despite the ease with which they talked, Thomas realised that he had been wrong to compare it to the days at the Residency. Both had been through much since then; not simply the flight across Erd Gellin. Here in Elaran both he and Lawrence had discovered talents that they had never known they possessed. His own status as a True Seer was stunning enough, but as Lawrence described his activities it was clear that the chaplain's talent, if more common, was scarcely less startling. Though Lawrence did not say so explicitly, reading between the lines it was evident that he excelled in his new profession; amongst the top rank of the *tarathinakii* here in the Citadel. A hidden talent, never before suspected, had suddenly been given the chance to emerge from the cloth of his vocation.

As they continued to speak, the conversation turned, inevitably, to the coming conflict. Thomas found that Lawrence was, surprisingly, more optimistic than he himself. But that, though he did not say so, probably reflected Ven Tychon's outlook upon life as opposed to the more realistic views of Euthymios.

"I wonder," said Thomas idly, "what view of it Piotr would take?"

"Why?" asked Lawrence.

"Oh, no reason really. He just always appeared very knowledgeable."

"Compared to us, yes. But I doubt he'd know more than the Elarani high council."

"You're probably right." Thomas stretched and stood up. "Shall we walk for a bit? It's too cold a day to sit still for long."

Lawrence rose and joined him. But as they neared the edge of the copse, Thomas felt something block out the sun. A harsh cry sounded overhead, too near, and a dark shadow dropped fast from above. Again the cry sounded. This was no *tarathin* that stooped upon them. Leaping back with a start, Thomas dived for the shelter of the copse, trying to escape.

Chapter Sixteen

Elders and Betters

Thud! Thomas felt as well as heard the impact of the creature's landing. The bare branches shook with the wind of its passage. Cowering, he tried to catch a glimpse of what it was, whilst simultaneously squirming deeper into the undergrowth.

To his surprise, he saw that Lawrence had not followed him into the bushes but instead was walking calmly towards the edge of the copse. Evidently realising that Thomas was no longer with him Lawrence turned and, seeing him crouching behind a tree, beckoned him forward with an exasperated gesture.

Feeling somewhat sheepish, Thomas trotted to catch up with Lawrence. He didn't think his action had been that unreasonable. After all, they'd been through enough on the flight from the Residency to make them sensibly wary of sudden surprises. And the thing certainly hadn't *sounded* like a *tarathin.* It wasn't his fault if Lawrence knew more about the creatures than he did: he couldn't be expected to recognise one on sight.

But when he reached the edge of the copse he realised that he had in fact been right. The creature that had surprised them was no *tarathin.* Sleek and powerful, the feathered, leonine body and eagle's head made the beast undeniably a gryphon. Thomas trembled. Gryphons were not native to the Triune Empire and were rare even here in Laurentia, the reclusive beings keeping predominantly to their eyries in the Elder Alliance and a few scattered locations in the Ventar range. The depictions that Thomas had seen in books had not remotely prepared him for the truth: whilst the basic details had been right, the pictures had been woefully inadequate at conveying both the beauty and raw strength of the majestic creature before him.

A gryphon might have a smaller wingspan than a *tarathin*, but those wings were more powerfully muscled by far, as was the body they supported. The foot-long talons – thankfully currently sheathed – and a beak large enough to snap him in half further amply illustrated additional very real differences between gryphons and *tarathin.* The only things that kept Thomas from bolting once more for the bushes was the beast's undeniably intelligent countenance and the fact that it was quite clearly sitting and listening to Lawrence telling them of their flight out.

"Grrreetings, Ambassador Maynard," said the gryphon and Thomas started once more to hear such a melodious, fluting voice issuing from that feral beak. "I am Kierrralllhion, of the Ellder Alliance.

"I have been lllooking for you allll over the Citadel. I couldn't find you anywhere but I fortunatellly I met Ven Tychon who tollld me that I might find you out here. You have not been here before, I belllieve? I have not seen you before, at llleast, and your frrriend, Lawrrrence, has told me much about you."

"No," stammered Thomas. "I mean yes – this is the first time I've been here. Why is it you've been looking for me?" Though he tried his hardest, it was hard not to flinch away from the stupendous creature.

"Ambassador Kvh‡r||xkltl!" – Thomas did his best not to leap away as Kieralhion snapped her beak sideways in frustration – "I can never prrronounce those Isp'te'rrran names – it needs a speciallll sorrt of mouth, not to mention chitinous forrre-lllimbs, which we gryphons simplly don't have. But the Ambassador would llllike to see you. And you as welll of course, Lawrrrence, but I knew where I would find you, wherrreas Ambassador Maynard here was much harder to find."

"Do you know what he wants to see me about?"

The gryphon looked at him in amazement. The feathered head was marvellously expressive. "Why, the Senrrrenites, of course. What elllse would he wish to see you about? I have never seen a Senrenite mysellf, but I am told that they make a magnificent sight, though no match for grrryphons, I am sure. But they are coming, arrre they not, and so he wishes to speak to you.

"Come on, come on," she continued impatiently, when Thomas did not respond immediately. "Lawrrrence can fllly you back to the palllace. Ourrr embassay is in a separate wing, on the south side of the Har Magisteris. They were worrrried about us disturrrbing peopllle, though why," – she arched her neck – "anyone should find a grrryphon disturbing I do not know. An isp'te'rrra, perhaps, but the Ambassador seldom ventures outside his quarters."

With that Kieralhion spread her wings – Thomas ducked, reflexively – and launched herself upwards. Thomas was still somewhat dazed from the rapid flood of words.

"But what do I have to do with the Senrenites?" he mumbled, but it was too late – the gryphon was already in the sky, climbing higher with each powerful wingbeat.

"I suppose we'd better do as she says," said Lawrence, with a shrug. "I've got so used to her ways by now that I'd forgotten what a shock she can be at first."

"It's not her ways," rejoined Thomas, "it's that beak. And those foot-long talons. She looks as if she could gobble us up in two seconds flat."

"Oh, come now – there are only a couple of instances each year of gryphons eating people." At Thomas's horrified expression, Lawrence laughed. "I'm only teasing. You should know that better than I. After all, you're the one who sat your Laurentian Service exams under a year ago – and I remember all those hours you spent studying Laurentian culture in the library.

"No," he continued, as he fastened first Thomas's harness, then his own. "Gryphons are entirely civilised, even if they are pagans. Kieralhion would no more dream of eating a human than you would."

Thomas nodded. He had known that really, but it was hard to remember theoretical facts when confronted with the living, breathing reality.

The *tarathin* laboured its way upwards with steady wing beats. This time, expecting it, Thomas was not so bothered by the motion. His mind, if not his stomach, had become accustomed to the motion. In fact, he was even beginning to enjoy it when his fragile composure was utterly shattered by a soul-chilling shriek from above.

Thomas screamed in unison as Kieralhion plummeted past them, wings swept back in a break-neck dive. Barely killing her speed she cleared the ground by a foot, wings unfurling and snapping out to bring her rocketing up once more, flashing up and over the *tarathin* like a bullet. Thomas forced himself to breathe steadily, fighting to bring his wildly racing heart under control.

It was then, watching the flashing antics of Kieralhion as she flew rings around their *tarathin* that Thomas learned an important lesson. Lawrence was a skilled *tarathinaki*, able to coax the very best out of his mount. But Kieralhion was a gryphon, a deadly predator shaped by nature over millions of years to be the master of the skies. A few tens of thousands of years of civilisation might have added a thin veneer of disguise, but it had done nothing to lessen the elemental strength and ferocity of the wild.

"So, how long have you been in Elaran for?" yelled Thomas as the gryphon darted past once more, seeking more to cause her to stop the aerobatic flying that was setting his teeth on edge. Despite twisting about like a teetotum – as much as one could on *tarathin*-back – he could never tell from which direction she was going to appear next.

Slowing, Kieralhion curved her wings back to sweep around in a long, slow arc, gradually losing height, until she intercepted their path a dozen *tarathin* wing beats further on.

"Since lllast spring. Alllmost a yearrr, now that you mention it. I came out rrright at the end of the yearrr; just before Midsummer; what you humans call High Scrrriansa. A short trrrip, but stillll, they allll flllapped their wings; clllacked their beaks..."

"A bit further away if you would, Kieralhion!" shouted Lawrence, fighting to control their *tarathin* which was reacting alarmingly to the proximity of the gryphon. Thomas's heart was in his mouth, the composure at flying that he had thought he had gained vanishing like the early morning mist.

Their mount fought Lawrence's commands; head bucking as it resisted the tugs of the reins. Had it been a simple bit and bridle that held it the head would long since have been free, but fortunately *tarathin* were held with stouter trappings.

"Away, further away!" called Lawrence again to Kieralhion. "Lean forward," he snapped at Thomas who obeyed with alacrity. Lawrence himself was flattened out against the beast, body stretched forward from the saddle, almost halfway down the neck. With one hand he held the reins, striving to maintain some form of command in the half-maddened beast, whilst with the other he fervidly stroked the *tarathin*'s neck, murmuring all the while in an effort to calm it.

Gradually the *tarathin*'s struggles eased as Kieralhion moved back to a less threatening distance. Thomas heaved a sigh of relief. The last few moments had been slightly too dicey for comfort. In the wild, *tarathin* would have been a natural prey of gryphons – in the fastnesses of the Gralbakh Mountains, where men seldom went, they still were. Some instincts were bred too deeply in the bone: even the best training could not prevent the natural terror that came from the close proximity of a predator. To expect otherwise, Thomas reflected, would be like expecting a horse to remain calm with a wild wolf totting by its side.

"I am sorrrry, Lawrrrence," trilled the gryphon. "I forget how stupid those beasts you rrride arrre. I rrreallly am not surrre why you bother: surrrely you humans could have found a better alternative by now."

Lawrence rolled his eyes. "We don't exactly have any other option. Unless you gryphons want to offer us your services."

"Oh no, that would never do! The necessary dorrrsalll muscllles would never suffice. And the indignity!"

"You were saying that the other gryphons were disapproving of you leaving the Elder Alliance," said Thomas, changing the subject. "Why was that?"

"Oh yes, so I was. What a to-do they made. You had never heard such a din; you would have thought I had suggested going acrrross the sea to your Trrriune Empirrre, or giving up flllying.

" 'Oh, Kierrralllhion,' they said, 'you arrre too young to leave the mountains; young grrryphons should stay clllose to theirrr eyrrrie; it is too dangerrrous outside; how willl you find enough to eat; what if yourrr featherrs fallll out...' and on and on untilll the skies falll in." A loud squawk showed Kieralhion's clear opinion of such nay-sayers.

"But someone must go on embassies, so why not me? It cannot alll be left to the *isp'te'rans*. We might find ourrrselllves llliving in caves! They would not do it anyway: the *isp'te'ra* have no great love for trrravellling far from theirrr hives. And so, why shouldn't it be me?

"I outflew everrry grrryphon from ourrr neighbouring eyrrries at the last Midsummer games. And this llittllle country is rrright next door. Therrre arrre stilll hillls, so I do not see why they should worrrry so. But still they carped like a flock of palsied lammergeiers. 'Send someone from another eyrrrie; why do you want to go away; we grrryphons should have nothing to do with the outside worllld.' The worllld could have turrrned purrrpllle and they would not be interested.

"But I ignored them. I received my name two summers ago and by custom, no adult grrryphon can be prevented from doing what they would, save that it harms anotherrr eyrrrie. So I went. Volllunteerrred for the embassy. And herrre I am."

With a pang Thomas realised that Kieralhion, for all her size and strength, was actually of an age with him. He did not know how long gryphons lived but they had both come of age within the last few years. No doubt she occupied a similar position in the embassy here as he had done in Erd Gellin.

"And do you enjoy it?" he asked.

"I do!" came the emphatic response. "You humans are strange crrreaturrres, but I am glllad I have seen you. Few come to the Ellllder Allllliance, and fewer stilll to ourrr eyrrries. Yes, verrry few – many in my eyrrrie have never seen a human. And some of you, lllike Lllawrrrence herrre, and otherrrs who can flly, I could alllmost think of as small gryphons." If Lawrence was startled by this comparison he did not show it. No doubt, Thomas reflected, he had heard it before.

"And these hillls arrre fascinating," she continued. "So lllow! How can you live without mountains? The high scarrrps; the snow-capped peaks; the delllicioussllly thin airrr of a crrrisp mountain morning? And the Citadelll; the other towns; why do you peopllle botherrr? It seems so much troubllle. But quite, quite, fascinating. No, I do not regret llleaving the mountains to see alll this!"

She turned a tight loop in the air, showing off her aerobatic skills once more.

"And herrre we arrre," said Kieralhion, gliding gently towards a tall tower that marked the end of the long south wing that jutted out from the rest of the palace like a peninsula. A large door stood at the base, the size of the great gate of his Chelmsthorpe college, though plain and without adornment. Clearly this had been designed for practicality, in deference to the large size of the creatures that would be using it, rather than for ostentation. The almost unweathered stonework surrounding the arch showed it to be of relatively recent construction compared to the rest of the Citadel. An equally incongruous pair of large shutters, about two thirds of the way up the tower, indicated the presence of an aerial entrance to what was undoubtedly Kieralhion's own quarters.

Delicately the gryphon landed followed, less gracefully, by Lawrence and Thomas. This time Thomas was able to unfasten himself from his own harness while Lawrence quickly went about the business of tethering the *tarathin*. Kieralhion watched impatiently for them to finish.

Inside, the room also had a subtle sense of difference. It was not the decoration or size; these could have belonged in any Elarani room in the Citadel. But the room still seemed more spacious. After a few seconds Thomas realised that it simply had less furniture – no chairs, for one thing, and fewer peripherals such as tables, ornaments and so forth. He reflected that creatures such as gryphons would have little liking or need for such clutter, not to mention the extra space that their larger bodies would need to manoeuvre easily around the dwelling. It was incredible what such small changes could make to the atmosphere of a room.

Trotting lightly across the ground Kieralhion led the way through a large archway at the far end of the room. Her claws sheathed, the footsteps padded softly on the polished marble floor. Thomas had half expected her to be ungainly on the ground, but for such a large animal she moved astonishingly agilely.

The two men followed her up a flight of unusually low stairs to a long landing on the floor above. Kieralhion gestured with her head towards a panelled door before them, extending her neck to indicate the direction.

"In therrre," she said.

Thomas looked at her with surprise. "Aren't you coming in with us?"

"No. The Ambassador has not asked to see me as welll. I willl see you anotherrr day, Lllawrrrence, and perhaps you alllso, Ambassadorrr Maynarrrd. But today is too fine a day to waste indoorrrs. If you find me laterrr you willl see some realll flllying, with no foolllish *tarrrathin* to slllow me down!"

The gryphon's absence left a tangible space. Without her, Thomas felt uncomfortably alone and exposed in the dimly lit hallway. Lawrence was no help. Now that he was out of his new-found element of the sky, the chaplain was visibly nervous, standing directly behind Thomas as if in that way he could hide himself. Tentatively, Thomas took a few steps towards the door.

Suddenly, from the shadows around the door a giant shape unfolded itself, though Thomas could have sworn there had been nothing there before. He stopped abruptly and took a slow step backwards, not wanting to inadvertently alarm this formidable sentinel. Behind him he heard Lawrence give a quickly suppressed yelp of alarm.

The creature, though roughly human in form, was as alien in its way as the outlandish shape fusion of the gryphon. Over ten feet tall, it towered over the two of them and in bulk was as solid and immovable as a mountain. The craggy form appeared to have been carved from the bedrock of the hills. This, then, was one of the famously reclusive *mokshtar*, the so-called warriors of stone, said to be kin to the mountains themselves.

"Go in," it said, in a voice of granite. As they hurried through the doorway, giving the *mokshtar* as wide a berth as possible, thoughts flashed through Thomas's mind of the myths that surrounded this ancient race, of the bitter wars of extinction that had been fought in the dawn of time between the *mokshtar* and their hated enemies, the *guradhak*. Long, brutal wars with neither mercy nor quarter that had left the *mokshtar* undisputed masters of the Gralbakh range, whilst the *guradhak* held sway in the fastnesses of the Har Meneth to the south. The Lays of Stone and Steel were ancient, dating to before the time of the Covenant, and the tales were millennia old even then, for the *mokshtar*, like the other elder races, had existed for aeons before humans had even crept out of their caves. Looking at the sheer power embodied in that massive frame, the legends seemed all too believable.

It was a relief to be able to enter the room and close the door behind them. Whilst an inch of wood might be a flimsy barrier to put between them and such a creature, the psychological difference was appreciable.

The Elder Alliance ambassador's quarters were even more dimly lit than the hallway outside. Only a pair of shuttered lamps gave off a faint glow. At first, Thomas could see almost nothing, but as his eyes adjusted he was able to make out more of the room.

A long, low shelf, perhaps three feet off the ground, ran around the room holding papers, strange ornaments and what appeared to be books, though some were made of an unusual material. In place of a conventional desk, two low, l-shaped tables, about the height of coffee tables, occupied each side of the room, similarly stacked with papers and documents in orderly, precisely arranged piles.

Between them stood the ambassador himself – or herself, to be accurate, though human convention dictated the use of the masculine pronoun for all neuter *isp'te'ran* castes. Jet-black, the long, low body was strangely beautiful. There was none of the repulsion that Thomas had expected to feel. Though the *isp'te'ra* certainly appeared ant-like – Thomas was aware that Linnarsonian scholars considered the *isp'te'ra* to be more closely related to termites but the distinction was moot, at least to him – its upright torso, distinct, if inscrutably alien, face and even its very size made it impossible to think of as an insect. Perhaps, he reflected, it was the contrast with what had gone before that made him so accepting. Whilst the *isp'te'ra* was undoubtedly a formidable warrior – he looked with a shudder at the wickedly elongated digit of each front claw that dwarfed the smaller, opposable digit – it was both refreshing and pleasant not to be facing a creature that would be able to snap you in two with a single blow.

The ambassador looked sharply up from the document he had been reading.

"Reverend Lawrence?" He turned to Thomas. "And you are the one they call Ambassador Maynard?" At their nods he continued.

"I am Ambassador Kvh‡r||xkltl, Ambassador of the Elder Alliance to Elaran." The *isp'te'ra's* voice was clipped and precise; its own name a mass of clicks and affricates that Thomas knew he could never have pronounced. Instinctively he bowed low. The *isp'te'ra* inclined his head in reply.

"Now," said Kvh‡r||xkltl, fixing Thomas in his gaze. "How much authority do you have over Triune policy for this region?"

"Very little, Your Excellency," admitted Thomas.

"I thought as much. Then we will waste no time on that matter. But you are also the one they think to be a True Seer. Are they correct?"

"I believe so, Your Excellency. I had found it hard to believe, but..."

"Very well. Now listen to what I have to say." Before that focused attention Thomas begin to feel like a bug being scrutinised under a microscope. Since the initial acknowledgement the ambassador had paid not the slightest attention to Lawrence.

"This country will be invaded within three months. It is likely to be defeated. Agreed?"

Thomas stuttered a reply. "With the Senrenites, and Euthymios has said..."

"Of course. The Queen believes it will hold. Perhaps it will. But the Senrenites will make less difference than people believe. One hundred men cannot hold back an army. Do *you* think this country can hold?"

"Perhaps." Thomas had had time to think now. "There is a chance. But the Queen is worried about her retreat from Hyrakos. She is not sure..."

"Exactly. I do not understand this. It was clearly the correct thing to do. One must not hesitate to sacrifice a member to save the hive. Thanks to this Elaran now has a chance. But now she is weak. She worries. It is why I feel this country will fall.

"I accept we cannot know the outcome yet. But you will admit that there is a danger of defeat?"

"Yes, of course..."

"And that if the Gellinese capture you they will kill you?"

"Yes." Thomas had learned to keep his answers brief.

"Then it is clear that you must flee. I offer you the shelter of the Elder Alliance. Come to us. We have lore that even Linnarson does not know. You will learn the art far faster than these petty priests can teach you. And the Archons' armies will never penetrate our mountain fastness. Your safety is assured."

That last was true at least. Two recent empires, the Variscans and the Pelagics, had broken their teeth upon the hard rock of the Elder Alliance. Although the Elder Alliance's territory bordered the northern Triune provinces on Laurentia, there had been no Triune attempt upon its lands. Thomas could well understand why. Even with modern weaponry, the thought of mounting an expedition against such formidable foes was daunting. How could cannon bring down an enemy who hurtled, shrieking, from the skies, or issued forth in a multitude from the ground beneath one's feet?

No, he would be safe enough from Erd Gellin there – so far the *isp'te'ra* was telling the truth. But what designs did the elder races have upon him? There must be something they wished. Even if their intentions were largely benevolent, the thought of being alone surrounded, day-in day-out, by such creatures filled him with horror.

"I thank Your Excellency for the offer," said Thomas slowly, trying to think of a polite way out. He did not wish to offend this powerful nation. "But things seem to be going well here. My instruction by the Velnerines seems to be having some effect and I wouldn't want to disrupt my studies. Besides, I feel some loyalty to them and to Euthymios and wouldn't want to desert them..."

With a loud clack Kvh‡r||xkltl cut him off. Thomas's heart fell. Somewhere he had said something wrong.

"Loyalty?" The *isp'te'ra* sounded puzzled, as far as that was possible. "They are not your hive. What obligation can you owe them?"

"Well, I..." he stuttered, but Lawrence came to his rescue.

"Loyalty and gratitude are admirable in the sight of Andur, Lord of Order. To show one's gratitude and honour one's debts is the Anduran way; Maynard here is..."

"Silence. Chaplain, you have no place speaking here. You speak of the absurdities of your religion."

"Our Lord Andur has..." Lawrence began but his words were cut off by a fusillade of staccato clicks. The door was opened behind them.

"Dwdwlch. Remove him." Still protesting Lawrence was forcefully ushered from the room and the door swung closed again with a thud. In the grip of the *mokshtar* his struggles had been as effective as those of a kitten. Thomas felt very alone; scared, but also outraged.

"You can't just do that to him! Where are you taking him?"

"Your companion will meet you outside. These are my quarters. I may control who is in them. Do you not agree?"

Thomas didn't answer. The *isp'te'ra's* point was unarguable, even if his manner of removal had been abrupt.

Taking his silence for acquiescence Kvh‡r||xkltl continued. "The distraction is removed. I have made you an offer. You have no reason to decline. Will you come?"

"Will the Elder Alliance send aid to Elaran if I come with you?" asked Thomas, suddenly daring. If nothing else it bought time.

"The Elder Alliance does not involve itself in the affairs of the outside world."

"But you're involving yourself in me, aren't you?" Thomas pressed his point. "And if you're doing that, then why not..."

"You do not seem to understand," snapped the *isp'te'ra*. "We are not here to bargain. I am here to offer you your life."

"Then no," said Thomas. Irritation, tiredness and disorientation at the rapid way he had been whisked about this last hour blended together to produce defiance. "I won't go to the Elder Alliance. I can't think of any place, bar Erd Gellin, that I would less like to go."

"Why not?" Kvh‡r||xkltl sounded genuinely puzzled. "It will be safer there. It is the logical thing to do."

Thomas stood mute and stubbornly held his ground. He was not going to be moved on this.

"Very well. You may go. I will not waste further time with you." Clicking, he summoned Dwdwlch to escort Thomas out.

"The Elder Alliance does not retract its offer. If Elaran is overrun then come to us. You will be escorted to safety."

Whilst an escape route might be good, as the door closed behind him Thomas fervently hoped that he would not be needing to take advantage of that particular offer.

Chapter Seventeen

Like Sunrise in Winter

In the distance a horn sounded. Leaning out over the parapet Thomas strained to capture a glimpse of the arriving Senrenites. Beside him Lawrence was doing the same, while Ven Tychon, for all his seeming nonchalance, was actually looking as hard as anyone else.

Half of the folk of Hyrnar were clustered along the northern wall. A messenger had sent word from Nerinth that the Senrenites were due to arrive today and nobody wished to miss seeing the first sight of them. Below them Rianda, Euthymios and the rest of the High Council were waiting to formally welcome their allies.

Nearer now the horn sounded, its clarion sound echoing through the hills even to the very gate of the Citadel. There had been no more than a few brief sights of the mounted column, rapid flashes of jingling metal and moving horse before they were once again lost to view behind the rocks. The steep, switchback approach to Hyrnar meant that the arrivals would not be seen clearly until they were under a mile from the walls.

It had snowed again last night, a sudden fall that temporarily reversed the spring thaw. Though Euthymios assured Thomas that it would not last long, for now the hills were once again covered in a carpet of white, sparkling under the bright sunlight of a brisk spring morning.

When the Senrenites finally rounded the last bend and came into full view Thomas felt he had been transported to another world. The splendour of the sight took his breath away; one hundred men in full panoply trotting rapidly through a fairytale winter landscape. The burnished armour of ruddy steel and rich brown flesh of the horses shone like a sunrise in winter. Under the glorious unfurled Crown of Senren banner the vibrant colours took on a life of their own against the pristine snow.

In perfect unison the cavalcade approached, not a man or horse out of synchrony from the rest. The discipline was superb. Thomas marvelled at the glorious anachronism of the sight of knights in full armour, their only concession to the modern era the fact that across each saddlebow lay a short-barrelled musket, rather than the lance that would have been carried in days gone by.

Yet it was no empty spectacle this, for all the trappings and show. These were warriors without parallel throughout the known world: perhaps a company of *mokshtar* could stand against them – Thomas remembered all too well his brief encounter of two months before – but no human force would be a match.

The incongruity of the Senrenites' battle array had even been noticed by Lawrence, despite his usual lack of interest in all things military that had been notorious back at the Residency.

"Why are they wearing armour?" he wondered aloud.

"To protect them," Thomas replied. "Sorry," he apologised, realising the inanity of what he had just said. "The Senrenites are mystics," he elaborated. "They're one of the great militant orders; warrior monks, essentially, as far as I understand it. They serve Andur through fighting in causes that they believe he favours.

"There used to be a number of such orders on Laurentia, like that of the Helm, Rochansza and Stirrup in the old Zechen-Rotliegendish Commonwealth, but all the rest have died out. The Senrenites were the only ones who adapted to the modern era – such as it is modern, here in Laurentia."

"But why do they still wear armour? Isn't it incredibly impractical?"

"Their armour is burnished in the sacred fires they keep burning at each of their five principal chapter houses. It's a month-long ritual, with constant holy chants and arcane prayers to invoke the power of Andur, but by the end of it the armour has become miraculously hard, able to protect them even against gunfire."

"It won't stop a cannon ball," said Ven Tychon, joining in the conversation. "Or even a bullet from a musket if it's at point blank range. But at any kind of distance – which is where most of the danger comes from on a battlefield – it will hardly even take a dent. And of course against swords or bayonets it's as good as impervious."

"And these heretical rites actually work?" Lawrence asked Thomas incredulously. But it was Tychon who answered.

"My father saw one of them in action in a border skirmish on the Givetian border and he said it had to be seen to be believed. He still talks about it sometimes, when he's in a lyrical mood. They say that his armour is a Senrenite's most treasured possession: they're given it at the completion of their novitiate and to lose it is the greatest shame that one of them can suffer, save for acting cravenly or violating one of their vows. But you'll see soon enough for yourself in a month or so."

Lawrence nodded slowly. Thomas was surprised. Tychon's influence upon the former chaplain had been even greater than he had thought if Lawrence was willing to even consider that Canonical rituals might have some validity. Below them Rianda and the other dignitaries had welcomed the Senrenites into the city and were busy escorting them to their place of honour within the Citadel. Even the least amongst that company would be treated with the respect due to a minor lord.

The arrivals were soon lost to sight amongst the maze of narrow streets and buildings, for even outside the Citadel itself Hyrnar was a city constructed for defence. There were none of the straight streets or wide boulevards that one found in other capitals such as Wenlock, Autigen or Iskarn. For some minutes Thomas, Lawrence and Tychon stayed staring out over the walls, but with the absence of the Senrenites the view was somehow lacking and drab. Reluctantly, the three of them turned and joined the crowds of others making their way down from the walls back to the realities of day-to-day existence.

As they patiently shuffled closer to the steps to ground level Thomas turned to Ven Tychon.

"You said your father had met one of them?"

"Not met, exactly. They were on the same side in a skirmish. But my father was in the air and the Senrenite on the ground: they had little contact.

"It was still something for him to remember. Elaran's further south than they usually come – surprisingly, perhaps, given that St. Senren's birthplace is here. It makes this occurrence even more noteworthy.

"They're quite unpredictable in some ways. For much of the time each knight is free to seek out whatever conflict he feels is most appropriate, according to his conscience. Most of them travel in small groups of half a dozen or so, but some are loners, like the one my father fought with. Sometimes you'll even find them fighting on both sides, though they'll never enter combat with one of their own order.

"A Servant-Captain can order one of his Hand – or a small troop, perhaps ten or fifteen knights – to take part in a battle. Or the command can come from the Vicar-General of course. But it's rare indeed that an entire Hand will come to the same cause: the Servant-Captain may have the authority to order that they follow him but it's rarely invoked. The full order has only been mustered twice: in the droghkar uprisings of the tenth century and, more tragically, against the Variscan Imperium. That was only two hundred years ago."

Thomas allowed his mind to wander as Tychon continued, letting Lawrence take up the slack of responding and asking questions. Thomas already knew much of what Tychon was saying. Embarrassed by his ignorance before Piotr on the flight from the Residency one of the first things Thomas had done once he had become settled in the Citadel was to fill some the holes in his knowledge left by his previous studies. Euthymios had only been too happy to grant him access to the Citadel library which, though hardly matching the great collections of some cities, was more than adequate for Thomas's purpose.

The news that had come soon after Longest Night, that an entire Hand of Senrenites would be arriving, had prompted him to return to the books once more. Now he knew much of the order's history, of its practices and habits, its adaptation to the modern era, of its tragic defeat in the Variscan Wars when it had intervened too late and of its subsequent rebirth and reclaiming of its former position. To his surprise their connection with St. Senren was very tenuous. They had been founded by Karanaven Jaeland in Aalenium more than five hundred years after the saint's death. Jaeland had, supposedly, been called to found the order by St. Senren in a vision but that was all, aside from the possession of a number of relics – most notably Senren's sword – which they had managed to track down and obtain.

What they had done was, through their errantry, to unintentionally succeed in binding much of northern Laurentia into an informal military convention. Because no Senrenite would serve in an army which condoned torture, the wanton slaughter of prisoners or similar such practices had gradually fallen into disuse. Though not entirely: Thomas noted that no Senrenite had served with the armies of Torridon since Niavon I's seizure of power eighty years ago.

The thought reminded him of Rianda and of the challenges she faced. Fending off the might of Torridon was like keeping a giant at bay with a blade of grass, yet the Nemessine line had done it for centuries. But now the giant had grown in strength and rapacity. All Rianda's skill might make little difference, even were Erd Gellin not pressing from the south. Or perhaps, as Rianda had suggested, it was that which was saving Elaran, for Torridon did not wish a common border with another hungry power. But for how long could Elaran manage to be the fulcrum about which span the two lumbering behemoths?

Longest Night had been a turning point for Thomas, in more ways than one. Since that chance, surreal meeting at midnight the stiltedness had entirely vanished from his relationship with Rianda. It was as if some barrier had been removed. They still met once a week and a certain formality was, of course, retained, but now Rianda talked to him openly, frankly, almost as an equal.

Not quite as an equal – more as someone who, coming from a different world, she could speak to without receiving an answer based on fear or favour. Though a degree of reserve remained it seemed, so Thomas thought, as if it were based upon something other than the need for a monarch's dignity. At times she seemed almost vulnerable, showing her age. It was then that Thomas remembered that she was almost the same age as he and, like him, striving to control events whilst thrust into a world that had suddenly grown in complexity beyond all recognition.

They crossed the last line of houses and entered the cleared area between the city proper and the Citadel itself. The last climb up was always steeper than Thomas remembered, despite the number of times he had walked it on his way back from the Velnerines. The crowds had thinned by now. Though almost all the inhabitants of the Citadel had turned out to watch the Senrenites' arrival most of those watching had still been from the city. There was no sign of the knights ahead of them: by now they must all have entered the Citadel. They were, no doubt, being escorted to their quarters. The stables by the Paddock would be filled to overflowing.

Thomas had been there many times since that first trip after Longest Night. His relationship with Rianda was not the only thing that had changed since then.

He had seen far more of Lawrence and Tychon than he had before. It was if it had taken that stimulus to remind them both how much they had in common, especially here, the only two of their countrymen within a thousand miles or more.

Tychon, too, had mellowed. The Air Captain no longer glowered at Thomas upon seeing him at the Velnerine hospice. Indeed, they had frequently walked down or back together, for Tychon, like a number of soldiers, was a frequent devotee of the Velnerines. The healing services they offered in war had aided many, and not a few old campaigners felt that regular prayers and donations were small enough things to offer in thanks for their own or a comrade's life. This time spent together had led Thomas to come to appreciate the Air Captain's laconic manner. Tychon had a dry wit which could, at times, be cutting, though never cruel.

Tychon came from a long line of *tarathinakii*; his father, grandfather and great grandfathers as far back as he knew had all been flyers in the service of Elaran. Not all had been Air Captain – that would have been too much to expect – but at least half had been. The talent and aptitude seemed to run in the family, along with a certain recklessness and daring that was essential for a successful military *tarathinaki*.

It was something that Thomas knew he did not share. Lawrence did; just to watch him fly for a few moments would tell you that. Tychon had confided to Thomas that the former chaplain had a gift possessed by one in ten thousand. Even that gift didn't extend to being able to transmit his enthusiasm to Thomas. At Lawrence's insistence he had been up with him several times but the experience was always terrifying. For Lawrence, to descend from a flight, even if he had not been steering, left him transformed, eyes shining with exhilaration. For Thomas, although he could feel the thrill, the slightest motion out of the ordinary would bring his stomach surging back into his mouth.

That difference was not enough to stand between them. Thomas amusedly tolerated Lawrence's excitement and, in turn, Lawrence did not press too hard. In fact, since Longest Night, the only thing that marred Thomas's contentment was the lack of progress he was making in controlling his visions. After the initial success, in which the Velnerines had prevented the recurrence of the scene of the massacre at the Residency, progress had slowed. About a month ago he had succeeded in being able to trigger a vision at will – his first breakthrough in over two months – but he was still utterly unable to control what he saw. Abbot Jarlod refused to be downhearted, saying that what they had achieved already was impressive given the lack of knowledge they were battling against, but it still sometimes felt like groping in the dark. It was sometimes galling to compare this slow progress with the ease with which Lawrence had mastered his new craft of flying.

Lawrence and Tychon's discussion of the Senrenites was drawing to a close as they re-entered the Citadel through the main gate. How much longer, Thomas wondered, would it be able to remain open and welcoming as it was today? For all the splendour of today's spectacle, the grim fact could not be hidden that it was in preparation for what would be a bitter war.

#

Hanyarmé Morentes strode into the Council chamber. Pausing briefly, he noticed Rianda gesturing to a seat near the head of the marble table. Sir Hanyarmé nodded with satisfaction. Things were as they should be: only two people would be closer to the Queen than he.

It was astonishing, Rianda thought, how others of her counsellors shrank into insignificance once the Senrenite entered the room. Very few could match his sheer presence. Euthymios, Nomiki, Chrysaor – they could equal him, but only they. Some, Eliud, Hesperos, Kadmos, these solid, loyal men did not dominate, but nor were they diminished: secure in their own roles, they would serve loyally until the end. But Actaion and Tarasios – both, in fact, of her disloyal or incompetent counsellors – were stripped of their pretensions, Actaion's trivial pecuniary complaint revealed as the mewling of a spoiled child.

Peremptorily silencing Actaion – a clerk could deal with him later – Rianda made ready to begin. Euthymios sat to her right; beyond him was Sir Hanyarmé. To her left was Nomiki's commanding presence. She sensed no hidden tensions, despite the new presence of Morentes. Like the weather outside, this council should be grey and uneventful: all that was necessary was to confirm plans made long before.

"I would like to welcome Sir Hanyarmé Morentes, Servant-Captain of the Knights of the Most Holy Order of St. Senren, to our company. All Elaran will be eternally grateful for your assistance in this time of great trouble." Rianda wasted no more time on introductions: this was a council of war, not a social gathering. All of her High Council had met the Senrenite the day before when he had arrived.

"We must discuss how best we can use you and your knights in the defence of our land. I know that First Chiliarch Nomiki has a number of ideas, but it may be that you have your own suggestions. You will know better than we your Hand's capabilities.

"Nomiki, if you would continue?"

"Very well, Your Majesty." The First Chiliarch clearly and quickly outlined the situation.

"There are three passes to the south of Elaran: Illapthos, the Thradfi Gap and the Pass of Istria. Through one of these the Gellinese army must come if it hopes to reach Hyrnar.

"Our spies report that the Archons have massed over ten thousand men against us, gathered on the Plain of Gadinno just south of Hyrakos. That is in addition to whatever foul beasts or demons they intend to throw at us. We can expect each of their men to be as well-armed and trained as our best, and in materiel and equipment such as cannon we are likely to be at a severe disadvantage.

"To set against that, we have the advantage of terrain and of loyalty. We are defending narrow passes, where numbers count for little and horses and cannon – at least for the attacker – count for even less. Furthermore, our men will be fighting on their own soil, to protect their homeland and their family.

"But make no mistake, we are facing a grim struggle where victory will be won at a great price, if it is to be won at all. Our regular army numbers only three thousand men. To add to that we have the muster, which I believe" – he looked questioningly at Euthymios – "has raised a further two thousand."

"The final contingent from Melnarion is expected within the week," the bishop confirmed.

"Good. But remember," he said, addressing the room again, "that these will be poorly trained. They are farmers, not soldiers. And even with them, we will be outnumbered by more than two to one.

"One chiliad, commanded by its chiliarch, will defend each pass. The most easterly pass, the Pass of Istria, is the widest. Over two hundred men could march abreast through it with ease. I myself will take command of the defence here, together with the first chiliad and one thousand of the muster. Added to that will be two hundred of Sword-Captain Kadmos's Household Guard, making a total of two thousand two hundred men, and leaving one chiliad and five hundred of the muster to defend each of the other two passes."

"If the Pass of Istria is so obvious a choice," questioned Eliud, "may not the Archons second-guess us and make their main thrust along one of the other routes?"

"It is something we have considered. But the advantages of Istria are sufficient to outweigh the fact that they will know we know they are coming. Should they attack in force along the others, the terrain is poor enough that we would be able to reinforce before they broke through."

"Then why must we defend these other passes at all?" The bovine stupidity could almost be heard dripping from Tarasios' tongue.

Before Nomiki could answer, Actaion responded, his tongue flaying his fellow counsellor mercilessly. Rianda thanked Andur that her enemies on the Council were not united. Actaion might hate and scheme against her, but he despised Tarasios.

"Of course, we could leave the other passes unguarded. They're not so narrow that a thousand men couldn't slip through and take us in the rear. Or raze Hyrnar to the ground, or perhaps Kaisoros. That would trouble you, wouldn't it? But perhaps we should take the risk; chance that the Gellinese won't have thought of attacking through more than one pass at once. What do you think?"

"I only wondered why we needed so many men," mumbled Tarasios. "I thought just a few would be enough."

Nomiki stepped in. "Even ten percent of the Gellinese army is a thousand men. They could send two thousand at each of the other two passes and still have over six thousand – more than our entire army – at Istria. No, each pass must be defended thoroughly, and fifteen hundred is the least that I and my fellow chiliarchi consider can do so effectively."

"What of us?" Sir Hanyarmé spoke for the first time. "Where do I and my knights fit into your plan?" His voice was sonorous and heavily accented with the cadences of his native Siluria. The voice of a courteous man, but of one used to absolute command and unaccustomed to being kept waiting.

"I had planned for your Hand to be split up amongst the three passes," said Nomiki. "If we were facing men alone, it might have been best to keep it united, but against demons they are the only troops we can rely on.

"Twenty-five men will go to each of the lesser passes, with fifty to the Pass of Istria. If, that is," he inclined his head civilly, "you are in agreement."

"I am. It is what I would have advised myself. I will accompany the fifty and take up station with you at the Pass of Istria. May St. Senren watch over us." Sir Hanyarmé paused, looking directly at Nomiki.

"My knights have fought demons before, though not in such great numbers as you report. If they are indeed present we will vanquish these spawn of hell as St. Senren once slew the *Soharadon*, and treat any other fell beasts similarly. But I believe you have overestimated their number. Such creatures have not been seen in the numbers your spies report since the days of the Variscan Wars."

"It is possible." Nomiki's reply, though polite, yielded no ground. "But it is as well that we are prepared for the worst."

"To that I cannot argue." Already, these two hardened warriors were winning each other's respect. Both were capable, intelligent men, skilled beyond the lot of ordinary men in the art of war. In each, compassion – stemming in Morentes's case from his service to Andur, in Nomiki's from his devotion to Elaran and the Nemessine line – had tempered ruthlessness in the forging. As they took the other's measure in this initial exchange, neither found the other wanting.

The moment passed. Sir Hanyarmé returned to practical matters.

"What of magic? We can counter some of the products of unnatural sorcery, but my knights are not mages. Will you be able withstand the Gellinese magecraft?"

"We will, thanks to good Euthymios here. His work in rallying and recruiting our mages to the cause has been incomparable. Thanks to him we have sufficient raw power to hold the Gellinese at bay. Neither scrying nor direct exertions of power shall pass our wards, nor direct combat spells. You must not expect us to be able to strike back."

"That will not be necessary. It is always easier to defend than to attack, and doubly so in wizardry. As long as the enemy cannot harry us or spy us out with unseen eyes I am content. And perhaps we may even be able to lay a trap or two of our own behind our lines.

"I am content. I do not need to know more at the current time, though perhaps your commanders and I could meet later to discuss precisely how our forces will act together when battle is joined."

"Of course," said Nomiki. "Lykourgos, Chiliarch of the South, is with the army at the current time, overseeing the preparing for the invasion. But I and Hesperos, Chiliarch of the North, will join you, together with Kadmos and Chrysaor if they wish."

"Chrysaor will not be joining you." Rianda's clear voice cut through the room decisively. "Or, if he does, it will be as an adviser only. My cousin will not be joining our armies on the field of battle."

The room froze. Even Sir Hanyarmé, new to the council, could see that this announcement had been entirely unexpected. Looking at Chrysaor he could see that the Royal Duke was as shocked as the others.

"Of course, Your Majesty, if you so command," said Chrysaor. "But may I ask why? Under your father I have commanded the armies of Elaran in battle for the last two decades."

Under your father. How simple those words were and yet how devastating. So much had changed since then, since that sudden grief that had snatched her father away from her in his prime. Less than a year ago: the time when she had not been queen seemed a distant age away.

"Yes, Your Grace. But I was not queen then. Now it is I, not my father, who must accompany our forces south. One of the Nemessine line must remain behind, to command the last defence of the Citadel if we are overwhelmed and to lead the last flight to the hills if all else fails. Our line must survive, for we are Elaran. And Elaran is us."

Chrysaor bowed his head. He had never wished to rule. His whole life had been devoted to the service of King Diarad. To stay behind in safety now, for the possibility of wearing a crown that he had no wish for, was a bitter draught to his palate. But he understood the necessity and, for Elaran, he would serve.

"Your will, Majesty."

Chapter Eighteen

Light into Darkness

Thomas tugged irritably at the tight high collar of his doublet. The thing just would not come straight. Who would have thought, he wondered, that the lack of a basic evening suit could cause so much trouble? Normally dressing for an event such as this would be the work of a quarter of an hour, at most, but he had been here for half an hour or more already.

Tonight was the night of Rianda's grand spring ball, ostensibly to celebrate the Day of Rebirth. In honour of the Senrenites it had been dedicated to St. Senren. In actuality it was simply a chance to give spirit to the populace – who would be catered for by a less formal but significantly larger feast in the grounds of the Citadel, provided entirely by the crown's largesse – and, more importantly, to put on a show of confidence to Elaran's neighbours.

Countries at war, Thomas had learned, depended no less than bankers, drunkards and the gentry on a ready and generous supply of credit. And for that to be available, the lenders had to be confident that they would be receiving their money back.

Thus the promised extravagance of the show tonight. Whilst the soldiers toiled in mud to improve the hastily constructed fortifications of the southern passes, their commanders, flown back from the front for the night only, would be socialising with the assembled nobility and dignitaries of Torridon, Linnarson, Rotliegendes and Givet. Costly food, music and lavish decorations; all as if Elaran was revelling in a long spell of peace rather than preparing to fight a war for its very existence.

Rianda, Euthymios and others would be putting on the performance of their life in the attempt to convince outsiders that Elaran was confident in its ability to beat back this invasion. No military aid would be promised as a result of this evening, but the promise of a loan or, just as crucially, a decision not to support a Torridonian or other incursion could mean the difference between life and death for Elaran.

Thomas reflected that for him it should be a pleasant enough evening. He would do his best to help of course, should anyone speak to him about Elaran's prospects. He had come to care about Euthymios, Rianda and others in this

Citadel that had sheltered him over the winter. But it was hard to feel as strongly when you knew that if the worst came to the worst you would be heading back to a safe post in the Empire.

Finally! Thomas at last managed to fasten the last button on the wretched shirt. Now it was just a matter of smoothing the fractious garment into place. In truth he welcomed this grand ball: the dismal pall over the Citadel had been increasing all winter, lifted only momentarily by high points such as the Day of Pledge and the arrival of the Senrenites. They didn't even celebrate Valadar here. The sombre period of Doren Mur had only made things worse. Taken far more seriously in this Canonical country than back in the Empire, the two-week fast of mourning had practically tipped half the Citadel over the edge into depression.

It was quite understandable. For all the bold words of the High Council, a sense of hopelessness had leaked out to infect the city. Perhaps the people could sense the desperation of their rulers; perhaps they could just look at the facts for themselves. Being snowbound in the dark depths of winter didn't help either. Rianda was right: the people badly needed something to raise their spirits. Thomas agreed entirely: he just wished he didn't have to wear these confounded clothes.

He had been in Elaran long enough to have assumed that he was prepared for any such occasion. His own clothes had been lost in the flight from the Residency, save for what he had been wearing at the time and they in any case had been little more than rags by the time he reached Elaran. More of course had been provided, in the Elarani style, and while they had seemed unusual enough at first he had rapidly become accustomed to them.

It seemed, however, that more was necessary for a Grand Ball. The worst was the colours. Though he had insisted on the relatively sober colour of russet, covered by a cloak of dark green, it still felt ridiculously gaudy compared to sensible Imperial evening wear. Uncomfortable too. Adjusting the white tippet draped about his neck he told himself that, viewed logically, it was no more absurd than a bow tie. But it didn't feel that way.

Suddenly Thomas felt cold all over. How could he be so blasé about the war? This might not be his fight, true, but he had heard the stories in the Residency back in Iskarn. The terrors of the countryside; by the Wheel, he had even seen the demons in the flight across Erd Gellin. He would not wish such things on his worst enemies, let alone the people of this Citadel. And if his vision of the desolated city – Hyrakos, according to Rianda – was true...

He shuddered. Maybe it wasn't true that he would not wish such things on anyone. The Archons – or whoever was ultimately responsible for unleashing such horrors – would justly deserve to have a portion of the same visited back upon them.

Feeling abashed by his former callousness he made his way to the Great Hall. Thank Andur that at least he had not spoken such thoughts aloud. Grimly, he determined that if there was anything he could do this evening to make up for them he would. The grandeur of tonight's celebration might seem a long way from the mud and toil of the southern passes, but it was no less crucial, nonetheless.

"Ambassador Maynard of the Triune Empire," announced the door warden as he entered the great hall. A few heads turned to look as he entered, but not many. The focus of the room was elsewhere tonight and, for all its power, the Empire was far, far away from Elaran. Losing himself amongst the crowd, Thomas accepted a proffered glass, a fine sparkling white wine from the Rhaetian Plains of western Siluria. The rich golden liquid sparkled warmly off the many facets of the delicate crystal goblet. Green wine it was known locally; a rare delicacy this far south.

Sipping slowly, Thomas scanned the room. Rianda had not yet entered, but that was to be expected. Others of the High Council were present, methodically working the room. It brought home to Thomas how few people he knew here. He had had a privileged access to some of the most powerful in the kingdom, but surprisingly little contact with those one step below. The language barrier contributed to that but still, many of the lesser dignitaries would also have spoken Dalradian.

Neither Ven Tychon nor Lawrence were here yet and Thomas knew enough of such gatherings from the Empire to realise that Euthymios would not appreciate him hanging on his coat tails at such a time. Feeling surprisingly lost, he threaded his way slowly through the crowd to a lavishly laid out buffet spread along the far side of the room.

He never reached it. Before he had travelled more than a dozen steps he had been intercepted by a middle-aged man whose lace-edged collar and attire proclaimed him as a native of Givet.

"Excuse me, Your Excellency," the man said politely, before introducing himself as the second secretary, trade to the Givetian embassy in Hyrnar. There followed an exchange of pleasantries and a brief discussion of the Elarani situation, before the man got down to the meat of the business: whether there was any truth to the matter that the Triune Empire might be considering a relaxation of the Navigation Acts.

No, said Thomas, there was no truth to the rumour, just as there had been none to the rumours a decade ago or the decade before that. The question, coming unexpectedly as it had, might have taken him initially by surprise but this was comfortable ground. The Navigation Acts were core to Triune policy, cursed as they might be by other nations. Triune goods were to be carried in Triune vessels and none but Triune vessels could dock at Triune ports. The Acts were key to Imperial Trade, and Trade was key to the Empire. The lines were clear; Thomas could have answered this question in his sleep. The justification to other nations of the Navigation Acts was a standard catechism in which all young aspirants to the Laurentian and other colonial services were drilled.

Disappointed but not surprised by the response the Givetian moved off, only to be replaced by a young Elarani noble who introduced himself as Ven Spyridon of Argosy, a second cousin to Duke Tarasios. Behind him in the crowd Thomas could see at least two or three others waiting to catch his eye.

This was a new experience for Thomas. He was unused to being the courted rather than the courter. Never before in a gathering such as this had he been one to whom so many others wished to speak.

He supposed it was only natural. The Triune Empire might be far from Elaran, but it was closer – much closer – to many of the nations represented here. And whilst, as an extremely junior ambassador to a distant land, he remained beneath the notice of the great and the good, to many of the lesser dignitaries he was a tempting target. It was ironic that but for the quirk of fate that had thrust him into this position – he was too young, by far, to truly be an ambassador, even a minor one – it would have likely been he courting them.

He soon fell into a pattern of dealing with them. A few pleasantries, then a firm statement of how confident he and the Empire were in Elaran's success in the coming war (here he overstated his authority, but he doubted anyone would ever know). What followed depended on the recipient, but the statement of a few standard lines on Imperial policy or recent activities usually sufficed. Thomas began to realise the real challenge of this type of thing. It was not each individual conversation – they were simple enough – but remembering the names, positions and attitudes of each, as well as searching for any nuggets of gold amongst the dross were where the skill lay. Despite his best efforts, after the first few they all began to blur into one.

All conversation broke off in an instant at the sound of a fanfare to announce Rianda's arrival.

"Her Nemessine Majesty Rianda of Elaran, by the Grace of Andur, Queen of Elaran, Lord of the Har Mareisch, thirty-eighth Nemessine monarch!"

Not through the side entrance through which Thomas and others had come in did Rianda make her entrance, but through the grand doors at the far end of the great hall. She walked with stately dignity down the sweeping marble steps, stunning the hall into silence with her presence.

A magnificent gown covered her shoulders and swept out behind her, myrtle green and bracken brown, the colours of the Elarani hillsides in spring. Upon her head rested the state crown of Elaran, a glorious construction of delicate gold resplendently set with five magnificent imbued gems – diamond, ruby, emerald, sapphire, pearl; one for each of the five major domains.

As she reached the base of the steps the hall began to buzz once more with the noise of subtle diplomacy and banal small talk. Thomas had taken advantage of the moment to escape from the most recent claimants on his attention and to snatch a bite of food. He was famished.

The chamber orchestra altered its playing while he did so. From its former banal series of undemanding fugues continuo, it now launched into the stirring chords of the Overture to Rzegotka's Commonwealth Suite.

The room stood to attention as if electrified. Across the great hall heads snapped round as the powerful notes filled the hall. Originally scored for choir and full orchestra, even in this lesser setting Rzegotka's masterwork still retained the power to move the soul.

As was customary for such suites, the overture contained the broad sweep of the entire piece within it. Depicting the glories of the long-dead Zechen-Rotliegendish Commonwealth, from its humble beginning, through to its zenith under Dominic the Great, thirty-seventh Sejm, and finally on to its decline: the bitter reign of Pavel Jitanski, the steady loss of power and the final divisiveness of the Pajderza War, when the Commonwealth was dissolved for ever. The Suite covered it all.

What did Rianda intend by having this performed at a time such as this? Or rather Euthymios, for Thomas could detect the subtle bishop's hand in this manoeuvre. A warning against hubris perhaps; a reminder to these powerful nations gathered looking on that they themselves could all too easily be brought as low or lower than Elaran? Or was it an exhortation to battle, recalling to their minds the triumphs of Dominic the Great and his adviser, Konelis Larach of Zarant against the droghkar hordes, in the hope that some today might decide to emulate their actions?

"I see that Queen Rianda has decided to honour my country's history," said a crystalline voice behind Thomas. The tone was faintly sardonic. "I wonder," it continued, "what could she intend by that?"

Startled, Thomas spun round to find himself inches away from a tall woman dressed in a gown of dark red velvet. He found himself looking up at her – by Andur, she must have been six feet tall if she was an inch – an awkward position from so close. Her pale skin and high, aquiline cheekbones proclaimed her to be of Tuevic race, as indeed did her words, which could only have been spoken by a native of Rotliegendes or Zechstein. She must have been beautiful in her time; even now she remained elegant and would turn men's eyes for more reason than her height.

"I'm not sure," Thomas stammered in answer to her question, even though he had been pondering the same question himself but a few moments before. "Perhaps it's just a coincidence."

She laughed, silvery peals that rippled around the room.

"Do not try to be disingenuous – it ill becomes one so young. The first rule of diplomacy is only to dissemble when it can be believed.

"But I will not press you on the point, Ambassador Maynard. Yes," she continued at his start, "I know who you are. Your Empire is hardly so insignificant that I would be unaware of your presence here. Though even your masters in Wenlock do not know all that you have to tell, unless I have misjudged gravely."

Thomas bowed, seeking to regain his composure. "I'm afraid you have the advantage of me, My Lady..."

"Von Wulffen. Baroness Von Wulffen of Olfensee, Ambassador Extraordinaire to the court of Hyrnar. And one of your few friends here, though you may not believe it."

"I have many friends here," Thomas protested.

"Do you?" She raised an eyebrow quizzically. "Well, we shall not argue the point, but did not Larach write in the *Annalia* that he who believes himself secure in the arms of Andur will suffer the greatest fall, but that Ruth will oft provide aid unlooked for, silently and unseen?

"Come now." She gracefully reached out to tap him lightly upon the wrist with her fan, revealing long white gloves embroidered about the wrists with the sacred wyvern of Rotliegendes. The pattern resembled drops of blood on freshly minted snow.

"Come, let us walk," and linking her arm in his she led him firmly away along the side of the hall. He could no more have resisted than he could have swum the ocean's depths.

"Consider, my young ambassador, why you are here at all. Here in Elaran, I mean, not here in Laurentia, for that is a mystery that only your Imperial masters can answer.

"But as to Elaran, is it not down to Rotliegendes? Has not Rotliegendes watched over you, helped you, succoured you – saved you? And this little kingdom" – she gestured airily towards the room, dismissing the assembled dignitaries as if they could have no more importance than a gnat – "well, it has served its purpose. It made a satisfactory enough refuge for the winter, I suppose, but I hardly think you intend to remain here for the rest of your life."

She leaned in towards him. "Tell me, Ambassador Maynard, do *you* think this court will still be here in three months' time?"

"They have a good chance. You haven't seen the preparations that I have, or the willingness with which these Elarani will die to defend their homes."

"Haven't I?" She pursed her lips. "I would not be too sure of that. There is very little that the eyes of Rotliegendes do not observe. You, of all people should be aware of that.

"Even if they do have a chance, it is a slim one. And not one that I would risk my life upon, were I in your place. As I said earlier, you can hardly be intending to spend the rest of your life here. Those Velnerines that are seeking to instruct you have done rather well, in their way, but for all their efforts they are still blind men groping in the dark."

"I'd planned to go back to the Empire, or possibly to Linnarson," said Thomas defensively.

"To the Empire? How can a nation that does not even admit the divinity of Our Lady of Silence instruct you in the use of one of her blessings? And those materialist scholars in Linnarson would be little better. No, you need an older expertise: knowledge from an earlier, deeper age.

"Listen to the music!" she commanded. "Rotliegendes was a great nation eight hundred years ago. The lore of the Commonwealth is not dead whatever the ignorant may say. It only sleeps. We are the nation that gave birth to the great Larach; Konelis Larach, author of the *Annalia*, monk, scholar, saint, martyr and seer. In Rotliegendes you will truly learn to use your gift.

"Will you not come to Rotliegendes?"

"I'll consider it," lied Thomas. Rotliegendes was even further from the Empire than Elaran. He could see no need to tangle himself further in their snares.

"Where is Piotr now, Baroness?" he asked suddenly. He had fenced long enough with this woman – let her see how she fared against a direct question.

"Piotr?" She appeared entirely unfazed by the abrupt change of direction. "I am afraid I don't know. He was back in Rotliegendes for a short time I believe, but as to where he is now, I couldn't say. I think I heard that he was in Scandia? Or was it Namuria? But that could have been someone else. He is such a wanderer, it can be hard to keep track of where he is at any given moment." She smiled apologetically.

She was lying, Thomas was sure, but there was nothing that she should be called on. The baroness allowed the conversation to turn to less personal matters, giving Thomas no little relief.

Hauntingly, the orchestra reached the conclusion of the Commonwealth Overture, drawing out the last, wistful cadence with a painful poignancy. When the last note had faded there was a moment of silence: the whole assemblage pausing in appreciation, before bursting into fierce applause. Meanwhile Thomas realised that the centre of the room was emptying, servants deftly guiding guests towards the sides until a large space had been created.

Now the orchestra was in motion again, bowing briskly as Rianda led her cousin, Duke Chrysaor, into the room. They acknowledged each other gracefully and then they were off, whirling rapidly around the room in the latest waltz from Aalen. Thomas could not keep his eyes off them.

As he would have expected, Rianda moved like a dream, footsteps as light as a fairy's, body floating gracefully as a gazelle in flight. In the arms of her cousin she spun, two bodies moving as one. Thomas reflected on the furore that the Aalenese style had caused when it had first reached the Empire's shores. Outrageous, they had said: disgraceful. Quite an unsuitable dance, particularly for an unmarried woman of under thirty. But here in Elaran there were no stuffy matrons from Home and the dance went on.

All too soon it ended. Rianda relinquished her cousin to his wife and turned for her next partner to Ven Atharden of Dorlan, Ambassador of Torridon, who accepted with polished grace. Other couples were taking to the floor, the elder with studied formality, the younger with poorly concealed enthusiasm and energy. For these the ball was truly a time of celebration and pleasure, marred for some only by the pressure to find a spouse. But for their elders – and, of course, for

Rianda – this phase of the ball simply meant a continuance of the earlier negotiations in a new setting. The subtle dance of diplomacy continued unabated around, through and during its physical counterpart.

For Thomas, it was an opportunity to escape. A single dance with Baroness von Wulffen could not, with courtesy, be avoided, but it was simple thereafter to make his excuses. A decorative young noblewoman was his vehicle of escape, and fortunately her Dalradian was poor enough to permit the avoidance of conversation. For the first time Thomas was glad that he had still not managed to learn more than rudimentary Elarani.

Now safely on the other side of the room from the Baroness, Thomas was truly able to make good his freedom. He bowed to his partner when the music stopped, the standard courtesy a heartfelt thanks for the service she had been. In truth he could afford to be gracious: it had been a pleasure rather than a chore, though he had no great love of dancing.

Lawrence, he knew, shared his feelings, and whilst still in the Baroness' clutches he had spotted the former chaplain and Ven Tychon across the far side of the room. Now, as he both hoped and expected, Lawrence remained firmly off the dance floor, near one of the corners of the room. Thomas threaded his way around the edge of the hall to join him.

"Finally I've found you."

"We've been here for a while," said Lawrence. "We've just been keeping out of the way as much as possible."

"You're lucky," said Thomas, with feeling. "It's been a nightmare out there; one person after another wanting to speak to me about some matter that they're sure I'll be interested in. I've only just managed to get away."

"Well, that's the price you pay for your eminence. A humble chaplain like myself is unbothered by such demands."

"You're meant to be deputy ambassador yourself!"

"Well, perhaps I've kept a lower profile than you. But is it actually just because you're the Triune Ambassador? Are you sure it's not because of...you know, your visions?"

"In one or two cases, yes," admitted Thomas. "The Rotliegendish ambassador had me cornered for a while because of that. Incidentally, I'm pretty certain that Piotr was a spy. But most of them don't know anything about the True Seer issue. I admire real ambassadors a whole lot more if they have to put up with this all the time."

"It doesn't surprise me. About Piotr that is. I never trusted him."

"He did save our lives," Thomas protested.

"Even so. He was a heretic. I always believed he was playing a deeper game."

"Lawrence, everyone here is a heretic," said Thomas tiredly. "Rianda, Euthymios; everyone: they're all Canonicals. So is Ven Tychon and you seem to get on well enough with him."

"Yes..." Lawrence squirmed, seeking a way out. "But they're not as fervent about it as Piotr. It was always the Blessed Ruth this, Our Lady of Silence that, but Konelis Larach wrote the other.

"Anyway, I was right. You've just said that he was a spy."

Thomas gave up. For all his recent changes, on some things Lawrence would never alter. He wondered what Lawrence would say if he knew quite how much attention Thomas had been paying to Larach's works in recent months. As the only True Seer to have written extensively about the gift, Larach was his primary source of guidance.

"Where is Tychon, anyway?" Thomas asked, changing the subject.

"Over there." Lawrence gestured to the dance floor. "He's been dancing since the music began."

Thomas looked in the direction Lawrence had indicated. Sure enough, there was Tychon, spinning and dipping with his partner through the ranks of couples. It could have been a comical sight: the stocky air captain was a good inch shorter than his partner, who herself was little more than average height for a woman. But it wasn't. Tychon's agility lent itself perfectly to this activity; the lessons learned from the sky translating perfectly to the dance floor. Like twin cranes he and his partner whirled across the room, graceful as a floating sycamore seed. Gossamer light, their feet barely seemed to touch the ground. Even when he had left his *tarathin* Tychon, it seemed, could not stop flying.

"Will you be going with the army when it moves south?" Lawrence's voice broke into Thomas's reverie. Reluctantly, he tore his attention away from the floor. Such a display was a delight to watch.

"What was that?"

Lawrence repeated the question.

"I hadn't thought so," Thomas said, startled. "Why would I?" He paused. "Why, are you?"

"I think so, yes." Thomas looked closely at him, but Lawrence appeared deadly serious.

"I've been training all winter and Tychon says that I'm good – very good. And I don't like the thought of the people we know here coming under the rule of those monsters to the south."

"But you wouldn't even take a weapon to defend yourself when we were escaping across Erd Gellin," said Thomas in disbelief. "Surely a few *tarathin* lessons don't change that!"

"No, that hasn't changed. Though the militant orders of the clergy here in Laurentia seem to have reached an accommodation...but no, that is my own personal decision. On *tarathin*-back I can do much good without needing a weapon. Scouting; carrying messages, and so on."

Thomas was slightly baffled. On the one hand he was filled with admiration, but on the other it was just all too strange. That Lawrence, of all people, was volunteering for what amounted to military service!

"And what, exactly," Thomas asked, "will their Imperial Majesties' Colonial Office think of one of their embassy chaplains gallivanting off to take part in some foreign war?"

"I've thought of that. I resigned my post as soon as I knew I'd made the decision. The message was sent by *variideshar* to Autigen last week. I'm now a free citizen of the Triune Empire, free, as you well know, to join the service of any nation – save for those with which we are actively hostile – as a benevolent neutral."

Thomas was dubious. "And the Ecclesiastical Commission? You haven't resigned your holy orders, I presume."

"Maynard," Lawrence said soberly, "if I get through this I'll happily face the Ecclesiastical Commission. The odds of a *tarathinaki* surviving a normal war aren't great and this isn't a normal war. The Elarani forces will be lucky to survive, let alone win. I've spoken to Tychon and the best that he hopes for is that we do enough damage to the Gellinese that they'll be unable to occupy this country thoroughly. Then some small part of Elaran may still survive in the hills and the future will not be wholly lost."

"But..."

"But don't you see, that's all the more reason why I'm going. These people may be Sanctists, but the light of Andur still shines upon them, for all their heresies. They are good people – you know that yourself, Maynard. Whereas all the forces of hell are leagued against them. We've seen Erd Gellin's demons ourselves. You didn't hear the stories that I did out in the countryside, before the massacre.

"Are you sure that you won't come?"

"What under the Wheel would I do?"

"What about these visions of yours? Aren't you meant to be a True Seer – can't you do something with that?"

"I still can't really control them. I couldn't do anything useful."

"You might. Andur might grace you."

"Well...yes. Or I might get lucky. But it seems a bit unlikely."

"So you're just going to stay here?"

"Or get back to the Empire, yes." Thomas felt uncomfortable, but he really couldn't see what good he would do by going. It was different for Lawrence: his talent for flying meant that he could really play a valuable part in the struggle. It was one thing, Thomas told himself, to risk your life when you might achieve something; it was another to risk it for no purpose whatsoever.

Fortunately, Lawrence did not press the point, though Thomas could tell he was disappointed. It was quite unreasonable really. Just because he wanted to be a martyr. Awkwardly, they stood beside each other, both pretending to be interested in watching the crowds.

"Where's the Queen?" asked Lawrence suddenly, breaking the silence.

"What?"

"Where's the Queen? I can't see her anywhere."

"Rianda? I don't know." Thomas looked around the room but found that Lawrence was right. Rianda was nowhere to be seen. Others of the nobility were still there – Euthymios, Nomiki, Chrysaor and so forth. But not Rianda.

"Maybe she's just had to leave briefly," he suggested.

"I haven't seen her for the last five minutes," said Lawrence.

Thomas paused. "That's odd. What could call her away from an event like this? Everyone of significance is here." Lawrence shrugged in reply and turned back to watching the room, but Thomas was puzzled. He began worming his way through the throngs in the direction of Euthymios. The bishop would know what was going on.

"Excuse me," said a clipped voice behind him. Thomas cursed under his breath. He should never have left his concealed corner.

"Yes, Your Excellency?" He turned and bowed to the outlandish creature that had intercepted him. Thomas hadn't spoken to the Elder Alliance's ambassador since that sole, intense, interview just after Longest Night and he would have been happy to keep it that way.

The *isp'te'ra's* black carapace gleamed lustrously in the bright lights of the room. Inconsequentially Thomas wondered if it had been polished specially for the occasion. After all, the *isp'te'ra* didn't have any other method of formal dressing. It added a certain majesty to the creature's countenance: as he had remarked before, though alien, the *isp'te'ra* was neither hideous nor repulsive.

"I had thought," said Kvh‡r||xkltl, a plethora of clicks and other harsh consonants supplementing the basic Dalradian, "that we might discuss briefly the matter that we discussed before?"

Thomas stalled. "Which particular matter was that?"

The evasion was met with a sharp, impatient clack. "I do not have time to waste, human! When will you be seeking refuge in the Elder Alliance?"

"I never committed to doing so."

"Come now. The storm is almost upon us here. Within a few days it will break.

"And what will you do? Sit here in fear, hoping against hope for an Elarani victory?"

"No. I will be going south with the Elarani forces."

There was silence. Only Andur could have told who was more taken aback, Kvh‡r||xkltl or Thomas. Thomas did not know what had made him say it: a combination of Lawrence's reproaches and the continued pressure by Kvh‡r||xkltl and, earlier, Baroness von Wulffen. But as soon as it came out he knew that it sounded right; that this was what he wanted to do.

The Elarani had at least been kind to him; treated him as a person, rather than as simply a perambulatory prophesying machine. Despite their troubles, none had ever pressed him to go south. Oh, he had no illusions. As sure as wood floated they were seeking to use his gift – he had not forgotten the blatant ploy that had kept him and Lawrence here over the winter. But they were subtler, more civilised about it. Form counted for a lot, even if some said it didn't. There were just appropriate ways of doing such things.

Kvh‡r||xkltl sidled, crabwise, to face Thomas head on. The *isp'te'ra* had let no emotion show outwardly – indeed, Thomas didn't even know if it was possible for that chitinous face to change expression – but Thomas sensed that he was surprised.

However, if that was the case, his voice did not betray it.

"Why would you do such a thing? You can gain no possible benefit from doing so. And there is a non-trivial risk to your own life." The flat, emotionless voice could have been making a statement about the weather.

"Because I wish to." Thomas felt no need to elaborate.

"But you cannot even be of any use. Your Seer talents are not yet so advanced." He clicked. "I am right, am I not?"

"Be that as it may, I'm still going."

"You are not making a rational choice. Not for yourself, nor for Elaran, nor for your own hive. Do you not see that this action does not serve your Triune Empire?

"I see that you will not be swayed." A trill of high-pitched clicks came from his throat. A sign of bafflement, thought Thomas, or of disgust? It was almost impossible to try to impose human emotions on to this creature.

Almost to himself, Kvh‡r||xkltl continued to speak. "Even after seventeen years outside my hive, I do not understand humans. And I was bred for this purpose. Why you will persist in making illogical decisions, when a simple weighing up of good and harm to oneself and to the hive gives clear answers I will never understand.

"It is possible," he admitted judiciously, "that one could argue for you to go to Rotliegendes, or to Siluria, or Linnarson, rather than to the Elder Alliance, though I believe that the logic would be flawed. But that any supposedly rational being could decide to go south?"

"Excuse me, Your Excellency," said Thomas, breaking into the monologue. "I have just seen someone I need to speak to." He bowed and escaped into the crowd.

Around the hall more people had begun to notice Rianda's absence. The atmosphere had changed subtly; the same half-felt, half-sensed feeling of pressure when the air was thick before a thunderstorm.

In one corner Euthymios was talking earnestly to the Givetian ambassador, a petite woman wearing a confectioner's fantasy of a dress, all frills and lace. Her honey-coloured curls were piled in an elaborate coiffure that added several inches to her height. Nodding solemnly, she appeared to be paying the bishop the fullest attention, but one glance at her face told a different story. Her eyes glanced rapidly back and forth across the floor, searching.

The approach of Ven Atharden gave her the chance she needed to excuse herself.

"Good evening, Your Excellency," she exclaimed in feigned surprise, bending enchantingly to kiss his proffered hand. "I believe I have not yet had the pleasure of speaking to you this evening."

"The pleasure is all mine, Your Excellency, I assure you," answered the Torridonian. Heads bent closely together, Ven Atharden's square countenance against the delicate oval of the Givetian they conferred rapidly – at least until Nomiki, ever alert to danger, made his respects and whisked her away in a rapid Aalenese waltz that left no time for conversation.

Disgruntled, Ven Atharden turned to the buffet table, irritably downing a glass of wine. Let the Elarani play at their court games while they still could. Soon they would find that the time when such things made a difference had passed long ago. He opened his mouth to speak as Baroness von Wulffen approached, but snapped it shut again as she glided past without a sideways glance, red velvet gown glimmering with a dangerous sheen in the shadows of the hall.

The baroness played her own game, neither Elarani, Torridonian nor Gellinese. For reasons known only to herself she would stop to exchange words with both the high and the low; treating all with the same effortless poise that made all but a few seem infinitely far below her.

But Rotliegendes and its schemes were the least of Elaran's worries tonight. Though the High Councillors did their best, they could not conceal the fact of Rianda's absence. Stubbornly they circulated, doing their best to keep troublemakers isolated: to reassure those who might be susceptible to becoming hostile. All their efforts could not prevent the mutterings or the whisperings in the corners.

It was a relief for all when at last – it seemed an age, though could not have been much more than half an hour – the queen reappeared. Both those of Elaran's party and those opposed were glad to see an end to the speculation, for better or worse.

Whole body erect, a model of perfect poise, she made her way to the front of the Great Hall, taking up a stand on the sweeping steps from which she had made her grand entrance only a few hours before. Only once did she stumble, the brief fumble giving a sickening glimpse of the chasm that lay beneath every precise step. Not even all her queen's dignity could disguise the deathly paleness of her face.

The gong was struck, its echoes quelling the last few murmurs of the hall into silence. All eyes were now rooted upon the slight figure that stood, alone, before their eyes.

"My lords, ladies and gentleman; honoured ambassadors and friends from other nations.

"It is with great regret that I must tell you that this morning, in the south of our blessed country of Elaran, the forces of Erd Gellin began to move. Three great columns are this moment marching north out of the fallen city of Hyrakos.

"The war has begun."

SEER

"To plunge oneself into the river of time is to taste the scent of eternity."

Konelis Larach – The Annalia, Volume Two

Chapter Nineteen

On the Eve of Thunder

From a small mound Thomas watched the Elarani forces digging in. It was astonishing the work that had been done in the short time that had been available. Across the centre of the Pass of Istria there now snaked two low earthen walls, each higher than a man was tall. Sinuous, they followed the contours of the ridges that criss-crossed the pass, stretching clear from one side of the slope to the other, up to the points beyond which no army could hope to keep formation.

Skirmishers would have to hold the line beyond those points. Skirmishers – and the two squat forts that terminated the earthworks at both ends, each able to hold eighty men. The walls curved forward at the ends like the horns of a bull, letting the men in those forts do far more than guard the flanks. From behind those rough and ready walls they could fire inwards along the line, shredding any advance that spread out too widely and keeping the Gellinese concentrated in the centre. Concentrated in a narrow front, that was the key: as long as the enemy couldn't bring their numbers to bear, the Elarani had a chance.

It had been Nomiki that had devised this strategy, just as it was he who had elected to first meet the enemy here, rather than further back, in the narrowest part of the pass. By laborious toil, the chiliad's cannon had been dragged into place on a spur just behind the lines and set into hastily constructed embrasures. It was a place without compare in the whole pass. From here, in relative safety, they could dominate the entire way before them – just four- and six-pounders they might be, but deadly in circumstances like this nonetheless.

Not content with this, two small emeralds had been sacrificed to bring down the sides of the valley before the defences. Elaran had few such resources, but any magecraft used in battle itself would surely be blocked by the superior Gellinese, and Nomiki had been in no doubt that their use beforehand would not be wasted.

The angry scars that had resulted were clearly visible on the valley sides, whilst the slough of rubble brought down in the landslide had effectively narrowed the pass by more than half, further channelling the enemy into Nomiki's central killing zone. Narrow enough to defend, with artillery behind and fortifications before, this position was where most damage could be done to the enemy and where there was greatest chance of victory.

More importantly than any of these factors, however, was that by ordering the first defence to be made here, the First Chiliarch had allowed for the possibility of one defeat. If by subterfuge, weight of numbers or sheer chance the enemy succeeded in breaching the defences all would not yet be lost. If the defenders were pushed back here they could still fall back and regroup further down the pass. Thus the presence of another wall at the narrowest part where, even reduced in numbers, the defenders would be able to stand at bay. If they had stood first at the narrows then a defeat would have meant there would be nowhere further to go.

Such was the theory, at any rate. There was no doubt that the plan was slightly discomforting. To defend at the narrows would have been simpler, more comforting and – according to Nomiki – ultimately doomed. The First Chiliarch had masterminded the strategy of defence for all three passes, but it was here, where the greatest blow would fall, that he was present in person.

Even now he was at work, somewhere off in the pass, urging his men to ever greater exertions. Not that they needed urging. Somehow, no one knew how, the news of the Desolation of Hyrakos had become common knowledge amongst the army and there was hardly a man unaffected by anger or the desire for revenge. Now they knew truly the nightmare they were facing; what the cost of defeat would be, for them and for their families. From the *hekatontarchi*, the company commanders, down to the lowliest recruit, every soldier strove his sinews to build the walls that inch higher, the ditches a hair deeper, the defences one iota stronger before the storm.

The intensity of work had not ceased since Thomas and the rest had arrived three days ago, flying south from Hyrnar into the coming storm. The three *tarath* had carried him, Rianda, the three chiliads and a few others south in a mere two days. Behind them in Hyrnar they had left Kadmos, the doughty Sword-Captain entrusted with the defence of the Citadel should the passes be lost. With him, to preserve the Nemessine line, stayed Chrysaor and his two children. The royal duke was bitter, but knew his duty. He had stayed behind willingly, if unhappily.

Only three of the *tarath* had come to the Pass of Istria. The other five had flown to Illapthos and the Thradfi Gap, where Hesperos and Lykourgos, Nomiki's junior chiliarchi, would be defending their passes.

There had been a bitter argument before they had separated, Thomas remembered. Nomiki and Hesperos had insisted that Elaran's *variideshar* be brought south with the army, two remaining with Nomiki at Istria with their linked partners at the other two passes. Thus the three forces could be sure of remaining in touch.

But Rianda would have none of it, insisting that only one came south, the others remaining in their usual places, at Hyrnar and the northern fastness of Melnarion. The three passes were close enough to maintain contact via *tarathin* – and if they lost control of the air so thoroughly as to be no longer able to do so, they were doomed anyway. To be able to hear word from the capital and the northern border was more important than the slight gain in speed and reliability that the *variideshar* would bring to the southern front. Had the chiliarchi forgotten

Torridon? Lykourgos, surprisingly, had stood with Rianda and, denied of even the united support of his own chiliarchi, Nomiki had grudgingly been forced to back down.

A similar debate had raged over the state crown but once again, Rianda had prevailed. Whilst Elaran's other gems might be spent like water in the defence of the passes, the five great jewels of the state crown would remain behind in Hyrnar, there to be used in the final defence of the Citadel or – at Chrysaor's discretion – carried to safety, should flight to the hills be deemed the best method of preserving some small fraction of Elaran for future years.

Thomas turned back towards the camp. The bulk of the army were at stations on the walls. Scouts had reported that the Gellinese were only a day's march away, a disciplined force with more than twice the numbers of the defenders. No one could take the risk that their were no small parties closer in and thus the defences were being kept manned, with one third of the army on duty at any one time and the remainder within easy reach.

But for some – clerks, Velnerine and other healers, smiths and those, like Thomas, whose roles were less well defined – it was both an obstruction and an unnecessary risk for them to be too close to the front. Nomiki had thus established a second camp, on the edge of the pass, behind the reserve wall. Placed there also were the two hundred of the Household Guard who had come south from Hyrnar. Whilst they would be needed once battle was truly joined, in the meantime the First Chiliarch had no intention of taking any chances with Rianda's life.

It was to this encampment that Thomas was heading as he trudged back through the mud of the pass. Euthymios was conducting a service for the Household Guard as he approached, his purple vestments a shock of colour against the dull background. The bishop did his part in helping to keep up morale, spreading his ministrations amongst the common soldiers rather than, as one might expect, saving them for Rianda and the high officers and nobility alone. Whilst Nomiki might have a better feel for the mood of the army than Euthymios, there were few others who could say the same.

They had got as far as the Creed by the time Thomas reached them. Slotting himself unobtrusively into the back of the crowd, he joined the soldiers in the remains of the service; the devotion, intercessions and Euthymios's final blessing. The words were in Dalradian, the traditional language of the church, and similar enough to the Scriptualist rite that he could join in without too much stumbling. At a time like this a prayer could hardly hurt. If ever they needed Andur's attention, it was now.

The Household Guard apparently felt the same for almost all were present. Few liked the thought of dying unshriven. Even these disciplined troops welcomed anything that took their mind off the coming battle.

The waiting was always hardest. Thomas had heard the saying frequently, but now he knew the truth of it despite – because? – he could play no active part in the coming struggle.

He envied Lawrence. Not that he actually wanted to be shot at, but it wasn't pleasant to feel like useless baggage. The former chaplain had barely touched the ground since arriving. Almost every hour of the day Lawrence spent scouting on *tarathin*-back, a valued member of Ven Tychon's *tarathinakii*. Meanwhile there was nothing that Thomas could do but wander aimlessly around, getting in others' way.

Of course the Velnerines – they had come south with the army as healers – were not yet busy. He had spent several hours each day with the Abbot, in more fruitless lessons. Today he had been too dispirited to even do that. He had not made any progress for months. But that had left him with the alternatives of either watching the army or sitting in the cold tent he shared with Lawrence, staring at the canvas walls.

The camp was bitterly uncomfortable. He supposed it was better than the conditions they'd endured in the flight across Erd Gellin, but a winter of living easy in the Citadel at Hyrnar had softened him. At least in autumn it had been hot.

Thomas forgot the oppressive sweltering conditions that he had endured, the true facts fading into a rosy memory of warmth. By the Wheel, it was cold today. They called it spring, here in Elaran, but it was not the sort of spring they had back Home.

The snow might have melted in the mountain passes, but the sun's rays had not yet warmed the ground. By the way the cold seeped through his bones when sleeping, Thomas could well have believed that a layer of ice remained frozen just below the topsoil as he had heard occurred in the northern reaches of Borallia.

He knew it was the altitude that caused it. That was to blame, too, for the winds, which whistled through the natural wind tunnel created by the pass like a cold knife cutting at his bones. It sliced right through his clothes as if he were naked. Thomas didn't know what was worst – the cold itself, or the way the countryside mocked him by ignoring it completely.

Grape hyacinths, anemones and naphlidin were flowering freely. All the beauty of the mountains was springing up around them whilst they prepared for war.

He shivered. A lone swallow flew across the mottled sky. In a week or two the skies would be alive with them, flying north for summer, but for now it was the only one to be seen, a lone traveller crying out harshly for its absent fellows. Thomas watched it until it disappeared, lost beneath the sharp line of the escarpment.

He turned away and stepped into his tent. It was empty. Lawrence was out, as was only to be expected. Thomas was glad. He did not feel in need of company at this moment. The outside world could do without him for now. The morrow would bring what it would bring.

Chapter Twenty

"The Droghkar are Extinct"

The host of Erd Gellin had arrived the evening before, long columns of men marching steadily into the south of the valley. The army had been placed on the highest alert since nightfall, though in truth no one had expected a night attack; not then, with the Gellinese weary from their long march and the defenders fresh and ready.

But now the morning was here, the bright sun glinting off the valley sides, bringing light but no heat, not yet. Thomas shivered on the knoll where he stood, Rianda and Euthymios by his side. Nomiki and Sir Hanyarmé were with the troops along the walls, bracing them against the charge. Down the valley the great war drums were beating, steadily, summoning soldiers to war.

They came roiling out of the valley mouth like a billowing cloud, pouring up the Pass of Istria: the incoming tide inexorably filling a narrow crevasse. Endless ranks with the Desert Palm of Erd Gellin emblazoned upon their breasts. By the Wheel, there were so many of them!

"They must have sent half their whole army against us," breathed Euthymios.

"Good," said Rianda. "The more we face here, the fewer in the other passes. It is what Nomiki has gambled upon."

"I only hope he has remembered what a high stake he is wagering."

As ever more troops marched into sight Thomas could understand Euthymios's qualms. Behind the solid squares of men – twice as many as stood in their path, at the least – came a veritable herd of artillery. No motley collection of firing pieces here: this battery would scarce have disgraced an Imperial regiment. Drawn by teams of mules and oxen the heavy guns lumbered slowly down the centre of the pass, their hollow barrels grinning like hungry mouths.

The men were close enough now to see distinctly. From the wall they must be able to make out their faces. In five disciplined squares they were arranged; each man with his musket slung across his chest in perfect order. Thomas counted swiftly. Each square was thirty men abreast: a thousand then, in each one. That made five thousand in total, give or take, not counting the guns.

And they were not all. Further back still stood ranks of darker foes. No uniforms were worn by these troops; twisted, goat-like creatures thought long lost and buried in the annals of history and myth.

It was thus that Thomas Maynard, junior official of the Triune Empire, first saw a host of droghkar and knew for truth that the deepest fears of the Empire had been confirmed. Beside him Rianda trembled, and Euthymios also and all the sturdy defenders of Elaran upon the wall, for this was their nightmare too and that of all men.

"The droghkar are extinct." So men had said for generations, taking comfort in its reassuring sound. But now that was true no longer; indeed, had never been true, and the creatures that had savaged Laurentia and Avalonia both during the Secession Wars, that had torn through the defences of the Zechen-Rotliegendish Commonwealth at the height of its power, were back, walking in open mockery upon Andur's green hills in the springtime.

What power could have yoked such evil; bound it to march in ordered fashion alongside the soldiers of Erd Gellin? What depths had the Archons plumbed? The wind veered to the south-west and a harsh scent wafted with it, the sterile odour of the western desert. Men shivered and whispered of the Forces of the Sand and of lost Atavus; of the Desolation of Hyrakos and the rumours that had come north.

But though they trembled, they did not break. First Chiliarch Nomiki strode amongst them, as did Sir Hanyarmé and all his Knights of St. Senren, with their own commanders; *hekatontarchi* with their Hundreds; *epimeleti* with their files; each taking strength from those above and steadying those around.

And so the men of Elaran stood as the forces of Erd Gellin marched closer under the dawn sun; the ranks of men; the great guns; the brightly garbed mages, more numerous by far than those of the defenders; the beating wings of the *tarathin* above, almost wingtip to wingtip shadowing the pass and, behind all, the twisted droghkar and the demons that marched amongst them.

The guns were coming forward alone now, moving ahead of the rest of the army. The Gellinese were rightly confident that the defenders would risk no sortie against them.

A cannon ball whistled overhead, plummeting down on to the Gellinese guns. Half a dozen more followed, bouncing through the ordered ranks and scattering men like ninepins. Now Thomas realised the genius of Nomiki's plan. The Elarani cannon, placed as they were upon their high spur, could bombard their Gellinese counterparts with impunity. To return fire, even had they possessed a mortar – which they did not – the Gellinese would have to move within musket range of the Elarani wall. Exposure unsheltered to such concentrated small-arms fire would be suicide.

But even this advantage did not compensate for the lack of firepower. Elaran had neither enough nor sufficiently powerful artillery. Thomas clenched his teeth. He was no soldier, but even he could imagine what could be achieved here by a battery of modern twenty-four pounders instead of the motley collection of primitive cannon that they in fact possessed.

The response from the Gellinese guns provided a partial answer. Their guns might be just as primitive as Elaran's, but by the Wheel, there were more of them. They roared out in a devastating salvo, shot smashing into the Elarani wall across the entire breadth of the pass.

Again and again the cannon blasted the line, even whilst the return fire from the spur dropped pitifully among them. The firing grew more ragged as some, more competent crews, drew ahead of their fellows. Great billows of smoke drifted up the valley, obscuring the lines of guns and carrying the sharp, acrid scent of gunpowder to Thomas's nostrils.

No battle of this kind though was ever won by bombardment alone. Perhaps half an hour of crash and thunder had passed when a long, deep horn sounded, calling the Gellinese guns back to their lines. Exposed so completely, even the feeble Elarani cannon had taken their toll. In any case, the damage was done. Though one could hope there the fortifications had at least protected the defenders' lives, the wall itself had been rent in a dozen places. Great breaches had been ripped out that the Gellinese could and would try to exploit.

Already the deep drums were beating again in measured tempo, sounding the Gellinese advance. Four regiments had come to the fore, widening and flattening until they had transformed into two long lines. Each was only ten men deep, but they stretched almost the full width of the pass. The discipline could not have been more perfect had it been a parade ground drill rather than a battlefield.

Steadily the Gellinese marched towards the defenders. Cannon fired as they passed into range but too few, far too few. The ranks swiftly closed up around the gaps caused by those shots that had struck home. The Elarani guns fired so slowly. All too soon, they could fire no longer for fear of striking their own side.

Now it was fire and fury before the wall, the Gellinese's steady fire answered by an opening volley by the defenders. Men screamed, fell, died; were trampled in the dust. The firing was furious now: a cacophonous crackle in Thomas's ears. He felt curiously detached. It was hard to comprehend here on this knoll that what he was watching was a battle with men being killed or maimed for life. The fate of Elaran depended on this, he told himself, little dreaming how far from uppermost in their minds was that thought to those fighting for survival on the wall.

They were holding, he saw. Fortunately it took less training and discipline to hold a line than to advance exposed and coverless to take it. The Elarani fervour and love of homeland was compensating for their inexperience.

Still, men were dying behind the wall as well as in front of it, shot down in the act of firing through a breach or whilst trying to reload. The air was alive with bullets: so heavy was the fusillade that to incautiously expose a limb or head above the parapet was to risk death or injury. But there had been no time to prepare knotholes, so expose themselves the defenders must.

Even as it seemed to Thomas that the carnage was at its height the deep horn of Erd Gellin sounded once more and the attackers closed ranks and began to fall back, leaving a trail of dead and wounded in their wake. Their ranks were not broken: not until they were well out of reach did the Gellinese cease firing. This withdrawal was a retreat, not a rout.

Behind the wall the defenders remained alert, Nomiki's iron will not permitting any slackening even now that the attack had ended. The minutes passed in eerie silence, save for the cries of the wounded on the ground before the wall. As it became clear that the enemy were not returning the tenseness of the defenders faded and then turned to exhilaration.

Fully one third of these men were militia, farmers and townsmen who had never held a gun before. Now they had faced fire, stood firm and won their first victory, all without grievous loss. Even the more experienced solders became infected by their mood and their captains, watching wisely, let it flourish. They knew that they had not yet truly been tested, but knew too that such a mood of confidence might yet be worth an extra thousand men.

Already, the white-robed Velnerines were moving forward, retrieving and ministering to the wounded. Like emissaries of peace they threaded their way amongst the slough of battle with grace and dignity.

"They're an odd crew," said a voice behind Thomas, laconically. "I always find it funny the way they've ended up, given the way their founder got himself killed."

Thomas leaped half a foot into the air. "Don't do that!" he yelped. "For the love of Order, we're in the middle of a battlefield."

Tychon – for it was he – just looked amused.

"Hardly the middle. And if the enemy managed to get this far without you noticing them you'd have to be stone deaf and blind. I know Our Lady of Silence has favoured you, but you've yet to receive those particular blessings."

Tychon appeared to be in fine fettle, not in the least disturbed by the fierce aerial skirmish he'd just been in. Thomas, like many others, had paid it little attention, distracted by the main action below, but though it had admittedly been brief, even so neither side had been without loss.

In truth, battle was what Tychon lived for: the speed and danger of such aerobatics were without compare and left him energised rather than otherwise. The presence of enemies simply added an additional fillip of risk. But whilst the air captain might be in high spirits, Thomas was less blasé about being startled at such a time.

"Anyway, what do you mean 'how he got himself killed'?" demanded Thomas, returning to the original statement. "I thought St. Velnery had established field hospitals in the Pelagic War until he got killed by mages."

Tychon laughed softly. "You Imperials. Everything you've just said is true, but you've still managed to completely miss the point. Of course, the Velnerines do like to try to keep quiet about it."

Thomas started to look annoyed as Tychon continued.

"You see, it wasn't Pelagic mages who martyred him – if you want to call it that – but Linnarsonians."

"What? I thought Linnarson was an ally in that war."

"It was. But the war itself had nothing to do with it, or at least only indirectly. It was the attempt by the Pelagics to assassinate the Gendarsh of Linnarson that started it all off. You're familiar with that?"

Thomas nodded, hoping Tychon wouldn't decide to press him on the details.

"Well, it failed of course, but the senior Masters were revealed for what they were and the shock almost split the coalition, which some say is what the Pelagics had intended all along. But whilst most people were content for the church synod to mull over the situation and reach a decision – which they did, a few years later – that wasn't enough for Velnery. He had to take matters into his own hands and 'root out the evil at its source' as he so poetically put it.

"He made a pretty good attempt at it too. Shattered the gates of Barnwell College with air elementals. My father said you can still see the scars where they've repaired it. But of course, that was as far as he got. You don't challenge the mages of Linnarson even if Andur is on your side, and especially if you only think he is. The Senior Masters obliterated him: all that was left were a few bones, like that one they've got in Hyrnar.

"And here are the Velnerines today, a peaceful order of healers. It's as if..."

He broke off as once more the drums began their rhythmic beat. Without another word he dashed to his *tarathin* tethered nearby and fastened the harness about himself with alacrity. Less than a minute after the drum began, Tychon was airborne, winging his way skywards beside the other *tarathinakii.*

Every one of them was desperately needed in an assault and, as with everything else, Elaran had too few. Somehow the bare score of them had to scout the battlefield and carry messages, all the while engaging the enemy flyers and preventing them from harrying the defence.

It was dangerous work even by battlefield standards, for the enemy was far more numerous and the threat of musket fire from the ground could not be discounted. Only speed, lightning reflexes and, occasionally, blind luck, could be relied upon to keep a *tarathinaki* alive.

Lawrence was in his element. Despite his relative inexperience the former chaplain possessed a flair that not even Tychon could match. Though he still refused to carry a weapon, for sheer flying quality he was without peer. The bond between him and his mount bordered on the uncanny.

This time Thomas watched his countryman throughout the assault as Lawrence swooped and dived across the skies of battle. One moment he would be soaring high above the battlefield, the next hurtling groundward in a terrifying dive before rolling up again at the last possible moment before anyone could react to his presence. Boldly, recklessly almost, he would urge his *tarathin* forward into the very teeth of the enemy, only to pass unscathed through a gap that one could have sworn did not exist a moment before and that vanished a moment later. Not a movement the enemy made was safe from his eyes, nor could the best efforts of their own *tarathinakii* keep him from relaying his news home.

Envy touched Thomas's heart, that Lawrence had so perfectly found his place here, but pride overwhelmed it, a great swelling sun beside which jealously was but a candle. To think that it was a man of the Empire doing this; a man, who with no prior training – a chaplain, by the Wheel! – could outmatch the best that Elaran or Erd Gellin could offer. Let these Laurentians see the mettle of the Imperial race. Lawrence's glory made up for his own inadequacies; his failure to master the strange gift that possessed him. Thomas watched his countryman until the horns once more sounded the retreat, and gloried in his skill.

Twice more did the drums beat that day, the first day of the war between Erd Gellin and Elaran in the spring of 1841. Twice more did the soldiers of Erd Gellin advance and twice more were they beaten back by the valour of the defenders, the stoutness of their walls and, not a little, by their sheer blind stubbornness. Even the attack, early in the afternoon, by two score *nasku*, winged horrors whose mouths dripped a deadly venom, was countered without great difficulties. Under the guidance of the Senrenites, the Elarani held firm, mastered their fear and trained their muskets upon the demons. And before that fire the *nasku* fell from the sky, neither their sharp claws nor their poison being of avail.

Only once did the Gellinese truly seem in danger of breaking through and that was in the last assault, when the bright spring sun had all but slipped beneath the rim of the valley wall.

The attack, as with the ones before, had been concentrated at one of the rents made by the morning's bombardment. This time, one particularly bold detachment of men had made it to the wall itself. Now fifty or more of them were in the breach itself, firing at the defenders from the shelter of the rubble. Though reinforcements rushed to force them back the Gellinese would not be dislodged from their hard-won position. And continuously more of the invaders were pouring into the breach, strengthening the position by the minute.

Clarion clear, a horn sounded. High and pure and sweet it was; in every way different from the deep war horns of Erd Gellin. Light itself seemed to live in that sound.

For an instant, the battle seemed to pause, an eerie tableau, and Thomas remembered the one time before that he had heard that wonderful noise, on a crisp white morning in Pilter when a full hand of the Knights of St. Senren had come to offer their services to the crown of Elaran.

From the western fort the fifty Senrenites thundered. Like a breaking wave they poured down the scarred flanks of the pass and along the valley floor in front of the wall, swords and carbines gleaming in the dying light. Desperately, the Gellinese tried to wheel their formations, to bring their fire to bear against this new threat. Shots rang out as, here and there, more adept units managed to react in time.

Better to try to halt an avalanche. Thomas watched incredulously as bullets glanced off the Senrenites' burnished armour as if they were no more than pebbles thrown by a child. The tales were true. Several horses fell, stricken, but their riders rolled unharmed from the dust and sped with celerity to the safety of the wall. And the charge went on.

At point blank range they fired their carbines, a sudden blast that shattered the already fragmented Gellinese ranks into disarray. Then, swords flashing, the knights were upon them, striking left and right with devastating effectiveness. The Gellinese reeled back from the onslaught, leaving their comrades in the breach isolated.

The defenders saw their chance. Pressing forward with renewed vigour they surged against the breach. The wall would be regained.

It was not easy, for the Gellinese were courageous men and, caught without a line of retreat, fought as desperately as rats in a trap. But eventually the futility of their position could no longer be hidden. The last man threw down his musket in surrender and the wall was Elaran's once more.

Only then did that glorious horn sound once more, calling the Senrenites back from their fight. Thomas counted their number as they withdrew. Two had fallen, only two, in that desperate sortie into the very heart of the enemy. Only two: but what a grievous loss.

Chapter Twenty-One

When Mountains Fall

"It is too easy," said Hanyarmé.

"Too easy?" Euthymios was quizzical.

Rianda broke in. "I object strongly to that statement, Sir Hanyarmé. Perhaps for your Senrenites a conflict like this is trivial, but I can assure you that for the men of Elaran dying on that wall it has most certainly not been easy."

Hanyarmé bowed low. "Your Majesty, the valour of Elaran's soldiers has been superlative. For my knights and me it has been an honour to fight beside them.

"But yes, I will say it is too easy. Four assaults the first day, three the second and only two today, not one of them pressed home. Valour alone is not enough in war. With their numbers we should be desperately trying to hold our own, not comfortably forcing them back from our walls."

Rianda was only partially mollified. "Have you considered that perhaps it is due to the strength of our defences and to Nomiki here's skill at strategy?" she asked pointedly. "Even so, on the first day they almost broke through."

"They should not have done. We were not yet practised at our defences. Since then they have not even come close."

"I see what you mean," said Euthymios, nodding slowly. "Even the *nasku* are far from the worst of what Erd Gellin might have thrown at us, if all that has been reported is true. And after that one attempt there have been no demonic assaults at all."

"Precisely. So what are they concealing? What is their real plan?"

"Perhaps they have no other plan," said Nomiki sombrely. It was the first time he had spoken. They looked at him, puzzled.

"Consider. In the last three days we have lost a hundred men, and praise be to Andur for the Velnerines, or the number would be three times as great. But even at that rate, within two months every one of us would be dead. The Gellinese could be in Hyrnar by High Scriansa.

"They lose more than we do," protested Euthymios.

"They can afford to lose more." He sighed. "But Sir Hanyarmé is right. I have been fighting the Gellinese on the southern marches for years and have never had reason to suspect their generals of incompetence. It would be unlikely for it to begin now. Nor do I think that the Archons would go to the trouble of binding demons and the long-dead droghkar to their cause only to have them sit by and do nothing.

"No, they have something planned, but the question is, what? All we can do is remain vigilant."

"I would feel more comfortable if we knew more of what was happening in the other passes," said Euthymios. "We've heard nothing since the first day. I know how ill even a single *tarathin* can be spared, but..."

"We should have brought the *variideshar*," said Nomiki flatly.

"Perhaps we should. For myself I remain unconvinced. I would not wish to be totally cut off from Hyrnar and the north." Rianda spoke coolly, every inch the queen. "However, the decision has been made for good or for ill and we must abide by it."

"You are right, Your Majesty. But I will send a *tarathinaki* tomorrow to Illapthos and the Thradfi Gap. It will do little good to hold here if we are overwhelmed there."

"You are First Chiliarch – our forces are yours to command. I think all of us are aware of how much we are relying upon your skill. To know news of the other passes would relieve us all.

"As for our success – is this not all we could have hoped for? We worry, yet where would we be had the Gellinese overwhelmed us? We have much to thank Andur for."

"Andur grant that it remain so."

#

"Your Majesty!" Rianda sat bolt upright, wide awake instantly. Her nerves had been placed on tenterhooks the moment the battle started and she had been sleeping restlessly ever since.

She looked around. The messenger's lantern was a lone light in the darkness. It was still the middle of the night. But there was no sign of gunfire or battle: at least the Gellinese could not be making a night attack. These thoughts flashed through her mind in a heartbeat. Her first fear at least was relieved – but then what could have happened?

She froze, her stomach churning. Her relief vanished as the thought struck home. The northern border. Surely Torridon would not have invaded so soon?

"Your Majesty?" The messenger spoke again. "His Grace the Lord Bishop sends his apologies but begs that you come urgently."

"Did he say why?"

"A messenger, Your Majesty. From Illapthos."

Not Torridon then, Andur's grace be praised. Trembling she let out the breath that she had not even realised she was holding. They could be thankful for small mercies.

They might be small enough at that. For Nomiki's messenger to have returned so soon was ill-omened. *Tarathini* flew neither freely nor willingly at night.

"Tell His Grace...no, wait. I will come immediately." Rianda pulled her great-cloak around her. Her night clothes were sturdy enough and this was no time to stand on ceremony.

"Take me to him."

Walking swiftly, she followed him through the camp. He had not expected her to go so fast: when they set off she had momentarily left him behind and he had had to half run awkwardly forward to catch up. He was very young, thought Rianda incongruously. Only a few years older than she.

A score of the Household Guard formed a circle on the outskirts of the tents, enclosing Euthymios and Nomiki. Though the night was clear the moon, still a few days before crescent, cast little light. Only inside the circle could one see; unshuttered lanterns cast dancing shadows across the ground.

Rianda shivered. The night was bitterly cold. Bowing, the soldiers stepped aside, admitting her into the ring. A shape became clear. From a distance it had seemed to be just a darker shadow in the variegated shades of the lanterns' flickering light. Now closer, the silhouette revealed itself as a body, motionless and indistinct.

"Why has he returned so soon?" demanded Rianda. "What has happened?"

Both her advisers remained silent for a moment, gazing down at the forlorn heap before them. It was Nomiki who spoke first.

"He's made it over the mountains from Illapthos from foot. Covered the distance in under two days, without food and with that gash in his side. He's Mareischi of course, from around Melnarion – one of the few who joined the army. No one else could have done it." The First Chiliarch's voice held a hint of awe.

"Two days? I don't understand. You only sent him this evening."

"This isn't our messenger, Rianda," explained Euthymios gently. "We don't know what's happened to him..."

"Dead, Johan's oath upon it," interjected Nomiki.

"Very probably. But this man's from Lykourgos's chiliad at Illapthos. The sentries say he came staggering in out of the night, crying out that he had to see Nomiki immediately. He'd passed out by the time we reached him."

"Andur alone knows what kept him conscious long enough to reach us," added Nomiki. "That wound in his side alone should have done for him after a few miles. And his other injuries..." He shook his head.

Rianda looked down at the man. Visible through the rips and tears of his tabard a great gash still oozed blood. Black and ugly, it snaked across his ribs before disappearing around his side beneath him. Half a dozen smaller cuts were scattered over his arms and torso. He had clearly made an effort to patch them, but his exertions had kept them from closing.

"Can he be revived?" she heard herself ask.

"We've sent for the Abbot. If anyone can save him, he can."

"We're fortunate to have the Velnerines with us."

Inwardly Rianda felt a sudden revulsion. Is this what I am? A man lies before me, near death, and all I can think of is what information he can give me. When did I learn to become so cold? When my father died, she answered herself. Since Elaran began to depend on me.

The Abbot arrived, interrupting Rianda's thoughts. Outwardly she had betrayed no sign of her emotions. To the world she must be queen.

"Your Majesty, My Lords," said Jarlod, sketching a hasty bow. "You asked for me?" His white robe, spotless as ever, lay askew about his shoulders. Like the rest of them he had come as quickly as he could. Ironically, his two young acolytes appeared to be in less disarray than him. No doubt detailed to be on duty that night, they alone had been awake when the summons came.

"Thank you for coming so swiftly, Father," said Rianda, smoothly taking charge. "This man here has come through the mountains on foot. He is grievously wounded and near death from exhaustion. Before he lost consciousness he said he was bringing urgent news from the other passes.

"Father, we need that information. Is there anything you can do for him?"

"I would try my utmost to save this man's life no matter what information he carried, Your Majesty." His tone contained the barest hint of a reprimand. "He does not look beyond hope. If St. Velnery grants it, he will be healed."

Losing no more time, Jarlod dropped to his knees. His acolytes followed suit. Gently, they turned the man over on to his back. Jarlod's hands ran tenderly and knowledgeably over the man's body, sensitively teasing out the location and severity of his injuries. Simultaneously, he began a steady chant, sotto voce, so low that no more than one word in ten could be distinguished. Supporting his prayer, the acolytes began a gentle crooning. The energy of the chant pulsed like a heartbeat, rising and falling at the edge of hearing.

The others could do nothing now but watch. As the esoteric business continued Rianda began to tremble. Her nerves, their effects thus far denied by the rush and urgency of the initial happening, took advantage of this lull to begin making themselves known.

What could make a lone soldier strike out for himself across the mountains? What calamity had overtaken them at the centre pass that not even a *tarathin* could be sent? This man had been running for two days. Two days in which not a whisper had reached them. Suddenly, Rianda was more frightened than at any time since the morning they had told her that her father had died.

"Are you sure he said nothing else?" she asked suddenly. She needed to speak; to hear human voices filling the silence.

"No more than what we have told you already, Your Majesty."

By the Wheel, she hated being helpless. Chafing inwardly, she watched the Velnerines continue their work.

The man was Mareischi, Nomiki had said. That much was obvious. The stocky, powerful frame and rugged features bespoke his origin as clearly as a written sign. The man could have been Eliud's cousin. Thought of the northern Marchwarden made her wonder how he fared, fighting in the Thradfi Gap, seven days to the west. Had disaster overwhelmed them, also?

"Your Majesty?" Rianda realised that the chanting had halted. Jarlod was standing before her, curiously hesitant.

"Yes, go on."

"Your Majesty, normally I would not even suggest this. I should heal this man, anoint his wounds and put him in a healing sleep from which he will awake, alive and well. But you have said that this man has already, of his own accord, put his life in peril to bring you the news he carries.

"If I put him in a sleep he will be unconscious for three days. Perhaps more. But I could try by my arts to revive him now..." He trailed off hesitantly.

"What is it that you are not saying, Father?"

"It could kill him. The odds are even, no better. I would not do this to serve you, nor any ruler, not for the Patriarch himself. But I ask myself, would he want me to revive him despite the risk? I do not know. Your Majesty, what would you have me do?"

Rianda closed her eyes. She remembered her thoughts of only a few minutes before. Blessed Ruth, she prayed, forgive me if there is something I do not see, some way I have missed. But what can I do? These are my people at stake.

"Revive him," she said.

Wordlessly, Jarlod bowed and, kneeling, drew out a long thin case from his cassock. Its surface was polished smooth, a dark, ruddy lustre that seemed almost to come from inside the wood, such was the smoothness of the grain. There were no carvings or designs on it save for the clasp, a cunningly wrought buckle of brass filigree. Deftly, the Abbot unsnapped it, carefully lifting the lid to reveal two small phials cushioned in rich velvet of the darkest green.

One at a time he withdrew the phials, kissing them reverently and holding them up in adoration before him. The cut crystal sparkled in the lantern light. In one was a colourless liquid that could have contained the stars themselves, such did the shining lights within it dance and twinkle; the other was golden, suffused with a warm, wholesome light.

"The tears of the holy St. Velnery," said Jarlod, in hushed tones, "and the elixir that bears his name."

Unstoppering them with great care he let fall three drops of the gold upon the man's brow, then used the star-filled liquid to anoint the wrists. He then delicately placed the phials back in the reliquary, closed and replaced it, before reaching out his hands in benediction over the wounded man, beginning once more to chant.

With a violent jerk the man sat up, staring Rianda straight in the face. There was a wild look in his eyes, an unnatural fire that burned too brightly.

"My Queen!" he cried out. "My Queen! We are destroyed."

"Who is? What has happened to your chiliad?"

"You do not know?" He fell back, stricken. "Then I am already too late."

"You are not too late. "Thanks to your courage in running the mountains, there may yet be time. But I must know all you have to tell. I must know!"

"It began when the host of Erd Gellin first marched up the pass against us. But oh, My Queen, it is a tale to make your heart weep."

He struggled to sit up again. The fell light burned less fiercely now, but a trace remained. The man still spoke with unnatural fervour for one so near death.

"Your Majesty, my name is Tasos. I was a *hekatontarch* in the Chiliad of the South, having served there for almost seventeen years.

"Like you here at Istria, at Illapthos we had constructed walls and fortifications across the pass. I and my Hundred were stationed on the left flank, where a shallow levelling provided a natural route of attack for the Gellinese.

"All that first day we held them, for all their numbers, their cannon and magecraft. We were fortunate, we told ourselves; the force that opposed us was not as large as we might have feared, nor were the demons or droghkar unleashed against us.

"But that evening, after the last assault had been turned back, the Chiliarch gathered us all together; every officer and most of the men, save for a few who remained on the wall. He spoke to us, telling us of the war, of the forces against us and of the Desolation of Hyrakos. We had all heard rumours, of course, of what the Gellinese had done, but now they were being confirmed, in brutal detail.

"We thought at first he was galvanising our resistance, warning us what the consequences would be for us and our families should we be defeated. But then he told us that he had received a message from you, Your Majesty. He said you had seen the forces that faced us, in all three passes. This was, he said, a war that we could not win.

"Knowing that we could not win, and knowing what would befall us if we resisted and lost, you had, he told us, signed a treaty. This was wise, he told us. No ruler should throw away the lives of her subjects to no avail, but it took courage to make such a decision. Too often, resistance seemed the easiest option. But now, thanks to your wisdom, Elaran would not be brutalised and enslaved, but instead become an honoured vassal of Erd Gellin; tributary, true, and subject to the Archons' will, but largely free to go about its affairs without interference."

"And you accepted this?" said Rianda in disbelief.

"Lykourgos was our Chiliarch, Your Majesty. What else could we do? Besides, it seemed possible. For all our bold words, we all knew it would take a miracle to win – and none knew the size of the armies at the other passes. Your Majesty, I have seen stranger decisions made in war. A soldier obeys.

"The mood amongst us was oddly mixed. You would have thought that as we had just been delivered from a battle we would be rejoicing, but it was not so. True, many of us who would have died would now no longer do so, but on the other hand, it was as if we had lost without a chance to try and win. No man likes to surrender, Your Majesty, and a soldier least of all. We had been prepared to fight and die for Elaran, but now that we were not needed, we were not sure how to live.

"The orders went out soon after that. We were to abandon our posts and let the Gellinese through. Then we were to arrange ourselves into companies of one hundred and put ourselves under the authority of the enemy. We were to be allowed to keep out weapons. That was to reassure us that we were being treated honourably," he added bitterly.

"They waited until we were all split up and surrounded. Then they destroyed us.

"The demons and droghkar were unleashed on us without warning. Terrifying monstrosities; creatures of dark legend come to life. For us it was a nightmare turned true.

"Unsuspecting as we were, fully half of us were cut down before we had time to react. What fools we were! But then why should we have suspected anything? Erd Gellin had already achieved its victory. Why did they need to massacre us?

"Even once the surprise had passed we could do nothing. Outnumbered, surrounded and in disarray there was no way of forming a line or square. A few officers did try to rally a defence but their resistance was as brief as it was futile. Most of us, Andur have mercy on us, simply fled.

"I ordered my men to break for the hills and then ran with them. We were amongst the lucky ones. My Hundred had been near to the edge so we had less far to go. It was all that gave us a chance. The demons were in a feeding frenzy, lashing out at anything that moved. That was how I took these wounds – I was lucky not to take more.

"But it was possible for a determined man to get through the mêlée. At least a dozen of us made it out. Then we scattered. I don't know what happened to them after that. There were *rahvashda* in the hills that night."

"Did they kill *everyone*?" said Rianda. She was still trying to take it in. The tale was incomprehensible: beyond belief.

"I don't know. I didn't stay to watch. They got Lykourgos though: that much I do know. Three droghkar pulled him down just as I made it past the outer line of guards. The great fool was still screaming about his agreement as they tore open his throat. As for the others?" Tasos shrugged. "I know that the screaming continued for a long time after I had escaped."

Suddenly he learned forward, the mad fire glinting in his eyes once more. Grabbing the front of Rianda's cloak he pulled himself towards her.

"You must not surrender, My Queen," he cried fervently. "They are terrible. Terrible! You must fight, My Queen. They will destroy us all, unless you can..."

His eyes rolled up in his head and he collapsed limply, the Velnerines' unnatural spell of lucidity ended.

The night wind sliced through the pass, but it no longer held any power to chill. Nomiki was the first to break the silence. Normally the most controlled of men he began to swear, steadily and methodically working his way through Elarani's worst epithets.

"Curse his soul to the deepest pit of the ninth circle of hell," he concluded. "Lykourgos was Hyrakine – how could he do this? How could any man do such a thing?"

"His wife and children were in the city when it fell," murmured Euthymios. "Who can tell what the Archons promised him? Their freedom perhaps, or perhaps just their release from torment."

Nomiki snorted with contempt. "And for such a thing he would betray his country and men to death?"

"Men will find strange limits in times such as these. No doubt Lykourgos had half convinced himself that what he told the troops was true.

"But I make no excuses for him, only explanations. Nor do I dispute your judgement. When his soul is weighed in the scales of Andur's justice, I fear he will be found wanting. The realisation of how he was betrayed in turn may have been just the start of his punishment."

"Tasos is alive, Your Majesty." It was Jarlod who spoke. When Tasos had passed out, the Abbot had returned to him immediately and was now able to give the fortunate outcome of his efforts.

"Good," said Rianda. At least one decision she had made had not gone awry. "Thank you for your efforts, Father." She turned back to her counsellors.

"We must deal with the situation as it is. Lykourgos has betrayed us; Illapthos is taken and one third of our forces destroyed. It matters not why he did so, but rather what the Gellinese will do now.

"Do you think they will march straight on Hyrnar Nomiki?"

"I am doubtful, Your Majesty. It is a possibility of course. But only a quarter or so of their army was attacking Illapthos. They cannot be sure how strongly Hyrnar is defended.

"Given this and their penchant for total destruction, I believe they will first turn their attention to the other two passes. With the centre taken, they can strike east or west at will. They will attempt to crush us from behind; then, united and unopposed, their entire army will march on Hyrnar."

"Very well: we must withdraw. But to where? Which way will they go?"

"Our own withdrawal is not absolutely pressing. Tasos may have crossed the hills in two days, but an army would take at least a week. I fear a graver problem is Hesperos's chiliad. The geography means that the Gellinese could block his retreat in just four days – and they have already had two. Without warning he will be taken completely unawares. His chiliad will be slaughtered as comprehensively as Lykourgos's men.

"And therein lies the crux of the matter," added Euthymios. "How are we to warn them?"

"I will go," said a voice from outside.

The three of them looked up, startled. Then they saw that beyond the ring of guards a crowd had gathered; officers, clerks, functionaries and off-duty soldiers. In all, perhaps half of the secondary camp had gathered to watch, listening in rapt fascination. It was testimony to the gravity of the situation that not only had Nomiki not rebuked such a breach of discipline, he had not even noticed.

Rianda recovered her poise quickly. "Who said that?" she demanded, scanning the crowd to try to make out individual faces beyond the barrier of lantern light.

"Come forward, into the light."

"I will go," said Lawrence again, for it was he. Stepping into the circle he stood, undaunted by the stares.

"I thank you for the offer, chaplain. But I cannot allow it."

"I am a *tarathinaki* now, Your Majesty. In truth, I no longer have a right to the nobler title, though I have endeavoured to remain a humble servant of Andur."

"Of course. As I say, I thank you for the offer, but I cannot allow it. Even a *tarathinaki* of your skills would never make it through."

"Really? Tell me, Your Majesty, what other choices do you have?"

"Euthymios?" Rianda turned away from Lawrence. "Will our mages be able to force a message through?"

"I fear not, Your Majesty. The spatial aspects may sometimes seem trivial, but with the Gellinese occupying Illapthos they're right between us and Hesperos. With their advantage in magical strength it will be child's play for them to block any arcane communications. Only an anchored line such as that between *variideshari* could hope to get through."

Rianda accepted the unspoken reproach. "And it is too much to hope that they will not realise this. It seems as if a physical messenger will be the only way."

"Precisely."

"But that also will not be easy," added Nomiki. "The same factors that our learned bishop has just described apply to sending a scout as much as any ethereal message. The Gellinese have punched a hole through our lines and the region will be alive with aerial patrols. A man would need the devil's own luck to get through."

"And it will not be you," Rianda said firmly to Lawrence. "You and your fellow countryman have already done much for Elaran: I cannot allow you to risk your life further in our cause."

"I am risking my life every day. Do you think flying over the battlefield is a stroll through the Elnesseyae Gardens?"

"To risk your life is one thing. It's another matter entirely to throw it away on a mission so dangerous it's close to suicide."

"It wouldn't be throwing it away. You have said yourself that this is the only way to save the men at the Thradfi Gap. If it is as dangerous as you say then you need the best *tarathinaki*. And that is me.

"Tychon," he continued, overriding Rianda's protests, "isn't that so?"

"I must admit," said Tychon, face carefully blank, "you are more skilled than any other flyer in my command. Myself included. But that does not necessarily imply that you should be the one to go.

"Your Majesty, as Air Captain of Elaran, it is my place to go. There is only a hair's difference in skill between myself and Lawrence. It is my place to go."

"Nonsense," rebutted Lawrence before Rianda could speak. "Your place? Perhaps if no one else was willing to go. But I have volunteered. And in something like this even that hair's difference that you mention could mean the difference between success and failure." He turned back to Rianda.

"Why are you so unwilling to let me go? Are you afraid I will betray you? We have already seen that Elarani birth confers no immunity on that count."

Rianda was stung. "Don't be absurd. It is simply that I do not wish our troubles to be the cause of you losing your life. By the Broken Wheel, you won't even carry a gun!"

"It has hardly hindered me so far. Tychon will confirm that. You wish me to carry a message, not carry out an assassination." With visible effort Lawrence managed to get his temper back under control.

"Majesty, I fully understand the danger. But I have made your cause my own. The droghkar and demons mean it is all humanity's, as the Senrenites recognise. I am the best *tarathinaki* you have: will you not use me?"

Nomiki was muttering in Rianda's ear. "If this Imperial wants to go, Your Majesty, let him. This is no time for scruples of conscience. He's right – he's our best hope and Andur's teeth, if we don't get a message through to those men in Thradfi we may as well sow our own fields with salt, for this war will be lost."

Defeated, Rianda caved in. "Very well. If you insist you may go. Nomiki, tell him what he must say."

"Tell Chiliarch Hesperos to retreat to Ad Cenyor with all speed. You know the background – tell him it all. Keep nothing back. It will take him at least five days to reach Ad Cenyor and then we will be near and will contact him again."

"By the grace of Andur I will get through. I will leave within the hour – even by this light I should be able to cover some ground." Bowing formally, Lawrence strode off, Tychon following.

Euthymios felt slightly stunned at the speed with which events had unfolded.

"What will be our course of action now?" he asked, pitching his voice low so that it would not carry beyond Nomiki and Rianda. "Surely we'll have to withdraw."

"Yes..." said Nomiki. "Yes, you are right. This position is no longer sustainable. But the question is where to make our stand. The Gellinese could take any of half a dozen routes through the mountains. If we don't choose the same as them we'll be doomed."

"Couldn't we simply withdraw to the Citadel?" asked Rianda. "That is what we had planned if we were overwhelmed."

"We could. That is always the option of last resort. But two thirds of our army is still intact and to retreat to Hyrnar would mean abandoning most of the country to the Gellinese. After the Desolation of Hyrakos and what we have heard today I believe we can do better than that."

"I agree. But how can we know where they are going?" She looked questioningly at Euthymios.

"I'm afraid not, Your Majesty. Just as we have done, their mages have put up screens against scrying. If we have been able to prevent them from breaking ours – which I fervently pray we have – you can be sure that theirs is utterly impenetrable to us."

"Much as I am loath to say it, it seems we must return to the Citadel. I will not risk being outflanked on the way to Hyrnar. Is there really no way? Mundane scouts, perhaps?"

"Unlikely, Your Majesty," said Nomiki shortly.

"I know of no mystical arts of the Senrenites or Velnerines that would give us the knowledge we need," added Euthymios. "What we need is a devotee of Ruth." The words hung in the air, the same thought rising as one in three separate minds.

"The Seer," breathed Rianda.

The three turned to face the spot whence Lawrence had come a few minutes before. The crowd seemed to pick up the cry.

"The Seer, the Seer," it murmured. "The Seer!"

As the whisper grew to a shout the crowd melted away before them, leaving Thomas standing small and vulnerable before their eyes.

There were a thousand things he could have said. That he'd never yet managed to control a vision; that the visions he'd had had been largely confusing, disjointed or allegorical; that even if he did see something of use, how would he recognise it? In the face of Lawrence's heroic gesture none of them was worth more than a handful of dust.

Did he not, ultimately, owe these people the best he could offer? Lawrence was risking his life; for him, what was the price of failure beyond a headache and nausea? And, of course, utter humiliation. But he was a citizen of the Triune Empire – would it not be worse to give in to cowardice before foreigners than to try and fail? He admitted to himself that Lawrence's casual valour was a bitter pill to stomach easily.

But most of all, Thomas gradually realised as he stood, exposed, before their pleading eyes, he cared for these people, for their dreams, their freedom, their lives. He was deeply grateful for the grace with which they had welcomed him, an outsider, into their home. He honoured their wish to live free and the price that they were willing to pay; he had no wish for them to be conquered, much less butchered and enslaved by the monsters of Erd Gellin. If there was any way in his power he could help them, he would.

Softly, he spoke. "I will do my best," he said.

#

"Do his trances usually last this long?" asked Rianda.

Euthymios shook his head worriedly. "Never. The longest I've known before is three or four hours. Unless he's taken longer with you?" Euthymios looked questioningly at Jarlod.

"Never."

The three of them had been present at Thomas's side ever since he had first triggered the trance. That had been shortly after midnight. As Jarlod had explained, Thomas had been able to bring on visions at will for some weeks now;

the problem remained how to control them. That was what he would have to do now.

Euthymios was unsure whether the abnormal length of the trance was good or bad, but in the absence of any information he had decided to take it as a positive sign. It meant that something different was happening which at least meant there was a chance. The Abbot, as was his wont, was more cautious and Rianda kept her own counsel. This time even Euthymios had been unable to penetrate her mask.

Nomiki had looked in on the vigil more than once in the night but they had not seen him since dawn. The First Chiliarch still had a battle to fight. Now it was past three o'clock – almost fifteen hours since the trance had begun – and a battle still raged in the pass. Euthymios deplored the waste but Nomiki had been firm: Lawrence must be given time to reach the third chiliad. Until then nothing must be done that could alert the Gellinese that the defenders were aware of Lykourgos's perfidy. Otherwise Lawrence's already slim chances would shrink to zero, the third chiliad would not be warned and they would be lost indeed. Besides, as Nomiki had said pragmatically, what was the use in retreating before they knew which way to go?

And so men fought and died desperately on the wall, all to protect the two outlander men who might yet save them all. Fortunately, or so Euthymios had heard, the assaults remained as desultory as on previous days. He would not have noticed even had it been otherwise, so engrossed was he in watching the frail, unconscious form in which their hopes lay.

All the three of them could do was watch and pray. Sometimes, especially recently, Thomas would moan or thrash about as if possessed by a nightmare or struggling against an invisible foe. But they could do nothing. Even Jarlod dared not intervene. The last True Seer had lived centuries ago and the three of them were sadly lacking in lore. With no other options, the three of them continued their interminable vigil.

#

He plunged into the maelstrom, a torrent of turbulence in the void. Buffeted from all directions the forces tore at him relentlessly, thrusting and pulling him every way at once. The power of even the smallest eddy awed him: he was at their mercy.

Desperately Thomas fought. Trapped in a river of fury all he could do was to remain still, resisting the impulses that would thrust him mind and soul into the grips of a vision. Once there he would be trapped, locked inside until it played itself out and vomited him back to consciousness no wiser than before. Such was what had always happened before.

Not this time, Thomas vowed as he doggedly fought on. For a long time he could do no more than that. Sometimes the nature of the void changed, the eddies and currents becoming a kaleidoscope of colours, garishly swirling and clashing around him. Then it would be black once more but filled with sounds, hisses and roars that deafened and befuddled him in an avalanche of noise.

How much of this was real, Thomas did not know. Did these protean forms truly exist, or was it simply his mind's attempt to make sense of something far beyond his ken? The void, so Euthymios had once told him, was infinitely mutable.

How long did this state of affairs continue? Time had no meaning here. Long ages passed whilst Thomas struggled; great empires rose, flourished and crumbled to dust in the blink of an eye. Each instant was its own and only entire reality.

Eventually some things began to change. Not in the void itself, for the void's nature is eternal. But Thomas began to make his first steps into fathoming its mysteries. Not much; he had as yet scratched only the barest fingernail of the outer crust of its surface. But it was enough.

No longer did the currents sweeping through the void appear entirely random. There was order to them, though an order so complex as to be all but indistinguishable from chaos. Through a shadowed lens Thomas began to discern the crudest outline of that pattern, to sense and predict where and how the powers would surge.

He was not always right. As yet he could predict only the coarsest structures of this fractal tapestry and even them not fully. However, that was sufficient to turn the tide of battle, to allow him to balance the tug of one current against the thrust of another; to circle, gathering momentum, around a dying eddy only to shoot off at a tangent across the chaotic maw of an emerging maelstrom.

It was not a place of calm that he had found. Calm implies stillness, peace and tranquillity and he had none of these. Suffice it to say that he taken the first tentative steps towards making himself the fulcrum, the pivot around which the madness turned, the true mastery of the void that only a True Seer can attain.

Given space now from the constant battle for survival, Thomas was able to probe deeper, for the first time exploring the void's true nature. Here, hidden within and beneath the turbulent surface, were indeed the great rivers of time that had been written of in the *Annalia*. Seeing it, Thomas understood why the book's descriptions had been so elliptical. It was not due to a desire on the part of Larach for mysticism, or to confuse the uninitiated. The truth was far simpler: it just was not possible to describe in words the complexity of this flowing fabric of time.

More aeons passed as Thomas contemplated its depths. From here, he sensed, he could soar to the dawn of time itself, when the spirit of Andur moved across the waters; walk with the great beasts of the past through antediluvian forests; survey the battles of the elemental giants in the Age of Chaos before history began; or follow the toils of an ant upon the far side of the world. In an instant he could be in Borallia, back Home in the Empire, or a hundred thousand years in the past or future.

Somehow, he suppressed the temptation to explore. Not now, he told himself firmly. There were pressing matters at hand. Later there would be world enough and time to unravel these wonders. Despite the possibilities, he sensed that there were as yet limits on his abilities. The world might lie before him but he could not yet choose with surety where he would go. It would take all of his current skill just to complete the comparatively simple task that he must fulfil.

Steeling himself he dropped into the River of Now. The great flood of time washed about him, hot and cold, wet and dry, fierce and tender. Around him and above him and through him it poured, smothering him, nourishing him, overwhelming him with bliss and pain.

Not so long ago he would have been swept under, caught and spun by its eddies and undercurrents until, helpless, he was hurled headlong into the waiting arms of an arbitrary vision. But he had learned much already.

Focusing, he made himself one with the current, moving with it instead of fighting. The void steadied; the dizzying colours slowed and settled; the deafening hubbub fading to a background roar. Moving downstream with the current he could move back and forth across its surface as if it were a meadow navigating the forks and confluences to reach the branch he wished. His senses kept one toe trailing beneath the surface to give warning of the dangerous rip-tides and undercurrents that could yet drag him down.

A sixth sense told him when he had found it. The channel was wide and full, a great low that pulsed, shining, like an artery that dwarfed the channels nearby into insignificance. Though it contained within it an infinite variety of themes and variations this, by all the laws of probability, would be the future. Opening his soul he embraced the vision.

Sunlight dazzled him. Below, in a wide valley, the army of Elaran was fighting desperately against the host of Erd Gellin. So few they looked scattered like grains of wheat across the breadth of the valley, straining to hold back the red tide that surged against them.

It was as he had seen it at Istria, but far worse. The Elarani seemed fewer whilst the numbers of the Gellinese had swollen to dwarf those who stood again them. Droghkar and demons marched in their ranks: *rahvashda, mernal, nasku* and great *barthantu*. Still the defenders fought gallantly, as if they truly had a chance of victory.

Thomas tore his eyes away from the scene. Where is this? I must be able to tell where this is happening if it is to be of use!

Will it be any help, even if you do tell them?" a little voice asked cynically. Look at the numbers below. Won't your information only let them die sooner, heroically, rather than later? Ruthlessly, Thomas forced the voice down and looked for landmarks.

What would suffice? A cluster of trees; strange rocks; a bulge in the valley side? Nomiki could hardly be expected to know every inch of every valley in

Elaran. It was only when Thomas lifted his eyes to the horizon that he saw something he could use.

Above the lip of the valley two hills, both forested, framed a double-peaked mountain, bare. It was west of the valley if one assumed – as was reasonable – that the Gellinese were coming from the south. To the left of the hills, two long ridges sloped down and crossed in a lop-sided 'v' and beyond that lay a cluster of higher hills, five of them, two considerably higher than the other three. One of the lower three had a strange bulge; another had a rounded dome-like peak. As fatigue swept over him, Thomas fixed the scene in his mind, repeating the details to himself until he blacked out.

#

Thomas looked up to find himself staring into Euthymios's face. He seemed to have done a lot of waking up like this in recent months. Owl-like, the old bishop peered at him upside down, a slightly concerned frown on his face.

Then the world righted itself and he realised that Euthymios was not upside down; rather he, Thomas, was lying down and Euthymios was standing behind him. As things swam into focus he made out Rianda, Nomiki and Sir Hanyarmé, the Senrenite. No Jarlod though. He frowned. He was surprised that the Abbot hadn't stayed near.

He pushed down the thought and struggled to sit up. It was almost morning; the grey light of dawn just beginning to get light. Jarlod, he knew, would have many demands upon him once the battle started.

Then it hit him. Dawn? He didn't know when he had gone into his trance but he had thought it had been well before dawn. How long had he been lost to the void?

"How long was I under?" he asked.

"Almost twenty hours," said Euthymios.

Twenty hours? Then this was dusk, not dawn. Thomas remembered the long aeons of struggle in the void and shuddered. He should be grateful it was not longer.

"None of us were sure if you were going to make it," said Rianda, with feeling. "You thrashed and moaned as if possessed. Even the Abbot said he'd never seen the like before."

Thomas could read the unspoken questions hanging from all their lips. Did you make it? We know you're back, but did you actually find anything? Or was it all for nothing; all our hopes lost?

He pre-empted them. "I know where they're going."

Relief, delight and more than a hint of surprise rose on their faces.

"Praise be to Andur!" exclaimed Euthymios.

"Elaran will be in your debt forever," added Rianda. "Where must we go?"

"The vision didn't tell me its name, but I can describe it." Systematically he did so. Before he had got more than halfway through Nomiki broke in.

"I know the place." He slapped his hands together. "It's the Yenestrine Valley. We couldn't have asked for better.

"It's the most direct route to Hyrnar, but one of the easiest to defend. The Archons are arrogant enough to think us beaten. Had they been willing to take a week or two longer to go through the eastern valleys we wouldn't have stood a chance. But now..." He smiled in anticipation.

"But I told you what I saw," protested Thomas. "How can you be so confident?"

Nomiki snorted. "Prophecy? You can't believe all that it tells you. Half of it is no more than mystic metaphors. In any case, you're no soldier. What looked to you like a rout may not have been what it seemed. We held them here, didn't we? And we still have two thirds of our army."

"Two thirds? Then Lawrence made it?" Thomas jumped up excitedly. "Where is he?"

An awkward silence fell. Suddenly no one would meet his eyes. Thomas felt a deep crack opening up beneath them.

"What is it? What's happened?" he demanded.

"Thomas, he's dying," said Euthymios gently.

In an instant the crack widened to a gaping chasm, a precipice upon the edge of which he teetered. A single misstep would send him plunging down into the abyss.

"Dying?" he asked uncomprehendingly. The news made no sense. It was only a few moments ago that he had seen Lawrence, bold and sure of himself, announcing that he would carry the message to the Thradfi Gap.

"He carried the news through unharmed," said Rianda. Her voice was hushed. Thomas could hardly hear it. "But then he decided that he needed to come back, to let us know he had made it."

"He was right," interjected Nomiki. "We needed to know."

"Yes. But even his luck couldn't hold twice. He hasn't told us much, but a patrol intercepted him. He was shot four times before he could get away."

"Isn't there any hope? The Velnerines..."

"Thomas, one of the bullets hit his lung. Abbot Jarlod is with him now but he says there's nothing he can do beyond make him comfortable."

"Take me to him," demanded Thomas.

#

When he pushed through the tent flap the first thing he saw was the Abbot. Apologetically, Jarlod stood up and moved back, giving Thomas space to approach.

"There's nothing I can do for him. I'm sorry. It's good that you were able to come in time – he's been asking for you."

Lying there prostrate on the bed Lawrence was a pitiful sight. Mercifully his wounds had been covered but the extent of his injuries could be inferred from his drawn, haggard face. With a shock, Thomas realised that the former chaplain looked old: worn out and tired. He was only thirty-eight.

"Lawrence," he said gently. There was no reply. "Reverend Lawrence?"

Lawrence's eyes opened. Unfocused they gazed about, wandering, locking on to Thomas for only a moment before drifting away.

"Maynard. Thomas Maynard, is that you?"

"Yes, it's me. They said what you did, Lawrence, when no one else could have managed it."

"You always had time for me, didn't you, Thomas. Always kind. We used to play sharom together.

"They used to laugh at me at the Residency you know." Thomas tried to protest but Lawrence took no notice.

"They didn't even bother to hide it. They thought it didn't matter. They're all dead now. I'll be dead soon too. I hope I don't join them. I think I'd rather be in hell than be put with them.

"But I did alright, didn't I, Maynard?"

Wordlessly, Thomas nodded. He wanted to weep, but no tears would come.

"I did alright in the end, didn't I?"

Thomas managed to find a voice. "Yes, you did alright."

"I won't see you again in this world. No, don't protest." Lawrence's eyes for a moment were keen once more, focusing abruptly on Thomas.

"We both know there's nothing to be done for me. The bullet's in my lung. Think of it: me, a minister of Andur, dying like this." He started to laugh softly but broke off, overcome by deep, wracking coughs. Thomas could see spots of blood in the spittle. When Lawrence spoke again it was quieter, more rasping than before.

"Tell Tychon..." He coughed again. "Tell Tychon that it was worth it, all of it. Even this. He gave me life again." The coughing overcame him again, worse than before. He began thrashing, as if to escape the wounds that were pulling him down, the blood in his lungs smothering him. Jarlod rushed back to the bed but let his hands fall, helplessly, to his side. He too could only watch now.

There was one more brief period of calm before the end. In the few moments of lucidity Thomas heard, weakly,

"I did alright, didn't I?"

Chapter Twenty-Two

Eye of the Hurricane

Lord Trevelyan gazed up at the fort, admiring it. Twenty-foot-high walls of wood and stone stood firm against any invader who dared to attack. Around the base, a deep ditch and sharply sloping earthen ramp added further obstacles. And this was only one of the line of twenty-five such forts under construction, stretching from the coast to the western foothills of the Gralbakh Range, all along the desert border.

Each was large enough to hold five hundred men, plus the armaments and supplies needed to keep such a force in operation. Further back, others under his command were constructing a highway, a military road that ran behind the chain of forts the entire length of the line to convey the Empire's might rapidly to whichever point might require reinforcements. Three great cantonments along the road, each fit for over ten thousand soldiers, would hold the rest of the army – once, at least, they had finished constructing these defences.

All this in only three months! As he watched, crews of men were at work putting the finishing touches to the fortification, drilling knot-holes, adding doors to store rooms and making living quarters habitable. A team was operating a block and tackle, hauling up a cannon to a recently constructed embrasure whilst another team waited patiently to settle it into its position. He could feel justifiably proud of what he had achieved.

A supply train had arrived this morning, bringing the supplies that would be the lifeblood of this fort no less than the soldiers who manned it. Building the defences was only half the story. Without the literally tonnes of flour and meat, not to mention the vast quantities of powder, shot, ammunition and other military supplies, these grand new structures would be nothing but empty shells. A steady stream of waggons had been flowing south from the heartlands of Pelagos ever since construction had first begun, carrying the necessary goods south and causing delight to the Pelagic merchants with their unprecedented demands.

A mounted figure detached itself from the throng surrounding the unloading waggons and made its way towards him. It was Browning, his private secretary. Those wildly flapping elbows would be recognisable anywhere: Browning still hadn't yet learned how to keep his arms steady while riding.

"Lord Trevelyan," he said, drawing up. "We're going to require more funds. The senior quartermaster advises that if we pay for these supplies we won't have enough to pay the army next month."

Trevelyan appeared unconcerned. "Don't worry, we'll just use the Requisitioning Act again. Start drawing up the necessary papers, will you?"

Browning hesitated, his Adam's apple bobbing nervously.

"But, My Lord..." he said tentatively.

"No, go on."

"I thought the Requisition Act was only meant to be used in times of war or a similarly disruptive civil emergency? It's just that we've used it twice already, and each time for larger amounts. You always talk of the Public Accounts Committee...

"I'm sorry, My Lord, I'm sure it's probably all in order, I just wanted to make sure that you were fully aware of all the details governing the Act before we used it again."

"Once. We've only used it once. Section 3(5) – multiple uses of the Act by the same person for the same purpose in the same emergency shall be classed as a single use for the purposes of accountability. That's very important.

"But you were right to bring it to my attention. It's the type of action we do need to keep a close eye on, because it's all too easy to step over the line without needing it. But I wouldn't worry. Atavus *was* invaded and our preparations here are against the same enemy. I think even the most hard-headed member of a Select Committee would have to concede that it's the same war, even if we had to bang their heads together a few times before we got them to admit it.

"I've been reading the Act fairly closely over the last couple of months, and while it's true we've been pushing against the limits pretty hard in places, I can assure you it's nothing that will raise any eyebrows *post facto*.

"Now, if you could see about drawing up those documents and get them to one before dinner, I'd be very grateful."

He would have to protect the lad, Trevelyan reflected, as Browning cantered away. No use getting a boy in trouble for actions that were none of his own doing. Better for him and all concerned if they were able to say in truth that they had known nothing of their master's doings. No, Browning would not have to suffer.

Whatever he might have said, Trevelyan knew that in recent months he had not merely been pushing against the boundaries of his authority but had left it several miles behind. A more flagrant transgression had seldom been seen in peace time.

Cannon and shot did not come cheap and he had been ordering them by the score. Nor did the sheer quantity of material needed to construct such a chain of defences. He had even been discreetly ramping up the number of local auxiliaries serving in the army. They would be needed to man the forts when the invasion came. Money had been running like water, and thank Andur that at least the local labour could be drafted cheaply, or the bill would have been even higher.

Only one thing was allowing him to act as he was, and for that he counted his blessings daily. The Governor of Pelagos had been so overawed by having a former Viceroy amongst his subordinates that he had essentially allowed Trevelyan to do as he pleased. Not only had he never asked for any reports from his newest High Commissioner, but he had accepted Trevelyan's flimsiest justifications for additional finance without question and done his best to supply them.

Really, thought Trevelyan objectively, it was a disgrace. He supposed that it would be difficult to adjust to a situation in which your immediate superior became under your command but, by the Broken Wheel, the man was a senior civil servant. One was meant to be able to cope with such situations; it was nothing more than basic administrative professionalism. If he, Trevelyan, had still been Viceroy the Governor would have found himself on the receiving end of a sharply worded reprimand.

But he was no longer Viceroy, which meant that the Governor's misplaced residual loyalty was a thing to be grateful for. The only question was how long he could continue as he was before being hauled up short. Even with the best will in the world, the sums that Trevelyan was spending were becoming too large for the Governor to hide even in the total budget for Pelagos. It was only a matter of time before the unauthorised expenditure came to the attention of his replacement, the new Viceroy in Autigen. And the Viceroy, new in post and eager to prove himself, would not tolerate such disobedience.

Trevelyan shrugged. That was now in the lap of Andur. Give him another month and the defences would be constructed. Once built, they would not be torn down, and by bureaucratic obfuscation he might even contrive to keep them fully manned for a year or more. By that time, the rest of the Empire might recognise the danger, and he would have done his duty.

The guards saluted as he strolled back into his field quarters. They were comfortable enough, though damned cold. The harsh climate of these northern steppes was a sharp shock to the system after the jungles of the south. He had been down in Scahania for too long; grown soft. After all, he was not significantly further north than the upper parts of the Empire, where he had grown up, though he was sure there was nothing back Home like this harsh wind that wailed from the ocean, right across Pelagos to the desert.

At his desk, the piles of paper never seemed to get any smaller. He had thought it would be better than when he had been Viceroy, but it seemed that paper, like water, distributed itself so as to fill each body into which it flowed to the same level. Here, too, there was more that he was unable to delegate; more matters that had to be kept for his eyes only. In circumstances like his one could not afford to spread information too widely.

Fortunately the reports from his intelligence network were still coming in regularly. Lord Trevelyan had invested considerable time and effort into building up the network – the state of play in which he had found it had been utterly feeble – and now, though still a long way from matching that of Rotliegendes, it was at least respectable. More importantly, given the way things had come to pass, he had invested an equal amount of effort into ensuring that as much of it as possible was loyal to him personally. That held true right up to the Head of Intelligence himself. Lord Trevelyan did not ask them to conceal any information from the new Viceroy – that would have been wrong – but he did make sure that he himself received copies of any reports that could be of interest.

As he had expected, the picture was beginning to come together quite satisfactorily. Those few spies who still reported from inside Erd Gellin told tales of a land paralysed by fear, where horrors stalked the countryside and ordinary citizens would disappear at random, never to be seen again, taken for Andur – or more likely the devil – knew what purpose.

Great armies had been reported marching north with creatures of nightmare in their ranks. Despite this, reported one agent, voluntary enlistment into the army had never been higher, as it was believed to be the only way a man could protect himself from vanishing.

In the Iskandin Palace, High Archon Lykaios's power had been all but absolute ever since the incident last autumn when the single Archon who opposed him had been found by his guards, brutally dismembered. No explanation had been offered for the event. There were rumours of a shadowed figure, with breath like the harsh sirocco, who came and went like the wind. Whether this was one and the same as the dark horseman who had been reported with the army Trevelyan did not know, though he had his suspicions. In both were reported to reside a fell power.

What had excited him the most, however, had been the first reports, that had reached him only last week, of sand elementals within the borders of Erd Gellin. Now for the first time there was a concrete piece of evidence to confirm his suspicions, indisputably linking the sack of Atavus to the events in Erd Gellin. And what power could control such primal beings, could simultaneously direct assaults on both the western and eastern borders of the vast desert, save for that ancient menace, almost forgotten, of the Forces of the Sand?

Damn Parrington. The blasted man had got his paper on sand elementals, much good might it do him, and was probably even now addressing a packed lecture theatre at the Imperial Society. Sir Walter Parrington FIS would be his new mode of address before very long, or so Trevelyan had heard. And that left him here without an arcanist worth tuppence to his name, and as good as no means of scrying or building defensive traps beyond the mundane. For all Parrington's flaws he had still been one of the most effective arcanists with whom Trevelyan had ever worked.

How was young Maynard doing now? he wondered. That was another person who might as well have dropped off the face of Edrith. The last report had been over a fortnight ago, but that had given every impression that a spring invasion was imminent. It was a pity: Maynard had handled himself with impressive competence for one not yet even of Principal rank, and Trevelyan would have enjoyed meeting him – one could always find an interesting position where a talented youngster could be made use of. But there was little hope he would be able to escape the coming maelstrom of conflict.

Elaran was doomed. Trevelyan doubted it would even last a week. The only question was where, when the blood and slaughter had ended, would the war be carried next? North, against the hardened legions of Torridon or the inhospitable slopes of the Gralbakh Mountains? South-east, against the fanatic hordes of Scandia? Or north-west, to slice like a knife into butter into the soft underbelly of the Imperial province of Pelagos?

The Empire would not be caught unprepared again, vowed Trevelyan to Andur. It would be no thanks to the new Viceroy. The man was a moderniser in all the worst meanings of the word, a cipher who believed radical initiatives and catchy sound-bites to be a substitute for sound administration. The fool didn't even have a clue what was really happening in his own palace, let alone in Laurentia.

No, thought Trevelyan, it was down to him. Two disasters had already occurred on his watch and he would not accept a third. When the Forces of the Sand struck at Pelagos they would find not a slumbering land, ready for the taking, but a solid wall of steel, steadfast and prepared, on which to break their teeth. And when their first assault had been blunted, then let them face the full fury of the Empire's wrath.

#

Thomas judged that they were almost halfway to the Yenestrine Valley. Nomiki had set a killing pace. For Thomas and the others of the army who were mounted it had not been so bad, though even for them there were places where the way became so steep that they were forced to get off and walk. But for those on foot – by far the majority in this hill-country where grazing land was rare and horses precious – the journey had been gruelling.

There were no objections though. Everyone knew that they could not afford to be beaten to the valley. There had been no sign of the army behind them but that did not mean they were safe. The Gellinese were coming from two other passes as well.

It was a curious mixture of ebullience and resignation that sustained them. On the face of it they had been defeated, forced to retreat. On the other hand, news of the last minute acts of heroism that had saved them had galvanised spirits. The tales of Tasos's trek across the mountains, Lawrence's daring flight against all odds and Thomas's miraculous vision had swept through the ranks like wildfire.

Unfortunately such exuberance did not go much more than surface deep, particularly amongst the army's leaders. The thought lay heavily on them all that even if they reached the valley in time, what could they do? In Istria, in well-prepared positions, they had barely held. What could they hope to achieve when the full might of the enemy exerted itself in earnest?

Such thoughts could not be spoken of out loud. They remained the dark shadow that hovered, a dark shadow over them, while everyone proceeded as if there was really a true chance of victory.

A forlorn hope of one hundred men, volunteers all, had been left behind at Istria to buy time for the army to retreat. The Senrenites had originally tried to claim this honour but Nomiki had refused point blank. Doing so had almost led to a rupture between him and Sir Hanyarmé.

Thomas remembered how Hanyarmé had announced his decision. Only the fact that they were in public, before the entire army, had prevented Nomiki from going ripping him to shreds.

"Out of the question," he said. "What can you hope to achieve?"

"By our martyrdom we will give you the time we need. My knights and I can hold this position for longer than any other contingent of your army."

"And it is for that reason I will not allow my fifty best men to throw themselves away!"

"Your best men, My Lord?" Hanyarmé's tone carried a hint of danger. "I had understood that my knights and I were allied to your cause, not your vassals."

"While you serve in my army you will obey my orders. A ship can only have one captain."

"In that case we will remove ourselves from your command. If we choose, independently, to place ourselves in defence here you can have no reasonable objections."

"By the Broken Wheel," exploded Nomiki, anger and frustration burst out. "You'll be swarmed over and cut down like striplings. We'll need you when we make our stand – this is no time for meaningless heroics."

"We are beholden to Andur and St. Senren, not to your worldly struggles."

"You swore an oath to fight alongside Elaran for the duration of this war. I thought that your order above all would hold such things sacred." With an effort Nomiki got his emotions under control. This exhibition was on display for all the army to wonder at.

"Sir Hanyarmé, I admit that I have no power to compel you. But still I ask, for the sake of the oath you swore, that you do not forsake us here, but rather retreat with us to the Yenestrine Valley, there to stand against the evil of Erd Gellin. By Andur Astartes and all his saints I swear that your swords will find more honour there.

"And," he added softly, "all of us may be martyrs soon enough without you needing to seek it here."

For a long time there was silence. For one long, heart-wrenching moment Nomiki thought that Hanyarmé would reject his pleas, condemning not only his own men but all Elaran for stubborn honour.

Hanyarmé nodded once, curtly, and bowed low. A great murmur of relief rippled through the ranks. Tension that had gripped them had been released. Nomiki himself, outwardly controlled, felt too a great upsurge of thankfulness within him as he received the tall Senrenite's submission.

"It shall be as you request, My Lord," said Hanyarmé. The crowd scurried to make way for him as he strode off, raising his voice in a command that carried clearly through the still air.

"Knights of St. Senren, make ready. We ride for the Yenestrine Valley."

#

"Not you as well," snapped Thomas. "For the last three days I've been crowded the whole time by people trying to talk to me and I'm sick of it."

"Of course," said Euthymios, unruffled. If the bishop had taken any umbrage at Thomas's shortness he did not show it. "I'll leave you in peace with your thoughts." With that, he urged his horse forward until he was alongside Rianda and quickly became deep in conversation with her.

No sooner had he gone, than Thomas regretted his hasty words. He had been short-tempered since they had left Istria and even the most casual remark could put him on edge. Earlier that day he had almost bitten off Abbot Jarlod's head for what he had thought at the time seemed an overly patronising remark about building on his first successful act as a True Seer. He owed the Abbot an apology he knew, but in his current mood attempting to deliver one would be more likely to end in another quarrel than in reconciliation.

Thomas knew what was driving it. He could barely move without someone coming up to him to congratulate him on how his True Seer's talent had saved them, or wanting to talk to him about how the gift worked and, inevitably, whether he could have a vision of the future for them. In normal circumstances Thomas was honest enough to admit he would have found such adulation highly gratifying. But in his current state of mind it was both irritating and insensitive. The idiots seemed to place what he had done on the same plane as Lawrence's sacrifice. It wasn't just the common soldiers but people who should have known better: Senrenites, *hekatontarchs* and other officers, members of Nomiki's staff.

Despite this it would have been a comfort to speak to Euthymios. On this occasion he had only asked Thomas whether his views on the Blessed Ruth had changed but Thomas had still driven him away.

The bishop was always a comfort: both sensitive and understanding but not afraid to give advice when necessary. Thomas recollected that first conversation last autumn. When he had been alone and friendless in Hyrnar, Euthymios had been the first to offer him friendship.

Wistfully, Thomas stared up the line to where Euthymios was now riding with Rianda. It was too late now to take back the words he had spoken in haste. The bishop was now deep in conversation with his queen, the young woman who had older and deeper claims on his loyalty than any outlander.

Ahead and behind them the column stretched out, a sinuous snake of marching men wending its way through the hills. The Senrenites, a steel knot, brought up the rear – a sop to Hanyarmé's pride – while the surviving *tarathinakii* beat a leisurely tempo above them, tacking methodically back and forth across the line of the column in order to match their pace to that of the soldiers below.

What were they, Thomas wondered. A defeated army, downcast in defeat, or a bold force, destined to arrive in the nick of time and save the day. Did it matter? What difference did it look like to the birds, the swallows, swifts and *therarni* winging their way north from their winter haunts of Scandia and Scahania to Torridon and the lush Rhaetian plains.

What did they make of this mysterious stain on the landscape? Did they just pass it by, two worlds slipping by each other like ships that pass in the night? Probably, decided Thomas wryly, his flight of whimsy coming back to reality with a bump. Few enough people outside Elaran cared about this invasion; it was too much to expect the birds to.

By all that flew or swam, he needed someone to talk to. Tychon was no help: the two of them had known such different sides of Lawrence's life that conversation now was just two people talking, each person's words sailing, untouching, past the other's and into the void. With the bridge between them lost, all connection had gone and they stood alone either side of a deep chasm that had never been closed, only hidden. And he had already done his best, albeit without meaning to, to drive away Euthymios and Jarlod, the only other people here he had been close to.

His horse snorted, tossing up its head, tired of the steady gait at which it was being forced to walk all day. By this point in the column the men ahead had long since torn the ground, freshly watered by spring showers, into a slough of mud. For a few minutes, the necessity of guiding his horse along the easiest route distracted Thomas from his thoughts.

Oddly enough, it was Rianda whom he had found easiest to talk to in recent days. Alone amongst the Elarani she did not weary him with false praise or demand answers to questions he was not ready to answer. She was bowed down by her own troubles; like him, she saw defeat and shame in something in which others saw only glory. Yet together they found a freedom, each able to talk and listen to the other and gain a comfort from it. Perhaps it was not so surprising. For all their differences, were they not almost the same age?

But that did no good to him now. She was busy, as indeed a queen must frequently be. Up ahead he could see her talking to Euthymios.

"You don't understand, none of you do," said Rianda. "You seem to think that all will be well now. Can't anyone see the ill that could come of this, the shame it brings to us and our country?"

"We see it, my daughter," said Euthymios. "But we know that you had no other choice."

"I know that as well. Sometimes it seems that ever since my father died I've had nothing but no other choices."

She had good reason to be bitter. Three days ago, when they had begun the retreat, Rianda had steeled her heart and done what she had sworn she would never do. She had contacted Lord Niavon of Torridon and told him that Elaran needed aid.

"At least," Euthymios pointed out, "it vindicates your decision to leave the *variideshari* at Hyrnar and the north."

"You think I care about that? It will take the rest of my life to win Elaran free of the concessions I granted. That is if they don't manage to bundle me aside with a convenient accident.

"Just think, Euthymios. An entire Torridonian legion on Elarani soil. My ancestors would roll in their graves. My father spent half his life fighting to keep Torridonian troops out of Elaran, only to see his daughter invite them in before he'd been buried a year."

"Better free, even impoverished by Torridonian demands, than slaves under the Archons."

"Oh, I know, I know. If it had not been for the Desolation of Hyrakos and then what happened to the southern chiliad I would have never done it. Better anything now than a Gellinese victory. But you know what they say of the man who invites in the wolf to protect him from the bear."

"What chance is there that they will arrive in time?"

"Some. The legion was on the border ready to march when I called. I somehow cannot believe it was there out of Torridonian benevolence."

"No. But it may yet work in our favour. Hyrnar at least will be saved. You realise, My Queen, that there is one question we have not asked. Even with the Torridonians, can we win?"

"Then what is left of the strength of Elaran will take refuge in the hills, if any of the Nemessine line survives to lead them." There was no give in Rianda's voice, weighed down though it was by despair. "We have done it before; under the Variscans, in the droghkar uprisings and at the time of the Givetian Ascendancy. Like them, Erd Gellin cannot endure forever."

Chapter Twenty-Three

Facing the Firestorm

The white sun lanced down the valley, scattering off the lazy surface of the River Yenestor and sending its ripples dancing like wings of opalescent dragonflies. The newly unfurled leaves of trees shone radiantly in the midday light. The valley was brilliant with the verdant glory of new spring. On a bend a kingfisher dived, a sparkling flash of colour.

"Our men will be fighting with the sun in their eyes," scowled Nomiki. He squinted down the valley. At this time of year the sun was still low in the sky and the valley could not have been worse positioned.

Mouth twisting in displeasure, he stamped on across the valley, trailed by his aides. He was not happy. As First Chiliarch, he could think of a dozen ways in which he could wreak havoc in an assault upon this valley and he harboured no illusions that his enemy would be any less competent.

"How does it look?" asked Rianda when he reached her. The young queen's encampment was set well back up the valley but today, like most days since their arrival, she was spending her time near the front. One had to admire her. Young, brave and beautiful; already half the men as good as worshipped her.

"Not good," admitted Nomiki. "We've done what we can, but this valley? I'd forgotten how wide it is compared to the southern passes."

"I thought you said it was the easiest place to defend on the way north."

"It is. But easiest is a relative term. It's still damned difficult. Just look at it."

Stretching north to south the u-shaped Yenestrine Valley stretched for over thirty miles before petering out. Carved into existence by glaciers in the last ice-age, when tongues of ice had fanned out from the Gralbakh range to the north, extending their probing fingers across much of Elaran, it was now one of the principal thoroughfares between northern Elaran and the lands of the south. Unlike the narrow pass of Istria the Yenestrine was a true valley: there were no narrow bottle-necks here that could be used to hold back an enemy.

Through the bottom of the valley wound the river Yenestor that gave the valley its name. A rushing torrent further north, on entering the valley it plunged in a glorious cataract over the Lyranthin Falls to the floor below and from there wove meandering round and through the gentle slopes of the valley, its wide flood plain all the space between the steep sides.

The sides at least were somewhat encouraging. They were no doubt what Nomiki had been thinking of when he had first pronounced upon the defensibility of the valley. Steep sided, it would be a precipitous climb to get atop them. In places, the force of ages had scoured away the top-soil to expose jagged white outcrops of limestone to the air, standing out sharply amongst the blooming *lissuin* and asphodel. On either side of the valley, half a dozen streams, many no more than trickles, gushed down the hillside to feed in to the Yenestor.

"You see?" said Nomiki. "It's just too wide. We don't have enough men."

Detachments of the northern chiliad had been trickling in over the last two days. They had scattered through the hills in order to better evade the Gellinese trap. Lawrence's warning had come in time for most of them had made it: according to Hesperos, who had arrived only today with one of the largest and slowest parties, containing many wounded, all of those who could be expected to get through were now here.

Even with these reinforcements the entire army numbered only a bare three thousand. Over a third of these were militia or recent recruits – though these, admittedly, had now survived three days of fierce fighting and a forced march retreat so could no longer be counted as entirely green. It was still nowhere near enough.

"So," said Rianda. "What has been done?"

Nomiki answered simply. "What we could. It has still been left for us to choose the site of battle – that at least cannot be denied to us. A sloping hill where the Yenestor runs close to the west side of the valley is our choice. The Gellinese will not be foolhardy enough to attempt to advance on both sides there, lest a pre-prepared swell upstream sweep them away. They will not gamble upon our paucity of gems.

"Rough embrasures have been dug for our cannon – though these are even fewer, relatively, than at Istria, for Hesperos's chiliad were forced to abandon the majority of theirs. We've also prepared breastworks for shelter as far as we are able. The chief problem is that the valley is simply too wide. Even if we had time to build a wall across we could never man it. We'd be stretched so thin that they'd smash through us like an egg shell.

#

"Is there no hope then?" Thomas asked her that evening.

Instantly she stiffened. "There is always hope, Thomas Maynard. The future is never certain: you, of all people here, should know that. Only when the last Elarani is in the grave will all hope be gone."

He smiled faintly. "Very well, Rianda. You know what I meant. Is there much hope?"

"Much hope? No, there is not much hope." Her voice was unnaturally high, as if the slightest gust of wind would dislodge and shatter it. "But then there never was much hope, was there? How much do you think we need?"

"Perhaps," Thomas said tentatively, "the Torridonians will get here in time after all. They passed Hyrnar three days ago."

"Perhaps they will. Or perhaps they will not. There is always hope, after all."

#

The Gellinese had taken their time. What was the need to hurry? Like the wheels of justice, the host of Erd Gellin ground slowly, but as it made its way through the Elarani hills it ground all resistance exceeding fine before it. Fully five days had passed since the Elarani had arrived in the valley, tired and weary from their forced march from Istria. They need not have hurried: it would have made no difference in the end.

For now the Gellinese had arrived at last and the valley itself had lost its verdure before them. Their numbers were vast; vast as the host of the Adversary when he raised his standard in defiance against the Lord of Order; vast as the grand army of Varisca when it swept through the Pass of Froude and overthrew all Scahania in fire and blood. So it seemed to Nomiki.

For it was not men alone which confronted the beleaguered defenders of Elaran. This would be no play battle as at Istria, though that in truth had seemed real enough to those who had died there. This was the true war now; battle was joined in earnest and now at last the full might of Erd Gellin and its newfound allies would be exerted in full.

Before the massed ranks of soldiery stood two great lines of droghkar, unbroken clear from one end of the battle front to the other. There were a thousand of the goat-like creatures in each line. Twisted and misshapen, the dark hordes quivered in anticipation of the moment when they would be turned loose.

They were not the worst. Standing forth at the forefront of the army were fourteen monstrous *barthantu*. Nomiki had never seen one before, but they were unmistakeable. Demons of brutal strength and hideous form, *barthantu* were amongst the most feared of the lower demons, those without true intelligence. Just one could wreak havoc against an entire company of men. Fortunately, even a single *barthantu* was difficult to summon and harder to control – the sheer power necessary to contain them put them beyond the reach of most mages. Nomiki shuddered to think of what could be powerful enough to summon fourteen.

He gazed at them implacably. He had heard tales of great beasts from the south – elephants, camelopards, hippopotami – but surely even if these could match a *barthantu* for size they could not possibly possess the palpable sense of bloodlust and evil that rose almost visibly like steam from the gnarled hides of the demons.

Every part of them spoke power. From the hairy bull-like head thrust forward atop a squat neck to the heavy-set body and the four powerful legs like pillars. Strength oozed from their flanks and sides. As he watched one roared revealing great banks of sharp pointed teeth. Even from this distance each tooth was clearly visible. How big did that make them? Not so large as the four over-sized tusks sweeping forward like scimitars on either side of the mouth or the six horns, splayed out like antlers, atop their heads.

Nomiki was unmoved. He had no illusions about their fate. These creatures would be hard to kill – in addition to their strength and power demons, even the lower orders, possessed an unnatural cunning that increased their danger three-fold – but he had long since passed the point where that made a difference. Even without the *barthantu*, Erd Gellin was throwing an overwhelming force against them. For all his reassuring words to Rianda, all that Nomiki now looked for was that he and his men would stand and sell their lives with honour.

No drums this time to sound the advance, only a single cannon shot to set the lines in motion. Forward the droghkar surged, gathering pace as they went, the ends of their lines sweeping forward to grip the defenders in a crushing embrace. And before them all surged the *barthantu*, the massive beasts leaving the smaller droghkar in their wake as they hurtled forwards.

Andur's teeth! How could things so big move so fast? The creatures had already closed more than half the distance. There was no order to their charge, no pretence at keeping a straight line, only a horrific intensity of demonic frenzy which within moments would be upon them.

Cannon thundered behind him but so swiftly did the *barthantu* move that they had already passed the ground upon which the Elarani guns were trained. The balls sailed uselessly overhead, scoring deadly lines through the ranks of the droghkar but doing no damage to the more dangerous foe. Save for one only that, by poor powder or gunner's error, fell short to strike the ground before the line and careen, by the grace of Andur, directly into a *barthantu*, bringing the beast down in a tangle of limbs. There would be no time for a second salvo: the *barthantu* were only seconds away, close enough that Nomiki could make out clearly the knotted hair on their foreheads.

"Fire!" he screamed and a fusillade of musket shots rang out. Then the beasts were upon them, goring to left and right as they ran amuck.

The line buckled like sheet metal beneath a dozen hammer blows. Men were on the edge of panic, helpless as infants against these demons whom neither blade nor bullet could bite.

Then the droghkar struck. Two solid lines of bestial death as impossible to turn aside as a tsunami. Prepared and steady, in disciplined lines, the men of Elaran would have done themselves proud. Shattered and broken as they were by the charge of the *barthantu* they had no chance against this second horde, a nightmare onslaught of grotesques who howled and cackled as they killed. The droghkar's wicked axes sliced with gay abandon through flesh and bone alike whilst, heedless of wounds and pain, their wicked claws and fangs were no less lethal. Maddened by the bloodlust no few of the creatures abandoned their weapons, launching themselves upon their foes in primal state, slashing with tooth and claw.

Only the Senrenites saved them. At the very moment when all seemed lost their horn sounded, crystal music singing through the air. In a glorious cavalcade they charged into the fray, trampling droghkar under foot.

It was a miracle, Nomiki thought. Not unexpected, perhaps, for this was what he and Hanyarmé had planned, but no less wonderful for that. He watched as, heedless of personal danger, the knights sought out the *barthantu*, five or more of them tackling each great beast.

A sickening scene unfolded. The Senrenites' armour, burnished though it was in the sacred fires of Andur, offered little protection against demons as powerful as these. Men were smashed out of their saddles and trampled underfoot, armour and limbs buckling and breaking. At least their swords bit deep, slicing into the *barthantu's* hides like a sharp axe into soft spruce. The holy weapons were anathema to such creatures of hell.

As he watched, a cluster was confronting the last. Seven of them rode at it, dancing their horses through the ranks of droghkar to converge upon the creature with devastating precision.

Quick as they were, it was quicker. With lightning speed it whirled, sweeping its antlers round and up to catch and toss two of the unfortunate Senrenites a dozen feet in the air. Screaming in agony, they flew through the air and fell, sickeningly, to the ground, bodies crumpling with the impact. Their bodies vanished beneath a tide of droghkar.

Undaunted, their companions pressed in. The *barthantu* bellowed in rage as five swords stabbed deeply into its side and rear. It lunged and they scattered back, evading its long tusks by a hair.

They tried to press in again but once more it moved too swiftly. No matter how they dodged and feinted, each sally was met by the suddenly presented teeth, tusks and horns of the demon, in the face of which there was no option but retreat.

Around them, the droghkar were crowding in once more. The time bought by their wild charge was fast running out and it would not be much longer that their companions could keep the creatures back. They must finish this demon rapidly or not at all.

As if of one mind, four of them darted forward, two to the left, two to the right. Confused the demon span, charging one pair. A horse stumbled. In an instant the *barthantu* was upon it, crushing the rider under foot while with its mouth it ferociously tore the horse apart in one bite.

In its triumph it had forgotten the fifth knight, the one who had not dashed forward to left or right. Now he moved. Spurring his horse forward the rider charged straight for the demon's unprotected flank and launched himself in a powerful leap from his horse's back to the back of the *barthantu* itself. He flew through the air gracefully – a heavenly contrast to his unfortunate tossed fellows – and landed upon his target as perfectly as an athlete at the High Scriansa games.

The beast went berserk. Wildly bucking, it did everything in its power to throw its attacker. To no avail. Its squat bull neck would not allow its head to turn far enough to reach the knight, perched as he was in a precarious position just behind the head. Stabbing his sword down into the creature's back the knight clung to it, making the wound itself the ultimate insult. Through all the wide bucking he somehow clung on, hands clenched around the embedded sword in a deathly grip.

Each time the demon paused for breath the man drew out the sword and thrust it in once more, seeking within the unnatural anatomy for some vital to pierce. Blood spilled out, scorching the man with its fiery essence, birthed of the fires of hell. Nomiki marvelled. The valour of this man was unbelievable. A lesser man – any normal man, himself included – would have let slip his grip long ago, defeated by pain or simple inability. But the Senrenite stuck again and again as the *barthantu*, utterly maddened now, charged wildly across the battlefield trampling droghkar and Elarani alike. The three remaining Senrenites who had attacked it pursued it, slashing when they could at its already scored hide; goading it to further heights of rage.

Finally it ended. Whether the Senrenite's blade found heart, lung, spine or something else, no one will know, but whatever organ was pierced, the wound was mortal. The demon's knees buckled and it collapsed, falling like a pole-axed cow. With it it took its slayer, true to its infernal nature even in death. For some time now the man must have been almost delirious with pain, clinging in the mist to two unyielding spars: to hold on and to keep striking. Did he even know he had killed the beast? Maintaining his death grip to the last, as the creature toppled he too fell, crushed beneath the body of the demon he had slain.

The horn St. Senren blew once more, loud and clear, rallying the Senrenites. They converged, slicing their way through the reforming droghkar to surround Hanyarmé. There were few enough of them left, thought Nomiki with a pang. Of the seventy who had charged a few moments before barely two dozen remained.

Their sacrifice had saved Elaran. The droghkar assault had been halted just when it had been at its most furious. Given time to recover – and with the *barthantu* dead – the soldiers of Elaran were beginning to rally. Yet even now the surviving knights did not cease their efforts but instead set their horses and charged into the heart of the reforming droghkar, scattering them wherever they were thickest.

"Form squares!" shouted Nomiki, bellowing across the battlefield. This priceless opportunity must not be wasted.

"Form squares!" He heard the command repeated, passing up and down the broken line. To try to retain that line now would be naught but a costly folly. At the command it coalesced into a dozen tight squares, islands in a sea of storm-tossed droghkar.

In each, three ranks of men faced outwards in each direction, a bristling hedgehog of musketry. Nomiki found himself in the middle of one of the largest. He recognised the ranking officer, a short *hekatontarch* from Altyrnal, of his own chiliad.

"Fire by ranks," bellowed the man, parade ground voice carrying easily over the tumult of battle.

"First rank, fire!" he cried and a volley of musket balls flew into the droghkar that surrounded them.

"First rank, reload! Second rank, fire!" Again the crash of gun fire.

"Second rank, reload! Third rank, fire!" In perfect discipline the rhythm continued, each man moving as part of the whole like the cogs of one of the great mill machines. In perfect unison the ranks knelt, fired and reloaded, sending volley after volley into the enemy. Across the sea of droghkar other squares were doing likewise, wreaking death amongst the disarrayed foes.

Of course, that was not the end. There were still very many droghkar and for all their savageness and cruelty, history has never accused their race of cowardice. Soon enough the brutish creatures rallied and a sea now driven by strong winds surged against the desperate islands of musketry in fury.

The squares held. Against every savage assault, against the steel axes, feral claws and sheer primal ferocity of the beasts, the squares held. Men fought hand to hand with droghkar at the boundaries, bayonet and butt fending off frenzied axe slashes until a rescuing salvo from their fellow behind could blast their attackers away. Men fell, dead and wounded; bodies were trampled underfoot; but the squares closed in, and held.

One of the smaller squares did go under, it is true. Pressed hard on all sides, a particularly stubborn assault punched through the third rank of defenders. Only momentarily but it was enough: in an instant droghkar had poured through the breach like water through a broken dyke, surging into the heart of the square and assailing the defenders from all sides. Men of other squares watched helplessly as the defenders were pulled down in an orgy of brutality. Not one man of that square was later found alive.

By then though the tide had already begun to turn, the tragedy the last revenge of an already defeated force. With cruel caprice, the droghkars' earlier good fortune in so completely overwhelming the defenders' position now contributed to their defeat. Initially the scattered men had been easy prey, but once the Senrenite's gallant charge had given the squares time to form it was the droghkar who were vulnerable. Caught in a cross-fire from every side they could find shelter nowhere, while the defenders' formations meant that every man faced danger on only one front. A more astute enemy might still have won the day but the droghkar, though possessed of a savage cunning, had never, with a few rare exceptions, been known for their mental adroitness. So they perished and died, falling by the score and hundred until at last they could take no more and fled, humbled and in disgrace, back to the Gellinese. For a moment the Elarani could savour the delightful smell of victory, a victory made all the sweeter since they had passed through the jaws of defeat to reach it.

Then the Gellinese attacked.

There were no more unnatural creatures being sent against them now, only ordinary soldiers, but the fighting was no less brutal for all that. Outnumbered four to one, what could the Elarani do but retreat?

Step by step along the length of the Yenestrine Valley they gave ground, the methodical retreat that Nomiki had orchestrated so carefully. There was no panic now. The near debacle against the *barthantu* and droghkar had achieved that for them, an anointment in fire after which no trial could break them. It was musket to musket and bayonet to bayonet now: this battle was fought at too close quarters for the cannon to find much use.

Every farmhouse, every hill, every knoll or terrace became a hard-fought-for place to stand until it too was abandoned in the continuous rolling retreat. Every inch of ground was contested; every furlong was paid for until the valley was paved with the bodies of Gellinese, but the men of Elaran fell too, and in no small number. Throughout could be heard the steady thunder of the war drums as they beat wave after wave of attackers into the fray.

No short assaults before the horns sounded a withdrawal. This day was constant fighting, a continuous wave that meant to carry the day by attrition and sheer weight of numbers. By midday, when the defenders were already weary and fatigued, Erd Gellin was still throwing fresh troops into the fray.

Somehow the Elarani struggled on. In squares, in wedges, in ranks; sometimes in ragged lines of skirmishers they fought to slow the enemy. What rest they had was garnered in brief snippets in the lull between Gellinese charges or in the few blessed moments when, having fallen back, they could rest and recover until their turn came again to cover their comrades. Constantly the Gellinese pushed forward, frustrated, determined to close with this elusive foe that refused to stand at bay.

When at last the long, low horn sounded the Gellinese retreat the men of Elaran found they had been pushed more than halfway up the valley. They had fallen back more than eight miles that day, but it had been on their terms, not the enemy's. They had not been routed. A defending force still stood in the path of the army of Erd Gellin.

They had paid a high price. In the fading light of dusk the valley took on a grey, washed-out visage: a dream landscape, or a nightmare's. The struggles of the day became unearthly, the torn-up land and detritus of war somehow worse than when it had been occurring. Such a place did not belong to the living, a colourless lich-yard where the shades of the fallen sighed and murmured at the edge of hearing. The dead held sway there now.

How many of their own lay out there, lost to that desolate land? Too many had fallen, too many by far.

There were some tales of hope amidst the despair. Nomiki had been found, unconscious, when all had thought him dead. A bullet, its force spent from a ricochet, had struck him in the very last engagement and he had passed out, a graze to the head the worse but otherwise unscathed, save for a light scoring along the side that he had taken earlier.

Others too had such stories to tell; men who had been swept apart in the chaos of the *barthantu* and droghkar onslaught only to find each other again, both hale, at the end of the day. But for every story of unexpected happiness there were a dozen of grief. So many had died. Hesperos, dour Chiliarch of the North, would grace Rianda's council no longer; nor would Sir Hanyarmé be seen again this side of heaven. He had found the martyrdom he sought, along with all but a handful of his knights. In all, fully half of those who had marched down the valley that morning now lay dead upon its floor.

They had triumphed for the day, but to what avail? Erd Gellin had paid a high price for its gains – two Gellinese had fallen for every Elarani – but so great was the initial disparity that the odds now were greater than they had been to begin with. The Elarani fought now for defiance, in stubbornness, pride and because they had no other choice.

Chapter Twenty-Four

On the Banks of the Yenestor

Thomas watched the troops flowing past. Company after company in a never-ending stream, they marched rigidly in perfect discipline, muskets slanted back over their shoulders. The Torridonians had come at last.

They had begun their day's march in darkness, arriving at the valley an hour after dawn. Now they marched swiftly down the banks of the Yenestor, smoothly supplanting the battered remnants of the Elarani forces to take up their defensive positions before the Gellinese assault.

Tychon and Thomas were observers from the sidelines as the new arrivals filed past. Tychon had taken a bullet to the arm the day before and much as he might wish otherwise, a broken and bound arm prevented him from flying as surely as a more serious injury. After the carnage of yesterday only the most grievously wounded could hope for the attention of the Velnerines.

The fiery Air Captain had never been one to bear injury or incapacity easily, his own least of all. Relegated as he was now to the company of the non-combatants he was constantly chafing against his restraints.

"By the Wheel," he said. "If only they could have got here yesterday."

Thomas shrugged. "At least they're here now. Last night we were praying for just this sort of miracle."

"I know, I know. Damn this arm! The first battle of the war we stand a chance of winning and I'm bound up like an invalid on the ground." He paused, staring out at the columns of men.

"Torridonians. Even when they're on our side they manage to plague us. But I can't deny that they're a fine sight."

A fine sight they were. A full legion had been sent to the aid of Elaran – as many men as Elaran could muster at full strength. Five cohorts of infantry, each a thousand men strong, plus the auxiliaries: artillery, war beasts, battle mages and the rest, with a mounted *ala* for scouting and harrying. Like the Gellinese, the Torridonians were wise enough to know cavalry was rarely of avail in these hills.

Companies filed passed them, blue tabards blazoned boldly with the black boar of Torridon. At the head of each cohort standards waved, signalling the order of battle, as drums and bugles marked the marching tempo.

Heavy gun carriages drawn by mules, a battery of artillery rolled by. Niavon I had reformed the obsolete Torridonian army when he seized power and then tempered the steel of his new weapon in his conquests; his successors, whatever else they had done, had kept it well honed. Archaic it might be compared to the Imperial army, it was still the most modern and professional fighting force on the continent of Laurentia. The cannon alone exposed clearly the deficiencies in the Elarani armaments.

"Riflemen," exclaimed Tychon suddenly, startling Thomas.

"What? Where?"

"Over there." He gestured, then cursed savagely as his wounded arm protested against the ill-usage. Gingerly, Tychon tried again with the other arm.

"Over there – just coming round that bend in the river."

Thomas squinted at them. The three companies had broad slashes of russet on their blue tabards and their guns did indeed seem different though he would have paid it no attention had Tychon not singled them out.

"Are you sure?" he asked suspiciously. His eyesight had never been that strong. "How can you tell from here?"

"Andur's teeth, it's unmistakeable. Look at the barrels and the shape of the stock and butt. They're Triune rifles or I'm a cloistered monk."

Thomas was outraged. Triune rifles here? Gun-running was a perpetual thorn in the side of the Imperial administration in Laurentian, impossible to stamp out despite the stiffest penalties and the best efforts of both the civil and military authorities. Half the blasted directors of the Farladan Company were in it up to their elbows, though of course nothing could ever be proved. Even the Triune navy couldn't patrol the entire coastline and even if you did catch one of the freebooters before they dumped the contraband overboard, there were never any links higher up and another would spring up to replace him a moment later. But seeing the naked evidence here before his eyes in blatant display was appalling.

"Illegal contraband! How did they get hold of them? If the Viceroy knew..."

"He would do nothing. We're a thousand leagues beyond Triune writ. The Torridonians are on our side at the moment, remember. A rifle can drill a man through the heart at a thousand feet. Those guns will be worth their weight in gold, never mind how they got them."

Objectively, Thomas could admit that Tychon was right, but that didn't stop him bristling with indignation. The Elarani's blasé dismissal of the illegality of the matter riled him. To any Triune stationed in Laurentia this particular crime was like a slap in the face.

A sudden rush of wind pulled their attention away as seventy-two *tarathin* swept down the valley, the upthrust from their wings buffeting bystanders. Six squadrons of twelve, one for each cohort and one for the legion. Wings beating in unison in perfect formation, they were a majestic sight. Tychon stared at them hungrily.

Below, a company of grakim was passing. The grotesque war beasts snarled and lunged at their handlers who brutally forced them onward with the aid of heavy pole collars and wicked iron goads. The beasts would not have been fed for two days in preparation for the battle and were now savage to the edge of uncontrollability. With eight eyes unnaturally placed in an even ring about their neckless heads, any direction was forward to them and all but their handlers gave them a wide berth, having no wish to run afoul of their sharp fangs or long, clawed arms.

Then, all at once, it was over. The last company had passed and an eerie stillness reigned.

The air was fresh with anticipation. The last drops of a fleeting morning shower were falling, bestowing a cool delightfulness upon the day. In the north the sky was already clear. Bright and still, it betokened another of those brisk Elarani spring mornings.

By noon it would be warm, but for now the air still carried a chill edge, funnelled through the valley on the back of a north wind from the Gralbakh range. Swifts and *therarni* called overhead and below, for one final time, the great war drums of Erd Gellin began their measured beat.

A *therarn*, had it eyes to see from its lofty vantage point high, high above the valley floor, would have been able to watch the Gellinese inching their way up the east bank of the Yenestor, creeping onwards like a red tide nosing its way relentlessly into the channels and gullies of a rocky shore.

What would it have made of their antics, secure in the sky above? The crackle of gunfire and motions forward and back with neither rhyme nor reference to anything of sense or reason? Would it have noticed any difference from the day before or would the marching of formations be to it merely a random fluctuation of patterns, one combination as unimportant as the other? In reality only the *tarathinakii*, those human knights of the air, could disturb the birds as the riders carried their struggle furiously upwards to trespass upon the sacred territory of the *therarn* and mountain eagle.

For Thomas and Tychon it was otherwise, lofty though their vantage point was. From their natural enclosure in the rocks – the same from which they had watched the Torridonians arrive – they could see all the battlefield laid out before them in miniature, each man and company in its place. But if their view was as clear and distant as a bird's, unlike the avians they were not dispassionate: they froze at every Gellinese assault, breathed again with each rebuff or sally and despaired whenever the line faltered; Thomas no less than Tychon, for all that his attachments were newer.

Their hearts were not to be too sorely tried that day. From the very first it was clear that the tone of the battle had changed. The Gellinese were lacklustre; even their fiercest attacks were desultory compared to the ferocity of the day before. Simultaneously the defenders were fighting with renewed vigour, their endeavours matching and overmatching those of their foes.

There was no reason why it should be so. The arrival of the Torridonians might have helped to level the playing field but the Gellinese still enjoyed a slight advantage in numbers and the defenders, pushed back as they had been the day before, had no fortifications to speak of to shelter behind. Victory could still have belonged to Erd Gellin, had it but chosen to grasp it.

Perhaps if they had faced the Torridonians from the beginning it would have been different. But the sudden appearance of five thousand fresh troops at a time when even the most pessimistic Gellinese soldier was confident that victory was certain was a deep blow to morale. For the first time since crossing the border last autumn, the army of Erd Gellin faced a battle that it could lose and the knowledge sapped their strength and left them unmanned and rudderless. The Elarani, already lions, grew stronger yet: if they had fought like saints for a dreamer's hope of victory, how much more reason to fight when the prospect of that victory had become a true reality? Andur had answered their prayers and they would show themselves worthy. As for the Torridonians, were they not soldiers of the finest army on Edrith, heirs to the heroes who had seized victory from defeat at the Battle of Karst and carried the banner of Niavon undaunted into Santon, Rodinia and Allende? Victory was no more than their due: they would not disappoint it.

The regiments advanced and closed. Cannonfire thundered overhead; the flurry of small-arms fire below. A point formed, was shattered, reformed and was repulsed again. Beneath the stately pavane of formations men bled and died, eyeball to eyeball with musket and bayonet. And the line held.

A bugle call came from above as a sharp-eyed *tarathinaki* signalled a new development. A company of Gellinese were seeking to outflank the left edge of the Elarani. Grape and chain tore through them, belched from the mouth of a Torridonian battery, placed on the eastern slopes for that very eventuality, and the Gellinese fell back, the heart torn out of them.

Time and again the Gellinese broke their noses against the brick wall of the defence. Things had changed since yesterday. No longer did they rush to the attack but instead manoeuvred cautiously, like a boxer who, bruised, has no real wish to expose himself too readily to the punishment of his enemy. In the centre the line was bulging, not outwards but inwards; the Gellinese were giving way and Thomas's soul soared to see it. He forgot that a year ago he had known nothing of this land or its troubles: in that instant he was Elarani in mind and heart and soul. If only Lawrence could have seen it.

The Gellinese were falling back in earnest now. Three cohorts of Torridonians had spearheaded the way, slicing into the Gellinese front like an assassin's knife. The sally had taken the Gellinese by surprise and now the space created was being filled by a solid phalanx of blue, dotted here and there with Elarani yellow. The advance crept forward inexorably until the soldiers of Erd Gellin had no option but to give ground.

From across the river riflemen opened fire, sending volley after volley into the retreating host. They had crept down the west side of the Yenestor early that morning and had kept their cover until just such a moment as this. Their way had been unopposed. Why should Erd Gellin watch the west bank too closely when the battle was here, on the east, and the river was too deep to ford. But now the Torridonian rifles were enfilading with impunity into the Gellinese ranks, their longer range allowing them to pick off their targets at will, knowing that even the most skilled shots amongst the enemy had only a miser's prayer's chance of striking home.

Under that debilitating rain the Gellinese flank began to wither. To stand and be shot at without any chance of returning fire was too much for already demoralised men to stand. The formations crumbled like soft loam as men fought to escape out of range. The whole line began to tremble. The left flank was collapsing into the centre before its commanders' eyes. Disorder and confusion spread like pestilence through the ranks.

A salvo of horns and the men of Torridon and Elaran forged into the shattered foe. The retreat became a rout. Orders were being bellowed amidst the carnage; men were firing with abandon. The grakim had been unleashed and the war beasts wreaked havoc amongst the broken ranks. Entire companies dissolved into masses of frightened men who fought only to escape from the deadly Torridonian wedges which wheeled with precision to smash into the enemy gain and again.

The Gellinese were in full flight now, running in a headlong rush towards the bottom of the valley. Grakim savaged the hindmost – until the bloodlust faded none could control them – and the *tarathinakii*, swooping low, took deadly aim at the backs of the fleeing soldiery. In the ranks of the victorious defenders officers fought to maintain order and to prevent a jubilant, foolhardy pursuit en masse. Drunk with victory, the Elarani in particular would have all too easily given way to such an impulse in the epiphany of triumph.

Discipline prevailed. The habit of obedience, helped in a place or two by the occasional hard fist, took precedence over the heady desires of the moment. What cavalry there was, was turned loose to harry the foe and behind them the ranks were reformed until, in orderly, disciplined rows, they marched in the footsteps of the fleeing enemy down the bank of the Yenestor. For the Gellinese had been defeated, not destroyed. Given time they could yet reform and become a threat. Lesser numbers could prevail over greater – had not this day shown that? – and even humbled, an army of Erd Gellin was not to be disregarded.

But for now, Elaran and Torridon were the victors.

Chapter Twenty-Five

The Price of Victory

The Gellinese have now retreated beyond the mouth of the Yenestrine Valley. They do not seem to be holding but instead are continuing to follow the Yenestor South. Whether they will regroup in the foothills near Hyrakos or abandon Elaran altogether only Our Lady of Silence can know, but for now the Elarani and their allies are undoubtedly triumphant.

Piotr paused, meticulously crossing the final *t*. The events of the last two days had been as much a surprise to him as to any, cut off as he was in the field from regular communications. But that, he mused, was frequently how Andur willed it. The Blessed Ruth alone could fathom the depths of His secrets.

It had been simplicity itself to gain a position in the Citadel at Hyrnar; rather harder to find a way of travelling south with the army that would not place him in the front line. However, a debilitating poison slipped in the food of a quartermaster's clerk had done the trick, the slow-acting potion leaving the man moaning and weak as a new-born child by the time the *tarath* were due to take him south. His superiors had been scrambling to find a man with the necessary skills to replace him; honest, literate men with a head for figures being in short supply in war time Hyrnar. No doubt the quartermaster had seen Piotr's appearance as a blessing from Andur.

The clerk should have recovered by now, Piotr hoped. The dose he had used was seldom fatal for a man of good health. It did not do to kill unnecessarily.

He had not had to worry about being identified. A dozen times or more he had even served Thomas personally without being recognised. A bowed head and downcast eyes did much to hide oneself especially when, naive, they were looking – if they were looking at all – for a pale, bleached Rotliegendan with the characteristic high-boned Tuevic features and never glanced twice at the olive-skinned Elarani servant before them. To alter such matters as these was simplicity itself to one skilled in the arts of concealment. As they should have known.

The boy's progress had been painfully slow. The winter had been one long, drawn-out period of frustration which had been almost as painful for Piotr as for Thomas. Why his superiors did not simply take matters into their own hands he did not know. While Thomas's breakthrough vision at Istria had been gratifying,

Piotr knew, as even one inducted into only the lowest of the Mysteries would know, how shallowly the boy had plumbed the great depths of the void.

He dipped his pen into the ink, carefully as always running the paper around the base of the nib to remove any stray drops.

What remains of the Elarani host will shortly be returning to Hyrnar. It is assumed that the Queen will go with them, accompanied by the Bishop of Hyrnar and the majority of the High Council, whilst a small force under First Chiliarch Nomiki remains in the south to harry the Gellinese retreat. If such occurs it is almost a certainty that Thomas Maynard will also return to the Citadel.

I will retain my position and accompany the army back to Hyrnar, maintaining my observation until and unless I receive orders to the contrary. You should be aware that this will make it more difficult for Elaran to justify holding Maynard against his will whilst simultaneously increasing their desire to do so. Thus far they have benefited greatly from his cooperation and sympathy but this state of affairs may not prevail for ever.

There is also the matter of Torridon to consider. Whether or not they were aware of Maynard's existence prior to their intervention is unclear, but that they will now wish to become a player in this game is certain. Measured by force of arms they are currently the strongest force in the vicinity. I would advise...

He hesitated, then crossed out the last three words. His place was to observe, to report and, within his limits and according to his judgement, to act, not to advise. It did not do to overstep one's place until one had been considered worthy.

Considering this, he tore up the last page and rewrote it, omitting his final presumption. There was in truth nothing more it was necessary to say.

My next report will reach you by the usual channels.

In loving memory of the Zechen Rotliegendish Commonwealth, eternal in spirit.

Piotr Alojzy

#

The leaders of the defending armies stood together on a promontory formed by a meander in the River Yenestor. They were only a short distance from the point where the tide had finally turned. Rianda, Euthymios and Nomiki stood together with Marshal Gelrin, the commander of the Torridonian legion. Around them, at a discreet distance, a ring of Elarani musketeers – what remained of the

Household Guard – stood watch, eyes flickering constantly around the perimeter. A larger, stronger, ring of Torridonians encircled them, equally ready. With victory won, no one wished to take any chances that could bring it to ruin.

Their mood was sober. After the initial flush of victory had faded, few had felt like celebrating. Truly, as St. Luderand had said, if this is victory, what price defeat?

"The *tarathinakii* report that the Gellinese are continuing to retreat without slowing," said Gelrin. Of them all, he alone was least downcast, but then Torridonian casualties – fighting for one day only – had been far lighter than those of Elaran and, if defeated, they would have had far less to lose.

"Our forces remain on their tail?" asked Nomiki sharply.

"They do. A small detachment remained to secure the cannon they abandoned at the mouth of the valley but the rest continued south."

Following the victory, two and a half thousand Torridonians had pursued the retreating enemy south to ensure they withdrew back to the borders rather than entrenching themselves in some defensible position inside Elaran. A token force of five hundred Elarani – almost all who remained fit to fight – under Eluid, March-Warden of the North had accompanied them to maintain Elaran's dignity. Even here, victory was poignant.

Rianda roused herself. Torpor was never acceptable.

"Then we can serve no purpose by remaining here. Nomiki, are the men ready to march?"

"Yes, Your Majesty."

"Then let us be underway. The pace must of necessity be slow out of consideration for the wounded, so let us waste no more time than necessary haunting this charnel house.

"Marshal Gelrin, you and your men will of course be our honoured guests at Hyrnar. Elaran can never express its gratitude for your aid too greatly."

#

A shadow lifted from the army of Elaran as it marched home to Hyrnar. With the victory in the Yenestrine Valley the soldiers had come out from a dark cloud. A great weight had been lifted from their shoulders and the extent of their deliverance was only now truly sinking in.

Many had fallen, it is true, but were they not alive and free in Elaran in the bright sunshine of spring? They had won a great victory, unlooked for, against great odds, seizing triumph when all hope had seemed lost. Their land had been delivered and now they were going home; going home to enjoy the fruits of that victory, returning to wives, to children, to parents, loved ones who would be rejoicing at their return. They had grieved for the fallen and would do so again but for now they were alive. And so praised Andur for their deliverance and sang as they marched, joyous with the sheer delight of living.

Rianda reined in her horse as they came near to Hyrnar. She rode at the head of the army with Nomiki and Euthymios beside her. As was their right, the surviving Elarani led the approach to the Citadel, the Torridonian forces following behind. Greater in number they might be, yet they were guests in this land and Marshal Gelrin understood this as well as she. Elaran was returning to its capital in victory. Her land was still free: despite all her mistakes, she had not disgraced her ancestors.

Nomiki and Euthymios beside her shared her triumph. The three of them sensed the men's mood and were glad of it, for they knew the ambiguities the surface exuberance masked. Like the rest they grieved for the dead, but the price, though high, had been worth paying. All too easily it could it have been a very different victorious army approaching Hyrnar; no rejoicing defenders but a grim-faced host of Erd Gellin ready to bombard the last refuge of Elarani freedom into submission and slavery. Another year would bring new trials, but for now they were free.

The journey home had been slow, for none wished to suffer any more deaths from injuries due to lack of rest. Every day, more of the wounded became well enough to walk, with the efforts of the Velnerines speeding the healing process four-fold. Thanks to the monks' powers there had been few deaths after the first day and the steady return of the wounded to fitness was a major factor in the rebounding morale. As the army turned up the final stretch of the road to Hyrnar only a few dozen remained waggon-bound.

The shadows drew in as they snaked their way up the switch-back canyon that for centuries had been Hyrnar's first line of defence. The precipitous walls and narrow bottom ensured that a small defending force could hold off a larger one until it was worn down by sheer attrition. Many an invading army had broken its nose here. Whosoever holds Hyrnar holds Elaran – such had been true since the first days of the Nemessine kings.

Rianda shivered and drew her cloak about herself. Little direct light reached the bottom save at noon. Since the victory at the Yenestrine Valley she felt the weight of such history more heavily. She too was now part of that history.

The steep walls drew in as they approached the city itself. The canyon narrowed. Behind them, the Torridonians formed a solid unit, blocking the pass from wall to wall behind the smaller formations of Elarani. In the gloom, shadows were hardly visible. After these claustrophobic confines it would be a relief to once again be beneath the open skies.

Sunlight lanced in from ahead, marking the end of the canyon. Resisting the urge to spur her horse ahead, Rianda forced herself to remain at a measured pace in front of her army. These last few hundred yards seemed to take an age. At last she rounded the last the last bend, stepping forward boldly into the sunlight.

Hyrnar lay resplendent before them, beautiful and strong; untouched by the ravages of war. The hidden valley was green with spring's growth and Lake

Cerynal glittered like a jewel at the base of Mount Karnitha. In the centre of it all stood the Citadel itself, strong as a rock, unyielding as adamant, heart and soul of the Elarani nation.

Above the Citadel's highest tower flew the Black Boar of Torridon.

Printed in Great Britain
by Amazon

32626583R00157